SAFARI

TONY PARK

Quercus

First published in Australia in 2007 by Pan Macmillan
First published in Great Britain in 2011 by Quercus Publishing Ltd
This paperback edition published in 2016 by

Quercus Publishing Ltd
Carmelite House
50 Victoria Embankment
London EC4Y 0DZ

An Hachette UK company

A CIP catalogue record for this book is available
from the British Library

PB ISBN 978 0 85738 792 9
EBOOK ISBN 978 0 85738 594 9

10 9 8 7 6 5 4 3 2 1

Printed and bound in Great Britain by Clays Ltd, St Ives plc
Cartographic art by Laura Whiddon, Map Illustrations

For Nicola

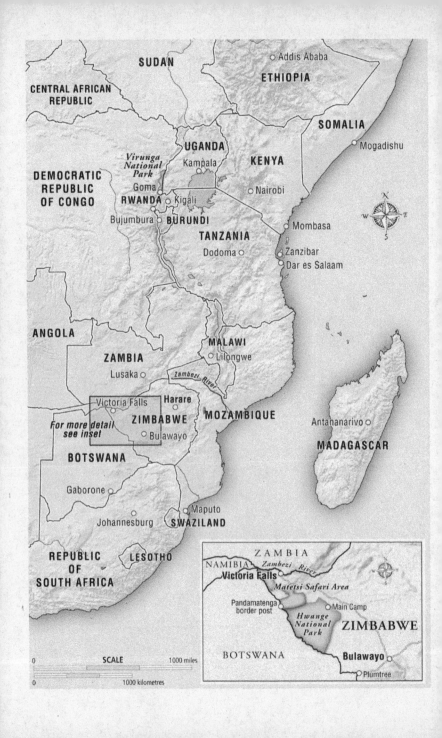

1

He killed to feed his family, and to make some money to buy clothes for his children and to pay their school fees.

He broke the law because it no longer existed in the country he had proudly served for more than thirty-five years. He had worn the green and khaki uniform of the national parks and wildlife service and he had been as proud and as well turned-out as any soldier on a parade ground, right up to the day he was compulsorily retired, on his fifty-fifth birthday.

He had taken a bullet from a poacher's rifle defending the black rhinos up in the Matusadona on the shores of mighty Lake Kariba. And then the bastard government that he had served for most of his life had taken his job and given it to a wild-eyed city boy from a different tribe, because he was a member of the party. They scared him, these youngsters, so full of hate and intolerance for other tribes, for other political beliefs. He prayed that when the government fell, as surely it must, these boys and girls would see sense again.

The scar still itched sometimes. He scratched it and thought it ironic that now he was the enemy of the state. Now it was him in the ragged trousers, carrying a black-market AK 47. He had become what he had despised for thirty-five years.

A poacher.

He knew this countryside like the wrinkles on the back of his hand, the furrows and clefts of his wife's ample body, the smiles of each of his children. The dry golden grass swayed with the wind that had long since sucked the moisture from every blade and leaf. What the wind had spared, the elephants had devoured, like a plague of seven-tonne locusts, eating everything in their path in their annual contest to survive until the rains came. In the old days they had culled the elephant – slaughtered them by the hundreds to keep the population under control, to spare some vegetation for the other animals, and to feed the poor people of his country. Culling had long ago gone out of fashion, because of the emotions it stirred in people half a world away from Africa, and the government and the party had long since stopped caring about feeding the hungry. Patrick shook his head. The world had gone crazy.

Four months ago he had made his decision to sacrifice his pride, his values, his honour and his honesty. A year into his retirement and he was starving. The pension the government paid him didn't increase fast enough to keep pace with the rampant inflation that was crushing the life out of the economy, like a python squeezing its prey to death. He had no trade – other than scouting for animals and tracking and killing

2

Zambian poachers. The only other skills he'd picked up in the service of his country's wildlife were a basic knowledge of mechanics and, most important of all, tyre mending. How many punctures had he repaired on Land Rover tyres in thirty-five years? Hundreds, for sure, maybe thousands. He had scoured the roadsides and dumping grounds for old inner tubes and two pieces of flat bar to use as tyre levers and bought himself some glue. Patrick Mpofu, senior ranger, holder of a bravery commendation for being wounded in the line of fire, vaunted tracker and scout, had found an old piece of cardboard and nailed it to a tree on the outskirts of the town of Victoria Falls and written the words *Tyre mending*.

His first business venture had proved spectacularly unsuccessful. There was no diesel or petrol in the country, so few people were driving. No driving, no punctures. Then, on a winter's night, the police had come. With bulldozers.

Patrick and his wife and four children had lived in a nice, albeit basic, house after he had lost his job, but the inflation meant they could not continue to pay the rent. They moved, with hundreds of others, to a shantytown on the outskirts of the Falls and constructed a home out of offcuts of corrugated iron and crumbling asbestos sheeting.

The government called it Operation Murambatsvina – a Shona word for 'drive out trash'. The untidy rows of makeshift homes were a breeding ground for criminals, state television had said. There were criminals living amidst the squalid settlement, of that there was no doubt, for many people had

3

turned to thieving to feed themselves. Most, however, were people like Patrick, displaced from their normal lives because of the shambolic economy and government mismanagement. Some of the people broke the law, but all of them were against the government and for the opposition. To survive, they made household goods out of scrap metal, wove baskets, carved curios out of wood and soapstone, and mended tyres. And they hated the government.

The police, who were supposed to be dedicated to the rule of law and the preservation of peace, had come with the bulldozers and destroyed what passed for Patrick's home. His youngest daughter had broken free of her mother's arms that night and raced back, into the dozer's path, to retrieve a rag doll. The police had apologised afterwards, but that would not bring back a seven year old's leg.

He sniffed the dusty, musty air. Elephant. He had no interest in killing one of them. Of course, there was money to be made in ivory, if you had the right connections, but Patrick knew from his time in the parks service that the poacher made a pittance from shooting an elephant, compared with the fortunes exchanged by the middlemen in the trade in white gold. He was not going to risk his life or a prison sentence, and leave his family destitute so that some wealthy Japanese businessman would have a nice seal with which to ink his letters. Nor would he hunt rhino. To kill a *bejane* would mean giving up his soul as well as his principles. It would make a mockery of the blood he had spilled, to cut off a horn of matted hair so that a Chinese millionaire could relieve the

4

symptoms of a fever, or a rich Arab could have a new handle for his dagger.

On the low rise, on the far side of the dry pan, he saw a branch move in the opposite direction to which the wind was blowing. His joints were stiff and his knees clicked as he walked, but he had the eyes of a boy, focused with the experience of a lifetime in the bush. He saw the telltale flick of the big ear. Hearing was a kudu's best defence, but its overly large antennae were also its biggest giveaway. It was a bull – alone, by the look of it – and he had hooked one curly horn into the branch of an acacia in order to pull it down to his mouth.

In his mind's eye, Patrick saw a day when his son could wear the uniform of the Zimbabwean Parks and Wildlife Service, when the government's madness had passed, and when his few months as a criminal could be forgotten, even atoned for.

For now, though, he dropped to a crouch and, as he watched the kudu feeding, his thumb slowly, silently, moved the safety catch. He told himself again he was hunting only for the pot, to feed his family. The money he'd make from selling the rest of the carcass would pay another month's school fees, so his son wouldn't have to grow up to be a criminal, like his father.

'Too young for Vietnam, too old for Iraq,' the American sighed.

'You sound like you're upset about it,' Fletcher Reynolds said. He dropped to one knee and pointed to an imprint in the dust the shape of two elongated teardrops, fanning out from the narrowest points into a 'V'. 'Kudu.'

The other man took off his khaki bush hat and mopped his scarlet brow. 'Should have worn this damn hat yesterday. No, it's not so much that I'm *upset*, Fletch, more, I guess . . . unfulfilled.'

Fletcher wouldn't have described war as a fulfilling experience, but he supposed he knew what the overweight, overindulged, overpaid dentist from Chicago was trying to say. They had been discussing military service – the American's time as a member of the Illinois National Guard, as opposed to Reynolds' four years on operations with the Rhodesian Light Infantry in the late seventies. The two men were of a similar age, and both lived for hunting, but that was where the similarities ended. 'You didn't miss much, Chuck.'

'Yeah, I know. But all the same, as one hunter to another, you'd have to say, Fletch, that there's nothing like the ultimate contest – man versus man.'

'Nothing like surviving an airline crash either, I suppose, but that doesn't make it right, or something you should feel bad about having missed out on. Quiet now, we're closing on him. Looks like a big bull from the size of the spoor.'

The American nodded and seemed to tighten the grip on his Weatherby Safari rifle. Reynolds was grateful for the momentary lull in the banal conversation. Occasionally he met a client he actually liked. All too occasionally. He heard the snapping of branches in the distance. Elephant. Best they steer well away from the herd. The dentist had at least been honest enough to

6

say that buck and zebra were more his league, rather than buffalo or elephant, which could do a man some real damage if things went pear-shaped. Talk of the war didn't usually bother him, but it irked him that the American thought that killing another man was something to aspire to – a rite of passage of which no man should be deprived. What a load of shit.

'Can you see it yet, Fletch?' the dentist whispered.

Mother of God, the man couldn't be quiet for two blessed minutes. He'd tried to tell him, on day one, that his name was Fletcher, not Fletch. He turned and glared at the overdressed, sweating millionaire. He was rewarded with a grimace and a mouthed 'Sorry' from the client. Reynolds forced a smile and winked at him. He couldn't afford to offend the man. He could barely afford to keep the hunting lodge running, in fact, so he needed to send Chuck the dentist home to Chicago with a smile on his face and a kudu's head with a magnificent set of horns. He squinted and peered through the thornbushes towards the low rise this side of the dry pan.

The dentist fidgeted behind him, breathing hard in the African heat and dust. Fletcher reminded himself that he hunted for a living, to feed the two teenage children he saw once a year, to pay their school fees, and to fund the jewellery and fashionable clothes his ex-wife wore to please another man. He shook his head at the absurdity of it all.

The kudu roamed alone. His brothers were dead – one taken by a lion, the other shot. He walked with a

7

limp, his left rear leg having been savaged by a big cat just days earlier. He had escaped the predator and the wound was not bad – it would probably heal well in the dry heat. But even if he did regain full use of it, he would not live long by himself.

He stood as tall as a grown man at the shoulder and his twin horns had three twists each, marking him as a veteran of twenty or more dry seasons like this one. The long shaggy beard that hung beneath his chin and chest had impressed the females once – now it just snagged on the acacia thorns. As impressive in stature and looks as he still undoubtedly was, he was getting older and slower as time wore on. The loss of his brothers meant his continued existence relied on one pair of eyes and ears, rather than three.

Patrick moved as a leopard – low and slow through the waist-high yellow grass. He paused and scooped up a handful of powdery earth and then let it trickle through his fingers, watching the fall of the grains and dust. The wind had changed direction, as he knew it would. He circled the antelope until he was on the rise, level with it, a hundred metres off.

Fletcher Reynolds put a finger to his lips. He couldn't believe they were this close to the prey and the dentist had been about to speak again.

He pointed to the kudu, which was still up on the rise. A warthog was ferreting in the black mud at the edge of the waterhole, its fat little bottom pointing skywards as it rested on its front knees and searched for tubers. Other than that, there was no other sign of life. Fletcher chewed his lower lip. He knew exactly where they were. He knew this country like the faces of his two estranged children, who now called another man Dad.

As they tracked the kudu he had been acutely aware that they were straying closer and closer to the border of Hwange National Park. The dry pan was in a shallow valley, a natural watercourse that marked the park's boundary, and the kudu had crossed it. Even though he and the dentist were outside the reserve – just – the animal was within it. It was illegal for him to let his client bag this magnificent trophy animal. To make matters worse, the American was leaving the next day. Chuck raised his rifle to his shoulder.

'No!' Reynolds hissed.

'Why not? It's a clear shot.'

Reynolds explained in a whisper.

'Aw, damn it to hell!' the American said.

The kudu's ears twitched and turned like revolving satellite-tracking dishes as it fixed the source of the noise. Startled, it leapt a metre into the air, its short white tail curled over its rump.

Reynolds saw the sun glint on something metallic, shielded his eyes from the momentary dazzle, processed what he realised he had just seen and yelled, 'Down!' He grabbed Chuck Hamley by the collar of his expensive khaki safari shirt and yanked him to one side as the gunshot echoed across the pan.

The bullet zinged through the air a metre to the

right of the dentist, leaving a shower of twigs, thorns and leaves in its path and carving a splinter from a tree which embedded itself in the American's cheek, causing him to howl in pain as he dropped to his knees.

Reynolds stood over his client, rifle raised, scanning the bush for another sight of the poacher.

Patrick realised his first shot had missed, so he continued to follow the kudu's arcing bound and squeezed off a second. As he did, he heard a voice. Fear welled from his stomach to his throat, almost making him gag. He looked past the fleeing antelope to where he thought the voice had come from.

The second shot was close enough for Reynolds to feel the air being displaced as the round passed his left ear. He hadn't been on the receiving end of a bullet for more than twenty-seven years, but his old reflexes kicked in and he dropped face-first to the ground.

Chuck, his face bleeding from the timber dart that hung from his cheek, was getting to his feet beside him.

'Get down!' Reynolds yelled.

The American ignored him. 'Dear Lord, I see him!' He raised the Weatherby to his shoulder, centred the black man in the crosshairs of his telescopic sight and pulled the trigger. Nothing.

The African had seen him now. The dentist locked

eyes with the man who had tried to kill him and his professional hunter. He realised that in his haste, he had forgotten to chamber a round. A sudden calmness came over him as he lowered the rifle and worked the bolt. He brought the weapon back to his shoulder and took another sight picture. 'Die,' he whispered.

Reynolds was on his knees now and could see the African. The man looked oddly familiar. He saw the man start to raise his rifle high in the air with one hand. It looked like he wanted to surrender. 'Chuck; wait, man, he's . . .'

The Weatherby boomed. The single shot echoed up the valley. The African was knocked backwards with the force of a stallion's kick. Reynolds was on his feet. 'Jesus Christ,' he panted as he ran forward. 'Stay there, damnit,' he ordered the American.

When he reached the man, the life force was oozing out of him, his breathing shallow and ragged. He looked up, into the sun, and the heavy-breathing white man. 'Mister Reynolds,' he croaked.

Fletcher dropped to one knee and took the man's hand in his. 'Patrick . . . it's you.' He swore under his breath. He had known the old ranger from his days at Robins Camp in the north of the national park. He had eaten with him, drunk with him, run him into the Falls occasionally on leave. Reynolds knew the government had been getting rid of the older rangers, but he had not given a second thought to what had happened to Patrick after his forced retirement.

'I . . . tell them I am . . . sorry, *sah*.'

Reynolds was a hard man who hadn't cried in

thirty years, not since the loss of his first friend during the war. He felt his throat tighten and the tears well behind his eyes as a series of violent spasms rocked Patrick's body. He heard heavy footsteps behind him. 'I told you to stay put, Chuck.'

'Praise be!' the American bellowed. He hopped from foot to foot, the adrenaline still coursing through his veins. 'Try and shoot us, you godless heathen, and you'll see what happens. That's right!' He lashed out with his right boot and delivered a hard, fast kick to the lifeless man's rib cage.

Reynolds was on his feet faster than a striking cobra. He dropped his rifle and grabbed the dentist by the lapels. 'Shit, man! He was trying to surrender!'

The American met his stare, not flinching, a new hardness to his reedy voice. 'I just saved our lives, Fletcher. That man was carrying a weapon inside the national park. If the rangers had seen him they would have shot him on sight – that's what you told me.'

'Yes, the bloody *rangers* could have shot him, but not us. He was probably hunting the same kudu that we were!' Reynolds let go of his client and ran a hand through his thick mane of silver hair. He had to start thinking.

'It was self-defence. I never saw a kudu, did you?'

Reynolds bit his lower lip. The Yank was right, damn him. It was their only defence, and it would work. The local cops might try to shake down South African tourists and local whites, but they'd have a hard time locking up a rich American. If needs be, a small 'favour' could ensure the desired result. 'At least let's make sure we get our stories straight.'

Reynolds looked down at the body of Patrick Mpofu, his blood pooling in the dust and dried grass, and wondered how his country had descended so quickly into hell.

The CID detectives from the town of Hwange exuded an air of professionalism but Reynolds reckoned most of it was show. One had a shaved head and mirrored wraparound sunglasses, the other a knock-off Kangol cap on backwards. The Samuel L Jackson and Will Smith dos and accessories were Hollywood, but their cheap, scuffed leather shoes were pure Republic of Zimbabwe.

Chuck's earlier bravado had waned on the trip back to Isilwane Lodge in the Land Rover that Reynolds had radioed for on his walkie-talkie. They'd placed Patrick's body in the old refrigerated railway container Reynolds used to store game meat, among sides of impala and buffalo haunches. Seeing those soulless eyes had reminded him again of the war, and how easy it had been for him to kill, when he had to. He'd given the American a brandy to steady his nerves, then told him to brush his teeth as the police Santana, a Spanish-built Land Rover, raised a dust cloud on the access road. They had quickly gone over their stories once more.

'This man was clearly breaking the law by being in the national park with a weapon. We investigated the scene where the shooting took place and confirmed that he was across the park boundary,' the bald detective said.

'And he fired on us first,' Chuck chimed in, repeating part of his earlier statement.

'So you say, Doctor Hamley,' the designer-cap cop said. 'But I am still concerned that you and Mister Reynolds were so close to the border of the park.'

'And as I said before,' Reynolds interjected, 'we'd given up on finding a good trophy. My concession has suffered severely from poaching and this hunt had turned out to be more of a walk in the bush. I was hoping to show my client some game in the park, even if we couldn't shoot anything.' Chuck nodded vigorously in agreement. The part about the poaching, at least, was the truth.

It was cool inside the airy, open lounge area. The steeply pitched thatched roof rose cathedral-like above them. The only sound was the ticking of an antique grandfather clock as the police reread their notes and waited, in vain, for the American or the professional hunter to fill the silence. Reynolds looked around his home. He had spent twenty-seven years since the end of the bush war building up his business, developing a rapport with officials who had once fought against him – bribing those who couldn't be sweet-talked or satisfied with permits and paperwork. The business had cost him his marriage. He had weathered drought and fire, political upheavals, invasion by disaffected veterans of the liberation war who coveted the lodge and his apparent wealth, and the country's slide into economic ruin. The truth was that the bottom had fallen out of the hunting business, as most of the well-heeled clients from Europe and America forsook strife-torn

Zimbabwe for more stable countries such as Zambia and Tanzania. If the police revoked his hunting licence, or even slapped a fine on him, he would go under in a heartbeat.

The bald detective, outwardly the friendlier of the two, pushed back his heavy mahogany chair. It scraped on the slate tiles. He extended a hand and said, 'Mister Reynolds, thank you for your time. It will be our recommendation that no charges be laid against you or your client. In fact, you have done us a service. These poachers are *ma-tsotsi*.' He turned to the American and translated, 'Criminals. Without the foreign exchange that visitors like yourself bring to this country we would be in great peril.'

Reynolds had to bite his tongue. The government, ably abetted by its police force, had done everything it could to imperil the country economically, politically and socially. A good man was now lying cold and dead in the back of a police vehicle as proof of that fact.

'I am sorry for any inconvenience,' the policeman said to the dentist. 'Please enjoy the rest of your stay in Zimbabwe.'

2

Shane Castle dressed for work in Iraq.

Boots. American Army issue, suede, desert tan with chunky rubber soles for good grip.

Trousers. Khaki cargo pants. In the right leg pocket, as per company standard operating procedures, were two field dressings – bulky pads for sticking in holes and soaking up blood. The left pocket contained a portable GPS.

PPE – personal protective equipment. A nylon vest with Kevlar chest and back plates inserted in pockets fastened with Velcro. The flak jacket was company issue, but Shane, like the other members in his team, had bought side plates as well. They spent most of their time in the car, and if a bullet were going to get you it would most likely come from the side of the road, rather than from the front or back.

Webbing. He wore the same Australian-designed chest rig he'd bought in Perth prior to his tour in Afghanistan in 2002, when he'd served with 1 Special Air Service Squadron. The gear had originally been supplied in the dappled green and brown disruptive-pattern camouflage of the Australian Defence Force, but he'd spray-painted it desert tan with an aerosol can. The paint job hadn't been wasted, as he'd dusted off the same piece of kit a year later when the SAS had crossed the border into Iraq. Here he was back again, in the same shit hole. Only this time the pay was better.

Ammunition. Two hundred and fifty eight rounds of 5.56 millimetre in nine magazines in the chest rig. Twenty-one rounds of spare .45 calibre pistol ammo in three single-stack mags.

Weapons. The tools of his trade. M4 carbine with a Wildcat sight and a night-aiming device. The rifle was a cut-down version of the long-barrelled M-16 still in general service with the US Army. In the black nylon holster slung low on his right thigh was a design relic from before the First World War – an M1911 Colt .45 automatic with seven rounds in the magazine and another up the spout. He'd bought the pocket cannon from an American contractor who had cashed in and gone home. The Yank, like many of his SF colleagues still in uniform, had swapped his standard nine millimetre pistol for the older, heavier .45 after it became clear on the streets of Fallujah and Baghdad that the newer, lighter bullets weren't enough to put down a hyped-up fundamentalist who was probably also wearing body armour and not averse to taking a few slugs on his way to his date with Allah and a bevy of virgins.

On his belt was a Leatherman Wave, which he mainly used for opening bottles and cleaning his fingernails; a US Marine Corps K-Bar combat knife, and an MBITR tactical radio. Around his neck on a chain with his company dog tags was a syrette of morphine.

He inserted the radio's earpiece into his left ear – he'd be sitting in the front passenger seat so he didn't want it visible to pedestrians on his side of the road – and taped its cord to the left side of his neck. Over the top of his webbing he pulled on a plain white cotton business shirt, a size too big for him and left unbuttoned to accommodate the bulk of his webbing. They were taking the blue Landcruiser today, the one with the CD dangling from the rear-view mirror, a garish strip of offcut carpet on the dashboard and a prayer in Arabic on the rear window beseeching Allah to take care of all on board. With his thick, wavy jet-black hair cut short, Saddam black moustache and white shirt he hoped he would be mistaken for an Iraqi civilian by a casual observer.

Shane checked his watch. Still twenty minutes to go. It was his military background that made him habitually early. He lowered his bullet-draped body into the fold-out camping chair that he'd bought from the US Army PX, like most of the furnishings in the airconditioned portacabin he called home for three months at a time. He lit a Marlboro and punched the button on the remote. The flat screen beeped to life. It was tuned to the Satellite News Network, SNN – twenty-four hour news, though usually it was the same thing rehashed twenty-four times a day. Mercifully the story was about somewhere other than Iraq. An earthquake in Turkey. Pictures of body bags. He shut his eyes and remembered the last car bomb, and the one before. His nightmare – everyone's on the team. The pictures cut back to the pretty Indian presenter, upper-class voice and pearls, a map of Africa behind her signalling a new story, more tragedy somewhere else in the world.

'In Zimbabwe, it's not only the country's human inhabitants who are feeling the effects of natural and man-made disasters. A worsening drought situation, political instability and economic ruin have lead to an increase in poaching of endangered wildlife. SNN's Africa correspondent, Sarah Thatcher, has more . . .'

He knew the location even before the blonde correspondent said it. Hwange National Park. Sweeping vistas of parched golden grass reaching for skies tinged blue-grey by the dust that hung over the place during the dry season. Pans that looked like a moonscape of dust after tens of thousands of elephant had passed through; mopane trees reduced to little more than ragged pachyderm toothpicks. A tight shot of a dry waterhole, Africans in parks uniforms carrying a mix of AK 47s and SLRs. An anti-poaching patrol according to the reporter '. . . *this thin green line is fighting a losing battle'*. The carcass of a rhino, its horn hacked off, vultures inside a belly hollowed out by hyenas.

Shane leaned forward in his chair, subconsciously trying to bridge the gap between past and present, and teleport himself back to Africa.

The reporter was talking about an American hunter getting involved in a fire fight with a poacher and nailing him. Bully for the Yank. The 'war on poaching' story was an old chestnut. The words didn't concern him, but the pictures of Africa hurt like a hook thorn branch wrapped around his soul. Like a child, he wanted to reach out and touch the screen, to reconnect with those tragically alluring flickering images. He was in Iraq for one reason only – to make enough money to get back to the continent of his birth. Africa.

His schoolteacher parents had left Zimbabwe for Australia in the mid-eighties, when he was fifteen. He'd been old enough to realise he belonged in Africa and the relocation was as much of a wrench for him as it was for his folks. His mother and father had wanted a better future for Shane and his younger sister, but all the boy wanted was to get a job as a game ranger and live in the African bush.

His parents had found jobs in the public school system in Australia, but hadn't earned enough for the family to return to Zimbabwe on holiday. He sensed, anyway, that having taken the decision to leave, they couldn't bear to see the country they had loved slide further into ruin.

Africa had its problems – the story on the TV concerned only one – but the continent was a model of peace and prosperity compared with Iraq. Shane had believed, when he'd taken his SAS patrol across the border in 2003, that whether Saddam Hussein was hiding weapons of mass destruction or not, the man was genuinely evil and needed to be taken down. Politicians and do-gooders could rail as much as they liked about what Saddam did or did not have hidden in his bunkers, but the simple fact was the tyrant had murdered thousands of his own people. That was where the straightforwardness stopped.

Sunnis, Shiites, Kurds, Christians, Iraqis, foreign Arabs, Americans, Australians, Britons, and a whole host of other nations for and against the Yanks, were all still trying to keep the peace or keep the war going, depending on whose propaganda you listened to. In the middle of it were people like himself – former soldiers from around the world working as contract security operators, and he wasn't the only one born in Africa. He'd met guys in their late forties and fifties who had served in the Rhodesian Army while Shane was a child.

Shane had done well at school, and transferred his love of the African bush to the Australian outback. The family could, at least, afford camping trips around Perth, where they lived. They wanted him to take a university degree, but he had his sights set on an outdoor life. The army seemed like a good compromise, and he'd studied science – with a view to specialising in zoology later in life – while learning to become an officer at the Australian Defence Force Academy in Canberra. He soon learned, however, that a life in uniform would be more rewarding and more exciting than sexing frogs in a lab or counting kangaroos in the outback.

Physically fit, intelligent and determined to succeed at whatever task was set him, Shane had naturally drifted from his first posting in an infantry battalion to special forces. The Special Air Service Regiment was based at Swanbourne, on the West Australian coast, not far from where he had spent his late teens.

His parents had been proud of his service in the

army of their adopted country, but he knew they disapproved of his decision to follow many of his comrades and leave to work as a civilian in Iraq. In their eyes, he was now little more than a mercenary. Today he and the other members of his team would be providing an escort for a senior female diplomat from UNICEF who was coming to Baghdad to announce more UN funding for schools. Didn't sound like a particularly sexy gig for a mercenary. There were others who had left the regiment to do things a lot worse. He slept okay at night, apart from the nightmares about car bombs – and that was just an occupational hazard, right? He stubbed the cigarette out and, without thinking about it, lit another.

The story on the television ended with a classic African scene – a herd of jumbos passing along a ridge at sunset, the big red ball sinking behind a flat-topped acacia. He could almost smell the dust and the musty tang of elephant. He switched the set off and sat there in the cool, dark cabin, the hum of the aircon the only sound now.

Another year in Iraq and he reckoned he'd have enough money to live his dream and buy his own piece of Africa. If Zimbabwe ever came good he would settle there, but for the moment he'd been eyeing properties on the Net in South Africa's Limpopo Province, in the hot, dry north of the country, around Musina. He had returned to Zimbabwe and travelled to South Africa and Namibia on half-a-dozen occasions over the years, at his own expense, on leave from the army. On one trip he had paid to attain a basic field guide's qualification, refreshing and enhancing the knowledge of the African bush he had gained as a child.

The years, he realised now as he smoked, had slipped away too fast. There had always been the dream of returning to Africa one day but, as the twentieth century drew to a close, the Australian Army had suddenly found itself busy. Shane's run of overseas deployments started with Australia's military intervention to restore peace to East Timor, which seceded from Indonesia with bloody consequences. After September 11, Shane knew his world would be changed irrevocably. First it was Afghanistan, then Iraq, as a soldier and now as a hired gun.

There was a knock at the door. 'It's open,' Shane called, stubbing out the cigarette.

'Ready?' Geezer, the Englishman, ex Special Boat Service, filled the doorway. Sunlight bright enough to make him squint peeked around the huge frame. The M4 looked like a toy in his meaty hand. 'See that shite on the telly about Zimbabwe?'

'Yeah.'

'Homesick?'

'Very funny.'

'Maybe you can find yourself a job back in Africa slotting poachers for a living.'

'I wish. I'd do anything to get back there.'

'Who'd want to live in such a fucked-up part of the world?' Geezer asked.

'What do you call what we're doing here?' Shane grabbed his rifle and slid in a magazine. He tapped the base with his palm to make sure it was well seated.

'Touché. Come on, sunshine, we've got work to do.'

*

Michelle Parker cried as though it were her child who had died.

She sat in the cab of her old Landcruiser, the tears cleaning streaks on her dusty face, as the lion glared at her and delivered the killing bite to the dog. It was stupid, she knew, and she was angry at herself for being so emotional. But Rembrandt had been the first African wild dog she had collared, nearly two years ago, and she had watched her mature into a fine alpha female who had led and protected her pack with courage time and again, and had cared as lovingly as any human mother for her litters of puppies. Michelle had decided, from the outset, that as the dogs were also known locally in Zimbabwe as painted hunting dogs, the new pack should all be named after artists.

Lycaon pictus, the scientific name for the dogs, once roamed all over sub-Saharan Africa, although now viable populations existed only in South Africa, Botswana, Kenya, Tanzania, Zambia and Zimbabwe. All up there were probably only between two and three thousand of them left in the wild, making them the continent's most endangered mammal.

Michelle wiped her eyes with her fists and, with a shaking hand, recorded the time and place of Rembrandt's death. *Nantwich Pan, Hwange NP*. This was, in her view, the most beautiful setting in Africa, but today it was a place of sorrow. A couple of tourists – a rare enough sight in the troubled country these days – sat in armchairs on the veranda of one of the lodges that overlooked the pan from a ridge, watching through binoculars the drama unfold below them. Michelle could hear their cooing and excited chatter

24

from her position in the tree line, on the edge of the vlei that surrounded the twin concrete water troughs. The tourists were ecstatic at having the exceedingly rare double experience of seeing Africa's most endangered mammal, the wild dog, and witnessing a lion kill take place.

For Michelle, Rembrandt's death marked not only the loss of a creature she cared about, but the end of a dream and thousands of hours of work.

That morning she had checked her emails via a satellite phone connected to her laptop and downloaded the message she had been fearing, yet expecting, for several weeks. The funding for her wild dog research program had officially been 'redirected' to another project. What or where, the message didn't specify, but she expected it would be somewhere like South Africa, or Kenya or Tanzania. With little support from the host government, researching animals in Zimbabwe was difficult and expensive. Also, there was little public pay-off for the wildlife organisation that sponsored her, given the reluctance of the local authorities to let foreign media crews into the country.

She had four weeks to wrap things up and return to Canada. At least they were paying for her air ticket. The trouble was, she did not want to leave Africa. She had seen the warning signs and had already been sounding out potential donors in case her principal funding source dried up. She had contacted local private lodges and safari operators, but all of them seemed on the brink of bankruptcy given the parlous state of the tourism industry. Thanks to the government's evictions of white farmers and black squatters alike, foreign tourists and hunters had all but stopped coming to Zimbabwe.

The sight of Rembrandt and her pack of eighteen other dogs at Nantwich just after dawn had momentarily lifted her spirits. At least she could leave the country knowing she had achieved *something*, having watched and recorded the creation of a new, viable group of dogs from the time Rembrandt had found another lone dog, a male Michelle had named Picasso. Rembrandt, long since accustomed to the sight of the old white Landcruiser, had trotted towards Michelle, sniffed the air and then returned to her latest litter of tiny pups. Michelle had smiled to herself, noted the behaviour and started to pour a cup of coffee from her flask, when she noticed the lionesses.

She had wanted to honk her horn or shout out to the dogs, but the tourists were up early, on their feet, watching in excited awe at the arrival of two types of predators at the pan. She asked herself whether she would have tried to intervene to save the dogs if she had been the only human on the scene. She shook her head. No.

The lionesses had seen the dogs first and all four had lowered themselves as one in the long yellow grass, their actions synchronised – a lethal killing team. Rembrandt had been shepherding her pups towards a flock of guineafowl and the young ones had yelped with delight as they chased the fleeing, clucking birds. Michelle's gaze flitted between the dogs and the cats, her binoculars swinging back and forth as the fear pumped through her body like a spreading sickness.

'No!' she whispered as the lionesses charged.

Rembrandt was the first to see them. She yelped her warning cry, scattering the sub-adults and the pups in a dozen different directions. Picasso raced away. 'Run, baby,' Michelle called futilely from the sidelines. The tourists up at the lodge had their cameras whirring away. They whooped in delight like Roman spectators at the gladiatorial games. Michelle bit her lip.

Three of the lionesses peeled off to follow individual dogs. Rembrandt ran from the drinking trough, straight across their paths. Michelle screamed, startling the tourists. The cats were confused by the dog's tack, and slowed to a halt as Rembrandt turned on them and started running towards the biggest feline.

Michelle had seen buffalo, in numbers, turn on a pride of lion and chase them away, and had even heard of a troop of baboon seeing off an attack by three lions. But one dog on her own stood no chance. Rembrandt stopped, bringing up a tiny puff of dust in the process. She bared her teeth and snarled. In the distance, Picasso, the juveniles and the pups disappeared into a line of bushy immature leadwood trees. Michelle had closed her eyes and heard a single yelp of pain as Rembrandt died.

The lionesses stood over her body now, looking in four different directions for the other dogs, who had long since gone. They didn't feast on Rembrandt – that was not their way. Michelle knew lions and hyenas killed wild dog and their pups simply to take them out of the hunting game, not for food. Of all of Africa's large carnivores, the painted dogs had the highest ratio of successful kills to attempts. They took game ranging in size from small buck up to zebra and wildebeest. Because they were so lethal they were a threat to other predators.

Michelle started the Cruiser, put it into gear and bumped and jolted her way out onto the pan. The lionesses stood their ground for a few seconds and then turned and trotted away. She could hear the tourists' curses from two hundred metres off. She didn't care about them. She wasn't depriving the lionesses of a meal, and she had to get the collar and valuable transmitter off Rembrandt's torn and broken body before some hyena crunched it into tiny pieces.

She stopped the truck and watched the tawny killers melt into the long grass. She eased herself out of the cab, long legs almost touching the ground from the driver's seat. She'd been sitting in the vehicle for nearly three hours and was grateful of the opportunity to stretch at last. She told herself to be strong, checked left and right and behind her in case there was anything lurking, and waded through grass as golden as the wheat on the prairie she had worked and studied so long and hard to escape. Now she'd probably end up back there, for a time at least. Her heart sank. No money, no research, no job back in Canada. The sum total of her last two years' work lay crumpled and mangled at her feet. She parted a clump of grass and felt the warm, sticky blood. That made her lose it again. Tears streamed down her cheeks as she used her pliers to unfasten the radio collar she had fitted. She'd known every brown and white and black blotch on Rembrandt's stunning patchwork coat. Now it was a mess of blood and gore. She reached out and ran her hand over the still-warm snout, closed the dog's eyes and smoothed back the distinctive, beautiful, oversized ears. Michelle took the collar back to the truck and returned with her digital camera. She sniffed and wiped her eyes with the back of her shirt sleeve, then took a series of photos of the body. She was a scientist, after all.

Charles Ndlovu coughed into his hand and bent forward at the waist to ease the weight on his legs. The canvas straps of the heavy pack dug into his shoulders and he ached all over, as though he had a fever. He used his self-loading rifle, the SLR, like a walking stick to steady himself.

'Come, old man, or would you rather us call the vehicle?' the young ranger said as he slapped Charles on the back.

If he hadn't been so incredibly tired he would have said something back to the man, or, in his youth, challenged him to a fight. Instead, he straightened himself and started to walk again. Had he been offered a lift home in a Land Rover he might very well have taken it, but that was part of the young man's joke. There was no diesel in the national park – virtually none in the country – so even if someone were taken seriously ill on the patrol, or wounded in a gunfight with a poacher, there was no prospect of a quick evacuation.

The callsign had been out for three days now. They

had hitched a ride part of the way on a trailer towed by a tractor that was ferrying a broken diesel engine, one of those used for pumping water at the pans where the animals drank, from Sinamatella to Main Camp for repair. The irony that the tractor driver was using the last of the camp's precious reserves of fuel to try to fix a piece of equipment that might not run again for weeks or months because the tanks were now dry, was not lost on Charles. At the Mandavu Dam picnic site the four men who made up the anti-poaching patrol, known in radio parlance as a callsign, had jumped off and spent their first night camped around the empty shelters that once brimmed with families on weekend outings and foreign tourists on safari.

An intrepid family of South Africans in a four-wheel drive, the only visitors to this part of the national park in the past fortnight, had reported seeing a campfire on the Sinamatella River three nights earlier. There were no tour operators in the park at the time, and no other callsigns in the area, so it was likely the fire had been lit by a careless or arrogant band of poachers.

Charles Ndlovu and his comrades had circled the dam in search of spoor, scattering a herd of grazing impala and arousing the curiosity of a lone bull elephant in the process. Charles had held his rifle above his head and tapped on the tin box of the magazine. Elephant were not stupid. The animal had seen the gun and knew it was wise to depart. After an hour of scanning the dirt, the dry grass and the tips of thorn-bushes, Charles had picked up their quarry's tracks.

Four men, two wearing rafter sandals; the other pair, new running shoes. This was normally the footwear of whites and tourists, though the poachers would be men of his colour. He guessed the men were from Victoria Falls or, more likely, its twin town on the Zambian side of the Zambezi River, Livingstone. The men with the shoes had money, which told Charles two things. These were commercial poachers – not starving men looking for food – and they were not Zimbabwean. At least one was armed with an AK 47 and he, as Ndlovu had just done, had rested the butt plate of the rifle on the ground when he'd stopped to rest, leaving a telltale imprint in the dust.

Now, on day three of the patrol, the callsign had picked up a new set of tracks, hence the urgency of the boy who chivvied Charles along.

'Take a look, old man,' the whelp, whose name was Lovemore, said.

Charles dropped slowly to one knee and wiped the sweat from his brow. The grey dust was as fine as talcum powder and smelled strongly of the *Ndlovu*, the elephant that had stripped the land bare and pulverised it underfoot. The animal was his family's totem, but Charles despaired at the damage they were doing to the park. '*Bejane*,' he said.

'*Chipmberi*,' Lovemore countered.

The third member of the callsign, Noah, broke the tension and the deadlock. '*Diceros bicornis!*'

Charles smiled. 'See what a good education does for you, Lovemore?' Whether in his native Ndebele tongue, Lovemore's Shona or Noah's Latin, it was still the same thing. A black rhinoceros. But Charles knew more than the other members of the team – he knew this one's name. 'They call her Chewore.'

He had known Chewore since she was quite young. His good friend Patrick Mpofu had cared for and guarded the female rhino from the time she was a baby, and not much bigger than a pig. Chewore had been orphaned by poachers about eight years earlier and, along with other rhinos who shared her fate, been relocated to Matusadona National Park in the north of Zimbabwe, on the shores of Lake Kariba. There she had been hand-reared and progressively reintroduced to life in the bush. Two years ago Chewore had been darted, captured and driven to Hwange National Park, on the western side of the country.

Charles was still amazed that Patrick, who had followed his horned charge on a posting to Hwange, was dead – shot committing the crime he had fought against all his adult life. He was certain, though, that Patrick would never have been involved in rhino poaching, unlike the men they were tracking now.

'You know this animal by name?' asked Lovemore, who was new to the park, having spent most of his career so far working in an office in Harare. He needed field experience to secure further promotion. However, being a member of the President's ruling Shona tribe, Charles doubted Lovemore needed to spend too much time in the bush to get his next pay rise.

'You can tell her by the nick on the sole of her right front foot. She likes to roam, this one. We've had to

32

bring her back from Botswana twice before. She is smart, this animal.'

'Why smart?' Lovemore asked.

'She knows there is no future in Zimbabwe,' Charles said. Noah, and the fourth man, Christopher, smirked behind Lovemore's back.

'Get on with your job.'

Charles straightened again. 'The rhino spoor is only a day older than that of the Zambians.' They had agreed the poachers were from across the border, as it was well known all Zambians were criminals. Their enemy, at least, united the members of the callsign. 'That means they will close on her in the next day or so.'

Lovemore nodded, as though he had already reached the same conclusion. He took a map from his pocket, unfolded it and studied it intently.

Charles leaned over his shoulder. He knew exactly where they were and did not want to antagonise the younger man any more than was necessary. 'Here,' he said, smudging the paper with his dirty fingerprint. 'Just north of Manzi Chisa.' While the rhino were theoretically concentrated in the Sinamatella Intensive Protection Zone, there was no fence around the IPZ and it was not unusual for the *bejane* to wander further west in search of water at this time of the year. The worry was that Chewore would run true to form and continue westwards, out of the national park and into Botswana.

'I know where we are,' Lovemore said testily. 'We need to catch these men before they leave the park, so we can shoot them.'

Charles imagined it would be a big feather in the young man's cap if he could claim responsibility for the deaths of the Zambians. All he wanted was to see the men arrested, for then he could go home to his wife for a rest.

Good lord, I am tired, he said to himself.

3

Michelle Parker brushed her long auburn hair and tried to imagine life after Africa. It was a grim prospect.

A ray of afternoon sun lanced through a chink in the curtains with the heat and intensity of a laser beam, warming the interior of the sparsely furnished national parks lodge at Robins Camp. Michelle had bathed and wore only a brightly patterned sarong, knotted above her breasts. The hot, dry breeze whistling through the gauzed windows on the shadowed side of the building cooled her still-wet body, producing a fleeting chill to be savoured. She'd grown accustomed to Africa's year-round heat and did not relish returning to Canada in the fall.

She pulled back her hair into a simple ponytail and scrounged in her toiletry bag for what little makeup she still had. She rarely wore the stuff, but tonight she was going to dinner. With a man.

Michelle had met Fletcher Reynolds earlier on in her time in the national park. There were few whites living in the area, their numbers having dwindled in recent years when the so-called war veterans invaded the white-owned farms, game ranches and hunting concessions, so it was inevitable that she would make contact with him. His hunting lodge was only a few kilometres outside the park's northern boundary and she was often in this area following her beloved wild dogs.

She hated hunting but, to her surprise, Fletcher had seemed genuinely concerned about wildlife conservation. However, she realised his overriding interest was ensuring a lifetime's supply of animals for his rich Americans and Europeans to kill at a later date.

At past fifty he was much older than she – maybe by as much as twenty years, though she had never asked – but she had to admit he was also a ruggedly handsome man. Age hadn't mattered to her in previous relationships – she had been with men older and younger than she. He was tall, too, which was of more than passing interest to a girl who stood perilously close to five-eleven. Tanned, strong-jawed with blue eyes the same colour as hers; and he seemed to be smart and witty. If he'd been a dog, she would have classed him as an alpha male – just as she would have said, to anyone who would listen, that human relationships should mirror those of the African wild dog. It was the alpha female who ruled the pack.

Fletcher had never made a pass at her, nor even asked her to come to dinner alone with him – until two days ago, when she'd stopped her Landcruiser beside his old Land Rover. In the past she'd been invited to Isilwane Lodge for parties, such as at New Year's, or when he'd had big groups of hunters in residence. He'd told her, candidly, that many hunters were looking for wildlife conservation projects they could contribute towards. She'd swallowed her pride and bitten her tongue at more than one such gathering and been rewarded with a few cash donations, which she was able to use to buy fuel, and batteries for her radio tracking equipment.

It had felt odd, though, accepting money from the hunters – almost as though she were prostituting herself on behalf of the animals she cared for. To his credit, Fletcher had sensed this, telling her on one occasion, 'Don't feel bad. We do what we have to do to survive in Africa these days. There's no shame in surviving, or honour in failing.' She had seen the sadness behind his eyes then, for the first time. Or perhaps it was loneliness, as she knew his wife and children had left him.

She wondered, as she stood in front of the mirror, what was behind this one-on-one invitation for dinner tonight. Perhaps he fancied her. Critically, she appraised herself, and frowned at the reflection. Too tall. Small boobs. She had a nice tan, though, and it had brought out her freckles, which she kind of liked. The funding for her project had never been lavish and she'd learned to survive on less food than she'd ever before had to in her life. Shortages of basic commodities such as sugar and flour had meant no sweet tea and no bread for months. That, at least, had been a blessing in disguise. She pirouetted slowly in front of the mirror, and stood up on her tiptoes. If nothing else, she'd lost a dress size or two in Zimbabwe. She sighed. If Fletcher were interested in her, he had left his run too late. She would have to tell him, tonight, that she would be leaving for Canada in a few short weeks. Silly, anyway, she mused, as she could never imagine herself seriously interested in a hunter.

Michelle rummaged through her pack and found the only dress she possessed. She dropped the sarong and pulled the simple flowered frock over her head. She riffled through her meagre supply of underwear and laid a pair of cotton briefs beside one of her two g-strings. 'What the hell,' she said out loud.

Fletcher Reynolds heard the rumble of the four-litre diesel and walked out onto the stone flagged veranda at the front of Isilwane Lodge. He saw the headlights bouncing up the dirt road from the gate. A nightjar winged its way out of the vehicle's path. His mouth was dry, his palms sweaty.

'Mary, light the candles, please,' he called to the maid. He imagined her smiling as she replied. He hadn't been alone, at dinner, with a woman since his divorce three years earlier. His failing business had cost him his marriage and, apart from the occasional unrequited amorous advance from a client's wife and a one-night stand in Houston, Texas, with a lonely American businesswoman when he'd still had enough money to visit the international hunting shows, the question of sex had rarely come up since his wife had left. He'd found himself thinking about Michelle Parker in that way often over the last few months, but he'd been in no position to take things further with her. He had determined, after his split with Jessica, that he would not even entertain the idea of becoming seriously involved with a woman again until his financial affairs were in order. That had seemed a remote proposition until a couple of days ago.

The night was warm, the moon on the rise drenching the bush in a ghostly blue wash. He felt his heart quicken as he saw those long legs swing out of the cab.

'Hi, Fletcher,' she called.

He sucked in his tummy a little and strode across to her.

'How's it, Michelle.'

'I hate coming empty-handed,' she said as he took her hand in his.

'No, don't mind that,' he said. Her skin was soft and cool. He wondered what it might taste like. 'Your company's enough.' The compliment came out awkwardly and he thought she might be blushing under her thin veil of makeup. 'Come in, come in.'

He followed her up the stairs into the lodge, unable to refrain from noticing the way the thin cotton rode her body. She wore sandals and her toenails were bright, bright red. He wondered if she'd done them especially for tonight. He wanted to blurt his news out to her. 'Thanks, Mary,' he said to the maid, who laid a tray with cold beers, spirit bottles, mixers and a silver ice bucket on a carved antique sideboard. The dining table was set for two. 'Can I offer you a drink?'

'My God,' she exclaimed. 'Tonic water! Who did you have to kill for that?'

He smiled and explained he'd been shopping across the border, in Botswana. 'I had to get some parts for the Land Rover,' he added, so she didn't think he had gone out to find a supermarket just for her. The truth was embarrassing. Tonic water was as rare as flour, diesel and single white women in this part of Africa.

'Bliss,' she said, sipping the drink from a tall glass, eyes closed in rapture.

He led her back outside, and said, 'How are your murderous hounds doing?' He'd teased her before about her research, explaining that for decades the wild dog had been viewed by livestock farmers and hunters such as himself as a pest that needed to be eradicated. A pack of wild dog could ruin a farmer's livelihood and clean a private game reserve or a hunting concession out of small buck in very quick time. She didn't bite, however, and he suddenly realised he'd said the wrong thing. 'What is it, Michelle?'

She looked away from him, unable to hold his gaze, and told him. The news about the cessation of funding for her research, the death of the alpha female, the inevitability of her return to Canada. He thought it silly that she gave her animals names – though he held his tongue now. He was touched by her sensitivity, by the vulnerability she tried to disguise with unconvincing matter-of-factness, and was secretly overjoyed that the news he had for her would now carry even more weight than he had expected. What he was about to do, tonight, would not only help him, it might change the course of this pretty girl's life forever. And she would be in his debt.

'I'm sorry, I'm being terribly self-centred. How are things with you?' Michelle asked.

He smiled. 'Oh, I'm fine. In fact, I haven't been quite so fine in some years.'

'More business?' She looked at him over her drink, trying to push aside her sadness.

'Yes, thanks to my last client. He's referred several new ones on to me.'

'Was that the one who shot that ex-parks guy, Patrick?' News of the dentist's run-in with the former-ranger-turned-poacher had spread throughout the national park even before the news media picked up on it.

'Yes, that's the one. I'll tell you more about him later. Are you hungry?'

'Famished,' she said.

He led her to the table and opened the wine, a South African Alto Rouge, as Mary served an entrée of Mozambican prawns the size of small lobsters, with an avocado vinaigrette.

He noticed the way she stared, wide-eyed, at the prawns, an extravagant luxury so far from the coast, in the wilds of a nation where people faced starvation daily. He noted, too, the effort she made to compose herself, as though she didn't want him to see how mere food could stun her so. She did offer some praise, however: 'This wine is my favourite.'

'I thought I remembered you saying that last New Year's Eve.'

She blushed for the second time that night, and he

was secretly pleased. New Year's had been nine months ago. He topped up her glass.

'Fletcher, I don't mean to sound rude, but is there a particular reason why you invited me here tonight, why you've laid on this lovely meal and wine?'

She was direct, as well as gorgeous. He wasn't arrogant enough to assume she would follow him to his bed that evening, but he realised he did genuinely want to impress her. He was sure his news would please her – it had to after what she'd told him earlier – but he also wanted her to like him, as a man, as a person. Sheesh, but he was getting soft in his old age. He'd never had a problem attracting women when he was younger, in the army, and later as a professional hunter. Many women were drawn to men in uniform, or to hunters, and not all of them had been locals. Foreign women often fell prey to 'khaki fever', a fixation on a safari guide or hunter. Where that became dangerous – and off limits as far as Fletcher was concerned – was when the woman was a client's wife or girlfriend. But Michelle was different. She'd been in the bush long enough to have gotten over any such romantic fixations on men like himself and, to make matters even more complicated, she was a green-dyed bunny hugger. A conservationist who hated the very idea of hunting. 'I do have some news for you. But first, tell me about your dog project. Where would you have taken it if your funding had continued?'

She sipped her wine and waited for Mary to clear away the entrée plates. 'Well, there are some viable packs here in Hwange. My work, apart from monitoring them, has been studying their preferred prey. This gives us an idea of the sorts of environments where new populations could be established, or where viable existing packs could be relocated.'

'Far away from my concession, I hope,' he said seriously.

'You're being too old-fashioned. FTs will pay big money to track and photograph wild dogs on private land – it's already happening in South Africa.'

He smiled at her use of the local vernacular for foreign tourists. The F had stood for something else when visitors to Zimbabwe were plentiful, but now no one in the country would bemoan the return of overseas guests and their cash.

She added, 'I'd be happy to take people along for a joyride as well to help attract funding and raise awareness of the dogs' situation. You might find that some of your rich killers like the idea of seeing the continent's most endangered mammal up close.'

'With those bloody things around I wouldn't have any game left to hunt,' he said.

She ignored the jibe. 'If I were staying – and had the money – I'd also start vaccinating the dogs as I collared the adults. They roam so far that they need to be protected against rabies and distemper, in case they come into contact with infected domestic animals.'

The maid brought out the main course, a rare roast of kudu bathed in a red wine and berry sauce. Michelle thanked her and nodded her approval to Fletcher.

'This is superb,' she said as she took her first mouthful, and he was pleased that she was finally admitting it. 'Just promise me when I'm gone, Fletcher, that you won't regress to the old days and go shooting or poisoning my dogs if they stray onto your lands.'

He had told her previously that from the 1950s through to the 1970s farmers and safari operators had been paid a bounty to wipe out the painted dogs, which were then considered vermin by the government. How times had changed. 'That would be breaking the law.'

It was her turn to smile now. 'I don't know anyone in Zimbabwe these days who hasn't bent the rules to the point of snapping. God, I'm going to miss this fouled-up, broken-down, ramshackle country.'

'What if I said you didn't have to go?'

She put her knife and fork down and wiped her mouth. She was buying time, he thought, a million thoughts flooding her mind. 'You're not asking me to marry you, are you?'

They both laughed at her joke. Many a true word spoken in jest, Fletcher thought to himself. 'I'm asking you to stay on and continue researching those bloody fleabags.'

'I'd love to, believe me. The thought of returning to Canada leaves me cold, literally. I feel almost an honorary African now. But in case you weren't listening to me earlier, there's the little matter of something called cash.'

'If you had your own source of funding, could you keep it going, without the involvement of those European greenies you've worked for up to now?'

'Yes, I suppose so. As long as it were enough money.'

He unbuttoned the top pocket of his starched khaki and green safari shirt and pulled out a folded piece of white paper. He opened it and held it out across the table so she could see the magnetic ink characters, the printed name at the bottom, the numbers and zeros. She read the payee's name.

'The Isilwane Wildlife Conservation Foundation? Don't tell me you've turned green, Fletcher, I'll have a heart attack.'

He laughed. 'You know I'm as passionate about saving the country's wildlife as you are. We just go about in different ways.'

'What's this supposed to mean, Fletcher? What are you going to do with fifty thousand US dollars – spend it on ammo?'

'Ha ha. I'm almost tempted to take it back now, woman.'

She grimaced. 'Take it back? From whom?'

'From you.'

She drained her wineglass. 'You can't be serious. You want to . . .'

'Yes. I want you to use this money, to continue your research, under the auspices of the newly created Isilwane Wildlife Conservation Foundation.'

She was, literally, speechless. She took the cheque from him and read it again, still not fully comprehending his generosity, perhaps wondering what strings the money came with. After a few seconds she asked, 'Who's the drawer on this cheque, Doctor Charles Hamley the Third?'

'The dentist.'

'The one who shot the poacher?'

'Correct, although it turned out he's not your garden-variety tooth-puller.' Fletcher explained that

'Chuck' was in fact the owner of twenty dental clinics across the United States and had a personal fortune, from the surgeries and other successful business ventures and investments, of several million dollars. 'He's nuts about hunting, and he's certifiable about saving endangered animals.'

'Probably helps him sleep at night, knowing he's saving as many as he's killing,' she sniffed.

'What's that about the hand that feeds you? You've been hanging around canines too long, my girl.'

'I don't know what to say, Fletcher.'

'Thank you might be a nice start.' They both laughed. 'Mary, fetch the champagne,' he bellowed to the kitchen. 'Is it enough?'

'Oh, it's enough all right, to keep me going, but I don't know, Fletcher. It's a wonderful gesture but, excuse me for saying so, it seems too good to be true, and I know business has been tough for you lately. Couldn't you have used this money in your own operation?'

He raised his hands to stop her line of questioning. 'I don't want to sound boastful, Michelle, but that's not all the money the good Doctor Hamley spread around after his last visit. He paid a handsome tip to me and my guides and camp boys, a contribution to the local school, and he's promised funding for me to appoint a full-time anti-poaching coordinator.'

'But why, Fletcher? All this must have cost him a fortune.'

'He got to see first-hand how magnificent our wildlife here is, and also how much it's at risk. He told me he donates a lot more money than this to community health clinics in the States each year, so you have to put it all in perspective. Also, I suppose it's a tax write-off for him.'

She did not look completely convinced. 'What will he want from me?'

Fletcher held up his champagne flute. 'He's left the administration of the conservation fund to me, though I told him about your excellent work and he seemed impressed. I also told him how photogenic you were, in case he wanted a PR spin-off for his investment!'

'You're joking, I hope.'

He saw the flash of anger. 'About the PR stuff, yes,' he said quickly. 'Chuck said from the outset he wasn't interested in media coverage of his charitable donations. He's a true philanthropist – he gives money just for kicks. But I did let slip that you were a very attractive woman. Forgive me?'

She frowned and was silent for a moment. She raised her glass, and a smile came to her despite her best efforts. 'You're forgiven.'

'Thank God you're going to accept my tens of thousands of dollars,' he beamed. They clinked glasses.

Afterwards they sat out on the veranda again, in heavy wooden armchairs placed in front of a fire in a circular brick pit, which had been started on cue by the night watchman. Fletcher had planned this evening in minute detail. He had arranged for their chairs to be set close together. They sipped Amarula cream liqueur poured over crushed ice, together with cups of freshly ground and brewed Kenyan coffee. He drew a cigar from his pocket. 'Do you mind?'

'It's nice of you to ask. I'm a nonsmoker and I hate the habit, but I like the smell of cigar smoke. Funny, huh? Go right ahead.'

He didn't think it funny, he thought it summed up the pair of them – at least, he hoped it did. There was so much of his life in Africa that she objected to, and yet they had a great deal in common. Perhaps it was true, about opposites attracting.

The moon was high, casting its floodlight on a waterhole set in a vlei below the safari lodge. A herd of elephant ambled out of the tree line a few hundred metres distant, then started to run when they caught the scent of the fresh water. They could hear a low, rumbling noise from the elephants' bellies as the animals urged each other on.

'That's how part of me feels now,' she said. 'Desperate to get to the waterhole and drink my fill of Africa, no matter what dangers might be lurking ahead.'

'There are no risks, no catches, Michelle. You'll be free to run your own programs and spend the money how you like. You've been doing this long enough for me to trust your judgement.'

He looked into her eyes and saw the conflicting emotions. He knew she saw accepting money from someone like him as a compromise, but at the same time she was just like him – leaving Africa would all but kill him. He wondered if there were anything more there, any other emotions. He suddenly felt dry-mouthed. Hell, he thought, this was worse than going into a thorn thicket after a wounded buffalo. He reached across from the arm of his chair and placed his hand on hers.

She hesitated a moment, smiled, then gently eased her hand out from under his. 'Please, don't think I'm not grateful, Fletcher, but . . .'

'No, no, of course. Think nothing of it,' he said quickly, to hide his embarrassment. 'I didn't mean to suggest . . .'

It was her turn to raise a hand to silence him now. Her smile came easier this time. 'Fletcher, you have saved my African life and for that I will always be grateful.'

'So, you're going to accept my offer?' He felt his pulse quicken as he waited on her answer, and prayed he hadn't blown it completely with his clumsy, adolescent advance.

'The offer of your money, yes, with gratitude, but nothing more, Fletcher.'

He nodded.

'Though we can be friends, as well as researcher and benefactor, can't we?'

He smiled. 'I never thought of myself as a benefactor. This do-gooding stuff is new to me. Friends, of course. I never assumed anything more.'

'I know you didn't.'

A lion started its low, wheezy roar somewhere across the vlei. While the other elephants slurped noisily from the waterhole, the matriarch of the herd, an old cow as tall as a house, lifted her head and raised her trunk from the water. She sniffed the air for danger.

'Shit, shit, shit!' Michelle railed as she pounded the steering wheel. The Landcruiser's suspension groaned and she left her seat as she bounced out of the unseen pothole. The condition of the road back into Hwange National Park was the last thing on her mind.

She'd been sitting next to him, almost close enough for their legs to be touching, her bare skin warmed by the fire, her insides deliciously cosy from the liquor, thinking of how she might spend the research money, when he had touched her!

The hide of the man, she had instantly thought. On one hand, she was offended that he had thought he could buy her body with fifty grand and a nice dinner; while on the other, she knew she had caught herself more than once over dinner being quietly hypnotised by those deep blue eyes and handsome, weathered face. Her cheeks burned as she remembered how, as he poured her wine, she had momentarily wondered what it might be like to feel the coarse skin of his fingertips on her flesh. She realised she had been out of the dating game for way too long. It had been a roller-coaster ride of a day, from dawn to after dark. A scrub hare darted into her headlights and she had to brake hard to avoid running it down. The stupid little creature continued to bound along the road in the glare of the lamps. She slowed and switched her lights on and off to confuse it back into the grass. Eventually it hopped away.

She had felt trapped, like the hare, frozen in his sights. Had he planned the whole evening, right down to the fireside drinks and that move with the hand?

The thatched gate that marked the northern entrance to the national park loomed into view at the top of a hill and she honked her horn to rouse the gate guard. The old man shuffled sleepily from his tin hut and squinted in the lights. He recognised her vehicle, then smiled and swung the gates open for her. She waved and juddered down the hill towards Robins.

One of three main rest camps in Hwange, Robins was named after a farmer who had donated his lands to the government of Rhodesia in the 1930s. His property had become part of what was then known as Wankie Game Reserve. The park's name had been re-Africanised to Hwange after Zimbabwe gained independence and majority black rule in 1980.

As a researcher, Michelle had a permit to drive in the national park beyond the normal sunset curfew and it was after nine when she coasted into Robins. The place was empty of tourists, as usual.

Michelle usually lived in a cottage in the staff area of Main Camp, a hundred and fifty kilometres to the south-east, but Rembrandt's pack had migrated slowly north and west, towards Victoria Falls and the Botswana border, which were only a hundred kilometres and forty kilometres from Robins respectively, so it had been logical for her to relocate temporarily to the park's northernmost outpost. The move had also brought her into increasing contact with Fletcher Reynolds. 'Damn him,' she said aloud.

She forced herself to analyse scientifically the evening with Fletcher, her reactions and emotions, as she opened the door to her spartan National Parks lodge. So what if Fletcher had set up the whole dinner and held back his news about the donation until late in the evening in order to seduce her? When was the

51

last time anyone had bothered to try? Perhaps she should be flattered.

It had been more than a year since Michelle had had an orgasm with anyone else present in the bed. There had been a graduate student, from Germany. Tall, blond, long-haired, muscled, intelligent, and ten years her junior. The boy was like a puppy – cute, eager to please, full of energy, but tired quickly. He'd technically been present for the climax of the evening, but unfortunately he'd also been fast asleep by then. She smiled as she slid out of her dress and eased herself between freshly starched white sheets stencilled with the words *Government of Zimbabwe* in red.

She would show Mister Fletcher Reynolds that she couldn't be bought, or led into a baited trap like some leopard he was hunting. She needed more time to work out what his motives were.

Once she'd sorted all that out, she might just allow herself to think about those eyes again.

4

Head turning, eyes scanning. Always looking. To daydream, just to look straight ahead, like any other passenger in any other car, was to fail, and the consequence of failure in this hunt was a fast trip home, in a body bag.

They were the tail car. The UN woman was in the armoured BMW, in the middle, and a Range Rover with the other four members of the team was in front. Geezer was driving, honking his horn like an Iraqi every now and then to keep up the charade. He wore a *kefiyeh*, the traditional male headdress, to hide his fair hair and skin. A Saddam Hussein double in a Mercedes tried to cut in on them, but the Englishman sped up and gave him the finger. Baghdad must have been a deadly town to drive in even during peacetime, Shane mused.

He was in the front passenger seat – the prime set of eyes. At the end of a day such as this his shoulders and neck would ache from the swivelling, from the tension. 'Two-one, two-two,' he said into the mouthpiece of the

MBITR clipped to his chest webbing strap under his flimsy disguise shirt.

'*Two-one*,' drawled the ex-US Navy Seal in the passenger seat of the lead vehicle.

'Stationary white Japanese sedan two hundred metres to your front, two-one,' Shane said. 'I just saw him pull over as we came round the bend, over.' He hoped the lead vehicle had seen it already. They should have.

'*Ah, roger that, buddy*,' the Texan said. '*We've seen it already. Woman driver, looks okay. She's getting out to check under the hood, though we won't be stopping to assist*,' the voice laughed. '*How about you concentrate on your end of the . . .*'

The explosion slammed the Range Rover sideways before the shock wave flipped it over on its side. The sedan was just a plume of smoke rising from a twisted, burning hulk. The woman, who had presumably activated the bomb via remote or from a switch in the engine compartment, had been vaporised.

Geezer floored the accelerator. 'Drive past it,' Shane said into his microphone.

There was no answer from the BMW, which slewed to the right, then back to the left before its driver's side fender clipped the smoking Range Rover. The car spun three hundred and sixty degrees and stopped.

'Out, out!' Geezer yelled. The road was blocked. They all knew what was coming next.

Shane opened the door and dropped to one knee on the road. He scanned the streetscape as he flicked the selector switch on his M4 to semi-automatic. Geezer was on the other side and the two men in the back, a Scot and a Fijian, both ex-British SAS, fanned out further on either side.

'RPG!' Shane called. He'd heard the rocket-propelled grenade's motor engage then seen the trail of white smoke streak from the gutted supermarket on the right, the building a victim of a past car bombing or mortar attack. The round was low. It glanced off the road, slid under the BMW and ricocheted up into the underside of the tossed Range Rover. It pierced the floor of the big four-by-four like it was paper, and erupted inside. If the car bomb and roll hadn't killed callsign two-one, then the explosive warhead at the tip of the projectile had.

No one needed to give the command to fire. Shane pumped four rounds into the window from which the rocket had come, and the Fijian let off a twenty-round burst from his M249 light machine-gun.

'Contact left, Shane . . .' Geezer was cut down as he called the warning. Shane swung his torso, leaning across the Cruiser's bonnet, and saw the distinctive long dark barrel of a Dragunov sniper rifle. His first round glanced off the Arab's weapon, forcing the man to drop it. The second and third shots tore holes in his chest. The man toppled from the window. Shane was on his feet, moving forward, before the body hit the pavement.

The Fijian sprayed the supermarket, but the RPG firer had moved. Another grenade whooshed down the street towards Shane. He rolled to the ground, just twenty metres short of the Beemer. Behind him he heard the Landcruiser being rammed into gear. The

RPG round slammed into the right-hand rear door of the black limo and detonated.

Shane's ears rang and his body felt as though a giant's open palm had slapped him from head to toe with one blow. Part of him wanted to lie curled in the foetal position in the gutter until it was all over, but his training took over. It was like SAS selection, back in the rugged hills of Western Australia. A man could be physically strong enough to endure the constant marching and running with packs as heavy as a dead body, but it took mental strength, determination and willpower to get up and keep going after the false peaks and the mind games the cadre staff played to make trainees feel like he did now, that he couldn't possibly get up again.

The adrenaline kicked in and he rolled over and sat up. The noise of machine-gun bullets was reduced to a dull thud somewhere in the background, and his vision was blurry. He blinked, and forced himself to observe and think. The armour-plated car was still intact. Money well spent, he thought. He ground the knuckles of his right hand into the bitumen and pushed himself up. He stumbled forward, loosing two rounds from the hip at a flitter of movement in the alleyway between the gutted market and the tailor's store.

The windows of the sedan were black-tinted. He rapped on one and pushed his face to the glass. The driver was slumped over the steering wheel; the passenger beside him – the German member of their team – was pinned behind an airbag, blood running down his face, no movement. The woman in the back was open-mouthed, screaming something, but Shane couldn't hear a thing now. He pulled on the door handle, the metal still hot from the explosion, but it was locked. Fucking reliable European engineering. He groped his way along the driver's side, reached in through the holed window, past the dead man, and opened the door. All of the locks popped.

Shane reached into the back and grabbed the woman by the elbow. She struggled, but he wrenched her out, so hard she fell to the road. He hooked an arm under hers and lifted her. The Landcruiser was reversing back towards them. The Fijian was grinning like a madman, walking down the street, firing burst after burst into the shops, laying down covering fire.

Shane heard sirens, and the wailing was getting louder, which told him his hearing was returning. He had to work hard to focus his eyes. He fell to the ground, the woman slipping from his grasp to land beside him. He put his left hand down to lever himself up and winced with white-hot pain. Blood streamed down his bicep, soaking the business shirt. The Fijian's face was grimly set now. He had a target. Shane watched him bring the machine-gun from his waist up to his shoulder and take careful aim at an Arab holding an AK 47. The terrorist was bold or crazy enough to have stepped out into the street.

The woman was screaming and crying. Shane looked at the bullet wound in his arm, then dragged her and himself to standing again. He shoved her into the open rear door of the Landcruiser. Plenty of these Arabs wanted a one-way ticket to paradise, but why step out in the middle of the road when everything seemed to be going their way? The Landcruiser wasn't armoured enough to stop an RPG, so they could easily . . . .

His thoughts coalesced. The AK man was a decoy. Shane couldn't fire the M4 effectively with one arm so he tossed it into the back of the Cruiser. It clattered over the UN lady, who was an incoherent mess on the floor. Geezer, he saw, was in the rear of the four-by-four, his face deathly white, blood pumping from a wound in his shoulder. He tried to raise an arm to point, but Shane already knew what was going on.

The man with the AK 47 crumpled to the ground, his torso nearly severed from his legs by the Fijian's burst, intestines slithering into the gutter like a snake let out of a bag. The Fijian backed up to the front passenger door and called, 'Shane, come on bro!'

Shane drew the .45 from its holster.

The RPG firer poked his head and his weapon around the corner of a fire-bombed restaurant, one shop further on from the tailor's. He had scurried through a back alley. That put him further away from the vehicles, but the launcher was still well within range of the idling Landcruiser. It would be a long shot for the pistol. Shane steadied himself, legs apart, and brought the weapon up, one armed. His left still dangled uselessly.

He squeezed off two shots, the heavy pistol leaping high in the air from the recoil of each of the .45 rounds. One slug knocked a splinter from the masonry beside the Arab's head, the second sailed high. Shane heard the squeal of rubber on a roadway slick with blood. The Scot had done what he would have done. The first priority was always the package – in this case the UN lady. The RPG firer still had a clean shot.

The man stared at Shane, unafraid of dying. That, Shane realised, was what made this whole thing so crazy, so unwinnable. The Arab stepped out from behind the wall and peered into the optical sights atop the grenade launcher. Shane was an excellent marksman, but at a hundred and fifty metres pistol shooting is more luck than skill.

He ran, his legs pumping faster until he was sprinting. He fired twice more on the go.

The RPG man looked up, wide-eyed with surprise, from his sights. Shane was obscuring his view.

Shane slowed and stood in the path of the anti-tank weapon. He fired again. The first round carved a bloody furrow along the right side of the man's exposed neck, above his body armour. He staggered, but didn't drop, and Shane cursed. A hit anywhere on the body, even on the man's flak jacket, would have knocked him over. As the Arab squeezed the trigger on the RPG launcher, Shane's second round pierced the man's right forearm, but it was too late to stop the rocket motor from firing. The grenade warhead leapt from its tube.

However, the wound had forced the firer to jink at the last second. Instead of flying past Shane, the accelerating missile was now coming straight for him. He threw himself face down on the unforgiving roadway, arms out. He felt the heat of the missile's exhaust on his back, through his shirt and flak jacket.

Shane rolled over and risked raising his head. The Landcruiser rounded a bend and the grenade sailed through the plate glass of a bank branch and detonated inside. Fortunately the place was closed for business.

Another shriek of rubber on road made Shane look up. A red pick-up truck hurtled down the street from the direction they had initially been travelling. The RPG man rolled painfully over the side wall of the vehicle and landed hard in the back. The driver turned as he reversed and, with a handbrake-induced skid, ended up facing back the way he had come. Shane stood and raised his good arm to fire again.

Another Arab had been hiding in the back of the pick-up. He sat up and laid the barrel of a Russian-made PKM machine-gun on the side of the truck. Dozens of projectiles lashed the road on either side of Shane, who dropped again and rolled. He was in the open, at the gunner's mercy as the vehicle drove forward. He thought of wide-open vleis teaming with wildlife, under a clear blue African sky, and waited to die as he blindly squeezed off his last bullet.

A deep-throated engine roar heralded the arrival of a US Army quick-reaction force – an RG-31 mine-protected four-wheel drive supported by two Humvees. Shane heard the deep *clunk-clunk-clunk* of a .50 calibre machine-gun cranking into action. Music to his ears, as long as one of the finger-sized bullets didn't head his way.

The red pick-up veered and smashed into a power pole. Steam hissed noisily from its radiator, which had been shattered by a lead slug. The man with the machine-gun knelt in the tray, trying to climb out, hampered by the loss of an arm. A glowing tracer round found the fuel tank and the truck erupted in a roiling orange-black ball.

Shane stood, his good arm raised, and staggered, half-dazed, towards the truck and the oncoming Americans. Instinctively, he ejected the empty magazine from his pistol, took a fresh one from the black nylon pouch on his thigh, and reloaded the .45.

'Hold it there,' a Southern voice called from the armoured gun mount high atop the RG-31. Nicely ironic, Shane thought, that he had been saved by a South African-manufactured armoured vehicle. He might yet live to see the continent of his birth again.

'Australian!' he called. 'Contract security.' He gave the name of his company, which was well known around the city.

'Stay there. We'll come to you,' the acne-scarred young sergeant called from his turret.

'What about them?' Shane asked. The driver, the machine-gunner and the RPG man in the pick-up were all alight. One of the two in the back – Shane couldn't tell which now – tried to stand, his body engulfed in flames. The man screamed like a dying buffalo.

'Fuck 'em, Let 'em burn,' was the pronouncement from the sergeant on high.

Shane stood back from the heat of the burning car. After a year in Iraq on contract and three years fighting these people in the war on terrorism, he had less of an idea now about what motivated them than ever. But they had fought bravely for their cause, whatever that was.

He cocked the .45 and raised his arm.

'Hey,' called the American. 'Put that down, buddy.'

Shane pulled the trigger twice. The screaming stopped.

Shane awoke the next morning between cool sheets in a room smelling strongly of disinfectant and slightly of urine. The painkillers had been too good. He blinked at the white overhead lights.

An American flag hung from the ceiling.

The nurse was in US Army desert camouflage fatigues and was holding a clipboard. 'Good morning. Open wide for me.' She smiled at him and slid a thermometer into his mouth. She had dark hair, pulled back in a ponytail, and her eyes were almond-shaped, exotic.

'Is he awake, Tenille?' an English voice asked from the next cot. Shane turned his head and winced through the pain. It was Geezer, sitting up in bed, a glossy men's magazine in his good hand. His right shoulder and upper arm were bandaged.

'He is,' the nurse said. 'And I've told you before, it's "nurse" or "ma'am".'

'Shane, this is Nurse Jamgotchian. She's from New York. She hasn't come to terms with it yet, but she's going to be my next wife.'

'Puh-lease,' she said, taking the thermometer from Shane's mouth and checking it. She made a note on the chart.

'Jam . . . ?' Shane's head felt fuzzy as he tried to read the nurse's name tag.

'Jamgotchian. It's Armenian-American,' she said.

Shane looked across at Geezer as the nurse turned around to adjust the drip, which he just noticed was feeding into his arm. Geezer winked and mouthed the word 'Hot'.

Shane wiggled his fingers and toes. Everything seemed to be working, which was good. He saw the face of the RPG firer again, in the second before he loosed his final rocket, heard the screams of the burning man in the pick-up.

'Rio,' Geezer said as the nurse walked from the ward, her rubber-soled boots squeaking on the polished linoleum.

'What?'

'Rio de Janeiro. South American women are sensational.' He held up the folded magazine, revealing a tanned girl on a beach folding her arms across her bare breasts. 'It's where I'm going on leave, if Tenille keeps playing hard to get.'

Shane shook his head. They'd both nearly been killed and all Geezer could think about was getting laid. Shane had been in a relationship for a while in Perth – she was a nurse, but not military. She'd been supportive, and supposedly remained faithful during his time in Afghanistan. Iraq – with the army – had been a strain. She'd complained about being lonely, hinted at marriage and kids. He'd wanted everything to stay the same. She'd been ecstatic when he announced he was leaving the SAS, then walked out of the home they had shared for six months when he told her he'd taken a contract job back in the Middle East. He hadn't asked her to move in, it had just sort of happened. He knew from his mates' experiences that precious few marriages survived the life men like him led. In busy times like these, professional soldiering – in or out of uniform – was hardly conducive to a happy home.

When he settled, in Africa, as he would some day soon, he hoped he wouldn't be alone. He thought of Amanda, the nurse, and her clutter about the house. At first he'd found the drying hand-washed underwear, the perfume bottles, the hair combs, the shoes, the shoes, the bloody shoes, so annoying. Later, when she'd gone, the place had seemed soulless. Clean, but soulless. He owned the house outright, but what good was a three-bedroom home when you lived alone?

'I said, where will you go on your leave?' Geezer said from the next bed. 'Still stoned?'

'What? Sorry. I don't know. Maybe back to Oz. Maybe to Africa again.'

'Hello, here's trouble,' Geezer said.

A short, bald-headed man walked in. Ross Goldman was a retired US Army colonel who ran the local arm of the company Shane and Geezer worked for. 'At ease, don't get up,' he said.

'Very funny,' Shane replied.

'I haven't told Shane yet about the generous terms of our compensation payment,' Geezer said. To Shane, he explained, 'Ross came by this morning while you were still in your drug-induced coma.'

'A moment, please?' Ross said to Geezer. Shane had pegged him long ago as the type of leader who thought men wouldn't respect him if he were too familiar with them. It was not the kind of management approach that endeared him to men such as those he led. Goldman pulled across the curtain that divided Shane's bed from Geezer's, then took a seat close to Shane's bedhead.

'There's been a complaint,' the American said.

'By who?'

Goldman explained that an Iraqi ambulance had pulled up behind the US Army vehicle that had set fire to the pick-up containing the Arab gunman. A doctor had seen Shane stride down the street and shoot a burning man in the head, killing him before the medical team had a chance to get near the vehicle to check for survivors.

'That's bullshit, and you know it, Ross.'

'I believe your version. But you know there are people in the Iraqi administration who'll do anything to undermine the American presence here – and that extends to foreign security firms.'

Shane screwed his eyes shut. This couldn't be happening. 'What about the sergeant in the RG-31 – the guy who told me to let the Arab burn?'

'He's under investigation too. This is going to get blown out of all proportion, Shane.'

Shane opened his eyes and looked into Ross's. The other man looked away. Bastard, Shane thought. 'You won't stand behind me?'

'It's their country and we have to play by their rules. You know there have been complaints about companies such as ours acting like a law unto themselves. We're bidding for a new contract right now with the Iraqi Government and we can't afford controversy.'

'So I'm finished?'

'You're a good operator and we don't want to lose you. You're due leave, right?'

'I'll be ready for work again in a couple of weeks.'

'It might be an idea to take a little longer.'

It dawned on Shane what his supervisor was suggesting. They wanted him out of the country – indefinitely. 'Shit,' he said. He hadn't expected a medal or a bonus for what he'd done yesterday, but neither had he expected virtually to be laid off.

'I can get you out of here on a C-130 to Kuwait tonight. I'll have our doctor say you need further medical treatment. If you're not in the country the investigation will probably peter out,' Ross said.

'All so the company can win another multimillion dollar contract.'

'We look after our people, Shane.'

'So it seems.'

Ross straightened in his chair. 'I'll try and ignore that attitude. Take six months' leave and we'll reassess the situation here at that time. In the meantime, you might be interested in this.' He handed Shane a piece of paper.

Shane felt betrayed, angry, abandoned. Reluctantly, he scanned the message. It was a print-out of an email. As he started to read, Goldman explained the originator was a friend of his, a retired South African Recce-Commando major who lived in Johannesburg. The major had been sounded out about a job in Zimbabwe, but was already engaged full time in his own security business. He had forwarded the original message, which had come from a professional hunter.

It was an informal job advertisement.

I'm looking for someone who can run anti-poaching operations on my hunting concession in Zim, north-west of Wankie, on the Botswana border. As the local law and order situation deteriorates things are getting worse up here. Not only subsistence poaching, but also organised gangs, heavily armed, who are crossing the border from Zambia in search of ivory and rhino horn. Ideally the person will be ex-special forces, with a good knowledge of the bush, and able to work well with Africans. I have funding in US dollars for the job. House and vehicle will be supplied. Initial contract is six months, with a view to extension.

The email was from a Fletcher Reynolds, of Isilwane Lodge, Matetsi, Zimbabwe. The name seemed familiar. Shane stared at the overhead lights, then remembered. 'I saw this guy on television yesterday.'

'Whatever,' Ross said. 'Are you interested?'

Interested? He could have kissed the American, if he hadn't been so pissed off at him. It was a chance to get back to Africa, make some contacts and earn US dollars at the same time.

Goldman left and a red-haired female doctor arrived to inspect Geezer's wound. As the Englishman flirted with her, Shane lay back, wishing he could light a cigarette, and closed his eyes.

The action replayed in his mind, in slow motion, but crystal clear. He saw the rounds from his rifle strike home on the sniper's weapon and body, his aim and actions as precise and cool as if he'd been on the firing range back home. He saw the anger on the face of the RPG firer as the man realised Shane's shot had spoiled his aim. It was the closest to his victims he had ever come. Man against man. It was a world away from calling in B-52 air strikes on Al Qaeda in Afghanistan, or the running vehicle-versus-vehicle gunfights of the early days of the Iraq invasion.

He had faced the ultimate test of a warrior. He thought about the burning man, and tried to remember how he had felt when he pulled the trigger. He told himself he had done the deed out of mercy for a respected foe, that he had wanted to end the man's incurable pain. He thought of the dead men lying in the street around him, the blood and the noise and smoke, and tried to remember if he had been scared.

The pictures still played in his mind, but when he strived to recall his feelings, and to analyse his emotions now, after it was all over, one shocking truth suddenly dawned on him.

He felt nothing.

5

The Sinamatella River wound its way across the dry plain like a brown snake. At this time of year it was a river in name only, its bed more sand than water, except for the odd puddle where the life force still oozed, reluctantly, to the surface. In some places there were damp patches of sand where determined elephants had dug for water.

Michelle watched a pair of white rhino through her binoculars. They might be a mating pair, she thought. It had been four days since her dinner with Fletcher. She set the glasses down on the stone-slab table at the Elephant and Dassie Restaurant and took a sip of bitter Zimbabwean coffee tinted grey with canned evaporated milk.

A cooked breakfast was pot luck at Sinamatella Camp these days. She sopped up the last of her runny egg yolk with a piece of home-baked bread and pushed the remains of her rather gamey pork sausage to the edge of the plate, then returned her attention to the view.

And what a view. The camp was situated on a mesa that rose steeply from the otherwise featureless plains. From this majestic vantage point, beneath an expansive thatched *lapa*, or shelter, with a bit of luck one could sit and see all of Africa's big five – lion, elephant, rhino, leopard and buffalo – though even through binoculars a two-tonne rhino was little bigger than an ant. Of wild dogs there was no sign, although a reported sighting by a ranger near Mandavu Dam ten kilometres from the camp had been enough to make her up-stakes from Robins for a few days.

She had packed reluctantly, having hung around Robins and its satellite camp, Nantwich, where Rembrandt had been killed, in the hope of running into the pack again, even though she had lost radio contact with Picasso's collar. Normally, when she received a new sighting report, she couldn't wait to get on the road, but yesterday she had wished she could stay in the north of the park a little longer – until Fletcher made contact with her again. There was no public telephone in the camp and her radio was tuned to the national parks frequency only. She could have gone to the warden at Robins or Sinamatella and found out Fletcher's frequency and callsign – they were sure to have that information – but she found herself unwilling to make the next move.

'Will there be anything else, madam?' the waiter asked.

'Just the bill, please,' she said as the man cleared away her plate. Poor guy had arms like an anorexic's. She remembered him, by sight, from her earlier visits, but couldn't recall his name. It saddened her to think that on her next visit – maybe in a month or two – he mightn't be around any more. The virus was a slow, silent plague that everyone in Africa had come to accept as a part of life – and death. She wondered if he would leave a wife and children behind.

Michelle heard a vehicle pull up in the car park beside the restaurant. Even though her view was obscured by the stone wall draped with pink-red bougainvillea, she recognised the clatter of a diesel Land Rover. She tried not to look as she heard Fletcher's booming voice as he greeted the waiter like a long-lost friend. 'How's it, *shamwari*?'

He strode across the flagstones after ordering a coffee and sat down beside her. 'You're harder to track than a leopard,' he said.

Oddly, he was carrying what looked to Michelle like a woman's woven cane sewing basket. She put down her binoculars and said, 'I kind of expected to see you again down at Robins, to talk about . . . business.'

'Ah, yes, business. First off, forgive me for not finding you sooner. Second off, please, Michelle, I hope you're not mad about the other night. You know I wouldn't want to do anything to offend . . .'

'No, no. Really, it's all fine. Still friends – and business partners?'

'Still both. Good, I'm glad that's sorted.'

'All the same, I did think you'd want to talk more about this research deal.'

'That's why I'm here, but I was called away on business, to Harare, the day after our dinner. There was no way to get word to you. I hope you didn't read too much into that.'

'Of course not,' she lied. She'd agonised for two days, thinking he might withdraw his offer of funding because she had spurned his advance. She breathed easier now, and hoped her relief wasn't too obvious.

Over a fresh pot of coffee Fletcher explained that one of his regular local clients, a brigadier in the Army of the Republic of Zimbabwe, had invited him to Harare to discuss a business venture. The army had been committed by the government to the Democratic Republic of Congo, formerly Zaire, a couple of years earlier to help prop up the regime of Joseph Kabila, son of the murdered Laurent Kabila, who had seized power from the Zairian dictator Mobuto Sese Seko in 1997. Stories abounded of how the Zimbabwean government and its military had become involved in business dealings in the DRC as a pay-off for their support of the regime. Fletcher's contact, Brigadier Winston Moyo, had been interested in exploring new hunting opportunities during his time in the war-ravaged country.

'Moyo's talking about a joint venture – him organising a concession from the DRC government on the Ugandan border, close to the Virunga National Park, and me running the hunting operation. Because the rains start much later up there than here in Zim, it means I can keep hunting in our off season.'

'I've read about the area you're speaking of. That's mountain gorilla country, isn't it?'

'Yes. Bad poaching, even worse than here. It's also

72

near the Rwandan border, and there are still refugees and militia from there living in the bush on the DRC side. They're hunting gorillas and other primates for bush meat, and also selling baby gorillas to illegal wildlife traders.'

'Fletcher, please don't tell me you're going to be hunting mountain gorillas?' She knew he wouldn't be, but couldn't resist goading him.

He ignored her flippancy. 'Leopard, forest sitatunga, giant forest hog, maybe some forest elephant and buffalo, if we can find any left.'

'No okapi?'

'They're protected,' he said, missing her sarcasm. The okapi, sometimes known as the forest giraffe, looked like a zebra with an impossibly long neck.

'What am I doing here drinking coffee with you?'

He smiled. 'Working out how to spend my fifty thou, I suppose.'

'What's in your dainty little basket there?' she asked.

'Ah, I was wondering how long it would take you to ask. It's for you. A peace offering.' He slid the basket across the stone table towards her.

'You don't have to make peace with me, Fletcher.'

'Then call it a belated birthday present.'

She lifted one of the top flaps and caught a whiff of bougainvillea and perfume. 'Fletcher, where did you get all this girly stuff?' Inside the basket was a tastefully arranged selection of scented soaps, bath beads, salon-brand shampoos and conditioners, nail varnish, and cleansers, interspersed with flowers and a kind of African ethnic potpourri made from seed pods, guineafowl feathers, leaves and even a couple of porcupine quills.

Fletcher looked across at her expectantly. He cleared his throat. 'My maid, Mary, did the arranging,' he said, as if to reassure her of his masculinity.

She laughed. 'I'm touched. Thank you, but where did you get all this stuff?' As her surprise receded, she fixed her eyes on his, trying to read what intentions there might be behind the gift.

He looked down, swirling the dregs of his coffee in the cup. 'To tell you the truth it was my wife's. She . . . um . . . left behind stuff she could buy when she and the kids moved to Cape Town. It's all unopened and it seemed a shame to throw it out. I hardly ever get clients visiting with their wives any more.' He looked back up at her.

She was touched by his awkwardness. He usually seemed so self-assured, yet here he was trying to do something genuinely nice for her, while not wanting to make it look like another come-on. At the same time, he was struggling with memories of his failed relationship.

'It's beautiful, Fletcher. Thank you, and thank Mary for me. Now, tell me, how's your local business going?'

He seemed grateful for the change of subject. 'More Americans coming in tomorrow. Some banking friends of the dentist. But, for now, how would you like to see some of your doggies?'

Her coffee cup clattered on the unforgiving surface of the stone table. 'You've seen them! Why didn't you tell me?'

'Relax, they're sleeping. On the edge of the road in some mopane, between here and Mandavu. Well, what are you waiting for?'

They travelled in her vehicle, as it was easier than transferring all of her monitoring, tracking and recording gear to his. Also, with fuel so short in the country no one ever took two trucks when one would do.

Fletcher was keen to see her in action, to assess the merits of her work and satisfy himself she was not just some overkeen graduate student on an extended holiday. As pretty as she was, he genuinely wanted to make sure he had made the right decision about committing the dentist's research grant. And he wanted to spend time with her. He'd been clumsy the first time around and, while he was disappointed, he was not deterred. Some hunts took longer than others.

The dogs were still where he had seen them on his drive up from Robins, on the side of the road resting in the shade, near the turn-off to Salt Spring.

She stopped the car and he whispered, 'Tell me about them.'

Michelle looked at him, pursed her lips and nodded. She understood what this drive was about, at least in part. She scanned the dogs through her binoculars. 'Three adults, four pups. The alpha male and female are on the far left. The other adult is a female, though subordinate. Both of the bitches are from the same litter, their mother was Rembrandt, the alpha female from the pack I was tracking last week around

75

Robins. The male is from a pack that originated south of Main Camp, near the Kennedy picnic site.

'Those youngsters are about three months old. They would have just started following the adults on hunts. Until recently they and the alpha female would have been fed by the other two, who would hunt and then regurgitate food for the others at the den. Look at the female.'

Fletcher moved his binoculars. The alpha female had raised her huge rounded ears and was looking intently down the road in the direction they had been travelling. 'What's she seen?'

'Watch the signal she gives the male in a second.' Michelle checked her watch and made a note of the time on the clipboard on her knees. 'There, about a hundred metres . . . impala.'

Fletcher followed Michelle's pointing finger and found the lone ram. The girl had good eyesight, and that was a rare compliment coming from him, though he didn't voice it. 'I see it.'

'They're up! Have you ever seen a wild dog kill?' she asked.

He shook his head. He had baited and shot plenty of them in his youth, and knew of their fearsome reputation as hunters and killers, but he had never taken the time to study or follow a pack.

'Then you, as a hunter, are in for a treat,' she whispered.

The dogs rose on their long, spindly legs. The alpha female yelped, her cry more a high-pitched twittering than a bark. She moved off down the corrugated dirt road, the pups scampering along behind her. She moved at a slow trot, as though pacing herself. The alpha male and the subordinate female split and took off at a faster pace, through the remains of elephant-shredded mopane trees, their paws raising little clouds of red-brown dust as they ran.

'They're the flankers,' Michelle explained as she put the Landcruiser in gear and slowly followed the mother and her pups.

'There's the impala! He's seen the male. I thought you said these things were good.' Fletcher saw how the antelope leapt high into the air then sprinted from the right-hand side, across the road, to the left.

Michelle smiled. 'Can you see the subordinate female?'

He scanned the bush on the left-hand side. 'No.'

'And neither can the impala. Watch and learn, big white hunter.'

There was yelping from the alpha male and the alpha female now, and the head dog picked up her pace, the pups finding it harder to keep up on their stubby legs. The adults, however, were made for the chase, with their greyhound-sleek bodies. 'There!' Michelle hissed. The impala broke right, running onto the road from the left.

Fletcher saw the subordinate female now, moving in from the same side. The alpha male closed in from the right. The impala had been funnelled between the two dogs.

'Here she goes,' Michelle said. The alpha female, who had been conserving her energy, shot forward like a bolt from a crossbow, her legs a blur, the pups left in her dusty wake. The impala skittered left and right, the other two dogs running on either side of it. Confused, it lost distance and momentum by jumping first to the left, and then to the right. It was a fatal mistake.

Michelle put her foot down on the accelerator, keeping a careful eye on the pups, who had moved off the road and were running parallel to the truck. They didn't seem to mind the vehicle's presence and, if anything, seemed curious about this newcomer to the hunt.

'They've got it!' Fletcher cried. He had seen lion and leopard kills, fights to the death between elephants, life and death in all its glory and tragedy, but this was like nothing he had ever witnessed.

The alpha female caught the impala by its tail and dragged it, still hopping, to a halt. The alpha male settled the prey's front by grasping its snout between his jaws. All three dogs then simply tore the antelope to pieces.

Michelle stopped ten metres away. Any closer and Fletcher reckoned they would have been sprayed. The carcass was unrecognisable, consumed in seconds rather than minutes – a mist of red blood, blue entrails and fawn-coloured hair. The pups caught up and chattered and squealed as they ran around the adults. Two fought over a length of intestine. Beside him, Michelle's digital Canon clicked away at three frames to the second, recording the whole thing.

As quickly as it had begun, it was over. 'My God,' he said. He was amazed. Not at the dogs' ferocity, or their success in the hunt – he had heard and read of those many times before. What impressed him – moved

78

him – was that this attractive Canadian girl had come to Africa and showed him, Fletcher Reynolds, professional hunter and bushman, something he had never seen before. He didn't know how to thank her.

'Impressed?' she asked.

'More than you can imagine.'

She looked at him and smiled and he thought his hard old heart might just melt there and then. She picked up her binoculars and followed the flight of the dogs off into the stunted bush. When they were out of sight she ignored him as she noted the time, the date, the distance travelled during the hunt – she had had the presence of mind to set her odometer when they had first spotted the dogs – and the size and sex of the prey. She edged the Landcruiser forward and noted how much of the impala remained. Not much.

Fletcher watched her work. His heart was still beating from the rush of seeing the kill. She was doing her job. And that only made him desire her more.

'She is walking faster, sometimes running,' Charles Ndlovu said, one knee in the dust and ash, his finger gently caressing the three-toed indentation. The tiny ant tracks and the leaves and twigs that filled the mighty creature's spoor told him they were still at least a day behind Chewore the rhino.

He started to speak again, but the cough wracked his body so much he could not get the words out. Some days were worse than others. This was a bad one.

'Perhaps she knows she is being followed by the poachers,' Lovemore said.

That was what Charles had been about to say, but he held his tongue. He didn't want another run-in with the young man, who was, whether he, Noah and Christopher liked it, the boss. He barely had the strength to speak, let alone argue. He nodded. They had been tracking the rhino, and the poachers who pursued her for days, and the younger men were losing patience.

'Ah, it will be dead before we catch those Zambians,' Noah said.

Charles spat. 'This is our job.'

Christopher sniggered, but it was Lovemore who came to the older man's defence. 'Ndlovu is right. Other people may not know or care about the work we are doing, but God knows, and the government knows.'

Charles smiled. So, it seemed Lovemore owed his allegiance to someone higher after all, or perhaps he put the Comrade President and the Almighty on the same plain. It didn't matter. The boys needed some backbone. 'We must be ready.' He wiped the spittle from his lips with the back of his hands. 'The Zambians are hunting rhino, so they will not be armed with spears. All of you, keep your eyes and ears open. If they see us first, then some of us will die.'

A fire had swept west from Dolilo, burning out what little vegetation remained after the elephants' annual destructive migration across the park. The wind gathered strength from the hot dry earth and whipped the ash and dust into whirlwinds that danced across the barren hills like ever-moving funeral pyres. They closed their eyes and shielded their weapons as best as they could as the cyclonic hail of dirt and charred leaves and twigs sandblasted their exposed skin.

After nearly a week in the bush they bore little resemblance to the smartly turned-out patrol that had paraded for inspection in front of the warden at Sinamatella. Only Charles still wore both his uniform shirt and trousers. In the old days, when the whites ruled the country, a man would have been charged and fined for being out of uniform. Discipline was not everything, but it kept men focused on the job and put paid to the whining and complaining that was going on now. Christopher picked at a scabby cut on his left upper arm, where a thornbush had drawn blood. The wound was caked with ash and grit and might become infected. The boy had taken off his shirt two days earlier and now wore only chest webbing on his bare torso. 'That wouldn't have happened if you had kept your uniform on.'

Christopher glared back. 'If I had left my shirt on, it would have got ripped, old man. And would the parks and wildlife service have given me a new shirt? Ah, no.'

Charles coughed again. There was no point in arguing against the truth.

Ahead he heard the distant *tukka-tukka-tukka* of a diesel engine. He raised a hand. 'Listen.'

They all stopped. 'Where is that?' Lovemore asked.

'Deteema. We are getting close to the dam and picnic site,' he said. 'We can rest and refill the water bottles there, if you agree, Lovemore.'

As well as the three main camps, dotted throughout Hwange were picnic sites where visitors could get out and stretch their legs, or camp overnight. The isolated compounds were staffed by an attendant, who kept water pumped to the pans – when there was diesel available – and tanks filled for humans to drink from.

'It will be good to stop for a while,' Lovemore said.

Charles wondered if they could really catch the poachers before Chewore crossed into Botswana. He doubted it.

If he were one of the Zambians his plan would be to pursue the rhino into the forest lands on the other side of the border and kill it there, out of Zimbabwean jurisdiction. A rhino's horns are not big. Once hacked off they could be stuffed in a backpack, and an AK 47 can be broken down into small pieces. The poachers could simply walk to the main tar road between Nata and Kazungula and flag down a passing bus. It was laughably simple.

Charles brushed the grit from the bare metal of the breech block slide that showed through the ejection port of his SLR. He would clean his rifle while the others drank and slept and ate at the picnic site. If they did meet the poachers, he would be ready.

6

It seemed like he had been flying forever. Baghdad to Kuwait on an Arizona Air National Guard C-130; a stopover at the military hospital at Ali Al Salem Air Base to re-dress his wounds and tell him he was fit to travel; Kuwait Airlines to Dubai; Emirates to Johannesburg; and now South African Airways to Zimbabwe.

Joshua Nkomo International Airport, at Bulawayo, the country's second largest city, was a tin shed. The new terminal, according to a sign, was under construction and passengers were offered an apology for the inconvenience. He'd been in worse points of embarkation and debarkation – at least no one was shooting here.

Inside, Shane Castle baked, along with rich black and white teenagers home for the holidays from private schools in South Africa; African businessmen – or maybe politicians, judging by their girth in this country of otherwise skinny people; women in bright-printed traditional dresses; and whites who had the same drawn faces and grim looks as soldiers reluctantly returning to a war zone after a couple of weeks' R and R. There were only two tourists that he could pick out, a hardy looking pair of Israelis with dreadlocks and backpacks.

He shuffled his way in the immigration queue, sliding his military backpack and green vinyl dive bag along the concrete floor of the hangar with his booted foot.

'How long do you stay in Zimbabwe?' the bored-looking clerk asked as he thumbed, slowly, through every page of Shane's Australian passport.

'Few months. After that we'll see.' He pointed to the six-month multiple-entry visa when the man eventually reached the page.

'Issued in Kuwait. And I see you have been in Iraq. What were you doing there?'

'Surfing.'

The man looked up, squinted, then smiled. 'Ah, but you are making a joke. There is water, but no surf in the Persian Gulf.'

'There isn't?'

'No.'

'How's the water here?'

The clerk raised the stamp and let it hover over the elaborate, hologram-embossed visa. Shane had a theory that the impressiveness of a country's visas was proportionate to the size of the national debt. 'We are a land-locked country, facing a severe drought.'

'Just as well I didn't bring my board.'

'I think you know all this already. I see you were born in a place called Salisbury, Rhodesia.' They were the old names for Harare and Zimbabwe, respectively.

Shane smiled. The man was sharper than he made out. 'So it says, bru.'

'I am not your brother and that place does not exist any more, Mister Shane Castle.'

After customs had finished searching his pack and bag, Shane, the last passenger to clear, walked past a flimsy wooden screen and saw a body builder clutching a piece of cardboard with his name on it.

With a grip that would have broken his fingers had he not anticipated it, the white Zimbabwean, Dougal Geddes, led him out of one hangar and across a concrete taxiway to another. 'I do charters – take all of Fletcher's clients up to the ranch. He tells me you might be working for him. Are you a hunter?'

'Kind of,' Shane said as he hoisted his gear into the back of the Cessna's cramped cockpit.

It wasn't nearly as hot as Baghdad in summer, but the haze rising from the runway snatched the moisture from under his arms before it had time to make itself felt. Dougal opened the throttle and raced towards the inviting blue sky.

'*Can't pick your accent, man. You from Australia or New Zealand?*' Dougal asked as the angular, colonial grid of Bulawayo slipped under them and wide, empty, golden-brown Africa bared itself to Shane again.

'I'm from here.'

*

Once they were over Hwange National Park, Dougal pointed out a herd of six or seven hundred buffalo. '*Poaching's getting worse, but the animals here are survivors*,' he said into the microphone attached to his headset.

Shane pressed his face against the Perspex and watched the smokescreen kicked up by thousands of hooves. He remembered their bovine smell from game drives in the family's old Ford on holidays. *Braais* at sunset, his first taste of beer. The smell of *boerewors* cooking and the sizzle of fat on the glowing red coals.

'*That's the place.*' Dougal pointed ahead and to the right.

Shane saw the long red-dirt airstrip carved from the grey-brown bush; a sprawling thatch-roofed lodge, open-topped hunting vehicles and two glinting town cars. Mud-brick buildings in a fenced compound – the staff area, he guessed – upturned faces and waving children. A Land Rover was parked on the edge of the strip, four white men milling around it. Dougal flew low over the runway, to check for animals, then carried on north, towards Victoria Falls, before executing a wide, lazy turn.

'*Hell, look at that, hey. Might be your first taste of business!*' Dougal's excitement was plain. He had coaxed from Shane the type of job he had applied for. He banked the aircraft to the left and started a tight circuit.

Shane looked down and saw a flock of vultures rise from a blackened, rotting carcass. 'Elephant. Looks like an adult – too big to have been taken by lions. Maybe old age?' The vultures organised themselves into a holding pattern, circling with the aid of a thermal over the hot dry killing zone.

'*I'll mark the coordinates.*' Dougal punched a button on the GPS mounted on the Cessna's dashboard.

The little aeroplane bounced a couple of times on the uneven surface then turned at the end of the clearing and taxied back to where the Land Rover waited. Dougal shook Shane's hand, said goodbye and explained that he would be taking off straightaway, with three hunters who had just finished their safari with Fletcher Reynolds.

As Shane hoisted his pack and grabbed his dive bag he caught snippets of the farewells, in loud American accents.

'Absolutely outstanding, Fletcher. The experience of a lifetime.'

'Unforgettable. Make sure you email the confirmation to me for our booking for next year. I want my son to see this place.'

Shane saw the tall, rangy owner of the ranch, dressed in a khaki shirt and denim shorts shorter than had been the fashion anywhere else in the world for decades. A scar ran up the hard-calved right leg. 'Let's hope it's safer for you next year, Hal.'

'Hell no, baby! The danger's the buzz in this place. Besides, the good thing is that we never felt threatened. You the man!' More hand pumping and then the Americans smiled and nodded to Shane as they squeezed into Dougal's aircraft.

Fletcher Reynolds shook his hand but held off speaking until the whine of the revving aeroplane engine had faded away to the other end of the airstrip. 'Welcome, Shane,' he said.

Shane passed on the information about the dead elephant and handed his prospective employer a piece of paper from the green hard-backed field notebook he habitually kept in his top pocket. 'Those are the GPS coordinates.'

Fletcher started the pick-up and handed the scrap back to Shane. 'That carcass is only three kilometres from here. I've known about it since it happened. I heard the shot, in fact. That group who just left were out with me when we came across the two poachers with their ivory. One's in hospital now with half his leg missing – a .458 will do that to you.'

'Who shot him?' Shane asked.

'Me.'

'And the other poacher?'

'Dead,' Fletcher said.

Shane nodded. He had hoped the news might have impressed the older man, but he'd been foolish to think Reynolds wouldn't have had a good grip on what was going on in his immediate backyard. He wondered, not for the first time, what skills he would be able to bring to anti-poaching operations that the experienced professional hunter did not have himself. The man had already been involved in at least two armed run-ins with poachers in recent times. He knew his business.

'That kill was unusual, in that it happened so close to the ranch,' Reynolds explained as he drove. The Land Rover was an old Series II, a museum piece the likes of which Shane hadn't seen since his childhood.

It was older than he was. 'Most of the poaching takes place on the boundaries of the concession and, of course, inside our neighbouring national park – Hwange. Some of the activity is subsistence, setting snares for antelope or shooting for the pot, and the rest is organised hunting of elephant for ivory or, if they can find one, rhino. I'm sure you're wondering where you fit into all this.'

Shane nodded again. A small herd of zebra panicked at the clatter of the old diesel engine and scattered.

'I need you to use the skills you've learned in the army and be my eyes and ears, Shane. I want long-range recce – the kind you Aussies are supposed to be so good at.'

Shane had been proud to serve in his adopted country's military, and he firmly believed the unit he had spent most of his time with was the world's best at what it did – long-range special reconnaissance – but he bridled at being referred to as a foreigner, when he was, by birthright, a Zimbabwean. He held his tongue, though.

Reynolds filled the void. 'I want you to train a team of your own and go out and find the *skellums* that are causing me grief. I want to know when, where and how the poachers are getting in here. Too much of our fight is reactive – we wait for an animal to be killed and then try and follow the poachers out. Usually they're long gone before we get near them. When you find these bastards, I want you to follow them, fix them, then let me know where they are. I'll call in the authorities and we'll catch them before they can do their business.'

'Sounds like a plan,' he said.

'You've come highly recommended, Shane. The only thing, and I'll be honest with you, that concerned me was that you've spent most of your life out of Africa.'

Shane nodded. He'd expected this line of questioning. 'I was born here, Fletcher, and I've got a field guide's qualification, so I know the basics about approaching dangerous game on foot and surviving in the African bush, but you're the professional hunter of animals here.'

Reynolds nodded.

'What you want me to organise is a military operation.'

Fletcher smiled. 'Exactly.'

Shane spent his first two weeks at Isilwane Lodge getting to know every road, fire trail, creek, river and kopje on Fletcher's hunting concession.

He had thousands of hectares to cover. His days were full of driving in a Land Rover given to him for the job, while his nights were taken up poring over a topographical map planning his next recce.

His guide for the first week was Fletcher's chief tracker, an Ndebele man of his own age, Lloyd, who was an expert scout with a genuine affinity for wildlife and the bush. Lloyd had been born in Hwange, the son of a ranger, and had worked for the parks and wildlife service for a few years before branching out into the private sector.

Lloyd had explained that given the parlous state of

the hunting industry – Fletcher Reynolds seemed to be the exception rather than the rule with his recent ability to lure more foreign bookings – it would not be easy to recruit younger rangers from the national parks to work on Shane's anti-poaching team. 'However, the government is retrenching the older men. You should start there.'

It was good advice and Shane wished he could have had more of Lloyd's time, but the tracker was needed by Fletcher to work on his next safari, which consisted of four Italians who worked for the corporate head office of a luxury car manufacturer.

Dougal, the pilot, occasionally helped Fletcher with flyovers of the concession to check on water points and game concentrations. When he brought the Italians to Isilwane he agreed to give Shane an hour's aerial tour of the ground he had painstakingly traversed by road. Shane had a map of the property taped to the wall of the two-bedroom manager's cottage where he lived, behind the main lodge. On it he had marked all of the known poaching incidents from the past twelve months. As Fletcher had predicted, the major incidents, involving elephant and buffalo kills, tended to take place in the north-west of the concession, near the Botswana border.

'Can you take us down?' he asked Dougal through the headset microphone.

'*Sure thing*,' the pilot replied. '*That's the border post at Pandamatenga below. Zim on that side, Bots on the other.*'

They followed a dirt road that paralleled the international boundary. '*We're getting close to the national park now,'* Dougal informed him.

Shane scanned the waterless bush through his binoculars. He recognised riverbeds and the border road. 'There's a hyena. Unusual to see him out in the middle of the day.'

Dougal nodded and pushed the control wheel forward, bringing them down lower. *'He's in a hurry. Must have the scent of something.'*

They passed over the loping scavenger and, as had happened when they spotted the elephant kill, it was an eruption of dark, slow-beating vulture wings that pointed out the scene of the crime. 'Elephant . . . no, wait, too small. It's a rhino,' Shane confirmed.

'Bastards,' Dougal spat.

That man is too low,' Charles Ndlovu said as the white Cessna roared overhead.

'Should we take his registration number and report him?' Lovemore asked.

Charles had found that since he had taken a conciliatory approach to the Shona, the man had not only become more amenable, but had started asking him for advice. However, when Charles had tried, politely, to suggest that they move on from the Deteema picnic site after refilling their water bottles, Lovemore had dug his heels in and sided with the two younger men, who wanted to rest the night. Charles feared the delay had cost them the rhino. 'No, Lovemore. I think he is low because he has seen something. Maybe the poachers.'

'Be alert, you men,' Lovemore commanded.

Charles noticed, with some concern, how their leader's finger curled with anticipation around the trigger of his AK 47.

Charles scanned the ground. The aircraft was definitely heading in the same direction as the fading tracks of the poachers and the wayward rhino, Chewore. The spoor of man and beast, however, was now the same age. He raised a hand and lifted his head. Mouth open, he sniffed the air.

He caught the first telltale whiffs of the stench. It sickened him. The smell of death was the smell of failure.

Shane leapt from the Cessna as soon as it rolled to a halt, and sprinted for the lodge. Behind him, Dougal had already taken off. If he hadn't been low on fuel he would have stayed and assisted with the tracking of the men who were responsible for the rhino's death.

Shane was on his own. A quick word with Fletcher's housekeeper confirmed the hunter and his Italian clients had wasted no time and had already left in search of game. He grabbed a radio and two spare batteries, then used his key to unlock the lodge's safe, and fetched the rifle Reynolds had allocated him, an old military 7.62 millimetre SLR. Just like Fletcher's Land Rovers, it was ancient, reliable and unstoppable. He doubled across the lawn to his own cottage.

His gear was packed and ready to go. It had been since his first afternoon, as he had anticipated the possibility of having to leave with no notice. In his chest webbing were four magazines of twenty rounds each. His web belt carried four one-litre military plastic water bottles and a hand-held radio. In his camouflaged pack was a lightweight one-man tent, poncho liner, food – cans, dehydrated potato and rice, and dried kudu biltong – two more one and a half litre store-bought bottles of drinking water wrapped in duct tape for extra strength, a collapsible shovel, a first-aid kit and a set of night-vision goggles he had purchased on the black market in Baghdad.

From the locked cabinet in his bedroom he took the valuables he was reluctant to leave lying about with his kit – Swarovski binoculars, a GPS, a digital camera and a satellite phone. These, along with fully charged spare batteries for all the gadgets, he stashed in the top of the pack, where he had left space for them.

He flung the heavy rucksack over one shoulder, the webbing and belt over the other, then piled the lot onto the front bench seat of his Land Rover. He left the Isilwane gatehouse behind in a spray of dust and gravel. It was five minutes since he had left Dougal's aircraft.

Shane navigated from memory, taking the main dirt road south towards the national park gate, then turning right towards Pandamatenga. Before reaching the final bend that would take him to the border post he branched left onto a hunting trail he'd driven just three days earlier. He remembered a spring, less than a kilometre from the line of white stones that marked the end of Zimbabwe and the beginning of Botswana. Perhaps the rhino had been heading for water. He checked the GPS. He was close to the spot he had copied from Dougal's aircraft-mounted navigation device. He pulled the Land Rover into the shade of a small grove of ilala palms. He shouldered his pack and webbing, clipped on his belt and loaded a magazine in his rifle. He took the GPS from the dashboard and set off to do his job.

It took him less than twenty minutes to find the carcass and he could have done it without the GPS – the circling spiral of vultures waiting for their turn, like jets in a holding pattern at a busy airport, was a better pointer than any modern gizmo. His hunch was right. The rhino had been plugged just fifty metres short of the spring. He watched the hollowed skin and jumble of bones for another fifteen minutes from the cover of a cluster of immature leadwoods. If there had been men nearby, the vultures would have been in the trees. Instead, the rhino's remains were being noisily picked and fought over. Most of the birds were white-backed vultures, though a lappet-faced, a monstrous thing whose ugly pink and purple head stood high above the others, occasionally bounded through the dust and gore, hopping on both clawed talons, to elbow the others out of the way. The lappet-faced, with its wicked hooked beak, was the can-opener, the one who cut through tough skin so that others could feed on the entrails. Because of his strength and size he also claimed the choicest morsels.

Shane had deliberately moved in downwind of the rhino, so as not to alert the poachers with his scent. As a result, he copped the full force of the rotting stench. He breathed through his mouth and scanned the surrounding bush. The illegal hunters were well gone, he reckoned.

He had established radio contact with Fletcher on the drive out from the lodge, alerting him to the find. He'd been quietly pleased that this kill, at least, was news to his employer. 'Niner, this is Taipan,' he said quietly into his hand-held radio. Fletcher had insisted on giving him the callsign Taipan, after Australia's deadliest snake. Shane had thought it a little corny – and also odd, given that he didn't expect to be doing any killing in this job. Whatever. As a mark of respect he'd suggested Fletcher be referred to as 'Niner' – Australian military radio-speak for the commanding officer of a unit.

'*Niner, over,*' Fletcher replied through static.

'Found the carcass, but it looks like the bad guys are long gone.' He read the coordinates from the GPS, then added, 'I'll follow their spoor to the border and see if I can pick up anything else, over.'

'*Roger, Taipan. We're not far behind you. RV back at the kill, over.*'

Shane acknowledged, then moved forward, walking slowly, scanning ahead, left, right, and up, in the trees. Just in case. The vultures erupted in a dark cloud as he closed on what was left of the rhino. He shook his head. He wasn't a sentimental man, and he had seen death in many forms, but this killing more than most seemed incredibly pointless. That men would kill such a magnificent beast for its horn seemed such a terrible waste. However, the man or men who had pulled the trigger had done this not for medicine or ornament, but for money. In that respect, was he much different from them? He circled the kill, looking for spoor. It was easy to pick up. Rafter sandals and running shoes mostly – four men, by the look of it. A scrape in the sand near the bloodied head where a sack had been laid. Cigarette butts. Careless. That told him something. His enemies were relaxed, self-confident, lazy, not expecting to be tracked. There was at least one imprint of the butt plate of an AK 47.

Shane checked his GPS. The spoor headed due west, the shortest route to the border. If the poachers had tried to conceal their tracks on their journey through the national park, they had given up any semblance of discipline. Their path through the long yellow adrenaline grass was as clear as a four-lane highway now. He moved off in parallel. The grass got its name from the risk of bumping into something deadly – such as a lion. He felt the familiar constriction in his chest and the beating pulse in his carotid as he set off. His adrenaline had kicked in and it was because he was hunting something far more deadly than anything on four feet.

The leadwoods and remnants of chewed mopane trees gave way to an open vlei, but Shane skirted the clearing the long way round, sticking to high ground, on his right. He smiled to himself. The basics of his military training would never leave him, no matter what occupation he ended up in. To be above your enemy was an advantage known since the days men fought with clubs and spears. The poachers' path through the grass was still clear, and he didn't want to risk being caught in the open if one or more of them were lagging.

Soon he came to a clearing and the first of the white-painted cairns that marked the border. He was just below the crest of a low hill. He dropped to his belly and pulled his binoculars out of his top pocket. To his left and right was a cleared trail – it hardly qualified as a road, though it might once have held such a title. He reckoned the poachers had crossed the border about a hundred metres to his left. He scanned the likely breach, and then looked left and right out over the featureless bush on the Botswana side.

Above the cooing of a dove and the rush of the merciless dry wind through stunted trees, he heard a voice.

He swung the binoculars to where he thought he had heard the sound and concentrated all his senses. He sniffed the air. Smoke.

He slowly raised the radio to his mouth. 'Niner, this is Taipan. Contact, wait out.'

Reynolds knew what Castle's message over the radio meant, and understood there was no point calling back asking for more information. The guy would give him more detail when he had it, and Fletcher should not call back before then.

The Italians were excited and nervous, whispering to each other at what seemed like a million syllables a minute. He had tried, politely, to tell them that they would never bag anything if they kept talking.

Lloyd led them from the road, towards the vultures that circled the kill in spiralling thermals. The tracker raised a hand, then pointed with his thumb towards the ground.

'*Shut up!*' Fletcher mouthed at the Italians. Reading the scowl on his face they immediately took heed. He crept forward, bent at the waist, and knelt beside Lloyd, who pointed silently through the bush. Fletcher didn't need his binoculars. There were three men in sight, wearing a mix of clothing – shorts, T-shirts, one with no shirt at all, just some ratty old green canvas webbing straps crisscrossing his muscled black back. They all carried AK 47s. Fletcher studied them as they circled the kill. It was odd, he thought, that they didn't seem to be doing anything. The rhino's horns were gone. So what were the poachers doing hanging around? It didn't make sense.

He had to risk letting Shane know that he, too, had found their quarry. He lifted his radio and whispered, 'Taipan, this is Niner. Acknowledge your last and I confirm that I have contact in sight.'

Shane cursed. The voice coming through the radio was soft, but to him it sounded as loud as a car alarm squawking in the bush. He pushed the transmit button once. The voiceless reply would tell Fletcher that he had received his message and – if the old man had half a bloody brain – let him know not to try talking to him again.

He leopard-crawled forward, praying he would not be called again. It confused him, though, that Fletcher could also see the men. He hoped no one started shooting, as not knowing where your friendly forces were in a fire fight was a recipe for tragedy.

He settled behind the fallen trunk of a dead tree – probably knocked over by an elephant. A bow in the log allowed him to peer under it. He could see the poachers now, perhaps a hundred metres away. Two sat on another felled tree, another stood. They were arguing with each other. One pointed repeatedly at his wristwatch – another shrugged his shoulders. Someone was late. Their pick-up, perhaps? The one doing most of the talking pulled a satellite telephone out of his khaki cargo pants and flipped up the stubby aerial.

Shane counted two AK 47s and one large-bore bolt-action hunting rifle. The fourth man appeared to be unarmed. He looked the youngest of the quartet – perhaps in his mid to late teens. In the centre of the circle of men was a hessian sack, darkly stained with the blood of the dead rhino.

The talking man spoke into his phone for a couple of minutes, displeasure plain in his voice and his gestures as he waved his free hand in the air. At the end of his conversation, he, too, shrugged and sat down on the log next to the other men. He said something to the youngest, who scurried forward and added more sticks to the small fire in the centre of the clearing. He arranged rocks around the growing flames and pulled a charred, battered metal teapot from a canvas rucksack. Brew time. These criminals were going to stay put for a while.

Shane marked the position in his GPS. He cradled

his rifle in the crook of his arm and started reversing from his hiding spot, using his elbows, knees and toes to propel himself – as slow and silent as the careful, deadly puff adder that concertinas its body, rather than slithers, when it is on the hunt. He smiled.

He was back in the fray. And he loved it.

Fletcher's head whipped around at the sound of a snapping twig. It was one of the bloody Italians. The man was as silly as his tailored four-pocketed safari suit jacket and leopard-print puggaree on his hat. The Italian knelt beside him and Fletcher scowled.

'Poachers, *si?*'

Fletcher said nothing, but raised his binoculars to his eyes.

The man with no shirt on looked their way and started to raise his AK 47.

The sound of the gunshot rolled across the bushveld and was carried on the wind.

Shane swore quietly. He had almost made it back to his pack. He slithered into a firing position, facing the direction where the poachers were, peering around the base of a leadwood. He heard alarmed chatter, orders issued. He imagined dirt being kicked on the fire; weapons, packs and booty being shouldered.

'Fuck!' he mouthed again to himself.

The shot had come from behind him, back where the dead rhino rotted.

He heard the men ahead now, making no attempt

to mask the noise of their flight. They were running further and further into Botswana. He gave it ten minutes and then crawled the remaining distance to his pack. 'Niner, this is Taipan. Shot heard. Was that you, over?' It was a hell of a time to be hunting.

'Don't shoot! Don't shoot! We're a hunting party, out of Isilwane Lodge, Matetsi Safari Area,' Fletcher called. The Italian cowered beside him, prostrate, clutching at tufts of grass with his hands, his weapon discarded.

Ranger Charles Ndlovu emerged from his position of cover, behind an anthill as tall as a man, his SLR still in his shoulder as he moved cautiously past the dead rhino.

'Charles, it's me! Fletcher Reynolds.'

Charles lowered the barrel a little. There was no smile on his face as Reynolds stood and walked out towards the carcass. 'What happened? Why did you open fire on us?' Charles said.

'I am sorry, *shamwari*,' Reynolds said. 'I saw your man with no shirt on, and when he started to raise his weapon I thought he was going to attack my party.' The Italians hovered nervously in the tree line.

'I am the senior man, here, Lovemore Sithole. And it was you who fired the first shot at *my* man,' said a man next to Charles, wearing a grubby brown T-shirt.

Reynolds appraised the shorter man. Charles, he knew well. This man was new, and looked like a

102

Mashona. 'I am sorry, Lovemore. I am Fletcher.' He extended a hand, but the other man pointedly ignored him.

'We will have to call the police,' Lovemore said.

Charles stepped between the two men. 'Mister Reynolds, you know we operate under a shoot-to-kill policy when we see armed men in the national park, but that does not mean hunters can open fire on poachers.'

Reynolds played his trump card. 'You know, Charles, that you are out of the national park. You are in the safari area.'

'That does not matter,' Lovemore said quickly.

Reynolds guessed the leader of the patrol, who seemed less confident than the older Ndebele, did not know that he had strayed out of the park and into the adjoining area. It was all government-controlled land, and the rangers had as much right to hunt poachers there as anywhere else, but by convention anti-poaching patrols in the safari areas bordering Hwange were coordinated through the parks and wildlife office at Matetsi, so that incidents like this could be avoided. Armed rangers wandering through an area populated with hunters could easily result in bloodshed. 'I hadn't received word from Matetsi that you would be here today.'

Lovemore scowled. Charles nodded, conceding Reynolds had made a valid point. Fletcher's radio cackled to life. '*Niner, this is Taipan. Have you in sight. I'm coming in.*'

Reynolds said into his handset, 'Roger.'

'Who was that?' Lovemore asked.

Shane jogged out of the bush, slinging his rifle as he entered the circle of men so there would be no mistaking him. The Africans regarded him with curiosity. He wore an American desert camouflage BDU shirt and his equipment was obviously military. His rifle, once black metal with a wooden stock and butt, had been spray-painted camouflage with tan and green stripes.

He beamed his widest smile, even white teeth splitting a face hurriedly camouflaged with spit and dust, and said, '*Sawubona*,' to Charles, and '*Kanjaan*,' to Lovemore. He nodded to the other two rangers, who stood back, and gave a casual salute to the Italians.

'*Yebo*,' Charles said in reply. Lovemore nodded curtly.

Fletcher smiled. The whole day had gone to shit, but Castle, the trained killer, had been able to put nearly everyone at ease with two well-directed greetings.

'*Ibizo lakho ngubani?*' Charles asked Shane.

'*Elami igama ngangu* Shane Castle.'

Charles smiled. 'You mean *ngingu*.'

'I have reached the end of my Ndebele,' Shane said.

Charles chuckled. Lovemore looked petulant and left out. 'What are you doing here?'

Fletcher answered for him. 'Mister Castle is our new head of security at Isilwane Lodge and I think that while we have been shooting at each other here the real poachers have escaped.'

Shane briefed all of the men, including the Italians, who had edged a little closer to the action and nodded sagely as Shane pulled out his map and pointed to the place where the poachers had been resting, presumably awaiting pick-up. He learned from Fletcher that shots had been exchanged between the hunters and the rangers – one and two respectively, though no one had been injured.

Shane's report had given them all something more to think about other than the near tragedy, but Lovemore seemed disinclined to let the matter rest.

'Christopher and Noah were out of uniform,' Charles said, his tone placatory, and he tactfully avoided pointing out that the only issued item of clothing Lovemore was wearing was his trousers. His brown T-shirt had a picture of Bob Marley on it. 'Perhaps instead of the police we should let the chief warden at Main Camp decide what action needs to be taken?'

Lovemore suddenly looked alarmed. 'No, I am sure we have all learned a valuable lesson from today. Mister Reynolds, just because you are white does not mean you can take the law into your hands.'

Reynolds nodded, swallowing the reply that almost came to his lips. He had lived for twenty-seven years under a black government and had not survived this long by always speaking his mind.

'You warriors look thirsty!' Shane interrupted. 'There is room for your men and gear in the back of my Land Rover. Lovemore, you might have to sit in the front with me, if that is all right. It is only fifteen minutes' walk from here. We can send word to the police in Botswana from the lodge.'

Reynolds smiled at Shane's easygoing charm, and picked up the hint. 'Beers for everyone at Isilwane!'

*

Charles and Shane sat in the shade of an umbrella thorn tree on the grassy irrigated lawn of Isilwane Lodge, each clutching a dewy brown 'bomber' of cold Castle Lager.

'You have the same name as the beer,' Charles said. He was into his third bottle, and smiling broadly, the tensions of the day and his illness forgotten for now.

'What, Lager?'

Charles laughed at the joke. 'Are you serious, about this offer you have made?'

Charles had explained to Shane that he would soon be retired from the parks service, because of his advancing age. He said, in a whisper, that that was the only reason he put up with incompetents like Lovemore. He did not want to risk losing his pension by being dismissed for disciplinary reasons, even though it was unlikely he could support his family on the meagre payments from the government.

Shane had explained that Reynolds wanted him to form an anti-poaching team to find the criminals before they struck. He had been impressed by Charles's obvious control of the situation near the rhino carcass, and with his breadth of experience as a ranger.

'I am an old man, and my health has been better,' Charles said, then took a long pull on his beer.

Shane saw the hollowed eyes, the thin limbs. It wasn't hard to guess what type of health problems Charles was referring to. 'I have six months to get the team established. I will need a good man to help me with a training program, and to monitor the radio twenty-four hours a day, from a room here at the lodge, when the patrols are out. Can you do that for me, Charles? The money will be good.'

Charles peeled the wet label from the beer bottle. 'Castle is a good name. A strong name.'

Shane looked into the older man's rheumy eyes. He thought the old man might be close to weeping. 'And *Ndlovu* is as strong as its meaning, the elephant.'

'I would very much like to come and work here,' Charles said. They clinked bottles.

7

'**W**hat do you think?' Reynolds asked as he stepped down from his brand-new Land Rover Discovery 3, in front of Michelle's cottage in the staff area of Hwange National Park's Main Camp.

A group of small boys in cast-off clothes suspended their game of soccer, played with a half-inflated ball in the middle of the dusty road, to stare at the shiny new SUV. A scrawny chicken clucked and pecked its way under the chassis.

'The old one had more character,' she said, wiping her wet hands on her shorts. She had been washing her clothes in the laundry tub when she'd heard the unfamiliar engine's deep purring. 'Where have you been these past couple of weeks?'

'Busy with business.'

'Looks like it's good,' she said, nodding to the car. 'Come in and I'll make you a cup of tea.'

The house had probably once belonged to a senior ranger. It was not big, but the ceilings were high and the two bedrooms were airy and cool, even in the strength-sapping heat at the end of the dry season. Outside she struggled to keep a small flowerbed alive, but she had not taken up a career in zoology because she was good with plants, and her results were mixed, at best.

'You know you could move up to the lodge – no strings attached,' Fletcher said, and thanked her for the tea.

He had made the offer twice before and each time Michelle had politely declined. It wasn't that she feared more lascivious advances, rather that she wanted to retain her independence and her good relationship with the park authorities. However, on a day like this, when the wind whipped the sandy soil around Main Camp into a stinging dust storm, she would have sacrificed all her principles for a dip in Fletcher's lawn-fringed swimming pool.

'Don't forget, I have a swimming pool,' he said.

She smiled. 'We have a pool right here at Main Camp.'

He laughed. It was an old joke. The cracked swimming pool hadn't had water in it for decades.

'Has your new mercenary killed any poachers yet?'

Fletcher shook his head and blew on his tea. 'Shane's doing a good job. He and his men are tracking a gang that's been crossing to and from Botswana. We think it's the same group that killed the rhino.'

'Well, I hope your dog-of-war kills the lot of them,' she said. 'By the way, when do I get to meet the war hero?'

'I'm not sure I want you to. He's about your age and I suppose some women would find him quite attractive.'

She was touched by his vulnerability, even though he punctuated the sentence with a false laugh. 'Younger men are overrated – trust me, I know.'

'I won't ask for details.'

'You won't get any.' She checked her wristwatch. It was three in the afternoon. 'What have you been doing in this part of the park, anyway? You're a long way from home.' It was more than a hundred and fifty kilometres back to Fletcher's lodge through the park, on bad roads, and even further if he went the long way around, back onto the main Bulawayo–Victoria Falls Road and into Matetsi from the north.

'More good news. I've just had a meeting with the chief warden at headquarters and I've joined the parks and wildlife service.'

She laughed. It must have been a joke. There had been a time, long ago, when there were many whites serving as uniformed rangers, but independence, affirmative action, white emigration and the fact that government salaries couldn't hope to keep pace with inflation had meant there were only two *murungus* – the local term for whites – left in the service that she knew of. 'You're kidding, right?'

'Honorary Ranger Fletcher Reynolds at your service.' Fletcher explained that his friend Brigadier Moyo had spoken to the senior management in the national parks office and suggested it would be a good idea to resurrect an old scheme whereby people could be sworn in as part-time rangers, to augment the service's meagre resources on the ground. There were other white land-holders, or lessees, like Fletcher, who still had properties on the boundaries of the country's various national parks, and many of them, like him, wanted to take a more active role in the day-to-day management and running of the government-owned lands. 'What it means is that I can work more closely with the rangers inside the park to coordinate my anti-poaching patrols with theirs, and it also gives me the same legal powers of arrest that the uniformed guys have, if I catch more intruders.'

'Do you get a uniform?'

'Yes, in fact I do.'

'Sexy,' she said.

'If that's all it took to woo you I would have dusted off my old army gear months ago!'

'Not so fast. I'm more a fireman-policeman-national-parks-ranger kind of gal. I don't go for professional killers, Fletcher – at least, not killers of men.'

'So I've got nothing to worry about when you meet my new *askari*?'

She laughed. She would never be interested in a security guard. She found she was enjoying their flirting – and his company. The other European researchers at Main Camp tended to be postgraduate students in their early twenties and she had a good ten years on most of them. They partied hard and had appalling taste in music. She realised, too, that an inability to recognise a single artist or band in some-one's CD collection was a sure sign of old age.

Fletcher, at least, made her feel relatively youthful. 'Hey, don't tell me you're driving home tonight. Where are you staying?'

'The safari lodge.'

'Get out! You're really flaunting your newfound wealth now.' The Hwange Safari Lodge was a former government-run hotel about ten kilometres from Main Camp. It was an expensive place to stay, even for local residents, who paid less than foreign tourists.

'Why don't you join me for dinner there, tonight?'

She studied his face. It looked as though the idea were spur of the moment, but she couldn't read him that well yet. She wondered if this were a set-up – an opportunity for him to make another advance, and what she would do if it was. 'Okay. What time?'

'Why don't we go right now? We can go in my car – I'll bring you home this evening. You can see what it's like to drive in a vehicle with aircon.'

She felt cornered again, and confused. She'd been enjoying their banter, but suddenly felt her heart leap. 'Um . . . I'm not really dressed for the lodge right now.' She wore shorts and an old cotton shirt knotted above her belly button.

'I can wait. Throw on a skirt and bring your swimming costume with you. We can have an hour or two by the pool before dinner. Come on, Michelle, it'll be like a holiday from this dustbowl. We can even talk about your research, if you want to make it business.'

She smiled. The hell with it. 'Yes, boss,' she said, giving him a mock salute.

*

Michelle broke the surface of the cool, clear fresh water to find a smiling waiter standing over her, bearing a silver platter with a gin and tonic in a tall glass.

'Right there, by the side of the pool will be fine,' Fletcher told the man.

Michelle stayed in the water, elbows resting on the warm tiled surround of the swimming pool, and sipped her drink. It really was a lovely spot. The hotel itself was an uninspiring low-rise concrete blockhouse, but its rooms and the pool overlooked a pumped waterhole in the centre of a wide vlei. A herd of sable was cautiously sniffing the wind before committing themselves to take a drink. The sleek black coat of the male and the rich red-browns of his harem of eight females gleamed in the slanting golden rays of the afternoon sun. A dry moat between the vlei and the hotel's verdant lawn kept elephant and other dangerous game out, but wasn't nearly enough to stop a cheeky baboon who barked with mischievous joy as he scampered off with a sugar bowl from a nearby table.

Fletcher lay back on the deep green canvas mattress on his sun bed and sipped a whisky and ice. 'Ah, life is hell in Africa.'

She smiled. It was an old saying but, at times like this, a good one. This wasn't the real Africa – not the heat, the dust, the drought, the sickness and disease, the corruption, the poverty – but it was a nice place to come for a break from all of that. She corrected herself – it was Fletcher's Africa. At least, it was his life indoors, alone in his luxurious hunting lodge. She was used to penny-pinching – a round of drinks here

113

was the equivalent of her weekly food budget – but she had no qualms right now about giving herself over to a taste of luxury. 'I could get used to this.'

She took a sip from her drink, did two more long, lazy lengths of the circular pool, then climbed out and dried off. She noticed him watching her, out of the corner of her eye, as she pretended to watch the sable. He was checking out her body. She didn't mind, as she had been unashamedly assessing him while she had chatted to him from in the pool. It was the first time she had seen him shirtless and she was pleasantly surprised to find he was in excellent shape. He had abs and pecs a twenty year old would kill for. His body was lean and tanned, not an ounce of fat on his big frame. Without his trademark bush hat he had a full mane of silvering hair. A breeze raised tiny ripples on the surface of the pool, and though the wind was warm it was enough to chill her wet body for a few delicious seconds. She felt her nipples stiffen, and self-consciously raised her towel to cover her breasts.

'You could use some fattening up, girl,' Fletcher said.

He was nothing if not direct, but she took his bluntness as a compliment. 'It's hard to get fat on a researcher's allowance.'

'If that's a cry for more money, it's falling on deaf ears.'

'You've been generous enough, Fletcher. I wish I could make it up to you – buy you dinner or something. But you'd be paying for it in the long-run – or, at least, your rich dentist would be.'

'Tonight is my treat. A business dinner where you

can tell me all about the faecal habits of canine predators or something equally stimulating.'

She changed in his hotel room while he waited downstairs in the bar for her. She fussed over her hair and frowned at the meagre choice of clothes she had to draw on. In the end she settled for a green skirt – the same colour as ninety-nine per cent of her wardrobe – and a bright yellow sleeveless shirt. Her palms were a little moist and there were butterflies in her stomach as she walked downstairs to meet him.

He wore tan chinos and a freshly ironed blue cotton shirt. He exuded an air of relaxed prosperity; cool and completely in control. He was the best looking man in the bar. In fact, he was the only man in the bar who didn't work there. The safari lodge suffered from the same malaise as the national park it bordered – a lack of custom. A grotesque elephant's head peered down at them from above the fireplace, as Fletcher ordered another gin for her.

Her diet contained too much pasta, rice and sadza – the bland mealie-meal paste that was the staple food of most Africans – so she leapt at the chance of a three hundred gram fillet steak, while Fletcher ordered fish. This was his excuse, he admitted, to order two bottles of wine, a red and a white. She hoped he wouldn't be too drunk to drive her home. She told herself she would take it easy.

He started with small talk, drawing out the details of her life in Canada, her childhood, where she had studied, and ended up with past boyfriends.

'One steady relationship, that lasted a year or so, just before I left for Africa. He knew I had my heart set on coming over here, and he talked about visiting, but . . .' She shrugged.

'He was a fool.'

'Not to come and visit?'

'To ever let you leave.'

She bridled. 'No one tells me what to do.'

He held up his hands in submission. 'I know. But life is sometimes about compromise. My wife hated the bush. Oh, she liked the idea of it all, the romance of it, at first. But later she complained about missing shopping and restaurants, and theatre. It got harder for her once the boys went to boarding school. She wanted us to keep a house in Harare, or maybe South Africa, for six months of the year and spend the rest of the time here. I wouldn't budge. She left.'

'I understand,' she said. She admired the fact that he didn't blame the failure of his marriage solely on his wife, as many men would have. 'But nothing could have stopped me coming here. It's where I belong. Besides, there shouldn't be a need for compromise if you find the right person.'

'To finding the right one,' he said, raising his glass of white, and they toasted.

They moved outside to the lawn after dinner, to escape a group of young African men who watched at full volume an English Premier League soccer match on the bar's satellite TV set. The rising moon lit up a herd of elephant rushing towards the reward of fresh water. Fletcher and Michelle had talked and talked over dinner, enjoying each other's company, and now they sat in silence over coffee, both aware the evening was drawing to a close.

116

'I should be getting you home,' he said.

'Maybe you shouldn't be driving after a bottle of wine.' As she spoke, she felt her cheeks colour. He raised his eyebrows theatrically. What she'd said must have sounded dangerously like a come-on. Was it?

He smiled. 'I'll take it slow. There are no cops on the road back to Main Camp. The main thing we have to watch out for are elephants.'

'My swimming costume – it's still in your room,' she remembered.

They walked back through the foyer area, between the darkened bar and restaurant, the soft slap of her sandals on the polished stone floor the only sound. He led her upstairs, to his room on the hotel's upper level, and opened the door for her.

She saw, in the moonlight, that the bed had been turned down. The crisp starched sheets looked cool and inviting. Her bikini hung from the back of a chair, his towel and swimsuit draped beside it. It looked like the most natural thing in the world. She heard the door close behind him, and turned in the narrow confine of the small hallway that led into the main part of the room. He was standing beside her in the half-darkness, saying nothing. She felt her heart trying to escape her body through her throat. What if he kissed her, now, or she kissed him?

'Let's get you home', he said.

'How about another cup of coffee – or something from the mini-bar?'

8

Shane and Caesar had been on the hill for four days, baking in the merciless sun, watching, watching, watching.

Their observation post was nestled amongst a cluster of granite boulders, over two of which they had been able to string a hutchie, a camouflaged Australian Army shelter sheet, which provided a little shade during the heat of the day and a place for whichever of them was not on duty to attempt to sleep.

From the OP they had a commanding view of the dirt road traversing the concession from east to west, and myriad back roads and game trails that ran off and across the main route like brown capillaries. Neither man had washed, but it had been two days since Shane had been able to smell Caesar – the stinks always cancelled each other out after a while in the bush. Even though they had used no water for anything more than a cursory wash of their hands and privates, they were nearly out.

And they had seen nothing. Not a vehicle, not a man, woman or child for four long days and nights. Of game, there had been plenty. Lion, thankfully far off in the distance – a pride of five sauntering down the road early one morning as though they ruled the concession; elephant by the hundred, roan and sable antelope, impala, kudu, buffalo, giraffe, zebra and even a pack of wild dogs chasing a warthog family. It had been a feast of wildlife viewing, which Shane had appreciated as a consolation prize, and he had made careful note of the number and estimated ages of the dogs, as he knew Fletcher was sponsoring some Canadian woman's research into the predators.

Caesar seemed content as he gazed out over the bushveld, while Shane cleaned his rifle and tried to ignore the tiny mopane flies that buzzed around his eyeballs and nostrils. Caesar was a good kid – an excellent choice by Charles, who knew his father. Like Charles, the twenty-three year old had grown up in Hwange as a ranger's son. He had first left the park to work as camp boy on canoe safaris on the Zambezi River, but the operation had folded due to lack of foreign business. He was a fast learner and a quiet, studious young man. Shane had told Charles he wanted thinkers and learners with the strength of a buffalo and the patience of a stalking leopard. Of the two new recruits Charles had brought in, Caesar was more suited to this type of work – long, boring hours of reconnaissance. Wise, the other newcomer to the team, had served in the Zimbabwean Army in the Democratic Republic of Congo. He was the louder of the two, and thirsted for action. On this, the first patrol since the two had joined, Shane had decided to leave Wise with Charles, to see how the young hot-head dealt with hours alone, cooped up in the radio room he had set up in the lodge manager's house. Shane and Caesar radioed sitreps – situation reports – every four hours, twenty-four hours a day, and Shane had been pleased to hear Wise's prompt replies, even at three in the morning.

Shane wiped the breech block and slide with a lightly oiled cloth. Too much oil and the working parts of the SLR would just attract excess grit. Also, when fired, an oily weapon gave off a telltale plume of white smoke. The rifle was spotless before he stripped it, and could have gone another day without cleaning, but he wanted to get Caesar, who had no military experience, used to the idea of sticking to a daily routine. Teaching by example was the best way with new recruits, and Shane had cleaned his rifle first thing in the morning on every patrol he had ever been on in fifteen years of peace and war.

Caesar grabbed his knee and shook it. Good man, was Shane's first thought. He had told him, during his training back at the ranch, never to speak in an OP when he could communicate by hand signal or gesture. Shane looked up briefly from the weapon and saw the dust plume of a moving vehicle. He cocked his head and heard the engine on the faint dawn breeze.

Shane tracked the dented blue *bakkie* – an Afrikaans term for a pick-up in common use in Zimbabwe – through his high-powered binoculars as it juddered along the dirt road. It was coming from the direction of Victoria Falls. In the back he noticed four dogs. That piqued his curiosity. Although the truck was heading towards Botswana he doubted anyone would be taking pets into that country, which enforced strict quarantine rules on the movement of animals and livestock.

'Log the time,' he reminded Caesar in a whisper. There were precious few entries in the notebook so far, other than *NSTR* – nothing significant to report – at each sitrep hour. 'Zero Alpha, this is Taipan. Contact, wait out,' he said into his radio. Given the time of day, Charles would be on the other end, in the operations room. The old man responded with one click of his transmission switch. Good drills, Shane thought to himself – Charles knew that he did not need to speak to acknowledge the report.

The *bakkie* slowed and turned left into a stand of long adrenaline grass and bounced another hundred metres into the virgin bush. The driver stopped in a clump of mopane trees and his passenger got out and returned to the dirt road. Walking backwards, a broken sapling in his hand, the man methodically obliterated the vehicle's tracks from the roadside. To complete the deception, the driver hacked off some more leafy branches and placed them around and over the pick-up's cab. He opened the tailgate and the dogs bounded down.

Shane lifted the walkie-talkie to his lips again and gave his report, following a set procedure he had worked out with his team. Charles would be writing down the information on a printed-out form.

'Two African male adults. Dented blue Nissan

121

bakkie. Believed hunting with figures four dogs. One Lee Enfield .303 rifle seen. Location . . .' he double-checked his map and read off an eight-figure grid reference. 'Heading south-west, following a family of warthog. Acknowledge, over.'

'*Taipan, this is Zero Alpha, affirmative, over,*' Charles replied from Isilwane, then repeated the details Shane had just provided. Shane was impressed with the calmness of the man's tone, and hoped it was a reflection of his.

'Zero Alpha, stand to, stand to. Relay information to Niner and report to parks and wildlife and Wankie police, as per SOPs, over.' Shane knew it wasn't necessary to tell Charles what was expected from him, or to remind him of the standard operating procedures they had hammered out together, but he wanted to make sure Caesar, who was listening intently while watching the poachers, was aware of everything that would be going on at the other end of the operation. The message to 'stand to' was to ensure that Wise was woken for duty in the operations room, while Charles made his report to Fletcher Reynolds.

All Shane and Caesar could do now was wait for a reply from base and watch. From their lofty vantage point the poachers' plan seemed clear. The men, who were presumably just after bush meat rather than ivory or rhino horn, had obviously spotted the warthogs as they ferreted along the edge of a dried river course. They had rounded a bend in the road and stopped downwind of the pigs. Shane had heard that warthog was good eating, but he had never tried one. With their knobbly faces, protruding tusks, hairy backs and antenna-like tails, they were amusing to watch, and cute, in a butt-ugly way.

The poachers were stalking through the grass and thornbushes, their dogs silent, though straining at their leashes as they caught scent of the prey. The man with the rifle kept his weapon slung. It seemed he would let the dogs do the work for him, rather than waste a precious bullet. The men looked about as well off as their vehicle. Poor and hungry, Shane thought. Yet they were criminals. He wondered what sort of sentence the courts would give them once the police rounded them up. It should be a straightforward operation – particularly as the men relied on their vehicle to get home. He just hoped the cops arrived before the men finished their morning's hunting.

The radio hissed. '*Taipan, this is Niner, over.*'

Shane nodded to Caesar to maintain watch on the hunters. He acknowledged Fletcher's reply. The man must have run straight from breakfast. Shane tried not to think about bacon and eggs and freshly squeezed orange juice. He knew Fletcher was hosting another party of American businessmen, so the dining table would be groaning.

'*Taipan, I am on my way to your location. Should be there in thirty mikes, over.*'

Half an hour. That wasn't too bad, Shane thought, although the plan was that if there were clients at the lodge, Fletcher would keep them well away from any poachers to ensure their safety. He wondered who would be looking after the Americans. Still, that wasn't his business. 'Niner, Taipan. What's the ETA for the police, over?'

'Unable to establish contact at this time. Will keep trying. Fix that vehicle, Taipan, I don't want them getting away.'

Shane nodded to himself. The plan had been for him to stay put as soon as contact was established, or to follow any poachers at a discreet distance if they were on foot and looked like they might get away. Ordering him to disable the men's vehicle – for that was what Fletcher clearly meant by 'fix' – was a departure from what they had agreed. Still, Shane remembered an old army saying he often repeated, that no plan survives the first ten minutes of action. Besides, it would be fun. 'Roger, Niner, over.'

'Taipan, once you have disabled the vehicle, move out . . . I say again, move out, to the pick-up point and stay concealed. You don't want to get involved when the police arrive, or have them open up on you if they see a couple of armed men in the bush. I'll send the rest of your callsign to pick you up.'

Another change in plan. Shane chewed the skin on the inside of his cheek. There was no way the police would spot them high up on the hill. Their original concept had been for him and Caesar to remain in their OP to keep an eye on the operation, in case other poachers showed up. Caesar had heard the message and turned to Shane and frowned. The youngster had clearly hoped to have a grandstand view of the capture and arrest of the criminals. Shane shrugged and responded that he understood. The pick-up point was a kilometre to the west of where they were. Mingled with his disappointment at not seeing the operation go down was his relief that all had gone well so far, and that he would soon be back at the lodge under a shower. 'Pack up, we're moving,' he whispered to Caesar.

Shane had to remind Caesar, through hand gestures, to slow down his pace as they walked down the hill towards the road. The boy was overexcited. Shane led, stopping every few paces to look and listen. He held up a hand and they both dropped to one knee. Shane heard the yapping of dogs – he guessed they had either made a kill or had cornered a warthog. He pointed in the general direction with the barrel of his SLR. Caesar, who had the butt of his AK 47 in his shoulder, nodded. If the poachers had done their business, they would be on their way back to their vehicle soon. Shane moved off, just as cautiously, but his paces were longer and quicker.

They stopped within sight of the *bakkie*. Shane nodded to Caesar, who smiled broadly and crept forward. Shane took up a position behind a stout tree, where he could watch the vlei the poachers would likely move through, and where he also had sight of the road. His heart pounded. He and Caesar had already placed their weapons at 'action' before leaving the hilltop – that meant each of them had a round chambered and sights up, though their safety catches were still on 'safe'. Shane had double-checked Caesar had not been too eager and let his safety catch slip to 'fire'.

He heard the hiss of air as Caesar pressed the tip of his pocket-knife blade against the valve of the truck's right rear tyre. Next, Caesar crawled under the pick-up, located the spare, and punctured it with his knife. There was no point in stabbing both tyres, as either Fletcher or the police would have to drive the *bakkie* out of the bush once the operation was over, and all of Fletcher's vehicles carried portable air compressors.

Caesar crawled back, the beaming grin on his face impossibly wide. Shane stayed stony-faced and nodded his approval.

The young man leaned closed to Shane and whispered in his ear, 'Eeeh, but I got a fright there, boss!'

'What?' Shane mouthed.

'There is a dead leopard in the back of that *bakkie*.'

'They've been busy,' Shane whispered back. 'Anything else?'

Caesar shook his head.

It wasn't over yet. He pointed the way they were to head, away from the poachers' vehicle, and indicated that Caesar should lead. The boy looked proud and determined as he stood and moved off. Shane was pleased. He let Caesar lead so that he could watch their backs, where the most likely threat still lurked. He heard the hounds barking louder now, and the chatter of voices. He assumed the hunt was over and the poachers were celebrating their success. He gestured for Caesar to get a move on. They melted away into the bush, staying parallel to the dirt road.

Shane checked his watch. It was fifteen minutes since the first radio messages. Ahead was the road junction that marked the pick-up point. He selected a spot where he and Caesar could keep watch on the rendezvous point but stay out of sight themselves. They lay down in the shade of an umbrella thorn that had miraculously lived long enough through decades of elephant migrations to reach maturity, and waited.

Ten minutes later they heard a vehicle. Not the rumble of one of Fletcher's lodge trucks, but the agonised whir of an old starter motor in need of service. Perhaps the poachers had not noticed their flat tyre. They soon would. After two more nerve-jangling attempts the engine caught. However, the motor ran for less than a minute, then stopped. Shane nodded to himself. He pictured the men on the side of the dirt road now, getting out of the cab and cursing at their bad luck, perhaps arguing over who would change it.

Another car noise. Caesar craned his neck to see, but Shane forcefully pointed in the other direction, reminding the rookie that his job was to watch along the road for their lift home, and any other intruders. Caesar mouthed an apology. Shane smiled. The other vehicle had to be Fletcher.

Shane pictured the poachers now, perhaps hurriedly throwing a tarpaulin over the carcasses in the tray of their pick-up, smiling at their luck. If they had already worked out the spare tyre was also flat, they would have thanked God for the appearance of the lodge's Land Rover. Shane allowed himself another mental taste of toast and pork breakfast sausage, and of the cool, cleansing rinse of the first cold beer down his throat. Life was looking up.

Then the gunfire started.

Michelle took her time driving through the national park, stopping for a light breakfast of cereal and coffee at the Guvalala viewing platform, sharing her morning ritual with a family of giraffe at the waterhole, then taking a long break and a siesta in the shade of the towering marula tree at the Shumba picnic site halfway through her journey.

She was on her way to see Fletcher, and to spend a couple of days in the north of the park following up a wild dog sighting reported to her by a ranger. She hoped it would be Picasso and the rest of Rembrandt's old pack. She was grateful for the time the long, slow drive gave her to think about things. Perhaps, she thought as she packed away her hammock and readied for the last leg of the trip through the hot, slanting afternoon sun, she thought about things too much.

They hadn't had their coffee in his hotel suite at the Safari Lodge – at least, not until the next morning.

As a scientist she knew it was a simple biological act, which she understood, brought on by some chemical reactions – ably abetted by a reasonable dose of alcohol – which she didn't really understand. It was hard to remember which of them had kissed the other first, but it hadn't been frenetic. There was no tearing of each other's clothes, hiking of skirt or popping of trouser buttons. One minute she was suggesting coffee or a raid on the mini-bar, the next minute they were sitting on the lounge making out. Their clothes had come off slowly, sensuously, teasingly. Piece by piece. It was orderly, but no less erotic than some of the fumbling nocturnal encounters she'd endured in the past.

Fletcher was attentive, even precise, as a lover. He

knew women and when he found her with the tip of his tongue her first orgasm had taken her by surprise with its speed and ferocity. Too long without, she mused now. She'd been content to lie there, on the deliciously cool, crisp hotel sheets, spread-eagled while he'd explored her and played her. The only break in his choreographed journey from lips to breasts to cleft had been a pause when he'd noticed her tattoo. It was a tiny fairy – Tinker Bell – hovering in the well of her hip, to the left of her pubic mound. He'd looked up at her, but she'd been unable to read the fleeting expression in his eyes. She sensed he disapproved of the permanent marking, though he'd said nothing about it – not then or since. Well, no one was perfect.

She'd been more curious about the puckered bullet wound in his left thigh, but he didn't seem inclined to talk about it. She'd licked and kissed it before going down on him.

Afterwards they had showered together and he had insisted on washing her, from shampooing to feet scrubbing. That was a first for her – a little weird, but lots of fun. Everything with Fletcher seemed meticulously planned and executed, though she couldn't fault him for that. She'd known men who couldn't have found a clitoris with a map.

She was looking forward to seeing him again, if not the company he wanted to introduce her to. She opened her eyes, put the Landcruiser in gear and left the picnic site. Fletcher's latest crop of Americans would be brimming over with tales of the bush and the animals whose lives they had snuffed out. She had heard all the macho bullshit before, about hunting being part of man's makeup, a primal rite, blah, blah, blah. Also, Fletcher could keep his argument that controlled hunting was a benefit for animal conservation. She might give ground on organised culling – though she was not a subscriber to the conventional wisdom that it was the only way to manage the elephant population in Hwange – but killing for sport turned her stomach. Still, she was a realist, and Fletcher had said this group were interested in learning about her work and, probably, in contributing to his conservation fund. For his sake she would be polite, listen to their crap and, hopefully, take some of their money.

And then there would be later – time to talk, hopefully, and maybe make love again. As she drove, she didn't know if it were the lowering sun, the heat of the big engine coming through the firewall into the cab, or just her, but it was getting hot in her truck this afternoon. Her mind was not made up. Part of her said just enjoy what might be a casual fling with a rich guy who was paying her to stay in Africa. The Canadian prairie farm girl side of her said she wasn't made that way. Deep down, she wanted a life partner, a soul mate. She had enough nieces and nephews and friends back home with babies not to be overly hung-up on having a kid, but it might be nice one day. With the right man. Was that man Fletcher, a hunter who was close to twenty years older than she was? God, but she overanalysed everything.

At Robins Camp she found there was no one booked into the satellite lodges at Nantwich, the place where Rembrandt was killed. Despite her still tender memories of that terrible day, she took up the desk ranger's offer of accommodation there for a night and signed the register. She also intended staying at Fletcher's luxury lodge for at least two nights. The comfort-factor aside, she wanted to confront him, to get him to state his feelings for her up front. He'd had to leave the Safari Lodge early the next day and there had been little time to talk over breakfast. Despite his physical attractiveness, his charm, his wealth and his position as the only eligible bachelor within a hundred miles, she still had to deal with the fact that he made his living killing animals. So she had decided to spend the first night in the rather more down-market national parks cottage at Nantwich, to buy herself some time. Besides, she wanted to stop somewhere and change and freshen up before arriving at Isilwane Lodge.

Michelle arrived at Nantwich just after four-thirty. The view, as she crested the hill on which the three cottages were set, made her sigh at the beauty of Africa. The sun was heading for the horizon and the grass out on the vlei surrounding the pan where Rembrandt had died was tinged red-gold. Africa's tragedy was part of her beauty – the everyday wonder of the struggle of life and death. As simple and as complicated as that. She wasn't an overly religious person, but the sight of a line of zebra and a small family of kudu queuing patiently for a drink at the trough while a mother elephant used her trunk to lift her tiny baby up out of the waterhole, touched her soul and made her believe there must be a God.

The attendant, a wiry man in shorts and a khaki

uniform shirt faded to near white, greeted her like a long-lost friend. She guessed he was probably just happy to see someone. As the attendant busied himself making a wood fire under the donkey boiler – a two hundred litre drum of water set in a brick fireplace and chimney to heat water for the house – she gazed over a picture-postcard image of the African bush, and there was not a tourist in sight.

She had been allocated the centre building of the trio, where the tourists had watched Rembrandt's death from their veranda. She hauled her backpack inside. The building was simple, yet spotlessly clean.

The sun entered the hazy zone above the treetops on the horizon and mellowed to orange-red through the dust that would hang over Africa until the rains came. She reckoned she had about half an hour. She stripped, wrapped a towel around herself, grabbed her soap and shampoo, an aluminium saucepan, and a cold can of Zambezi Lager from her cool box and slapped outside in her half-fastened rafter sandals.

Beside the donkey boiler was a chipped enamelled bathtub, fed direct from a cold tap plumbed to a tank resting precariously above her on some timber scaffolding, and a hot tap protruding from the brick fire structure next to the bath. While there was a perfectly useful bathtub inside the cottage, there was nothing like an outdoor bath while watching the sun set over Africa.

The hot water was already close to boiling, the fire roaring like a distant freight train in the furnace next to her, the bricks giving off a pleasant warmth to counteract the mildly cooling effect of the breeze as she hooked her towel over some plumbing and lowered herself into the water. A kudu raised its big ears at the *pop* of her beer can, even though she was a good two hundred metres from the waterhole where it drank. The animal settled back to drinking the muddied water.

'Bliss,' she said aloud, taking a long swig then sliding down to wet her hair. As she closed her eyes and lathered, her only regret was that there was no one there with her to share this magical experience.

When Michelle sat up and opened her eyes again she glanced across at the pan and saw the kudu and zebra had vanished and the elephant herd was tramping purposefully through grass so long that it obscured the babies and juveniles. A matriarch let out a long trumpet blast and two lionesses skulked guiltily into view, skirting the approaching herd. Elephant hated lion, and Michelle, naked in an outdoor bathtub, suddenly felt very vulnerable.

Shane, Charles, Caesar and Wise sat around a Formica-topped dining table in the kitchen of the manager's house where Shane lived. A bottle of beer was in front of each of them, a bowl of chutney-flavoured chips in the centre. Real food at last, Shane mused.

Shane wore a Billabong surf T-shirt and a pair of British Army desert camouflage trousers, hemmed to shorts at the knee. He and Wise were sharing from a pack of Zimbabwean Madison cigarettes. Charles wore his off-duty uniform of dark slacks and pressed white shirt, while the two younger men were dressed casually, similar to Shane.

'Right, thanks for coming over, guys. I'll keep it brief, as I know some of you need to get your heads down for the night. First of all, well done to all of you for today,' he began.

He had held off debriefing his team until after the police had left Isilwane. It had taken a long time for the detectives to interview Fletcher and each of the four American hunters about the morning's action. Shane had given his employer space as he knew he had his hands full, not only with the police, but with his guests, who had literally been whooping with joy when they arrived back at the ranch. Shane had followed Fletcher's intent to the letter and had kept the team away from the police and the guests. The Africans had gone to their quarters, a long building with five single rooms and a communal kitchen, and, under Shane's orders, had stayed there all day.

Shane recapped the mission, starting with their preparation, orders and with the insertion of Caesar and himself into the bush four days earlier. That had all gone like clockwork, with Charles taking out his own vehicle, a beat-up old Nissan Sunny, in the predawn darkness and dropping Shane and Caesar a kilometre from their eventual observation post atop the hill, barely stopping on the side of the road to let them leap out of the still-running car. If there had been poachers in the area, Shane did not want to give away the presence of an anti-poaching patrol by arriving in broad daylight in the back of an Isilwane Land Rover.

The reconnaissance had been uneventful until the final morning, but Shane summed up the first phase with some well-deserved words of praise. Caesar had proven he had the patience to endure long, boring days in the OP, and Charles and Wise had never missed a radio call, no matter the time of day.

Wise broke in, 'But why didn't Mister Reynolds wait for Charles and me to help him drill those poachers?'

Ever the loudest of the small band, Wise was running true to form. 'We'll get to that soon, Wise,' Shane said, and went back to his rundown of events from the time he and Caesar had spotted the poachers until they had heard the shots fired. For Caesar's benefit, Shane recapped what Charles had told him, namely that he and Wise had arrived just after Reynolds, and seen the bodies of two African men lying on the side of the road next to the disabled pick-up. Reynolds had waved them on, telling them to proceed to the pick-up point.

Shane had spoken to Fletcher late in the afternoon, though not for as long as he would have liked. 'Mister Reynolds decided that he could handle the poachers on his own. When you look at it from his point of view, he probably made the best decision.'

Charles looked across the table at Shane, who nodded it was all right for him to comment at this point. 'Shane, I thought the plan was for Mister Reynolds to keep his clients away from any poachers we found, for their safety.'

Shane nodded. It was the element that concerned him most. 'Yes, that was the plan. The information we

135

passed to him was that there were two men, with one rifle, and four dogs. He probably thought he could handle that sort of opposition on his own.'

Caesar said, 'It is true, there was only one man with a rifle, and he had it over his shoulder most of the time.'

Shane was reluctant to add the new piece of information Fletcher had given him to the mix, but that was what the debrief was for – reviewing the events of the day from every perspective and, hopefully, learning from them. 'The problem,' he said, looking at each of their faces, 'was that there was a second weapon.'

'No!' Caesar said.

'Relax, mate, it's not a drama,' Shane said, lapsing into Australian vernacular. Like his accent, his vocabulary was half-Aussie, half-African. 'Mister Reynolds said the second man pulled an SKS from the back of the *bakkie* when he showed up.'

Caesar looked puzzled, so Charles explained. 'It's an old Chinese or Russian semi-automatic rifle. They were common amongst the freedom fighters during the bush war. It's longer than an AK 47, but with a smaller magazine and not able to fire on full auto.'

Shane did not want the debrief to turn into a witch hunt. 'I told Mister Reynolds that I, personally, had watched the men all the way from their vehicle to where they were hunting and that definitely,' he repeated the word again, 'only one of them was armed. I told him at no time did we see any sign of a second rifle.

Caesar fidgeted with the label on his beer bottle.

Without looking up, he said, 'I checked the back of the *bakkie*.'

'I know you did – and for the rest of you, I want to say, on the record, that I neglected to tell Caesar to check the tray of the truck. He did that on his own initiative when he went to flatten the tyres. That was good thinking.' The others nodded in support.

Caesar still plainly felt guilty of some mistake. He looked directly at Shane, eyes wide and beseeching. 'There was a dead leopard in the truck, but no other gun.'

'Perhaps it was under the carcass?' Wise said. 'Hey, just a suggestion,' he added hurriedly when Caesar shot him a malevolent glance.

'Enough,' Shane said. 'We'll never know where the man had his weapon hidden – or why he chose not to take it out on the hunt with him. Rest assured, all of you, that no one – not Caesar, nor myself – has to take any blame for what went on. Mister Reynolds is an ex-soldier. He knows things don't always go according to plan, and he was pleased with the work of all of you today.' He went around the table, asking if anyone had any questions. They had none, but Charles, as the second-in-command of the team, echoed Shane's earlier praise, telling each of the younger men in turn that they had done well.

'One more surprise,' Shane said, stilling them before they rose from the table. 'Two days' extra leave from tomorrow. I'm taking the Land Rover to Victoria Falls and you're all welcome to come along. Mister Reynolds has donated the first crate of beer and a *bonsella* for each of you to spend.' Wise whooped and did a little victory dance in his seat. Charles smiled, but Caesar still looked worried. Shane excused himself, saying he had to dress for dinner with Reynolds and his guests. The men got up to leave.

Seeing them out, he put a hand on Caesar's shoulder. 'It's nothing. Don't dwell on it. It was my patrol and I made the report. Everything worked out well in the end.' Except for the dead poachers, of course.

Shane battled through another rugged cigarette as he changed into trousers and hiking boots and a long-sleeved cotton shirt. It was the closest he could get to smart casual. In truth, he felt bad about the day – much worse than Caesar, who had youthful inexperience to fall back on. He hated to think of the consequences of Reynolds and his hunters facing a man armed and ready with a semi-automatic rifle.

Reynolds had been magnanimous about the mistake, and only gently reproving of Shane and Caesar's failure to identify the other weapon. 'They probably had it behind the back of the seat in the cab. Not even a poacher would be silly enough to leave an illegal weapon lying in the back of a *bakkie*,' Reynolds had said. But that simple statement had carried an implied accusation – Shane and Caesar had failed to search the interior of the vehicle as well as its open tray.

Shane didn't tell his men his view why Fletcher had ignored the plan and gone after the poachers himself. It was, he reckoned, the man's ego running his mind. The safest, easiest thing would have been to call the cops – or to keep trying them until he made contact, given that his earlier attempt had failed. The second-best course of action, in Shane's view, would have been for him and Caesar to disable the vehicle – and search the bloody thing properly this time – so that at least the poachers and their dogs would have been hampered. He would have then maintained surveillance on the two criminals until the authorities could arrive. However, Fletcher had wanted to grandstand in front of his rich overseas clients. As a newly sworn-in honorary ranger he had the power to arrest the men. It was a risky action – perhaps foolish – but five armed men against one old Second World War bolt-action rifle could be seen as reasonable odds.

Lessons had been learned, though, and that was important. After their leave, he would take the men through vehicle search techniques, and show them tricks he had learned in the SAS about rendering enemy weapons inoperable. He recalled that Fletcher had an SKS in the gun collection in his safe, so he would ask Charles to borrow the rifle and show the patrol how to strip and assemble it. It would be good training, and a reminder for them to be always thinking a step ahead of the poachers.

Shane combed his hair, brushed his teeth to remove the smell of alcohol from his breath, and girded himself for his next battle – dinner with four American millionaires.

9

He stood out from all of them, even Fletcher. He was conspicuous by his silence, and notable for his dress – the most casual of all of them. The youngest male, the tallest, the fittest.

Michelle studied him, from her seat in the lounge area of the lodge, like the scientist that she was. She started with the physical characteristics – a thick mass of barely kempt jet-black hair; broad shoulders, narrow waist, firm everywhere he should be. Dark eyes to match the hair; big hands; long, almost elegant, fingers wrapped around the frosted beer glass. The only flaw – physically, at least – was the nose. Squashed, with a kink in the centre almost like a zigzag in the cartilage, presumably the result of a fight, perhaps on a sporting field.

He stood there, on the fringe, saying nothing as the others dribbled on about baseball, ice hockey, football, rifles, hunting. His reluctance to engage was not shyness, or politeness.

Arrogant. That was how she summed him up. As

attractive a specimen as he was, she had the feeling he would rather have been anywhere else in the world than in the comfortable surrounds of the hunters' lair that night. In that, at least, they had some common ground.

The eyes – hard to study without him catching her – were so black as to be empty. No, that was the wrong word. There was something going on behind them, certainly something more than sport and shooting. They moved slowly, taking in each of the men sitting around her, until they finally rested on her.

Michelle looked away, too quickly, and asked one of the Americans about the route of his flight home, whether he would be stopping off anywhere. She realised he had been doing exactly the same thing as she. Quietly, methodically appraising every individual in the room, including her. It made the downy hair on the back of her neck stand on end, though when she looked back at him he wasn't looking at her. Instead he said something that made the maid smile behind her hand as she scurried away to fetch another bucket of ice from the kitchen.

They had been introduced, as he'd arrived, and she had offered her hand. The fingers might have the reach of a piano player's but they were coarse, like sandpaper. His face was wind and sunburned. Fletcher had said something about him being out on 'patrol', whatever that entailed, for four days.

'I hear you've been out bush,' was all she'd thought to say to him.

'For a while,' he'd replied.

They had left it at that.

The Americans were similarly dark featured, but that was where their resemblance to the Australian – who apparently had been born in Zimbabwe – ended. They were uniformly overweight, balding or with thinning hair, and their accent was from New York. Italian-Americans. Chunky gold pinkie rings, chains, protruding chest hair, designer safari clothes.

'I'm in sanitation – I clean up other people's shit, pardon my French.' Laughs all round. The others were in construction, newsstands and trucking. All in their late forties or early fifties. Money to spare. The shit, news, building and transport worlds paid inordinately well, it seemed.

Fletcher paid just the right amount of attention to her during pre-dinner drinks. She would have shuddered if he had been cloying, or overly attentive. Instead, he'd been friendly, giving each of his guests, including her, the same amount of time. He'd been as stand-offish with Shane Castle as the other man had been with the rest of the crowd. Something going on there for sure, Michelle guessed. She wondered if it concerned the day's events, which were being retold ad nauseam.

'You shoulda seen this guy,' the sanitation man said to Michelle, not for the first time, as he scraped his heavy mahogany armchair over the polished stone floor to get closer to her. 'Like Billy the Kid, he was! Boom, boom, bada-boom. Two shots in each of them scumbags – first one, then the udda!'

Fletcher smiled modestly. 'Bit of luck and some old training.'

'A regular John Wayne,' the newsstand magnate chipped in.

'Just like Fancy Paulie in Brooklyn,' the trucking king added, though this earned him an elbow in the ribs from the shit man.

Michelle smiled at the repeat of the story, though the whole thing alarmed her, for a number of reasons. First and foremost, poaching really did seem to be on the increase in their part of the country. Secondly, Fletcher Reynolds, a man she had recently become intimate with, was in the thick of this war on crime, almost on a daily basis, trading bullets with armed men. It scared her a little, but as she looked across at Fletcher, who shrugged off the accolades, she saw him in a new light. He was a man who could face the prospect of death and kill to protect Africa's wildlife, and then sit there a few hours later playing the convivial host with effortless nonchalance. Courageous. Modest. Ruthless, when he had to be. Completely in control. Kind of exciting.

'Two shots, that's all they got off,' the construction man said to Shane, trying to involve him in the conversation.

'Fuhgeddaboutit,' Shane said, raising his glass.

Michelle put a hand to her mouth and coughed, to stop from laughing.

The builder, with a brow that overhung his narrowed eyes, fixed Shane with a cold glare, then broke out in a bellow of laughter, raising his bourbon in response to the toast. 'You Italian? You should be!' The others joined in. There was no dampening their revelry, and Fletcher's glance at Shane ensured he stayed quiet until dinner.

Eventually Fletcher prised the businessmen from their leather-upholstered cushions and spirits and led them into the lodge's dining room. The stuffed heads of all of Africa's big five glared down at them through dinner and almost turned Michelle off her meal. She had eaten in a smaller, more intimate dining room when she had visited, one without any dead animals, except those on the plates, of course.

'So, you was in the special forces, huh?' the builder, whose name was Sal, asked Shane over marinated impala steaks.

Shane nodded. 'Special Air Service Regiment.'

'I gotta son in Iraq right now. He's US Marine Corps. Tell me, is it as fucked-up over there as the news media says?' He muttered an apology to Michelle, who waved it off, interested in hearing Castle's answer. She had protested against the invasion of Iraq by America and her allies before leaving her job as a university science tutor in Toronto to come to Africa. She was no fan of Saddam Hussein, but she detested the way the American and British governments had trumped up charges of a horde of weapons of mass destruction in order to start a war over oil.

'It's like anywhere else. There are good people and bad people, Sal.'

'Fuckin' A-rabs,' the sanitation man said. 'Kill 'em all and let Allah sort 'em out, I say.'

Michelle held her tongue.

Shane continued. 'The ordinary people in the street – most of them – just want an end to the killing. But there are too many outside influences there at the moment with a vested interest in not letting that happen.'

'Like America and Britain,' Michelle spoke up from the end of the table.

Fletcher sat back in his chair, watching with a half-smile on his face.

'And Al Qaeda and Iran,' Shane countered.

'They didn't start the war in Iraq, but it's giving them a chance to show the Muslim world they can give Uncle Sam a bloody nose,' Michelle said.

'Someone once said that all that's required for evil to flourish is for good men to do nothing,' Shane said.

'Fuckin'-A, bubba,' the sanitation man said, and pounded the table. He had clearly had a couple of sundowners too many and made no attempt at all to apologise for his language. Not that Michelle minded too much. She had a pretty foul mouth herself at times, though this self-righteous, jingoistic justification of the war really did offend her.

'Saddam was evil, for sure,' Shane continued, 'but I'll agree with you, Michelle, that the main thing the coalition's achieved so far in Iraq is giving Al Qaeda a battleground on which they can hurt the West.'

His concession surprised her. She had been getting herself ready for a fight.

'So what, now you're saying we should bug out? My boy hates that kinda chicken-shit talk,' Sal chimed in.

'Nope. We've got a job to finish, but there are better ways of fighting terrorists than invading a sovereign country – smarter ways.'

'So, if you say we gotta job to do, how come you're

here and not there?' the American asked. Everyone else listened intently.

Shane looked up the table to where Fletcher sat, at the head. 'Because it looks like we've got ourselves a better war here to fight.'

The Italian-Americans banged the table in applause and the sanitation man stood and raised his glass of red wine, again, to Fletcher Reynolds and the monumentally successful safari they had all enjoyed.

Michelle rolled her eyeballs during the toasts and, looking across the table, saw that Shane Castle was watching her. Smiling.

During dessert Shane said little, and noticed that Michelle seemed uptight. Every couple of minutes she fidgeted in her seat and, at one point, made a loud scraping noise that almost stopped the dinner table conversation as she shifted her chair to her left.

The sanitation supremo, whose name was Anthony, was sitting next to her, on her right, and his left hand was under the table while he ate.

She excused herself as orders were taken for coffee. 'I'm going outside for some fresh air,' she said to Fletcher. It seemed to Shane their host either ignored or missed the pained look on her face.

'Hey, wait up, I'm coming too,' Anthony said. 'I been dying for a cigarette.'

'This isn't America, you know,' Fletcher said, waving a hand dismissively. 'You can smoke inside and no one will sue.'

'Well, I don't mind if he goes outside,' Sal said. 'Ever

since I quit those damned things I can't stand the smell.'

Shane produced his pack from his pocket, excused himself with a nod to Fletcher and followed Michelle and Anthony out. Fletcher resumed his conversation about Zimbabwean politics with the newsstand magnate.

Outside, Shane put his cigarettes back in his pocket and moved silently along the veranda, sticking to the shadows under the overhanging thatch roof.

'Look, please don't take this the wrong way, but I'm attached,' Michelle said in a pained voice.

'Hey, whose gonna know out here in the middle of the bush? You want some more money for your research – I want a little companionship. Strictly business. Name your price, baby.'

Shane heard the stinging crack of an open palm on flesh, and stepped out of the shadows to see Anthony rubbing a flabby jowl. 'What the fuck!' the American said. He grabbed Michelle by the elbow.

Shane was starting to move when Michelle raised her right knee up hard and fast into Anthony's groin. The big man doubled in pain, wincing and drawing a breath as he tried not to yelp. Shane paused behind a tree, ready to cover the few metres between himself and the other two in less than a second, if he needed to.

Michelle twisted her arm out of the panting American's grasp and stepped back a couple of paces from him.

'Jesus Christ . . . what the fuck did you do that for?' he groaned. He stood and glared at her, then started towards her.

147

Shane emerged from his cover. 'Everything all right here? I heard a noise.'

'Anthony here has a sore tummy,' Michelle said, winking at Shane.

Anthony looked at him and was plainly sizing him up. The man already knew something of Shane's background. 'Yeah, right, musta been something I ate.'

Anthony straightened his safari jacket and walked back inside.

'Were you following me? I can take care of myself,' Michelle said.

Shane held up his cigarettes and offered her one. She declined. 'So I see. I hope you don't wind up with a zebra's head in your bed.'

'God, can you believe that asshole?' She brushed a strand of hair from her forehead. 'He was trying to feel me up under the table. Creep.'

'Did he hurt you?'

'Not as much as I hurt him!'

He smiled. He guessed you had to be tough to live out in the African bush all by yourself, male or female. 'I just remembered, I've got something for you.'

'If you're going to proposition me, beware. That was just a warm-up.' She made a fist.

Shane put his cigarette between his lips and pulled the army notebook from his pocket and flipped through some pages. 'Eighteen wild dog. Zero-five-thirty-five. This morning, on the road between here and Pandamatenga. I can give you the GPS coordinates, if you like.'

'That's Rembrandt's pack! It has to be!'

'I didn't ask their names. Four adults – one male, collared, three female; three sub-adults, undetermined sex; and eleven pups. The male's collar was day-glow orange with reflectors. Quite a healthy pack, by the look of it.'

'That's them.' She explained about Rembrandt's death and the two years she had spent tracking wild dog in general, and this pack in particular. Michelle said the reflective collar was one of a number of initiatives that had been trialled to improve the endangered dogs' chances of surviving. As well as being preyed on by lions and hyena, many dogs were also killed by drivers, particularly at night. Hence the reflective collar.

'I'll let you know if I get any more sightings while I'm out,' he said.

'While you're out hunting?'

'I wouldn't quite put it that way.'

'But it's true, though, isn't it. You're hunting men. Don't get me wrong, I don't have any sympathy for poachers, but don't you find it difficult to sleep, knowing that today was the end result of your work – two more bodies in the morgue?'

She was very direct – surprisingly so. He'd picked up the vibe from her over dinner and had no plans to engage her in conversation – other than to report the wild dog sighting – until the lecherous gangster intervened. 'Whatever,' he said. 'I should go in and say goodnight. I haven't had much sleep the last four days. Are you going to tell Fletcher what his guest wanted from you?'

He saw her indecision, and it surprised him. The

man had assaulted her, physically, even though he had come off the worse for it. 'I don't know. They're going tomorrow, and Fletcher's business is just starting to take off. I can deal with losers like Anthony.'

Shane started to go, then thought of something. 'When you first tried to give Anthony the brush-off you said you were "attached". Was that true, or were you just trying to get rid of him?'

'Everything all right out here?' Fletcher's silhouette dominated the French doors leading to the dining room. Shane heard the note of concern in the older man's voice. He must have guessed something was up.

'Just chatting,' Michelle said brightly. 'I'm coming back in now if you're offering coffee and port.' Fletcher made way for her, nodding to Shane as she walked back in.

Shane finished his cigarette and ground it out on the grass. She hadn't answered his question. She didn't need to.

The dining room was empty except for her and Fletcher. The Americans had retired, led by Anthony who had only stayed a few minutes after Michelle's return. Shane had drifted away without returning to say goodnight to any of them. She sat opposite Fletcher, facing him across a white tablecloth stained with ruby drops of wine.

Her heart had been pounding when Shane had emerged from behind his tree. She had never been accosted like that before and, while it was unnerving, she was proud of the way she had handled herself.

She wanted to tell Fletcher, but didn't want him to make a big deal out of it, as she sensed he might. He was so damned old-fashioned he might challenge Anthony to a duel, or take a horsewhip to him. The thought made her smile.

'What's so funny?'

'Oh, nothing,' she said, draining her wine.

He inspected the bottle of South African red. 'Empty. I'll open another.'

'Not on my account,' she said, placing her hand over her glass.

'Tired?'

'It was a long drive today, and quite an eventful night.'

'Eventful?' He raised an eyebrow. 'You must have been daydreaming about another party. I thought you would have been bored stiff – or repelled by my guests.'

She gave a little laugh to cover her mistake. 'No, it was fine. They're . . . interesting characters.'

'You can say that again, but they're loaded. I've met some terrific people hunting, of all nationalities, but these guys . . .' He let the sentence hang there.

'Have money?'

'Precisely. And while I'm no longer a beggar, I can't afford to be too choosy right now, although hopefully that will change one day. You looked a little edgy when you came back inside from the garden.'

'Edgy?'

'Did someone say something to upset you, Michelle? Shane?'

'Oh, no. No, no, no. Shane was fine. It was nothing.

It was a little warm inside and I just needed some fresh air.'

'Was it Anthony?'

'I was *fine*, Fletcher. Though I have to admit, I think Anthony probably spends more time around strippers and whores than educated women. Even if he offers you money for research, I don't want to take it. I don't trust him and his cronies.'

'Michelle,' he reached across the table, laying his hand on hers. She didn't move, and looked into his eyes. 'If I thought someone had hurt you, or wanted to hurt you, I wouldn't have them in my home, and I would do anything – *anything* – to ensure no harm came to you.'

'That's sweet, but I can take care of myself. I'm not a little girl.'

'I know that. Will you consider staying here tonight, in one of the spare rooms, rather than driving back to Nantwich?'

After asserting her independence and saying nothing was wrong, she couldn't very well tell him the truth: that she was nervous about being under the same roof as Anthony and his gangster buddies. She looked down at his hand on hers. It felt nice. His skin was cool and dry, and the gesture seemed more one of reassurance than romance. 'I've got all my stuff back at the cottage. I should go.'

He withdrew his hand and smiled. 'Fair enough. I'll walk you out.'

'Fletcher . . . we still haven't had a chance to talk about the other night. I don't know if we should . . . if we ought to . . .'

'Why not?' he asked.

It was a damned good question. Her reservations, her concerns over what he did for a living, over whether or not there was a future for them, suddenly evaporated.

They lay in the outdoor bathtub outside her bungalow, bubbles and hot water cascading over the rolled enamel top when either of them moved. He had followed her into the national park in his vehicle, not questioning her preference to sleep at her place rather than in his luxurious lodge. Her back was against his chest, his muscled arms around her. She held his left hand in hers, inspecting it by the mellow light of the full moon. His other hand was under the water, covering her mound – claiming it.

They had made love on her single bed. She had climaxed again under his soapy caress when he'd made her stand in the tub, knee deep in water under the night sky, while he sat on the edge and washed her. He had stilled her embarrassment, wanting to show her off 'to the gods,' he'd said. He still made no comment about her tattoo. A herd of elephant had drunk noisily at the waterhole on the vlei below them as she'd slipped beneath the warm suds.

'I have to leave at dawn,' he said. 'The Americans are flying out early.'

'I'll head up around ten,' she said, then kissed his fingertip, before licking the length of the digit.

He kissed the sensitive skin behind her ear and she

squirmed playfully. 'Will you be bringing your *kitundu* with you – your clothes and whatnot?'

'Yes,' she said.

He hugged her and kissed her cheek. 'Good. I'm pleased.'

10

S hane showered and dressed in the morning, still thinking about Michelle Parker as he ate a simple breakfast of cereal, tinned fruit and coffee. He was glad he had taken it easy on the booze, but resolved to make up for his temperance that evening in Victoria Falls.

As he lit his second smoke of the day and walked out to his old Land Rover he dismissed the thoughts of her. If she had been single, he might have made an effort. She was certainly attractive. He liked the way the sun had bleached some pale highlights into her auburn hair. She was tall, and had the angular grace and poise of a giraffe – a little aloof and, at the same time, a little vulnerable on her lofty perch. 'Enough,' he said out loud as the starter motor put on its usual whining protest before finally coaxing the engine to life.

Shane was an habitual early riser – something the army had indoctrinated in him – so even though last night was his first in a bed for ages, he was still up at five am. Outside, smoking his first of the day in the cool dawn light, he had been surprised to see Fletcher's vehicle coming up the driveway. His boss, who hadn't noticed him, was dressed in the same clothes he had worn to dinner. There was nowhere else he could have been except with Michelle. Pity.

Shane drove the Land Rover out of the main gate to the lodge's airstrip, which paralleled the main dirt road north to the Falls. Dougal's Cessna roared overhead on final approach. He was coming to collect the gangsters. Shane had no wish to see the men, but Fletcher would be there to farewell them and Shane wanted to catch him to discuss the following week's patrols before he and his men left for their two-day leave.

The Americans were already aboard the aircraft as Shane pulled up next to Fletcher's Discovery. His employer, freshly changed, was leaning into the rear passenger area. Dougal was obviously in a hurry or, more likely, short of fuel, so he wasn't wasting any time. Fletcher turned and strode back to the Discovery, and returned to the aircraft carrying a brown and green canvas suit bag.

Shane strode over to the aeroplane. 'Hey, what's happening?' he yelled to Fletcher over the engine noise.

'Change of plans. I have to fly to Bulawayo for a couple of days. I got a call this morning from a senior army contact of mine, Brigadier Moyo, who wants to talk urgently about some work in the Congo. Wants me to meet some other investors tomorrow. There's a note for Michelle on the front seat explaining everything.'

He pointed back to the four-by-four. 'She's coming up later this morning. Can you give it to her?'

Shane nodded. The discussion about the forthcoming patrols would have to wait until he returned.

Fletcher leaned close to Shane's ear again. 'I promised to take her shopping. Could you be a pal and take her to the Falls with you and your boys? I've left her some money for a hotel room – it was supposed to be my treat.'

'She doesn't strike me as the kind of girl who needs looking after,' Shane observed.

'She mightn't get there without you. The diesel tanker I was expecting today has been delayed at the South African border. It won't be here for another three days. Unless she's got enough fuel in her Landcruiser, she won't be going anywhere.'

'Right,' Shane said. He swore to himself. The last thing he wanted to do on his leave was chauffeur someone else's girlfriend around. 'I'll take an empty drum with me and cross over the border into Livingstone for fuel. It'll keep us going until the bulk delivery arrives.' Zambia, unlike the rapidly deteriorating Zimbabwe, had no fuel shortages.

'Good man.' Fletcher clapped him on the arm in thanks and climbed into the Cessna. Shane waved a hello and goodbye to Dougal, slammed the door shut, and the aircraft raced away.

Babysitting. That's all it was. He took his annoyance out on the road, driving hard and fast on the corrugated dirt surface.

'Hey, careful. I think you missed a rock back there,' Michelle chimed in from the passenger side. Charles, Wise and Caesar were having an even rougher ride in the open back of the four-by-four.

From the lodge to the Falls was a little less than a hundred kilometres, the first half on badly rutted secondary roads. The Tarmac of the main Bulawayo to Victoria Falls road, when it finally came, was like a balm. He relaxed his grip on the wheel and got over his earlier resentment. He felt for the girl. Although she tried to hide it, she was clearly disappointed by Fletcher's sudden departure. As Shane had predicted, she had initially rejected the offer of a lift, saying she would drive herself. A check of her fuel gauge had changed her mind.

'So, what have you guys got planned for the day?' she asked him.

He told her the surprise he had in store for the rest of his team. He had asked them to give him three hours, in the morning, and after that they could go their separate ways. Charles was planning on spending his leave with his family, who lived just outside of the town; Wise would ensconce himself at the first shebeen he came across, while Caesar was going to the library, church and his girlfriend's place, in that order. Shane thought that Wise's parents had named him well.

'What about you?' he asked.

'Shopping. Food and clothes. You know, the funny thing is that I've been to the town of Victoria Falls maybe twenty or thirty times since I got to Zimbabwe, but I haven't seen the Falls themselves since I first visited as a tourist, nearly ten years ago.'

'The last time I saw them was when I was fifteen years old, just before my folks moved to Oz. I have to cross over to Livingstone on the Zambian side of the river to fill up with diesel,' Shane gestured over his shoulder to the empty two hundred litre drum around which the men sat in the back of the Land Rover's tray. 'I've never seen the Falls from the other side.'

'Me neither, and I've got my passport with me.'

He hadn't meant it as an invitation, but he supposed there were worse ways of spending a day than sightseeing with a pretty girl – even if she were a left-wing greenie pain in the arse who belonged to his boss. However, it seemed that she was trying to make amends for her brusqueness the night before. 'Okay. Right after we drop the guys off in town.'

A billboard for Zambezi Lager welcomed them to Victoria Falls but, short of the town itself, Shane took a left turn to the airport. Some African women had set up a stall selling lace tablecloths in the hope that the few international tourists who still visited the town might stop on their way.

'Are we collecting someone else?' Charles asked as Shane stopped the truck outside a cluster of hangars in front of which were parked a row of single-engine privately owned aircraft.

'No, we're training.'

Charles's hacking cough was getting worse and they had had to stop the Land Rover twice on the relatively short journey from Isilwane for him to scurry off into the bush, with barely a shred of dignity, to void his bowels. Shane was getting worried about the man's deteriorating health and he had suggested Charles visit a doctor during his leave. When Shane had hired him, the first thing Fletcher had said to him was, 'You know that old *gondie's* Henry the Fourth?' *Gondie* was one of the myriad derogatory terms used to describe black Africans, but it had taken Shane a moment to realise the second colloquialism meant H-IV, HIV-AIDS. 'The virus'; 'the big A'; and 'slow leak' were just a few of the many euphemisms for the plague that lowered life expectancy to the early thirties in parts of sub-Saharan Africa. He'd explained to Fletcher that he intended on primarily using Charles's skills for training and patrol coordination. He looked at the old man's bloodshot eyes and said, 'Training for Wise and Caesar.'

'Are we going flying?' Caesar asked. 'I have never been in an aeroplane.'

'I have, in the army,' Wise said.

Shane said nothing, but motioned for the men to follow him into a small demountable building that advertised joy-flights over the Falls and skydiving. 'Hi, I called ahead. My name's Castle,' he said to a young white man with dreadlocks, sitting behind a desk.

'*Ja*, free-fall rig for one, accelerated free-fall first jump for two, right?'

Charles was relieved, Wise was excited, Caesar was scared to the point of wetting himself, Shane was in his element, and Michelle was laughing until he said, 'How about you?'

'Oh, no, no, no,' she protested. 'I'd forget to pull the ripcord!'

'There are ways around that. Have you ever seen a tandem jump?'

'I won't jump unless the madam jumps,' Caesar said defiantly.

'Okay, I'll do it!' Michelle exclaimed. Caesar looked sick.

Shane had done his static line and free-fall parachute courses in the army as part of his SAS training and had often jumped for pleasure back in Australia at weekends. He'd later qualified as a parachute jump master and then as an instructor and was a veteran skydiver, with more than six hundred military and civilian entries on his respective parachute log cards.

He inspected the tandem rig and explained to Michelle that all she had to do was cross her arms, trust him, and start her legs moving in a running motion as they neared the ground. In an empty hangar, Wise and Caesar were being taught the first of the drills they would need to know to qualify as free-fall parachutists. 'Arch!' the instructor commanded and the two men, lying face down on trolleys resembling cut-down hospital gurneys, raised their feet and arms in the starfish position they would need to adopt when they left the aircraft.

Heat haze rippled from the Tarmac and the temperature soared inside the cramped Cessna as they waited for permission to take off. Shane sat on the floor with his back to the fuselage wall. Michelle was in a harness clipped to the front of him, her back against his chest. The air was thick with the acrid smell of sweat and fear, but all he noticed was the scent of the shampoo in her hair. He gave her a thumbs-up and she returned it, her face a little pale. He smiled broadly. Wise was sitting opposite them with two instructors, a muscled African with a shaved head and yellow-tinted goggles, and a white man with peroxided short hair, who turned out to be a New Zealander. The pilot yelled back over his shoulder for them to hold on and the aeroplane raced down the runway. The wind through the open door provided some welcome relief.

As their aircraft gained altitude it passed over the majestic Victoria Falls, and the sun made a rainbow through the mist of spray that rose like smoke over the tumbling water.

'Awesome,' Michelle called in his ear, craning her head back so that her silky hair brushed his chin for a fleeting moment. He tried to concentrate on revising his parachuting drills instead of the presence of her lithe body.

They circled the drop zone, a secondary dirt run-way carved into the bush, and the African instructor climbed out onto a step above the right-hand wheel of the Cessna, gripping the strut with his right hand and offering his left to Wise, who forced a smile for Shane's sake and stepped out. The second instructor followed him, and hung half in and half out of the aircraft. It was a complicated aerial ballet, but they had rehearsed it several times on the ground. At the jump master's signal the three were gone, hurtling into the clear blue nothingness, each instructor hold-ing one of Wise's arms. Shane heard the brash young man's scream as he fell away.

'Oh my God!' Michelle wailed as she and Shane left the aircraft.

'Arch!' Shane reminded her and she mimicked his spread-eagled arms and legs. Their fall stabilised as he deployed a small drogue chute, to slow their descent, and he yelled, 'How's that?'

'Incredible!' she hollered back.

He looked left and right over a broad expanse of Africa and spotted three brightly coloured parachutes deploying as Wise and his instructors slowed their descent to earth. He reached for the 'bunny tail', a nylon tab low on the right-hand side of the parachute, which did the same job as a ripcord, and said, 'Here we go!'

The stillness under the open canopy was a sharp contrast to the mad, freight-train rush of adrenaline during their freefall. 'God, it's beautiful,' Michelle said as she took in the Falls from a bird's perspective.

She started pumping her legs as they neared the ground and Shane pulled down on the steering toggles, flaring the parachute and allowing them to sink gently to the baking earth. Michelle whooped for joy as Shane unbuckled her harness, then she turned and gave him a hug. 'Thank you so much!'

For a moment he wondered if she were going to kiss him. He took a half-step back, remembering that she was another man's woman.

Her cheeks flushed and she held out a hand, which he shook. 'Welcome to the airborne fraternity,' he said.

Wise's first question was when could he jump again. Shane explained that he had convinced a reluctant

Fletcher Reynolds to pay for a free-fall course for both Wise and Caesar as a team bonding exercise. Wise, if he wanted, could stay at the airport and do another two jumps that day, putting him well on the way towards the nine he needed for an initial qualification. 'This is better than beer, man,' Wise replied, eagerly taking up the offer.

The group waited for Caesar, who was in the Cessna orbiting above them. They watched, heads tilted to the sky, hands shielding their eyes, as the three rectangular parachutes blossomed against the blue. Caesar smiled weakly as he stumbled towards them, the gathered folds of his canopy billowing in the warm breeze.

'Well?' Shane asked.

'Ah, this is for the birds, not for man.'

They left Wise to continue his training, and Shane dropped Charles and Caesar near the Wimpy hamburger bar in the centre of the small tourist town, with a promise to meet at the same spot the following afternoon for the return trip to Isilwane.

Victoria Falls looked like an ageing whore down on her luck and damn near out of business. Once pretty, now tatty, she struggled along, barely eking out a living as the customers passed her by for a new face. However, there were still shops open in a new-looking arcade on the main road heading down to the Falls. Shane parked the Land Rover out back in the shade of a tree and tagged along with Michelle as she wandered through stores selling curios and clothes.

He waited in a shop full of T-shirts, board shorts, bikinis, hats and ladies' wear with complex African prints. Michelle emerged in a sleeveless shift dress that reached halfway down her thighs.

'What do you think?' she asked.

He wasn't wild about the lime green or the child-like elephant print, but the total look – her showing acres of skin and dressed like a woman rather than a unisex bush baby – was 'Fantastic.'

She smiled, told the sales assistant she would take the dress, then ducked back into the change room. Shane felt odd, waiting for her. The girl smiled at him, as though he were a husband or boyfriend bored with waiting for his woman to finish shopping. He didn't feel restless or ill at ease at all. In fact, he reckoned he could watch Michelle Parker try on clothes all day. But there were precious few other boutiques on offer.

There were a few tourists wandering the streets of the Falls as they emerged from the relative cool of the shop into the muggy, stinging heat, but they were out-numbered by young men in shiny football skirts and baggy shorts offering to change money and sell drugs. There was too much hassle and not enough cash to feed either the legitimate or the black market.

Shane and Michelle agreed that they should press on to the border post and cross into Zambia, then view the Falls from that side. Neither had a place to stay in mind, and Shane assumed they would part company at some stage and then rejoin each other at wherever they were spending the night.

Customs and immigration was a crush of tourists and locals, a human traffic jam exacerbated by the presence of two overland trucks full of road-stained young backpackers from a score of different countries, and a long-distance bus that seemed to carry as many caged chickens as people. Shane bought bananas and Cokes from an enterprising bicycle-based vendor as they waited in the sun in a queue to get into the immigration hall. The monotony of the wait was briefly relieved when a baboon – one of a cheeky trio who danced along the tin roof of the building – stopped to urinate, the stream falling on the wide-brimmed hat of a temporarily unaware African man. The women and children on either side of him hooted at his embarrassment, and some young boys tried but failed to hit the primates with rocks.

'Why is it,' Michelle asked rhetorically, 'that the busier a border post is, the slower the clerks work?' An hour and a half later the Land Rover rolled onto the road and railway bridge that spanned the gorge between the countries. A bungee jumper leapt off the structure and, after a few bounces, ended up dangling like a tea bag over the one hundred and eleven metre drop.

'I can think of better ways to part with a hundred bucks,' Shane said.

Livingstone, on the Zambian side, was the fortunate twin sister of her Zimbabwean counterpart – an old girl who had suddenly undergone an extreme makeover. Zambia's infrastructure and economy had crumbled away under decades of mismanagement after majority rule was granted to the former Northern Rhodesia in the sixties. The newly independent Zimbabwe had stolen a march on her poor neighbour after independence and the end of the bush war in 1980. Tourism had boomed in Victoria

Falls as Livingstone had all but slid into the Zambezi River.

'Wow, this place is heaving with people,' Michelle said as they passed sign after sign offering accommodation and tourist activities, in search of somewhere to stay. Livingstone was undergoing a facelift on a grand scale, with new hotels and shops under construction and once-flaking old colonial homes being rejuvenated with paint and money, to be reborn as curio shops and cafes. There were still the money-changers and the touts, but unlike the Zimbabwean side, there seemed to be more than enough tourists for the enterprising and the criminal to fleece.

African music blared from stores; backpackers wandered the streets consulting guidebooks, and a policeman with an AK 47 slung over his shoulder kept an eye on some youths leaning against parked cars. Livingstone was on the up while her sister city was on the slide, but it would still take some time before the Zambian side attained the same manicured finish that Victoria Falls had had in her heyday, and it would take time for the Zimbabwean side to fall as far into disrepair as Livingstone once had.

'What are you smiling at?' Michelle asked, handing Shane a dewy bottle of cold Coca-Cola as he leaned against the truck. They had stopped at a service station to fill up the Land Rover and the two hundred litre drum.

'Africa.'

'Some people would say there's not much to smile about here. Rising international debt, AIDS, corruption, megalomania, tribal violence.'

'The beat, the noise, the smell, the vibe. It's like here and Vic Falls. Yesterday's economic basket case is tomorrow's tourism powerhouse.'

'Or vice versa,' she said.

'Depends which way you look at it, I suppose.' He paid the pump attendant with tens of thousands of Zambian kwacha. The skyrocketing inflation and devaluation of currency in Zambia used to be a source of jokes in Zimbabwe, but even if he could have bought diesel back on their side of the border he would have been counting out millions of Zimbabwe dollars.

They checked into separate rondavels at a small budget lodge on the banks of the Maramba River, a tributary of the Zambezi overgrown with weeds. What the river lacked in water, it made up for in birdlife. Michelle would have been happy sitting by the swimming pool with her field guide to southern African birds by her side, but there was a bigger natural marvel to take in.

They drove back to the Falls and walked along a winding track until they came to the edge of the drop-off, where they stared in awe at the millions of litres of foaming water falling away beneath them. On an island in the middle of the fast-flowing Zambezi, wild-eyed noisy backpackers leapt from a rock into a pool perched near the top of the gorge, white water roaring past them on either side.

'That makes what you do for a living look safe,' Michelle said to Shane.

'What's life without a little risk?'

'You don't really believe that, do you?'

'No,' he admitted. 'Still, I've never not done something because I was afraid of the risks or consequences.'

That made her think about Fletcher. She had been more than disappointed when she'd arrived at Isilwane to find Fletcher had left for Bulawayo. Deflated was a better word. She had been full of excitement, bursting with a mix of pleasure, curiosity and hope about what their trip to the Falls would involve, where it would take the two of them.

She'd sensed from Shane's lack of conversation on the drive up that he was not exactly thrilled about being lumbered with her. Fletcher's note had been full of apologies and promises to make amends, as well as three hundred American dollars in crisp new bills. That had weirded her out at first. Her initial reaction was that he was treating her like some kind of kept woman, but the more she analysed the gesture, and Fletcher, the more she realised he was just trying to do the right thing. He had explained in the note that he wanted her to spend the money on some clothes – which would have normally been out of her budgetary means – and a nice hotel. It was, he had said, money that he would have spent on her, rather than an advance on her salary. He assured her, too, that the cash was from his personal fund, and not from the money Chuck had donated to fund wildlife research.

She wished she could appreciate the full magnificence of the Falls, but she was too lost in thought. She had been afraid of the risks and the consequences of sleeping with Fletcher – workplace romances were hard enough in the Western world, let alone the isolated reaches of Africa – yet she had still gone ahead and done it. And now he was paying her extra.

In the shop in Victoria Falls, where she had tried on the dress while Shane waited for her (bored out of his skin, she imagined), she had made another rash decision – or rather, changed her mind. On the road, she had decided she would return the money, along with some polite advice to Fletcher about the inappropriateness of giving a girl money after sex. However, when she'd looked at the price tag on the dress she had decided to use it. Did that make her cheap, she wondered, or, in a funny way, even more self-assured – acknowledging that she could take his money and not feel like a tramp? She hadn't bought herself anything nice in two years and, although she had trouble admitting it to herself, doing so made her feel special.

She walked beside Shane away from the Falls, the spray delightfully cool on her bare arms and the back of her neck, back to the Land Rover. She still had change from the three hundred – more than enough to find a nice hotel room – but she had drawn the line at using Fletcher's funds to stay somewhere different from Shane. That would have been downright rude.

'The cook gave me a list of things he can't get in Zimbabwe. I have to find a supermarket – do you want me to drop you at the lodge?' he asked her as they neared their accommodation.

'No, I'll come with you, if you want me to, that is.'

He shrugged. A man of few emotions, as well as words.

Shane parked the Land Rover outside the Barclays Bank in the centre of Livingstone town and they were immediately surrounded by a gang of young boys, all jostling and calling for attention. 'Let me mind your car, sah!'

Michelle looked at an urchin, dressed in the dirty remnants of shorts and a T-shirt. His forehead was creased with a nasty cut, which wept blood and clear fluid. 'How did you do that?' Michelle asked.

'One of the older boys hit me,' the lad said. 'He tried to take money from me.'

'Oh my God, that's terrible,' she said, and looked across at Shane.

Shane peeled off five thousand kwacha – the equivalent of one American dollar – and handed it to the boy. 'There'll be more if the truck's still here when we get back. Which boy hurt you?'

The youth pointed across the square to an older teenager affecting a rapper's beanie despite the heat. Shane nodded and started walking across to the other boy, who had been watching the transaction but now pretended to be engrossed in a chat with another young man.

Michelle watched and waited for Shane to return. Other youngsters pestered her to buy carved wooden elephants and precious rubies and emeralds. She declined, politely and persistently, knowing full well the 'precious' stones were ground-up glass from broken traffic lights. She didn't hear what passed between Shane and the standover merchant but, after

171

a brief moment of concern when the teenager squared up to the taller man, the boy turned and walked away from the car park.

'What did you say to him?' she asked as they crossed the busy main road.

'Enough.'

It seemed he was being only as polite as he had to in order to discharge some duty to his boss. Still, the last thing she wanted was for Shane to become interested in her. It was hard enough working out how to deal with one man, let alone two. Their visit to the cluttered, fragrant, eclectic Indian trader's store that sold everything from coriander to coffins, took her mind off men for the moment, though the following trip to the crowded OK Supermarket reminded her of her mother's sage observation that men were useless shoppers. Shane had left the cook's list in the Land Rover, and had decided he could remember enough of it.

'Maybe you'll be overseeing the kitchen from now on?' he commented, as she insisted that he buy two large sacks of potatoes, instead of one.

She scoffed. 'I can barely boil an egg. Besides, what makes you think I'm moving to Isilwane?'

He shrugged and pushed the wonky, overloaded cart down the aisle. As they neared the checkout, the lights went out in the supermarket. Zambia might be moving ahead faster than Zimbabwe, but it was still part of Africa.

After waiting half an hour in the queue for the power to come back on and the tills to work again, they loaded their groceries into the Land Rover. Their young car guard was grinning in anticipation and there was no sign of the older thug. Shane told him to stay with the vehicle a little longer. 'Maybe we can get a decent coffee in this town,' he said to Michelle. They started walking back down the main road in the direction of the Falls.

'These houses must have been beautiful in their day,' Michelle said, as they passed a third colonial-era villa under renovation.

They stopped outside another old home, which was now a cafe and curio gallery. While they waited for a latte and a cappuccino, Michelle browsed amongst the carvings, jewellery and printed fabrics. She tried on a bracelet of twisted brass and copper, holding it up to the light.

'Nice,' Shane said. 'Coffees are ready.'

She paid for the bangle and joined him at an outdoor table in a shady garden. Water bubbled in an ornamental pond beside them. 'This place is an oasis,' she said.

He sipped his cappuccino and closed his eyes. 'You should ask Fletcher to buy an espresso machine for the lodge.'

'What makes you think he'd listen to what I say?'

'The way he looks at you, you could make him jump through a hoop and fetch your slippers.'

She laughed, wondering where that had come from. 'I think you might be reading too much into things.'

He shrugged. 'You're staying at the lodge, aren't you?'

'Yes, but only for a couple of days. I don't have any plans on moving in full-time, Shane.'

'I'm guessing it's a lot nicer than wherever you live at Main Camp.'

He was right, of course, but she didn't like his inference that she was selling out in some way. 'I'm my own person. I'll live where I want to.'

'Sure, but wouldn't you prefer a four-poster, a swimming pool and a Jacuzzi?'

The waitress came and cleared away their empty cups, leaving the bill. Shane reached for it but Michelle beat him to it, snatching up the piece of paper. It allowed her to ignore his last question.

'Boss paying for that too?' he asked, leaning back in his chair.

She scrutinised him. Had he peeked inside the envelope Fletcher had left for her and seen the three hundred bucks? God, she hoped not. Suddenly she felt cheap again, though he *was* right about her wanting to move into the lodge. She'd started allowing herself to fantasise about it that morning, lying in her single bed at Nantwich after Fletcher had left.

'He's given me some money for expenses, yes.'

'For both of us, or just you?'

'As a matter of fact, he told me to pay for both our hotel rooms and left some money for that,' she lied.

'Really? He didn't say anything to me about it. I should have checked us into the five-star joint down at the Falls.'

She laughed. It was good to see Shane Castle off balance for a change.

Later, over a simple dinner of grilled bream and chips in the lodge's open-walled restaurant, she said, 'I had a nice day, Shane. Thanks for bringing me.'

'Me too,' he said, meaning it, though he felt bad for baiting her in the coffee shop.

'I'm sorry if I came across as rude last night, talking about you killing people for a living.'

'It's cool.'

'It's just that . . . what I was trying to say was, do you think you'll spend your whole life hunting other people? Being a soldier?'

'I hope not. You'd have to be a nutter to want to go out and kill people.'

'And you're not?'

He smiled. 'It's a catch-22 situation. If you're crazy enough to want to kill people, the army won't let you join. However, when you do join, you have to be able to do it. That's the difference.'

'Sounds like a fine line to me,' she said, sipping her South African white.

'What I'd like,' he said, 'is a little piece of Africa all of my own. A game reserve or a farm.'

'For hunting?'

'No,' he said. 'I've got no problems with what Fletcher and his clients do, but I've got no urge to kill for sport.'

'Just for business.'

'Now you're teasing.'

'You know, I was staunchly anti-Iraq,' she said.

'So was I. My guys and I killed plenty of Iraqis.'

'That's not very funny. I marched.'

'I fought. And no, it wasn't very funny at all. But it was my job. I did it as well as I could, and we didn't use any more force than we had to.'

'Aren't you worried about the danger? Are you ever frightened?'

'Sometimes – to both. Sometimes war is as boring as hell. Hours, days, weeks of watching, waiting, doing nothing at all. But once things start happening, instinct and training take over from fear.'

She shook her head. 'I could never kill another human being.'

'Everyone is capable of killing.'

'Not me.'

'What about if you had a family – kids – and they were being threatened, and you had to kill to save them?'

'I don't have kids and don't intend on having any in the near future.'

'No wedding bells with Fletcher?'

She pursed her lips, as though the question were none of his business. 'Fletcher and I are friends. Good friends. And you changed the subject. How do you feel, after you've killed someone?'

He drained his wine glass. 'Another bottle?'

'If it'll make you talk.'

'Maybe you should be getting to bed.'

'I'm a big girl. I decide when I'm going to bed.' She summoned a waiter with a wave. 'Same again, please.'

He looked down at his glass as the waiter refilled it.

'Shane, look, I'm sorry. I didn't mean to pry.'

'Nothing,' he said.

She looked at him quizzically.

'You asked what I feel, after I've killed someone. Nothing. That's what I feel.'

She sipped her drink, and he wished she would say something right then, but she stayed silent. It was an interrogation technique, though he doubted she knew about such things. If she stayed silent he might say something more, just to fill the void. 'I guess that sounds pretty weird, huh?'

She shook her head. 'At least you're honest. But you must feel *something*. I don't know – sad . . . elated that you've survived?'

He looked into her beautiful, innocent eyes. 'If I try to analyse it, the fighting, the risk, the action; all produce some intense emotions. Fear, elation, the whole box and dice. But when I think of the men who've died, the ones I've killed, I feel nothing for them. And that worries me.'

Fool, he told himself. Why was he going on like this? Acting like some headcase. He had to get out of this situation before it got out of control. He heard a munching noise behind him, from across the weedy river. 'Hey, look!'

She followed his line of sight and saw the elephants, feeding under the cover of darkness. They watched in silence, along with the other dozen patrons in the restaurant, as the big matriarch waddled down the slope to suck from a gap in the choking water hyacinth. Behind her, a tiny baby half walked, half belly-skidded to her side.

Shane looked at the simple beauty of the family feeding and drinking together, caring for each other, watching out for each other, and felt a lump rise in his throat. Get a fucking grip, he said to himself. He thanked God for the darkness, and the distraction.

In the shower, as Michelle soaped herself and touched the tenderness in her armpits and at the tops of her legs where the parachute harnesses had bitten, she thought about Shane.

In the aeroplane, in the dress shop, in the super-market, she'd felt totally at ease with him, and she realised now that for those brief few moments she had stopped agonising over her blossoming relation-ship with Fletcher and just enjoyed being in a man's company.

She was not scared of him – worried that he might be some sort of psychopathic killer – but she was acutely aware that he was suppressing things more terrible than she could imagine, and that she should not try to coax him into revealing any more to her. It was not fair on him, her, or even Fletcher.

Instead of thinking about the future she let her mind drift back to the previous night. She closed her eyes and gave herself over to the sensation of the hot jets of water pummelling her body, and of her own touch.

11

S hane had seen little of Michelle Parker since their trip to Livingstone and that was just fine by him. He'd recognised the early signs of attraction to her and was embarrassed by how easily she had opened a window onto his private concerns about himself. While he had no idea if she had any other interest in him, it was against his personal code – and common sense – to entertain feelings for his employer's girlfriend.

Michelle had lost contact with the pack of dogs that had moved from the north of Hwange into the Matetsi Safari Area, and had returned to her normal base in the south-east. Fletcher had invented a couple of excuses – or so it had seemed to Shane – to visit her in between client bookings.

'Hell, this place is looking *lekker* now,' Dougal said between sips of tea.

Shane and the pilot sat at a wrought-iron table in the garden of the manager's house, though Dougal had been gesturing to the main lodge. A quartet of

African workers was busy rethatching the building's roof, while a new gardener raked a truckload of gravel across the driveway. The lodge had been painted, inside and out, the clean smell of it still strong. 'Yep, it's in good shape,' Shane agreed. He explained that Fletcher had been reinvesting a sizeable proportion of his newfound wealth in the property, and on the anti-poaching patrol's equipment.

'I just wonder how he's doing so well while other hunters are struggling,' Dougal mused.

'PR.' Shane had finished his tea and was cleaning his SLR, the pieces spread out in a neat row on the garden table. He and Wise had returned from a five-day patrol the previous afternoon, and Shane had spent the morning checking and repacking his gear. 'Word's getting around that Isilwane Lodge is in the front line of Zimbabwe's war on poaching. Rich Yanks and Euros like to be on the fringe of the action, see the battle up close, I suppose.'

'Well, he hasn't killed a poacher for weeks, so I hope the clients don't get bored and stop coming.' Dougal laughed at his own joke.

Business – if that's what it could be called – had been quiet for Shane, Wise, Caesar and Charles. To keep them busy, Shane had taken his men on sweeps around the north and eastern borders of the concession, looking for snares set by subsistence poachers. The work was mundane but necessary. He explained to Dougal that much of this petty theft was being done by 'new farmers' – veterans of the country's liberation war and, more commonly, faithful members of the ruling party who had taken over the former white-owned farms on the border of the hunting concession. 'They can't feed themselves because they've let the farms go to ruin, so they poach game from the fringes of the national park, or fish illegally in the rivers.'

'Perhaps a few shots over their heads might clear them off.'

Shane shook his head and started reassembling his rifle. 'Fletcher's not dumb. He doesn't want to pick a fight with the government's cronies.' Shane slid the gas piston, spring and plug home, cocked the empty weapon and raised it to his shoulder. He took aim at a tree. 'In the meantime we keep looking for the gang that killed the rhino. They've slotted a few elephant in the park lately. That's what Wise and I were doing the last few days, trying to get a fix on them, but so far,' he pulled the trigger and it clicked on the empty chamber, '*hapana*.'

'Nothing, hey. You're starting to talk like a Zimbo again, *shamwari*,' Dougal said, slurping his tea. 'Maybe we should go for a flight, see if we can pick up anything from the air?'

'Needle in a haystack' didn't do the difficulty of the task justice. Fletcher had imported some drums of aviation gas and a pump from Botswana, specifically so that Dougal had extra fuel on tap if he had the time to assist with the anti-poaching operations, though so far they hadn't had enough of a lead to justify using the fuel. Fletcher had left on safari with a trio of the rich American dentist's national guard buddies from Chicago. Doctor Chuck Hamley the

Third had been the best thing to happen to Isilwane for decades.

Charles Ndlovu announced his arrival with the hacking cough that now punctuated most of his sentences. 'News, boss,' he said to Shane. 'Parks and wildlife at Matetsi just called. A callsign from Hwange has advised they are crossing into the safari area in pursuit of a gang of up to nine poachers. They think it may be the same Zambians that killed the rhino, with some extra help. They have asked for our assistance.'

Shane carried his rifle into the manager's house, followed by Dougal. Charles read out the coordinates of the patrol's location and Shane marked it on the clear plastic overlaying the map on the wall of the bedroom that served as their operations room. The radio hissed static in the background. 'They're close to the Botswana border,' Shane said. 'How many guys in the national parks callsign, Charles?'

'Three. Lovemore, Noah and Christopher,' Charles said. It was his old patrol. 'They say the poachers' spoor is very fresh, but they are worried they will not catch them before they cross the border.'

'With three men against nine, if I was Lovemore I'd be more worried if I *did* catch them.'

Dougal studied the map. 'The patrol's kilometres from the nearest roadway, Shane. You'll never get to the border to head them off in time.'

Shane smiled and clapped Dougal on the shoulder. 'Not by vehicle, we won't, China.'

'*You* ouns *are crazy, you know?*' Dougal said into the microphone. Shane heard the tinny voice in his headphones and laughed. He looked across at Wise, smiled and gave him a thumbs-up. The African tried to grin.

Shane leaned over the back of the Cessna front passenger seat and stabbed the map with his finger. Dougal glanced down. 'There's the border. Stay high, Dougal, we don't want to tip them off.'

'*Roger,*' Dougal said.

Shane saw the flare of sunlight reflected off something man-made. He stuck his head out of the gaping hole where they had removed the Cessna's rear side door prior to takeoff. The slipstream tore at his thick dark hair as he looked down. 'Vehicle,' he said. 'A *bakkie*, just across the border.' He sat back in his seat and rechecked the map. 'That'll be their pick-up.'

Shane radioed Charles again with the new information and asked for a sitrep from the national parks callsign. Charles informed him that Lovemore and his men were less than three kilometres from the border, and closing on the poachers, who were somewhere between the rangers and the dirt track that marked the international boundary.

'Wise!' Shane yelled. 'Are you okay?' Wise looked up and nodded. Shane admired him at that moment. The boy had only just completed his ninth jump. As a parachutist he was still a novice, but he had agreed without hesitation to accompany Shane.

Charles had radioed Fletcher, who, predictably, was heading as fast as he could towards the scene of the possible showdown. He had, under Shane's orders, stressed and restressed the estimated size of the poaching gang, and conveyed a formal recommendation from Shane that Fletcher's hunting clients be kept well away from the area. Orbiting over the border, Shane hoped his boss and the foreigners didn't stumble into a fire fight.

'*Shane, up ahead*,' Dougal said.

Shane leaned into the front of the cockpit again and Dougal pointed to a grassy vlei. Shane checked his topographical map and saw a prominent ridge line rising up from the left of the clearing. The rise, which was heavily treed, flanked the vlei. That was where they would position themselves. If the poachers kept to their straight course for the border, they would cross the open plain. For now, it would make an excellent drop zone. 'Perfect. Circle around, Dougal.'

It was madness – jumping without a safety crew, the nearest hospital more than a hundred kilometres away. His ground support, in the form of Caesar in a Land Rover, was still two hours' walk away. However, he wouldn't have been anywhere else in the world right then. Shane was jumping with the bare minimum of equipment. His chest webbing was crammed with six magazines of twenty rounds each, his handheld radio and three wound dressings. He carried three water bottles on his belt and his K-Bar. Stuffed in the bulging pockets of his camouflage tunic and cargo pants were matches, a map, a GPS, a compass and enough basic rations to last a night – although he planned on being back at Isilwane for sundowners. He had slung his SLR over his right shoulder, barrel pointing down, before strapping on his brand-new free-fall parachute rig. Two chutes had arrived from Australia while he was out on his last patrol – a donation from an ex-army friend who now ran a civilian parachute training school. He'd been intrigued by Shane's request to supply parachutes to help aid in the fight to save Africa's wildlife. Shane had envisaged an operation such as this, but not so soon, and with so little preparation or planning.

He knelt on the floor of the aircraft and checked Wise's parachute and gear, making sure the AK 47 was firmly seated under the parachute harness straps. He made the younger man talk through his flight drills, and the actions he would take if his main canopy malfunctioned and he had to use his reserve chute.

'Are you ready?' Shane barked.

Wise croaked a feeble, 'Yes.'

'ARE YOU READY?'

'*YEBO!*'

Shane felt the Cessna come out of a turn and level off. Dougal looked around and held up crossed fingers. Thirty seconds. Shane motioned for Wise to dangle his legs out of the opening where the doors had been. He held the African's left hand, steadying him. The fierce slipstream snatched at Wise's green trousers.

The last trip of the season and it had been a good one. Soon the rains would come, dispersing the animals, who would no longer be forced to congregate around the meagre water of the pumped pans and the trickling natural springs.

The whores and bartenders in Livingstone would grow rich from their wages tonight, as soon as the ivory was delivered and paid for, in Botswana. They were nine for this trip – four hunters, the boy, and four bearers who carried the four mighty tusks between them, slung from mopane poles. And such tusks! The one pair weighed at least forty kilograms, the other probably fifty. Where the booty was bound for, Leonard did not know. All he cared about now was getting his men and himself home safe.

Maybe he was being extra cautious because it was the last trip of the season, but Leonard had the feeling that they were being followed. An earlier foray into Zimbabwe, to kill the rhino, had been a close call – someone had been shooting at a person behind them, but by then they had been safely across the border. The Botswana national parks authorities and their army also mounted patrols, but they used vehicles. Patrolling in a truck might have been easier on the feet of the rangers and soldiers, but they were also simple to avoid, as one only had to listen for the engines. The Zimbabweans might be short of diesel and spare parts, but they were good on their feet – and they shot to kill. Leonard had sent Samuel circling back on the route they had taken, to see if he could spot anyone following them.

Leonard looked up at the sky. A small aeroplane droned across the clear blue sky, very high, too far up to notice them. He smiled at the four bearers, who trudged past him as he stared at the aircraft. Following them, in reserve, was his brother's son, just a boy of fourteen, but so very keen. He had boasted that he would take his fill of beer and women that evening too. They would see about that, but for the time being the boy looked as though he had never been happier in his life.

He raised his rifle at the rustling of some bushes to his left. Samuel emerged, panting. 'You were right, Leonard. Three men. Parks and wildlife. AK 47s. Moving fast.'

Leonard scanned the horizon, checking the familiar landmarks. They were still a few kilometres from the border. 'How far behind us?'

Samuel sucked greedily on a water bottle, then wiped his mouth. 'They will catch us, Leonard. Even if we run, with the ivory, we will not make it.'

Abandoning the tusks was out of the question. They represented close to a year's wages for the gang. Three rangers, versus four hunters, all with the same weapons. Also, one of the bearers carried a .303 and another had an old shotgun. Six guns against three, and the Zambians would have the element of surprise. 'We fight them, Samuel. And that is three less of them we will have to evade next year.'

Samuel licked the last drops of the water from his lips. 'Leonard, let us hide the ivory, in an anthill. We can come back for it in a week or two.'

The others had stopped and were listening now. The boy, whose name was Daniel, spoke up. 'Uncle, give me Samuel's AK. I will fight.'

'Shit,' Samuel said. To be shamed by a boy. He would take it out on the whelp later that night – if they lived that long.

'There is a big vlei ahead. You know the one, Samuel?' Leonard said.

Samuel nodded.

'We will wait for them there, where the land rises. We will kill them. And you, young man,' he said, pointing to Daniel, 'will have your first rifle, courtesy of these men who would make us poor and hungry.' The teenager beamed.

'Isilwane, Isilwane, Isilwane, this is national parks callsign Whisky One,' Lovemore repeated into his radio. There was only static on the other end.

'What's happening?' Noah asked, breathing heavily, as he scanned the bush ahead of them.

'Ah, but this radio is buggered. The batteries, I think.'

'Shit,' Christopher said.

Lovemore scanned the spoor again. They were so close he could almost smell the Zambians. 'We know from Charles Ndlovu that Isilwane was trying to deploy a callsign to head the poachers off. We do not need communications to kill. Let us proceed.'

Christopher looked worried. 'There are nine of them, Lovemore, you said it yourself.'

'They will not stand and fight. They will run as soon as they see us. Between us and the *murungu* Castle and his men, they will be caught in a trap.'

Noah looked at Christopher and shrugged. 'It is our job, Christopher.'

*

As the more experienced parachutist of the two, Shane had decided that Wise should jump first. Shane would follow him and be better able to steer towards where Wise landed, so they would not be separated on the ground.

He tumbled out of the Cessna a half-second after Wise had pitched forward into the blue nothingness. Wise had taken to parachuting like a bird and Shane noticed the near perfect way the other man arched his body as he plummeted earthwards.

As soon as he saw Wise's canopy deploy, Shane pulled the ripcord on his own parachute and felt the jolt as the leg straps cut into his crotch. Wise was steering for the middle of the vlei and Shane followed him in, touching down before all the wind had spilled from the rectangle of panelled fabric over Wise's head.

'Good work,' Shane said as he unbuckled his harness. Wise kept watch, kneeling in the grass, looking down the barrel of his unslung AK 47 as Shane hurriedly field-packed the parachutes so that they could carry them. 'Come, on, let's move,' he whispered.

Shane had taken the time to orientate himself thoroughly with the surrounding countryside as he had hung beneath his parachute. He led Wise to the south-west now, using a game trail ploughed through the shoulder-high adrenaline grass by elephants. Wise dragged a dry-leafed mopane branch behind them to obscure their tracks. Shane doubted, however, that the poachers would be looking for spoor ahead of them. They would be too busy beetling for the border.

They climbed the ridge line that rimmed the vlei on one side, and from the cover of a termite colony's earthen mound they had a commanding view of the grassland. Shane called Charles on the radio. 'Zero Alpha, this is Taipan, radio check, over.'

Charles replied. The signal was loud and clear, but he explained that he had lost contact with Lovemore's callsign. First problem of the day, Shane thought to himself. While they waited and silently prayed that the poachers would continue on in a straight line, Shane took out the map and showed Wise exactly where they were. 'You know which way to head, to get to Caesar and the pick-up Land Rover, if anything happens?'

Wise nodded.

'No heroics,' Shane said to him.

With the benefit of radio communications between Isilwane and the national parks patrol, Shane's plan had been to guide the rangers as close as possible to the poachers, and provide support if called upon. As a civilian, he had no legal justification for opening fire on the Zambians, unless of course they saw him and fired on him first, in which case he and Wise could act in self-defence. They had hurriedly discussed a couple of ruses they could use to slow the gang down, if it looked as though they would cross the border before the Zimbabweans caught them. They might start shooting, though not at the criminals, in the hope that they went to ground for a few precious minutes. Another idea of Shane's was to light a campfire, in the hope that the Zambians would alter their course and therefore take longer to reach the border. All that was out the window now.

Shane called Charles again, hoping that the old man had somehow been able to re-establish communications with his former comrades. He felt a tap on his arm. Shane slowly raised the binoculars to his eyes and focused on the area at which Wise was pointing. They watched the eight men moving, like a line of black ants, four carrying valuable white crumbs between them. Shane noticed a ninth figure, shorter than the others and trailing behind. Only a kid. He shook his head. The lead poacher gestured with his hands and the gang followed him off to the right, to the north, up out of the long grass onto the high ground on the other side of the vlei. The head man stopped his followers at various points of cover and concealment – a fallen log, an anthill similar to the one Shane and Wise hid behind, a stout leadwood. Shane and Wise faced the poachers across the open expanse of grass.

'Ambush,' Shane whispered. 'Shit.' He crawled closer to Wise and whispered the new plan, so close his lips almost brushed the other man's ear. It was so simple, it was stupid.

Lovemore walked with a permanent stoop, his eyes fixed on the spoor in front of him. 'Hurry, hurry,' he chivvied the other two.

Noah tightened his grip on his rifle, his palms damp with sweat. Christopher closed up to his friend. None of them had killed a man before.

191

Ahead of them the bush thinned to a grassy plain, set in a shallow valley between two opposing ridge lines. 'We can make fast time through here.'

Leonard had not survived two decades of forays across the border in search of rhino horn and ivory without honing all his senses. He saw the first national parks green cap bob into view above the tall yellow grass.

He nodded to Samuel, who passed the silent message down the line. Six fingers tightened slowly around triggers.

Shane peered around the anthill and saw the first of the rangers, a dark shape almost obscured by heat haze and swaying yellow grass. He looked heavenwards, decided it was too late in life to become god-fearing, and climbed up onto the anthill.

'LOVEMORE!' he bellowed, his words echoing across the vlei. '*Hokoyo! Ambush! Ma-tsotsis, kurudji kwenyu!*'

He had the satisfaction of seeing the capped head bob down instinctively as the first bullets slammed into the anthill and whip-cracked in the air around him. He dived and rolled, using his parachute training to take the force of the landing along his right side and thigh.

Lead slugs scythed the grass above his head as he leopard-crawled away from the mound, which made a perfect target for most of the poachers' rifles.

Wise, on Shane's orders, had repositioned himself behind a fallen tree, fifty metres from the anthill and closer to the poachers. He had a perfect view of the man they had identified as the leader. He took a breath, as Shane had taught him, then exhaled. The poacher was visible through the circular sight as he paused at the end of the breath. Wise squeezed the trigger. His first shot fell short, raising a geyser of dust in front of the old Zambian, who ducked his head. Wise fired again, until he could not see the man, then shifted his aim to the right, to another of them. This man was obviously unaware, through the cacophony of shots, that anyone was shooting back at the gang, for he rose on one knee to try to see Shane.

Wise centred the poacher in his sights, controlled his breathing again. He exhaled and squeezed. The man was knocked flat on his back. Wise whooped with joy. In the Congo, despite what he had told Shane about being an infantryman and the veteran of several fire fights, he had only ever driven a truck. Today he was a warrior from the sky.

Shane's pulse raced, but his mind was clear and calm. He reached the leadwood's trunk and raised his head. He saw one poacher fall, and heard the man's screams of pain. He stood, braced himself against the tree, took aim at a crouching man with an AK 47 and fired. He felt the satisfying kick of the old rifle in his shoulder. The man was gone, swallowed by the grass. A poacher yelled something in his own language and Shane was aware of fire being redirected. They had seen Wise. He hoped the boy did as he had instructed and backed away to the reverse side of the ridge. They had spoiled the ambush and saved the national parks callsign – for the time being. It was now up to Lovemore to make the next move.

'Mapenga!' Lovemore muttered as he shook his head. The white man was crazy, but he had saved their lives.

'Let us wait for help,' Christopher pleaded as he lay in the cocooning warmth of the grass.

'There is no help!' Noah said. 'Lovemore, what do we do next?'

Lovemore risked a peep through the swaying blades of gold. The fire was directed away from them now, and the Zambians were shouting. At least one was crying in pain. 'Right flanking attack. Now!'

Shane moved across the middle of the vlei now, from south to north. Only the grass covered him, but there was nothing between him and the Zambians solid enough to stop a bullet. If he was seen, he would die. His mouth was dry, his heart thumping. A poacher was firing on automatic, long bursts of six or seven rounds, away from Shane, towards Wise.

There was movement to his right. He dropped to his knee and pointed his rifle down an elephant trail; a flash of green as a man darted across the path. 'Zimbabwe, Zimbabwe,' he hissed.

A second man reached the trail, turned and raised an AK 47, his eyes wide. Shane opened his arms, his SLR held high in his right hand. 'Friend,' he said. He recognised one of the men from Lovemore's patrol.

'Lovemore!' the man whispered urgently, and tapped the tin magazine of his AK 47.

Shane joined the patrol. Lovemore explained that he was hooking around to the right, to try to outflank the poachers. 'Lead on,' Shane said.

Splinters of wood flew off the fallen tree behind which Wise sheltered. He remembered he should retreat, but was sure he could account for another Zambian. He had seen and heard nothing of Shane since he had climbed, like a madman, onto the anthill.

Wise rose, grinning and yelling an incoherent war cry, exposing himself above the deadfall for a second and a half as he squeezed off two more rounds. The firing pin of his rifle clicked on an empty chamber. 'Magazine!' he yelled and started to duck down.

Two poachers, who had already zeroed in on the tree, fired bursts of automatic fire at him. A third, the bearer with the .303, had been waiting for such a chance. He took careful aim and pulled the trigger of his fifty-year-old rifle.

Wise screamed and fell back.

Shane had seen the younger man's foolhardiness, and he cursed under his breath. But Wise's fall had given the poachers a false sense of victory and distracted them. Shane and the rangers used the poachers' jubilant cries to their advantage, moving stealthily up behind them.

Two of the gang rose and started to advance on Wise's position. Shane, Lovemore, Noah and Christopher opened up on Shane's command. The two Zambians pitched forward, shot in the back.

'Forward! Fight through!' Shane commanded. They had seized the initiative and needed to maintain it. They walked, line abreast, along the ragged ambush line.

Shane came across the lifeless body of a man, a shotgun lying by his side. He kicked the weapon aside. 'One dead enemy!' he yelled, then continued moving, his SLR held high into his shoulder, finger curled around the trigger.

Lovemore came to one of the men armed with automatic weapons. He echoed Shane's call, adding, 'AK 47.'

'Leave it, we can . . .' Shane began, as Lovemore stooped to prise the rifle from the dead poacher's hand. 'Down!' Shane saw the movement in the bush, then spotted the long wooden stock of a Lee Enfield rifle. He turned at the waist and fired two quick shots. The second found its mark, and the man's head flicked back.

Lovemore was wide eyed at his narrow escape. 'Keep moving,' Shane cajoled.

Noah flung the dead man's bolt-action rifle away when he reached the corpse. Christopher came across the body of another man armed with an AK 47.

'Eyes peeled, men,' Shane said, his voice steady and calm.

'Over here,' Noah called.

Shane crashed through a thicket of leafless bush,

ignoring the thorns that snatched at his fatigues and skin. A grey-haired man sat with his back against the trunk of a tree, his AK 47 on the ground beside him. Weakly, for blood pumped thick and bright from a hole in his right shoulder, he tried to raise his hands, and moaned in pain with the effort.

Lovemore walked ahead of Shane and kicked the man, hard, in the ribs. The man screamed.

'Enough,' Shane barked.

Lovemore turned on Shane, eyes wide and nostrils flared in anger, then the fear and adrenaline seemed to subside. He nodded to Shane, dropped to one knee beside the older man and tossed his rifle out of reach. 'Where are the other four?' Lovemore asked the man. The other two rangers stood by, watching.

Shane left them, striding into the bush, looking for tracks and other signs. There was one armed man still on the loose.

'WISE!' he called.

There was no reply. He noticed and ignored the four elephant tusks, tied in pairs and slung from timber poles. Shane kept his rifle raised as he moved, at a crouch, through the tall grass, which had been flattened by men on the move. He ran down into the shallow depression, then scaled the ridge to the fallen log behind which Wise had sheltered. He braced himself for the worst as he crested the ridge.

Wise lay on the ground, on his back, beside the two parachutes, which he had dragged to his new position after he and Shane had separated. His neck and left shoulder were drenched red. Lying face down across Wise's lower torso and legs was another man, dressed in three-quarter length pants and a tan bush shirt. Wise was conscious, but silent, and he stared up at Shane. In his right hand was a US Air Force pilot's survival knife, the top edge of its blackened-blade serrated, for cutting wood. It was Shane's spare and he had given it to Wise before the flight. The weapon, like Wise's hand, was coated in blood.

Shane looked around for signs of danger. Wise's AK 47, which had been painted camouflage, lay two metres away. The cocking handle and working parts were locked open – a sign that Wise had not been able to reload after he called 'magazine', which meant he was out of ammunition. It looked as though he had dropped the rifle after being hit in the neck by a grazing shot.

The dead man's weapon lay beside the pair.

Shane grabbed the poacher by the waistband of his shorts and dragged him off Wise, staining the grass the same colour as Wise's clothes. He checked the man's pockets and found a bundle of banknotes, still damp with sweat, and a grubby-covered Zambian passport. He opened the document and looked at the face of Samuel Mumba. Shane pock-eted it, and the cash, then extended a hand to Wise. 'All right, mate?'

Wise blinked at him and finally seemed to under-stand. He raised his hand. Shane took it and hauled him to his feet.

'I . . . I think I fainted for a few moments. When I woke, he was . . . he was searching me.' He held the knife out for Shane's inspection and stared at it, as if unable to comprehend what he had done.

'It's okay. Pick up your weapon and reload.'

'But . . .' Wise looked down at the man he had killed.

Shane grabbed him firmly by the shoulder with his free hand and stared hard into his eyes. 'You did good. Get your rifle, reload it, and grab his as well. That should be the last of the ones with guns, but we're not safe until we're back at Isilwane.'

'He could have killed me, Shane . . .'

'Yeah, but you got him first. That's all that matters, mate. Let's go home.'

Wise was able to walk and, when they returned to the rangers, Lovemore told them the ringleader had died of his wound.

'The bullet had hit his lung, I think. He was an old man.'

Shane wondered if Lovemore had administered first aid to the poacher – or done something else.

Lovemore kept looking down at the body, then back at Shane. 'He told us they were from Zambia. Asked us not to harm the boy if we found him.'

'What did you say?'

'I told him we would shoot any Zambian we found in our country.' Lovemore ran his hand through his close-cropped hair.

Shane shook a cigarette from his packet and offered the rest to the Africans. Lovemore and Noah accepted and Shane lit their smokes. He couldn't judge these men. They were fighting a war, but he didn't want any part of tracking unarmed fugitives, especially not a child.

'We should go. Wise is injured.'

Lovemore nodded, and Shane sensed the fight leaving him, along with the adrenaline.

They left the bodies where they had fallen, hoping that the police could be raised before hyenas and vultures discovered them. They were all tired and thirsty from the aftermath of combat, and Wise needed medical attention.

Fletcher Reynolds and his three American hunters were parked next to Caesar on the side of the road when the rangers, Shane, and Wise straggled out of the bush.

'How many got away?' was the first thing Fletcher asked Shane.

Shane had a wounded man with him and thought some words of compassion, let alone congratulations, might have been in order. 'Three. One of them is just a kid. They were unarmed bearers.'

'Shoot! We heard you nailed some of them, though, is that right?' a beer-bellied, balding American in camouflaged fatigues asked.

Shane looked at the man in silence, then nodded. 'Six.'

'Let's go take a look,' another of the hunters suggested.

'Have you picked up the spoor of the *tsotsis* who escaped?' Fletcher asked.

Shane lit another cigarette and ran a hand through his dirt- and sweat-matted hair. 'I've got a wounded man who needs to see a doctor. Where are the cops?'

Fletcher smiled. 'You've done a great job, Shane. You really have, as has Wise. But we can't let the others get off scot-free. They'll only be back to kill again.'

'Yeah, let's get some!' the third of the Americans said.

'You're not seriously considering taking these . . . your clients out on a man-hunt, are you?' Shane asked.

Lovemore strode over to the two men. 'Mister Reynolds, parks and wildlife will coordinate the search for the other men with the police, when they arrive.'

Shane thought the Americans looked like a pack of dogs who had just seen their fox disappear down its burrow.

'Awww, shoot, can we at least go take a look at the dead guys?' the fat hunter pleaded.

'Come, we'll go and collect the ivory,' Reynolds said to them. 'Shane, I'll see you back at Isilwane.'

Shane washed his hands with antiseptic soap in the kitchen sink of his house, watching as the blood and filth sluiced down the plughole. He shook them dry and reached for a pair of latex gloves.

'I am clean. I have been tested, and I always use a condom,' Wise said. The young African sat bare-chested at the kitchen table, a cigarette burning in the ashtray, two open beers on the table.

'I'm wearing gloves so that I don't infect you with bacteria, not because I'm worried about catching anything from you,' Shane said.

'You did good out there today,' he continued as he peeled away the shell dressing, which was crusted with dried blood and dirt. Shane had qualified as a patrol medic in the SAS and, after checking the wound again before the drive back to Isilwane, had decided that he could patch Wise up from his own first-aid kit. Wise had a nasty furrow on his neck, but if they kept the wound clean and dry it would heal without stitches. 'What do you think about Charles? He's very ill.'

'He has HIV-AIDS for sure.' Wise pronounced the last word in two syllables, for added emphasis. He winced as Shane squirted saline solution into and around his wound. 'He's like all the old guys. They're good family men, but after every payday they go to the shebeens, get drunk and screw a prostitute. Then they go home to their wives and kids. It's just the way it is.'

'How long has he got, do you reckon?' Shane asked as he sprinkled antibiotic powder into the graze.

'I watched my uncle and my older brother die. I think Charles will be dead in a month – maybe two.' Wise said it with the matter-of-factness of a generation for whom death had become an everyday occurrence. Shane had been surprised at first by the commonality of death, and the burgeoning funeral industry, on his return to Africa. There were roadside stalls advertising headstones, and you could buy a coffin at any hardware store. In Australia, Shane could count the number of funerals he had been to on the fingers of one hand. Boys like Wise had lost most of their families before they reached manhood. 'It will be very hard on his family, with only the national parks pension to live on,' Wise said.

'I'll have a word to Reynolds,' Shane said.

He dressed the wound with gauze and Elastoplast. 'Keep it dry. We'll change the dressing every day.' After checking that Wise wasn't allergic to penicillin, he gave him some generic antibiotic tablets he had filched from the army before discharge. While the physical wound would heal, Shane knew the scars could run deeper. 'Do you want to talk about today?'

'About what?'

'The shooting – getting wounded. The dead guy.'

'I saw a lot of dead people in the DRC, boss,' Wise said. 'I drove a truck that carried the bodies to the morgue.'

'You had a close call today, but I was proud of you. Your training got you through – though you should have got off that ridge line like I told you to, instead of sitting up there like Rambo.'

He looked sheepish, then said, 'It was good, Shane.' He held out a hand and Shane clasped it.

'It was good,' Shane repeated. 'Go get cleaned up. Debrief at eighteen-hundred hours tonight.'

'*Yebo.*' Wise saluted, then winced as the muscles in his neck contracted.

Shane smiled and waved him out. He removed the gloves and washed his hands again, then lit a cigarette. He replayed the day's battle in his mind as he sipped his beer. He saw the first man fall, then the guy with the .303 – close enough to him to see his eyes widen as the bullet hit him. Then the other two that he and the rangers had drilled at close range, from behind. He closed his eyes and pressed his palms to them. He needed to piss.

In the bathroom he closed his eyes again, but the

ghosts returned. The antlike figures in the Tora Bora Mountains of Afghanistan, vaporised by the B-52s' J-DAM bombs as his patrol had called in air strike after air strike from their vantage points; the rolling contacts in the Western Desert of Iraq as he and his men had raced towards Baghdad in their long-range patrol vehicle; the burning terrorist he had killed in that city; the dead bodies of the poachers in the African dust. He was moving closer to death, not further away from it. There were no air strikes and little technology to rely on out here – he was close enough to see, hear and smell death at its most intimate. Wise had been there too – even closer – and he seemed okay.

From outside, he heard the return of Fletcher's Land Rover. As he stepped onto the veranda he saw a herd of elephant emerge from the shelter of the trees and amble down to the waterhole outside the perimeter fence.

The voices from the truck were brash and exuberant, though when the men strolled into view, waving to him as they entered the main lodge, Shane saw that all the noise came from two hunters. The third looked pale and a little unsteady on his feet.

'Aww, come on, Larry,' the beer-bellied American said to his subdued friend. 'Get *over* it, man.'

The quiet man looked unconvinced. Fletcher told the men he would see them at dinnertime, then walked over to Shane.

'I was a little abrupt with you earlier,' Fletcher said.

Shane shrugged. 'It was nothing. The boys did well today.'

'Don't let them catch you calling them that. *Boy* is a derogatory term.'

'They're good men.'

'That they are. As are you. I checked the scene of that contact. Man, you drilled those *okes* one time!'

Shane smelled beer on his breath. 'What's wrong with that American, the one who wasn't talking?'

'Larry? These guys are all part-time soldiers – national guard, they call it in the States. Today was the first time any of them had seen the results of some 7.62 surgery. Two of them loved it, the third one lost his lunch.'

'Did you go looking for the bearers who got away?'

Fletcher narrowed his eyes. He looked a little unsteady on his feet, then he smiled. 'Yes, you got me, man. Guilty as charged. After we checked the bodies I gave the Yanks a little lesson in tracking – took them maybe a kilometre into the bush – but those guys were long gone, into Botswana. Still, they loved it.'

'What would you have done if you had caught up with the ones who got away?'

Fletcher shrugged. 'You said they were unarmed. I would have tried to stop them, but we wouldn't have shot them, if that's what you're thinking. I don't play that way.'

12

'I t's so wonderful to finally meet you, Doctor!'
Michelle gushed, as hard as she could, as she
shook hands with the diminutive Doctor
Charles Hamley the Third.

She towered over him. He motioned for her to sit in
a lounge chair in the lodge's bar, as if he owned the
place. Fletcher didn't seem to mind, she noticed, and
with the amount of money the good dentist and his
friends had put Fletcher's way, he could nearly have
bought Isilwane outright.

While she detested the little man's love of blood
sports, he, as much as Fletcher, was the reason she
was still in Africa.

'I'm so keen to hear about your work, Michelle.
And call me Chuck,' he said, pushing a pair of thin
gold-framed spectacles up his nose. He was dressed
in pressed safari clothes – khaki bush shirt with a
reinforced padded patch on his right shoulder and
matching trousers. A finely cropped fuzz of grey hair
barely covered a scalp reddened by the merciless

African sun after only a day back in the bush.

Fletcher's maid brought drinks, and Michelle opened her laptop and delivered a twenty-minute PowerPoint presentation she had prepared about her research program, its goals and her achievements to date.

'Fascinating stuff, Michelle. And you say a pack of dogs has relocated to the hunting concession?'

He seemed genuinely interested in her work. 'Yes, once I got Fletcher to promise not to eradicate any of the dogs, they seemed to take to the place.'

They all laughed. 'I heard from Shane Castle, just before you arrived,' the dentist said. 'He and Fletcher have had some very encouraging results in their anti-poaching operation, so that's probably made a safer environment for the wild dogs as well.'

'Anti-poaching operation – more like a full-scale war, if you believe the newspapers,' Michelle said.

'It's been quiet lately, ever since that big *hondo* with the Zambian gang,' Fletcher said, using the Shona word for war. 'I think our gamekeeper has put the fear of God into the local poachers.'

'Praise be to Him,' the dentist intoned.

Michelle rolled her eyes as the dentist closed his. She gave a cheeky smile when Fletcher shot her a look that told her to drop it.

'Anyway,' Fletcher continued, 'Shane hasn't had a contact since the big one. He's had his guys out patrolling for snares, and the figures he's kept show a ninety per cent drop in the number of traps found over the past two months.'

'Hardly surprising. Who'd want to get nailed by

Bruce Willis and his gang of mercenaries?' Michelle intended it as a joke, but Fletcher took his cue from his benefactor and looked sour. 'Hey, don't get me wrong, if I found someone who'd set a snare that caught one of my dogs I'd tear his balls off!' That approach, involving crudity – the dentist might have called it 'cussing', she thought – went down about as well as her earlier remark.

'Anyway, it seems we can drink to success all round at Isilwane,' Chuck said brightly.

'Amen,' Michelle said.

'*Amen*, indeed!' Chuck said, beaming. 'Now, my dear, has Fletcher told you the real purpose of my visit?'

Michelle looked at Fletcher, then shook her head.

'What do you know about the Democratic Republic of Congo?' Chuck asked.

'Lots of wars and gorillas?' She'd heard from Fletcher that his contact in the Zimbabwean Army, Brigadier Moyo, had offered him a joint-venture stake in a hunting concession near the Virunga National Park, in the north-east of the DRC. The park, she knew already, was part of a network of reserves that straddled the Ruwenzori Mountains – the so-called Mountains of the Moon – which were spread across the Congo, Burundi, Rwanda and Uganda. What those countries had in common, aside from a virtually ceaseless round of conflicts and civil wars over the past few decades, was that they were home to remnant populations of the endangered mountain gorillas.

'I'm very interested in investing in wildlife conservation in that part of the world, Michelle, not only in support of the mountain gorillas – which already attract a good deal of funding from various international organisations – but also in the protection of other game in the area.'

She found the use of the word 'game' coming from a hunter mildly distasteful, as though any animal were fodder for his guns. She would have used the term 'wildlife'. 'To ensure there are sufficient numbers for future hunting.' She said it not as a question or an accusation, merely a statement.

'Exactly, Michelle. Hunting can bring foreign currency into a devastated area long before mainstream tourists return. If, for example, you tell me there are viable populations of unusual trophy animals, such as sitatunga or giant hog in the forests around the Virunga National Park, then we spread the word and start getting that country back on its feet again.'

He seemed so earnest, almost caring. Michelle found it bizarre. 'I'm not sure, Chuck. I mean, it sounds like a great offer, but I'm pretty attached to my work here.'

'I could find half-a-dozen pro-hunting ecologists back home who would go over there, spend time in the concession that Fletcher is looking at, and tell me, hand on heart, that it is safe for me to go in there all guns blazing and kill whatever I want, Michelle.'

She sat back in her chair and regarded the pair of them. Fletcher looked back at her, eagerly awaiting her answer. She guessed he wanted her to accompany him to the jungles of the DRC – for other than scientific reasons. He had visited her at Main Camp three times since her altercation with the gangsters at Isilwane, and he had been smart enough to realise that he had fouled up by standing her up over the trip to Victoria Falls. She had snubbed his advances that first time – keeping it to just dinner – then slept with him on his subsequent two visits.

She had returned to Isilwane five days earlier, ostensibly in search of the wild dogs again, and had stayed at the lodge rather than in the national park. It was a world away from her cottage at Main Camp, and while she found the idea of having servants on call initially a little uncomfortable, it only took her a couple of days to get used to the maid tapping on the door of the master bedroom every morning to deliver a tray of tea and coffee to Fletcher and her.

'What would happen to my work here with the dogs if I moved to the Congo? It's just as important.'

'Don't tell me you don't get requests for people to come and help you?' Chuck asked.

'All the time.' She had a drawer full of unanswered letters from fellow scientists and graduate students who wanted to assist her with her work, which was becoming better known now that she had published two papers in conservation journals.

Chuck explained that he had been so impressed with what he had seen at Isilwane that he wanted to double his contribution to the lodge's conservation fund. It was his wish, if the details could be ironed out, that the wild dog research continue, with funding allocated for an assistant, perhaps a postgraduate student under Michelle's supervision. 'But I'd like you to do the initial work up in the DRC, and maybe fly back down here to Zimbabwe once every couple of months to check progress on the wild dog research.'

'That sounds very generous, Chuck, but why me? You hardly know me.'

'Fletcher knows you, and I've seen some of the work you're doing. I'm a generous man, Michelle, and the good Lord knows I can afford to be. But I detest the idea of giving money to a big conservation organisation, not knowing if it will be spent on protecting animals or the drinks bill for the next international convention on walrus-tooth smuggling!'

She laughed. She felt her resolve weakening. The simple truth was she was there at the grace of men such as Doctor Charles Hamley and, like it or not, they had the final word on where their money would be spent. She had never been to the DRC, but it fascinated her – a land of dense, mysterious jungle filled with wildlife she had only ever read about.

Chuck continued, 'I prefer to invest in people, such as you, Fletcher and Shane and his guys. That way I can see results for myself.'

'Besides,' Fletcher interrupted, 'the rains will be here soon. You know very well business comes to a halt once the wet season starts. The game disperses and the roads are rubbish, so it won't matter as much if you're not here. Up in the Congo, their serious rains won't start until next March. They have what they call their small rains from October to December, but we can still hunt. It dries out again in January and February.'

She nodded in agreement. It was the time of year when she allowed herself a vacation from Zimbabwe. The year before she had returned to Canada for Christmas, though she was looking forward to avoiding family commitments this year and maybe travelling to parts of Africa she hadn't yet visited. The offer on the table would take her to an exotic part of the continent she might never see otherwise. 'What about the security situation up there?'

'It's been bad,' Fletcher explained. 'The Virunga Park and the areas around it have been a haven to several different refugee and militia groups in recent years. They had the Rwandan Hutu rebels spill across the border after the genocide there; the Lord's Resistance Army from Uganda hides out in the DRC's jungles when they're on the run from their government; plus there are the various rebel factions from within the Congo itself.'

'Sounds dangerous. I've heard poaching is terrible up there. I read somewhere the elephant population in the Virunga has dropped from seventy thousand to fourteen thousand in the last few years.'

'That's true. And the hippo from Lake Edward have been decimated to feed starving refugees. All of that could be a problem, but . . .'

'Knock, knock,' Shane said, striding into the bar. 'I've just finished the debrief with my guys,' he told Fletcher. 'Hi, Michelle, and hello again, Chuck.'

Michelle smiled a greeting at the tall, dark-haired ex-soldier. The hunter of men, was how she still thought of him, and she still hadn't made up her mind if that sobriquet put him a notch above or below the likes of Fletcher and Chuck. All that aside, shaved and scrubbed he was a handsome specimen.

'Perfect timing, Shane,' Fletcher said. 'We were just about to start talking about you. Grab a drink from the girl.'

Shane ordered a beer from the maid. 'Are they trying to talk you into relocating to the DRC as well?' he asked Michelle.

She nodded. 'I gather Fletcher was just about to say that you and your band of mercenaries will be coming along to protect us and kill some more poachers.'

He shrugged. 'I've just told the guys,' he said to Fletcher. 'Wise was a bit reluctant. He spent time up there with the Zim Army, but when I explained the pay and conditions he came around. Caesar just wants to stay with the crew, but old Charles is looking like he's on his last legs. Shame.'

'There will be funding for Shane to recruit more people for his anti-poaching team,' Chuck said to Michelle, in an attempt, she assumed, to allay her fears further.

'Out of the frying pan into the fire, sounds like to me,' she said.

Shane looked at her. 'The security of the new camp, and the personal security of Fletcher, his clients . . . and you if you're in, will be my team's first priority.'

She was about to say something glib, but then she saw the sincerity in his eyes.

'Come! No decisions now,' Fletcher said. 'Let's eat and we'll make sure, Chuck, that Shane and Michelle are both pie-eyed when they sign their new contracts!'

'I'll drink to that,' Chuck said, raising his soda water.

After dinner, over coffee, Fletcher asked Shane to join him on the lawn, while Chuck, and an increasingly interested Michelle, talked about the details of the proposed new research program, and the unique wildlife of the DRC's jungles.

'What's up, boss?' Shane asked.

'It's about Charles. I'm worried.'

'Me too, his health is getting worse and —'

'No, it's more than that, Shane. It's very serious, in fact. And, AIDS or not, I don't want him coming to the DRC with us.'

'What's up?'

Shane listened, stunned, as Fletcher recounted the details of a meeting with the chief warden of Hwange National Park and the senior ranger from the parks and wildlife station at Matetsi, which administered the hunting concessions, including Isilwane's.

The warden and the ranger had said that on four occasions over the past three weeks national parks callsigns – anti-poaching patrols – had radioed Charles at the Isilwane operations room and advised him of possible poaching gangs moving through the concession. The parks officials had put Fletcher on the spot, wanting to know why no sign of assistance had been rendered.

'I haven't received any messages asking for support from parks since the shoot-out with the Zambians,' Shane said.

'I know. You would have told me if you had, Shane,' Fletcher said. 'I hate to draw conclusions, but . . .'

'You think Charles has been deliberately holding back information? I've been relying on his local knowledge, while things have apparently been quiet, to suggest areas for our snare sweeps.'

'I don't like saying it, but it appears that Charles may have even been deliberately sending you and your guys to areas *away* from where the poachers are. I have to tell you also that he asked me for money recently.'

'What?' Shane was alarmed that Charles hadn't gone through the chain of command if he wanted a pay rise, but Fletcher explained that what Charles was after was not a salary increase but a commitment to ongoing support for his family after his death.

'I'm afraid I was a bit short with him. He's my employee, but he hasn't been here long enough for me to offer him a death benefit pension for his family. I sent him packing. Besides, his wife and kids will have his parks pension when he dies.'

Shane wished Charles had come to him first. He might have been able to negotiate something on the old man's behalf. He realised that as the commander of the anti-poaching team it was an area he should have looked into earlier – what compensation payments would be made if one of the team were killed or incapacitated in the line of work. He had his own life insurance – the premiums were astronomical – but his Zimbabwean foot soldiers would never be able to afford such protection. 'Bloody hell,' he said, shaking his head. 'You reckon he's on the take?'

Fletcher nodded. 'You'll have to sort him out, Shane. He's your man.'

'I'll do it now,' Shane said, draining his cup of coffee. It would be the worst and hardest job of his life, he thought.

The wind, for the first time since Shane had arrived back in Africa, blew cold and from the south, instead of from the vast hot plains and saltpans to the west. The dry season was ending. He thought he smelled rain, far off.

Michelle retired to her bedroom before Chuck and Fletcher, but had hardly gotten undressed and between the sheets when she heard the soft knock on her door.

'That was quick. Where's the dentist?' she whispered.

'Jet-lagged. I think he was only waiting for you to go to bed.'

'What happened to Shane? He left without saying goodnight.' Timber shutters rattled on their hinges outside her window.

Fletcher explained briefly that he had trouble with one of his men, a disciplinary matter that needed sorting out.

'So, what do you want, *Bwana* Reynolds?'

'You.'

'I don't come easy,' she said.

He smiled. 'That's not what I've noticed.'

She laughed, then the grin vanished. 'And I can't be bought, Fletcher. I'll come to the Congo out of curiosity, but don't think it's Chuck's dollars that are attracting me.'

'The ball's in your court, Michelle,' he said, sitting on the bed beside her. He reached out to stroke her hair, which was fanned across the starched white pillowcase.

The rounded top of her left breast was visible above the sheet. He let his fingers trail down her neckline. 'What do you think of him?'

'He's a little creepy. I don't know what it is about him, but I think there's a nasty streak under all the Christian do-gooding and polite manners.' A shiver ran through her body. It could have been the stiffening cool breeze that exploited the gaps in every door and window frame in the lodge.

'You're a tough judge of character. He's absolutely besotted with you. Thinks you're a goddess.'

She sniffed. 'Have you told him about us?'

Fletcher nodded. 'I hope you don't mind.'

'I'd rather he thinks that I'm attached than imagining he can woo me by increasing my research grants.'

'Are we?' he asked, his finger hooking the sheet, drawing the crisp whiteness down, slowly.

'What?'

'Attached?'

Her nipple stiffened at the touch of the sliding cotton. A shiver ran through her body as his skin met hers. 'I've a feeling we're about to be.'

Shane brooded over a cup of coffee and a cigarette in the operations room. The radio hissed in the background. Caesar was in the kitchen making mealie-meal porridge for breakfast. Wise had hitched a lift with a national parks vehicle to Victoria Falls, taking two days' leave.

The sky outside was gun-barrel grey and the chilled breeze swayed the long dying grass out past the cottage's trimmed lawns. There was no game at the lodge's waterhole. The resident sable herd would be huddled together unseen, taking shelter amongst the trees. It was a good time for predators, when the wind rustling in the bush masked the sound of their movement as they searched for prey.

Charles had not been in his room the night before, when Shane had gone to confront him. Neither had his clothes, his bag, his toiletry gear nor, more ominously, his AK 47, which, according to Caesar, he had that afternoon taken from the safe where the weapons were stored, supposedly to clean it.

On Charles's bed was a note. Shane had it on the table in front of him now.

Shane. I wish to thank you for the opportunity of employment that you extended to me in a time of great need. I am leaving because I cannot continue to serve you and the others. Please understand that nothing I have done was ever intended to harm you, or Wise or Caesar. I am ashamed that my decision to leave has been brought about by something as petty as money, but that is the way of life – I must think of my wife and children first. My life is near its end, and I must do what I can to protect my family, and to atone for my sins. May God keep you safe. Charles Ndlovu.

Shane ran a finger over his stubbled chin. Normally by this hour of the morning he would have been shaved and dressed in the lodge's uniform of green bush shirt and khaki trousers. He wore an old army T-shirt and a pair of running shorts. It was cool outside, but inside, out of the wind, it seemed as if the house's walls had absorbed enough sun during the dry season to keep it warm for months. When Caesar came in he was similarly casual. The younger man looked sullen, and spooned his porridge in silence. Shane knew it was time to show some leadership, or all of them would sink into a morass of inaction and depression over Charles's apparent defection.

'Come on, Caesar, it's time for work. I want you dressed and ready for the firing range in thirty minutes. We'll have some target practice today and —'

The radio crackled to life. *'Zero Alpha, this is Niner, over.'*

Fletcher, his guide Lloyd and Chuck Hamley had left to go hunting sable early that morning. Shane keyed the handset, 'Niner, this is Zero Alpha, over.'

'Zero Alpha, contact! Two shots fired. Wait, out.' Shane heard the alarm in Fletcher's voice. After days of inaction, the boss and his client had stumbled into a fire fight. It was a bad time to be short two men.

'Move!' Shane barked at Caesar.

By training and habit their packs and webbing were lying waiting to go in the front room of the cottage. Caesar slung the gear into the rear of the Land Rover. Shane snatched up a portable radio and sprinted for the main lodge and the gun room.

Michelle Parker was padding barefoot down the hallway in a sleeveless blouse and incredibly short shorts, a cup and saucer in her hands. 'Hello. You're in a rush.'

'Can't stop, sorry.'

'What is it?'

He heard the rising alarm in her voice and debated whether or not to tell her. 'Nothing to worry about.'

The radio betrayed him. '*Zero Alpha, one African male adult, automatic weapon – probably an AK. Grid reference follows.*' Shane grabbed a pen off the telephone table and wrote the numbers down on the back of his hand as Fletcher read out his location. '*Request support. Where are you, Shane?*'

Shane heard the crash of china and was vaguely aware of her gasp and a spatter of tea on his bare leg. Then he was gone, without further explanation. When he came back into the hallway he had his SLR in his hand and Caesar's AK 47 slung over his shoulder.

'I'm coming too,' Michelle said.

'No.'

'Yes!'

Shane swore. 'The best thing you can do is wait here. We might need someone to telephone the police.'

'Bullshit,' she spat back, hands on her hips. 'You've got a satellite telephone.'

He had neither the time nor the inclination to stand there arguing with her. He jogged out the door as the Land Rover pulled up with a crunch of gravel. Shane hauled his chest webbing out of the rear of the vehicle and buckled it over his T-shirt. He pulled a magazine from one of the camouflaged pouches, fitted it to the rifle and snatched back the cocking lever. It chambered a round with a satisfying snicker as he let it fly forward.

Shane climbed in and slammed the door. 'Go!' he commanded Caesar.

'But, boss . . .'

He looked over his shoulder and saw one long leg hooked over the side wall of the pick-up's rear tray. He ran a hand through his thick hair. 'Fuck!'

She glared back at him through the cab's rear window, blue eyes burning into his. She was fully in the truck now, sitting on Caesar's pack. He slammed a fist down on the dashboard. 'Drive!'

It took twenty minutes of breakneck bouncing over potholes and corrugations. Shane had the satisfaction of seeing, in the rear-view mirror, Michelle slide off the pack and land on her butt at least twice. He scanned the bush ahead of him. He hoped the stupid woman didn't get herself killed. Still, she obviously cared for the old man. Maybe even loved him. None of it was any consolation.

Shane checked the GPS. 'Slowly now, Caesar. We're close. Kill the engine and coast down the hill.'

The Land Rover creaked to a halt. Shane leapt out of the cab. 'Please, Michelle, I'm asking you nicely. Stay here in the back of the truck. Lie down, out of sight. I promise you I'll come back and tell you what's happening.' He grabbed his pack and passed Caesar's to him.

Michelle started to say something, but a single gunshot cut her off. Her eyes widened in fear. 'It's okay,' Shane said. 'I'll come back for you.'

She nodded and did as he ordered, dropping from sight in the back of the truck.

'Coming in, from the east,' Shane said without preamble into his radio handset. Fletcher pressed his send button once in acknowledgement. Thank God, Shane said to himself. At least someone was still alive.

221

Shane took point, scanning the ground until he picked up the spoor of white men in expensive boots.

'Over here!' Fletcher called.

Shane hurried ahead, rifle up, just in case.

'Relax,' the grey-haired hunter said as Shane and Caesar broke out of a stand of wicked thornbushes. Shane's exposed arms and legs were tattooed with scratches.

Fletcher and Charles Hamley stood over the face-down body of an African man. Blood welled from a hole the size of Shane's hand in the left side of the man's back. It looked, to Shane, as though the poacher had been heart-shot as they were staring down at an exit wound. At least it had been a quick death.

'Bastard took aim at us as soon as he realised we'd seen him. Look, the *tsotsi* nearly drilled me,' Fletcher said, holding up one arm. Shane saw the neat holes in the long sleeve of the shirt, near the bicep.

'That's right,' Chuck said. The words tumbled out of him as he described how the African had fired half-a-dozen or more shots at them. 'He was holding his ground, not running. Bold as brass!'

The dead man had worn a wide-brimmed green bush hat, which had been fastened with a string chin-strap, so it was still on his head.

'Caesar,' Shane ordered, 'circle the body, look for more spoor. There could be others.'

'He was alone,' Fletcher said.

'How do you know?'

'They would have backed him up,' Fletcher said. 'We heard no other voices, saw no other movement.'

'Better to be sure.' Shane nodded to Caesar, who moved off.

Fletcher shrugged. 'Let's take a look at this floppy.'

Shane grimaced. Yet another euphemism for a dead body, from the good old days.

Charles Hamley the Third dropped to one knee, removed his hat and looked skywards. 'Lord, we thank you for your divine intervention today; for guiding the eye and the hands of your servant, Fletcher Reynolds; and for delivering your judgement on this wrongdoer who was taking from your bounteous kingdom that which was not his.'

Shane thought the prayer an insult to the man on the ground. Poor bastard had probably only been trying to feed his family. And Chuck had robbed God's kingdom of more than his share of its bounty.

A peal of thunder rolled through the grey clouds overhead, echoing across the veld. The hairs stood up on Shane's arms. He smelled the rain coming on the wind, musty, like wet washing left too long in the laundry.

Fletcher slid a toe under the body and Shane saw how the suede of his *veldskoen* absorbed some blood. Chuck had stopped praying and was standing, hat clutched in his hand. Fletcher flipped the dead man, like he was a sack of farm produce.

The brim of the bush hat fell back.

The eyes looked to heaven, as Chuck had just done, but they were those of a man who had glimpsed hell.

'Well, well, I should have guessed,' Fletcher said.

'Thou shalt not steal,' Chuck intoned.

Shane turned away from the body of his friend Charles Ndlovu and started walking back towards the Land Rover.

Michelle pushed branches out of her path and was twisting her torso side on to avoid some thorns when the first fat blotches appeared on her shirt and stung the top of her head.

She looked up and a drop hit her square in the eye. She started and blinked at the wonder of something so everyday in some parts of the world. Here, its return seemed miraculous, like a favourite, half-remembered dream come true.

Shane walked towards her, eyes fixed straight ahead.

'What happened? Is Fletcher okay? Shane, what's the matter?'

He was gone, past her without a word, lost in the downpour.

The boy, only fourteen years old, was drenched by the rain in seconds. It was the closest he had come to washing in weeks. In a discarded plastic shopping bag, wrapped tight and folded into his shorts, was his travel identity document, which proclaimed him a citizen of the Republic of Zambia.

Folded inside the creased, stained piece of paper, was a hundred and forty-four American dollars.

He did not cry, for his tears were long exhausted. He smiled, because his luck had finally changed, and he would be able to go home, though to what he had no idea.

He had wept like a baby after the ambush, after the killing spree. He had cowered in the lee of a fallen tree, curled like a *picanin*, and sobbed for his dead uncle to come back to earth and rescue him. He cried no more now, because he was no longer a child.

To be a man was to look evil in the eye, to survive it, and then take revenge. He had accomplished the first two tasks, and wondered still, after all these weeks, how he would achieve the third.

After the deaths he had walked westwards, numb with shock, uncaring what wild animals he might encounter. Lion, leopard, buffalo and elephant seemed as harmless as the fieldmouse after what he had witnessed.

When he had passed the white-painted cairns, which he knew marked the border with Botswana, he had carried on through the forest lands until he reached the ribbon of wide black tar that shimmered like a basking cobra in the midday heat. He had walked. And walked.

At the tiny border outpost of Pandamatenga he had melted back into the bush and lived, like a pecking crow, off the meagre scraps of that pitiful settlement. Just a filling station, a couple of shops, some wheat silos where the burly white farmers brought their crops, and some houses belonging to the government men and women who manned the crossing point. He had slept under a piece of offcut tin, stolen shorts and a shirt off a washing line, drunk water from the taps at night when people were locked inside watching satellite television behind mud-brick walls. Compared with his native Zambia, Botswana was a prosperous land, where the men and women were fat and the cars were shiny and new. And there were tourists, plenty of them, but few stopped at the out-of-the-way little cluster of bureaucracy that was Pandamatenga.

He had moved on, northwards towards his home, and tried hitchhiking. For days no one stopped, and he had to turn back to the township to steal more scraps from the waste bins, more water from unguarded taps.

Today he had been lucky, though his fortune had brought him close, dangerously close, to another type of evil.

The *bakkie* was new. A twin-cab Toyota with a canopy on the back and a stowed fold-out rooftop tent. The blue and white registration plates contained the letters GP. It was from South Africa's Gauteng Province, home of *egoli*, the City of Gold – Johannesburg. He had another uncle who worked there in the mines and sent money home.

A *mzungu*, the Swahili word for foreigner, was behind the wheel. Old, with a mane the colour of salt, gold chains tangled with matted hair on his chest. Shorts, sandals and socks. Two things were unusual. Firstly, that the man had stopped, where no one, black or white had stopped for the lone African boy in days; and secondly, that the man was alone. Where was his woman? His children?

In halting English the man had said his name was Herman and he was from Germany. The boy thought

226

Germany might be in Europe, but he was not in school because he was not as smart as the others in his class; he found the books and the pens and the teachers could not hold his attention in the way his uncle Leonard could. He had been eager to be a man, to learn the ways of the hunter, and had seen no use for books and letters and numbers.

Now, however, the boy just wanted to fall asleep in the cool airconditioned interior of the *bakkie*, which enveloped him like a numbing ice bath after his days and weeks living rough in the bush. The man was talking, but the boy found it hard to keep his eyes open. Soon he was lulled to sleep by the whine of the tyres on the blacktop, the soft music coming from the car radio.

The boy awoke with a feeling half arousing, half terrifying. Something – someone – was touching him. He blinked, then recoiled as he saw the white man reaching across the cab. The boy's nylon shorts were pulled halfway down, exposing him. His first thought was that the man was trying to rob him, but all he had in his pants was his travel permit. Then he stared, horror dawning, as he saw the zipper on the *mzungu*'s shorts was undone, and a limp, tiny white penis lay across the man's thigh. The old man, Herman, moved his hand, with its gold rings, to the boy's face and cooed something at him. The boy did not understand the words, but he understood the man.

He struck, fast as the mamba, launching himself across the cab and grabbing at the steering wheel. The man shrieked, like a woman, and hauled back on the wheel, overcorrecting the turn that sent the front tyres juddering off the tar and onto the sand at the side of the road.

The boy lashed out with fingernails long and ragged from weeks in the bush, scratching and gouging at eyes and cheeks as the man, his thing bouncing ludicrously against his leg, fought to control the truck. Top-heavy, with its bulky tent, spare jerry cans of fuel and containers of water on the roof, the hired vehicle's right front and rear wheels left the surface of the highway as the left ones slid off the edge, towards the bush.

One minute they had been careening along the road at a hundred and twenty kilometres an hour, the next they were rolling, over and over, into the mopane sticks and thornbushes.

The boy screamed. The man wailed. When the rolling stopped, all was silent, save for the hiss of steam escaping from the upside-down radiator. The boy lay on the inside of the roof of the *bakkie*. The old man hung, silent, unconscious, or maybe dead, in his seatbelt.

The boy righted himself in the confines of the shattered vehicle. His left shoulder was powerfully sore, but his legs seemed to work all right. He felt in his shorts for the travel document, which was safe. His hands roamed over the inert body of the man, in his pockets, and into the money belt that was damp from the sweat of the folds of his belly that hung over the top of his shorts. Careful not to touch the thing, the boy unzipped the hidden compartment and withdrew the money.

A hundred and forty-four American dollars. A fortune.

The boy allowed himself the first smile for weeks as he trudged along the highway through the enveloping rain. The sign said *Kazungula 20 km*. He was almost at the ferry which would take him from Botswana to his home in Zambia. He had enough money in his pants to eat, buy clothes, and get home. He had survived, and he would tell his story.

He would be a man, a warrior, and he would seek his revenge.

13

Shane, Wise and Caesar stood side by side as the cheap wooden coffin was lowered into the new cemetery outside the town of Victoria Falls.

Wise had been against going, calling Charles a traitor. Shane had convinced him they all needed to say goodbye to their one-time friend and colleague. He didn't know whether it was the right decision – if it showed weakness on his part in front of his men – but he did know he couldn't hate the old man, whatever he had done.

They were far from alone in the graveyard. Around them, a dozen other services were going on.

The cemetery reminded Shane of pictures he'd seen of the aftermath of First World War battles – row after row of fresh graves, mounds of red earth, most unmarked by any headstone. The lack of grass or vegetation on the newly cleared plot of land meant that the hot winds could gather speed and substance. The breeze whipped up the newly turned earth into eddies of dust that coated the mourners, in their best clothes, and scattered bouquets of cheap flowers, poorly anchored photographs, dead children's toys. The rain had not yet reached as far north as the Falls. When it did, the grassless graveyard would become a quagmire.

AIDS and economic mismanagement were decimating the continent. The only things growing in Africa were bone yards and the funeral business. He shook his head at the futility of it all, and his lack of understanding of why a good man would, so close to death, turn his back on the law. To protect his family, of course. Fletcher wasn't at the service, conducted by a priest in fraying robes.

Caesar moved forward and reached into his pocket. From it he pulled Charles's old green parks and wildlife beret, with its polished badge featuring a waterbuck's head. He nodded to a plump woman – Shane guessed her to be Charles's wife – and laid the hat on the coffin. He stood, for a second, head bowed, hands clasped in front of him, then stepped back.

'He dishonoured that uniform,' Wise hissed.

'He was a victim,' Caesar said.

After the coffin was lowered into the ground, between the last resting place of a twenty-year-old man and a five-year-old girl, Shane broke the small knot of relatives and introduced himself to the woman.

'I am Miriam,' she said, extending a hand. She was flanked by a weeping teenage girl in a maroon and white school uniform, and a young man in a hand-me-down black suit, who nodded stiffly when introduced. 'My son and daughter. He spoke so highly of you, Mister Castle. I know – I am sure – he was sorry for what happened.'

'He thought of you and your children first and foremost, and always told me so,' Shane said. It was true. For all his faults, including the philandering that indirectly cost him his life, Charles had made it abundantly clear that he lived for his family.

'Try not to think ill of him, Mister Castle.'

'I'll remember the good times, when we were together as friends.'

She dabbed the corner of her eye with a damp handkerchief. 'He would never have hurt you, Mister Castle, or your men.'

Shane started to feel uncomfortable. While he understood Charles's motive, nothing excused betraying the team. 'I understand.'

'He did nothing wrong, Mister Castle.'

'I should be going, Miriam. It was nice to meet you.'

Tears rolled unchecked down her cheeks as her son took her by the arm. Miriam looked back over her shoulder as she was led away. 'He did nothing wrong, Mister Castle.'

He looked away from her. The gravediggers' bodies glistened with sweat as they worked. Shane lingered long enough to see the beret, once proudly worn, covered with dirt.

'Hello, are you drunk?' Michelle asked.

At the sound of the familiar voice, Shane turned slowly on his stool at the long bar in the Sprayview

Hotel. He looked, theatrically, back at the three empty green Zambezi bottles in front of him, and calculated how many there would have been if the bartender hadn't slowly been taking them away. 'Statistically speaking, yes.'

'I heard you buried Charles today. I'm sorry.'

Shane shrugged. He smiled, though, as it was good to see her. Wise and Caesar had stayed for a few drinks then gone their separate ways in search of female companionship: Caesar to his girlfriend, Wise to a whore. Shane had allowed himself to feel alone and morose for a while, a stranger in a bar full of tourists off two overland trucks. They were all young backpackers – half-naked and half-stoned on one substance or another.

Michelle looked around and, with a tilt of her head, drew Shane's eyes to two girls sitting at a nearby table. One was pointing and saying something to her friend. 'I think I might have muscled in on someone's turf,' she said.

Shane looked over his shoulder at the girls and shrugged. 'Jailbait.'

'Mind if I join you, then?'

Shane dragged another seat over, with the toe of his boot, without standing.

'Please, don't go to any effort.'

The sarcasm was lost on him. 'What'll you have?'

She ordered a gin and tonic. He signalled for another beer. 'I hope you're not driving home tonight,' she said.

He told her he had booked himself into the hotel for the night, so he didn't have far to stagger.

'So you're writing yourself off in memory of Charles,' she observed.

'Call it a tradition.'

She didn't press him. She changed the subject instead. 'The dentist, Doctor Charles Hamley the Third, left this morning.'

'Our wealthy benefactor.' Shane realised he was slurring a little. 'Gimme an ice water as well,' he said to the barman.

'What do you think of him?' Michelle asked, raising the drinking straw to her lips.

Her lips were full, soft, shiny with newly applied lip gloss. He'd noticed she had only started wearing it since she had moved into the lodge. She was wearing the green dress with the elephants on it, the one she had tried on in front of him on their trip to the Falls. He wondered what that glistening mouth would be like to kiss, how it would feel caressing his body. 'Um . . . don't know. Bit of a weasel. Call me old-fashioned, but praying in the middle of the bush after a fire fight seems a little odd.'

'Surely there are religious soldiers.'

'Sure,' Shane said, waving a hand. 'No atheists in foxholes and all that crap, but mostly it's just, 'God, get me through this and I'll never cheat on the missus again,' or, 'Thanks, big fella, I owe you a few Sundays' . . . that sort of stuff. No one I know goes on about the Lord smiting down evil-doers when they look at a corpse.'

'He gives me the creeps. Are we doing the right thing, packing up and heading for the Congo because Chuck says so?'

Shane shrugged. 'Fletcher pays my team's wages, so we go where the money is.'

'Spoken like a true soldier of fortune.'

Shane raised his beer. 'Nice work if you can get it.'

She frowned. 'But don't you feel a little apprehensive about going up there? I mean, there's been a war going on there for decades.'

'That's been the story of my life lately.'

'Sure,' she said. 'But I still feel uneasy about it.'

'Fletcher might not go if you don't.'

She leaned back on her bar stool. 'What do you mean by that?'

'He's in love with you, isn't he?'

She looked away. 'I don't know. His marriage went bust because he ignored his wife in favour of his work. Now his business is doing really well, I don't think he'd change his mind over me.'

'I would,' Shane said.

'What?'

He instantly regretted letting the words slip out. He felt foolish and, all of a sudden, drunk. 'Sorry, I didn't mean anything by that. Forget it.'

'No,' she said, appraising him, as though trying to work out how sincere he had been. 'That's nice. But I wouldn't want to stand in his way. What we've got, it's not like a marriage. I don't want him to give up business opportunities to stay with me, and later regret it.'

'But I'm guessing you don't want to give up Isilwane Lodge for some national parks rat hole, either.' He took a swig from his beer.

'What are you insinuating?'

'Don't get all huffy. Tell me you don't prefer conducting your ground-breaking research from an airconditioned gin palace with hot and cold running servants.'

She laughed. 'It is kind of nice having my underwear ironed and my eggs over easy.'

'Fletcher told me he's planning on taking you to a hunting show in Dallas next year. Are you going to go and sell out to help him get more business?'

'You're drunk,' she said sternly, then smiled. 'And nasty. Truth is, I don't know about the States. Other conservationists go to those international gun love-ins to raise money, so part of me thinks, why not? On the other hand, I might not want to give up that much of my independence.'

He pondered how much he would give up to be with a woman like Michelle Parker. He realised he was getting maudlin. 'So, are you coming to the Congo or not?'

She stirred the remains of her G and T with her straw, then looked up. 'I'm in. It can't be any more dangerous than Zimbabwe.' She checked her watch. 'Sorry, I've got to run. I only drove up to get my camera repaired. Don't know if there'll be any camera shops in the DRC. I've got to get back to Fletcher . . . I mean, the lodge, before dark.'

'See ya.' Shane watched as she walked away. He considered following her, but ordered another drink instead and looked around the bar.

He thought he saw one of the backpacker girls at the table, now sitting alone, attempt to catch his eye, and rather than look away he stared straight back.

Shane thought that if he half closed his eyes she could pass as Michelle, but when she walked over, he realised it was an illusion. Still, she was attractive – blonde curly hair, green eyes and a nice smile – and very young. Shane guessed she was no more than nineteen. Her colourful skirt was low on her hips and she wore a white cotton singlet with the top few buttons undone.

'Hi,' she said.

'Hi.'

'Where are you from?'

'Here.'

'You sound like me – like an Aussie, I mean.'

'I grew up there.'

Shane said nothing as she talked about where she had been and where she was heading. He noticed that she wasn't wearing a bra and when she leaned closer to talk over the noise of the bar, he could see her nipples and feel them firm against his arm. As he started to pay more attention, she put her hand on his arm, and he felt himself stirring. He had a quick vision of Michelle's disapproving face, but quickly brushed it aside. She belonged to another, so how the hell could he feel guilty?

'By the way, I'm Shane,' he heard himself saying.

'I'm Annie. It's nice to meet you. You look like you've had a lot more African adventures than I have. Have you been to Kenya yet? I really want to go there and I'd love to know where you reckon the best places are.'

They moved from the bar to a table in the corner as Shane began to tell the girl of his travels and his work.

He tried to downplay what he did for a living, but her eyes got wider and her interest mounted when she drew out of him what a 'contact' with poachers actually entailed. She hung on his words and Shane was enjoying the power he felt. It was reassuring to know that, unlike Michelle, Annie was actually impressed by his job. As he described how he lay in wait watching the rhino poachers on the border, she moved her hand up his thigh until it rested in his crotch.

Annie started to stroke his jeans, and Shane felt himself harden at her touch. He leant across to kiss her, but she turned her head.

'Not here,' she said, standing and taking his hand. He let himself be led through the swinging doors at the side of the bar, and through another door into the female toilets. He pushed her up against a basin and kissed her deeply. He probed her mouth hard and fast, and she matched him. Hungry.

She wrapped one leg around him and ground herself against his leg. He reached under her skirt and pushed the flimsy g-string aside. She grabbed his hand, untangled herself and dragged him into a cubicle, locking the door behind her.

She was wedged hard against the tiled wall as he sought out her hard nipple and sucked deeply. She moaned, so he bit down on it. Annie gasped as he pushed two fingers deep inside her. She fumbled as she undid his belt, button and zipper. He grunted encouragement as she took him in her hand and found a rhythm.

Annie slipped down the wall and sat on the toilet seat. She sought out his cock with her mouth and

Shane leant back as she sucked him deeply, wrapping her tongue around his balls and returning to the head in quick succession, never losing the rhythm.

Then she stood again, pushing him onto the seat, and sat astride him. He slipped inside her with almost no effort, and felt a flood of warmth engulf him as her body squeezed his. He bucked up against her, and she responded, pushing down on him hard and then pulling away to the point where he could bear it no longer. The sound that left his mouth when he came was animalistic, and she shook above him for what seemed like minutes before they were both still.

'Thanks,' she said as she stood up and adjusted her clothes. Before he could reply, she had left the cubicle and was washing her hands and face at the basin. As he buckled his belt, he heard her laugh with a friend in the hall outside the ladies' room. Shane shook his head and thought again about Michelle.

'All yours,' Fletcher said, pushing the chair back from the computer desk in Isilwane Lodge's office. He stood and rubbed his back. 'Damn machine is killing my eyes and back. Give me the bush any time. I don't know how people can sit in front of these things all day.'

'You're not wrong,' Shane said. He sat his beer down on the desk and nodded his thanks to Fletcher. Once a week he used the computer to check emails and to surf the Net in search of properties for sale in Africa. With each passing month his bank balance was getting closer and closer to the figures listed on the real estate pages for small game farms and lodges.

It was only two days until Shane, Caesar and Michelle would depart for the Democratic Republic of Congo. Fletcher was leaving the next day, with Wise, to organise transport, supplies and last-minute administration on the ground before the others arrived. All of them were packing and preparing themselves for a stay of at least three months. Michelle had made good progress in recruiting a new research assistant to look after her wild dog program – a young English guy named Matthew Towns who was already in Zimbabwe on holiday. As a result, Michelle was ready to travel to the Congo immediately and start her assessment and recording of game on the concession where Fletcher would be hunting. Lloyd, Fletcher's chief guide at Isilwane, would be staying in Zimbabwe to manage the lodge during the wet season. Fletcher had already organised a new tracker in the DRC, who would know the mountains and jungles around the Virunga National Park – an environment that would have been as familiar to Lloyd as the surface of the moon.

Shane had been busy organising flights and equipment for the team, but realised he had left himself precious little time to learn about the country they were heading to. He wanted to see what he could dig up on the Internet.

Shane entered *www.cia.gov* in the web browser's address bar. The Central Intelligence Agency might not have been able to predict or stop the greatest terrorist act of the twenty-first century, but they could tell you the gross domestic product, population figures and currency exchange rate for any country in the world. He clicked on 'The World Factbook' and scrolled down a list until he came to 'Congo, Democratic Republic of'.

The Factbook was a mine of basic information for someone like him – he thought of it as a Lonely Planet guide without the tips for gay and lesbian travellers and budget places to eat. The country formerly known as Zaire and, before that, the Belgian Congo, was colonised by the tiny European nation in 1908. He studied the map of what was now known colloquially as the DRC. It was a huge chunk of Africa, bordered by nine other nations. The country touched on nearly every type of climate and landscape the continent had to offer – a transition zone between the dry bushveld Shane was familiar with in southern Africa, through to the equatorial rainforests of central Africa to the west and north, the jungle-covered mountains of the Ruwenzoris to the east, and even the deserts of Sudan on its north-eastern border.

Laurent Kabila had led a rebellion that in 1997 toppled the country's longest-serving dictator, Mobutu Sese Seko, who had stayed in power, with a little help from the sponsors of the website Shane was browsing, for thirty-two years. Kabila changed the name from Zaire to DRC, but no sooner had he taken power than he faced his own insurrection, which was backed by his neighbours in Rwanda and Uganda. Other African countries, including Zimbabwe, Angola, Namibia and Chad, rallied in support of Kabila and sent troops, but the international effort wasn't enough to stop the new president from being assassinated in 2001. Laurent's son, Joseph, inherited his power.

Shane knew the country was still far from stable, and the situation wasn't helped by the continued presence of refugees and fugitive rebel soldiers from some of DRC's neighbours – many of whom were hiding up in the region where Fletcher would soon be taking wealthy hunters. The rumour mill in Zimbabwe had it that their own government had been lured north to support the Kabila clan on the promise of mining concessions and other economic sweeteners. Shane read that as well as diamonds, there were mines extracting copper, uranium, silver and something called coltan, which was apparently used in computer chips.

He sat back and scanned the pages for other information that might be of use to him and his men. Poaching was listed as a major environmental issue, along with deforestation by refugees looking for firewood and building materials, and mining. The AIDS rate was high among the sixty million inhabitants, and the adult life expectancy was less than fifty years.

There were, he noted, more than two hundred ethnic groups in the country, the majority of them Bantu. That was bad news for him, because Wise and Caesar were Ndebele and therefore spoke a language closer to Zulu than any local dialect. To top that off, the official language was French, with Swahili also in common use – two more tongues neither he nor his men spoke. He wondered if Michelle, having been brought up in Canada, spoke French. Bottom line was that they would need a translator if they picked up any poachers.

Shane exited the CIA page and did a Google news search on the DRC. He found another online story about endangered wildlife and ecosystems in the country's five national parks, including the Virunga, near where they would be operating. It was bleak. Park rangers had been engaged in gunfights with armed refugees and rebels, some of them Rwandan Hutus with blood on their hands from the massacres in their own country. Poachers, whose ranks included government soldiers as well as rebels from within and outside the DRC, had decimated all wildlife species with an economic value.

He whistled softly to himself as he read an account of four hundred armed men attacking a national parks outpost. Shane leaned back in the swivelling office chair and clasped his hands behind his neck. He was heading into what journalists – with only a little licence – would call a war zone. Himself and two men.

Why, he wondered, would Fletcher want to risk taking well-heeled American and European clients into such a dangerous area?

'Safari.' Michelle said the word to herself again. She loved it. The way it rolled off her tongue, its myriad meanings, the promise of travel and adventure.

It was derived from an Arabic word for journey, but used in different contexts it conjured up so much more. It could mean harmless game viewing or a hunting trip. In Zimbabwe, a safari area, such as the Matestsi, where Fletcher operated, was a place where game could legally be killed, under a strict quota system.

To Michelle, it was travel. Packing her meagre belongings into a backpack, saying goodbye to a place she had called home, and venturing out into the unknown. She felt the same as she had when she left Canada. A mix of excitement and anticipation, leavened with a trace of fear. It made for a heady combination. She relished it.

The relocation to the Congo would be fascinating for her professionally, and equally intriguing on a personal level. A couple of times she had gotten the feeling that Fletcher had driven down to her place, when he was between safaris, for the sole reason of getting laid. She didn't necessarily see that as a bad thing – he had reawakened her sexual appetite for sure – though she had thought it would have been nice if just once he had come for a chat, or so that the two of them could go out and do something as a couple. It would have been good, she realised, with a touch of surprise, if she could have spent time with him as she had done with Shane, in Victoria Falls and Livingstone.

With Shane she had talked and walked and eaten and drunk and gone sightseeing – the things some people normally did before they started sleeping together. She had thought Shane might make a move on her at some stage. He was a good-looking guy, still single in his mid-thirties, and she'd no indication that he was gay. She wasn't conceited enough to think she was beautiful, or irresistible, but she imagined that a handsome soldier would fancy his chances with her.

The fact that he had studiously avoided proposition-ing her was kind of nice, though. If it was because she was attached to Fletcher, it showed he had a personal code of honour.

Which made her question her own morals. Despite the way Shane had drunkenly taunted her about being a 'sell-out', inferring she was with Fletcher because of his wealth, when she left him in the bar of the Sprayview Hotel at Victoria Falls she had felt an intense pang of irrational jealousy when she noticed the backpacker girl rise from her table and noncha-lantly saunter over to the bar to be next to him. The whole time Michelle had talked with Shane she had watched the blonde girl casting furtive glances at the pair of them. Michelle wondered what she would have done if Shane *had* made a pass at her.

She zipped her pack closed and carefully disassem-bled her two cameras, separating the lenses from the bodies, and packed them into a padded photographic bag. On the research side, she was confident that her new English assistant, Matthew, would work out just fine. Matthew had the right qualifications and seemed to have a good work ethic. Michelle planned on initially spending about two months in the Congo, doing the initial wildlife assessment of the concession, and then returning to Zimbabwe to check up on Matthew's progress with the dogs. She smiled to herself. Not too long ago she had faced the prospect of winding up her research and flying home with her tail between her legs. Now she was starting a new project, employing an assistant *and* she had enough funding to fly from one country to another.

She still found Doctor Charles Hamley the Third loathsome, but without his money she would probably be back on the prairie teaching high school science or breeding lab rats in a university somewhere cold.

Michelle heard the buzz of a light aircraft overhead and darted to the window. She recognised the registration letters of Dougal's Cessna and was just in time to see him waggle his wings as he droned low over Main Camp.

'All set?' Matthew asked, popping his head through the open door.

Michelle looked around her at the first place she had called home in Africa. She hadn't spent much time there lately. Aside from some hand-stitched curtains and a few dog-eared paperbacks on the makeshift brick and timber bookshelf, there was little evidence that she had ever been there.

'I guess,' Michelle said. She closed the door.

14

It was in Africa, but that was where the commonality between Zimbabwe and the Democratic Republic of Congo ended, Shane thought as they headed north, on an atrocious road, from the decaying regional town of Goma on the shores of Lake Kivu, north towards the Virunga National Park.

'Ow!' Michelle cried as the Landcruiser lurched sickeningly in and out of a pothole. 'What gives with this road?'

Fletcher laughed. 'You'll never complain about dirt roads down south again after spending some time up here. We're actually driving on an old lava flow. It's solid, so you don't get bogged in the wet season, but there's not much the Congolese can do about the holes until Nyiragongo erupts again and resurfaces it.'

It was a pretty callous joke, Shane thought. The volcano's last eruption in 2002 had displaced hundreds of thousands of people and cut the town of Goma, where they had landed, in two. The mountain smoked behind them as they headed north. Civil war, a virtual invasion by rebels and refugees from neighbouring countries, and natural disasters – even for an African country, the DRC had more than its share of misfortune. In the past ten years, Fletcher had told them, about four million Congolese had died as a result of warfare. Battles were followed by organised rape. It was the way of this part of Africa.

Shane had no regrets about leaving Goma behind them. From the air it had looked pretty enough – the sun glinting off Lake Kivu, which looked cool and inviting; opulent villas lining the water's edge; and lush green fields of crops thriving on the volcanic soils. The airstrip spanned the gap between the volcano and the lake, and Shane had marvelled that the ramshackle white brick terminal had somehow survived. The end of the runway jutted into the disorganised cluster of stone and tin huts that made up the town and Shane was surprised to see a gaggle of women with baskets of fruit balanced on their heads strolling across the Tarmac, even as the pilot of the aircraft he and Michelle had flown in on was bringing his engines up to full revs and swinging out onto the strip.

The terminal – such as it was – was like others he'd been to in Africa. Frantic jostling and shoving amongst the passengers to grab their bags off the single belt – perhaps their rush was to beat the local thieves – followed by interminable queues and questioning by immigration and customs.

Up close, the evidence of war and the volcanic eruption was everywhere. About eighteen per cent of the town had been destroyed and buried under lava and black ash. In the years since the natural disaster, people had begun rebuilding on top of the wreckage of the old town, rather than excavating and clearing. A new layer of misery was rising from the black earth. Once whitewashed buildings were stained and crumbling, some pitted with bullet holes. The only structures that looked as though they had encountered a lick of paint in the past decade were a cluster of banks at the first roundabout they went through, and the Primus brewery at the second. 'The mainstay of the economy,' Fletcher noted, pointing to a billboard advertising Primus beer. The town centre was bustling and chaotic, and had a bit of a Wild-West feel to it, Shane thought.

'Not much for us here, unless you need fuel, beer, gold or illegal diamonds,' Fletcher noted. A couple of soldiers in camouflage uniforms, toting AK 47s, watched their progress through mirrored sunglasses as Fletcher geared down and accelerated out of town.

Fletcher swerved, yielding a few inches of road space to an oncoming truck whose tray was stacked high with hundreds of little woven reed baskets, each the size of a shoebox. 'What's in those?' Michelle asked, pointing to the load as they drove through a brief smokescreen of black diesel fumes.

'Smoked fish,' said Fletcher, who had collected them from the airport in a new Landcruiser. 'The baskets are called pockets. The different coloured bits of rag tied to them shows which family has caught them from the lake.' Pick-ups crammed with people sitting on bench seats in the back – Kimalumalus, they were called – whizzed past them at breakneck speed.

Wise and Caesar were ahead of them, bouncing along the rutted road in a shiny, dent-free late-model Land Rover Defender, along with Fletcher's newly employed Congolese guide, Patrice, whom they had all met briefly at the airport. Each of the vehicles towed a trailer packed, like the vehicles' roof carriers, with tents, tools, supplies and all the other odds and ends needed to create a safari camp out of nothing, in the middle of a jungle. Zimbabwe's roads weren't getting any better with age and the crippling effects of inflation and government mismanagement, but the narrow tar routes of his homeland seemed to Shane like German autobahns compared with the track they were traversing now.

A class of schoolchildren, barefoot but dressed in clean white shirts and blue shorts, yelled and waved at them as the convoy bounced past. Fletcher pointed out a man freewheeling downhill towards them on a homemade scooter. Its wheels were simply rounded cross-sections of a fallen tree trunk, and the timber running board was piled high with bunches of bananas. It was an ingenious-looking contraption that even sported shock-absorbers, though Shane wouldn't have trusted his life, let alone his fruit crop, to it.

Shane wound down the window and breathed in the thick, hot, wet air, savouring it. It was the smell of the tropics – rain, wet earth, year-round perspiration, rotting food and vegetation. It was, in his experience, more Asian than African. The smells took him back momentarily to the dank jungles of East Timor where he had hunted Indonesian-backed militiamen hell-bent on disrupting the former Jakarta-ruled colony's transition to independence.

The dense vegetation that still grew in pockets between villages and subsistence farms was vivid emerald. Luscious, impenetrable, and speckled here and there with the bright colours of flowers and tropical fruits he'd not seen since leaving Australia. As they neared small villages he saw patchy groves of banana trees. Women sat behind tomatoes, carrots, cabbages, beans and potatoes, all piled high on mats on the side of the road. Skinny kids, who realised they wouldn't make a sale from the two four-by-fours, chased after them down the rock-hard road, hands outstretched. '*Jambo, Monsieur!* Give me money, give me ballpoint!' a little boy with a potbelly yelled as Fletcher down-shifted to tackle a steep hill. Two young women dressed in brightly printed *bikwembe*, which reached from their hips to ankles, carried curly-haired babies on their backs, bundled tight in matching wraps.

Here, more than in Southern Africa, was evidence of an economy dependent largely on aid. In Zimbabwe, as bad as things were, it was still relatively unusual to see anyone other than the poorest of the poor begging. The only other new vehicles they passed now were the ubiquitous white Cruisers of the UN.

In Shane's Africa a man could walk or drive for hundreds of kilometres and not see another human being. Here it seemed they couldn't move more than a hundred metres without doing so. People thronged the roads, staring blankly at them, as if they had arrived from another galaxy instead of another country. Here, they spoke French – with the exception of the kids' begging English – and drove on the wrong side of the road. There was more litter than one encountered in Zimbabwe, with plastic bags scattered along the roadside.

It had amused and annoyed Shane the way outsiders often thought of Africa as a single entity, a basket case that would only survive with billions of dollars of foreign aid and the goodwill of middle-aged musicians who would have passed into obscurity had it not been for mass concerts which perpetuated the myth that money would solve the continent's myriad problems.

Africa was as unified as Europe. This was so in name, perhaps, through some largely ineffective institutions that allowed overfed politicians to congregate and talk at a different luxury tourist destination each year, but in practice, it was ridiculous and insulting to suggest that Ethiopia shared the woes of South Africa, or that Namibia should be lumped in the same leaky boat as Nigeria.

Fletcher seemed to read his mind. 'About the only thing this place has in common with Zim is AIDS.' In the front passenger's seat, Michelle's face was perpetually turned to the parade of life flashing past them. Shane was in the back seat.

He could tell when they were about to reach another village, as the bush on either side of the road thinned out, replaced with stacked sacks of charcoal on the verges and fields of unweeded crops – maybe potatoes, he thought. The roadside rubbish was worse as well. As they cruised through each ville their senses were assaulted with music, played African style, at full volume as every tiny shop or bar tried to compete with its neighbour in an eardrum-bursting competition. Those without radios made their own music, on drums made of up-turned tins. Young girls danced and swayed as boys, still too young to pay much mind to them, kicked an improvised soccer ball made of a balloon filled with rags and wrapped in string.

'White caps,' Fletcher said, pointing to a roadblock ahead, manned by local policemen. 'Patrice will sort them out with a packet of cigarettes or two. He knows his way around the law, that one.'

Shane nodded. He tried never to pay bribes to officials in Africa. He found a ready smile and an inexhaustible supply of patience usually got him around any requests for money or gifts, or spurious fines dreamed up by shifty policemen. Whatever Patrice said or did worked, though, and they moved through the roadblock without hassle.

Apart from the rich greens of the vegetation, the dramatic relief of the countryside on either side of him was a source of wonder and, at the same time, concern. He and his men would be operating in this tough, hilly terrain. Shane knew from studying a map that they were headed north through the western arm of the Great Rift Valley. Off to their right was the chain of Virunga volcanoes, dividing the Congo from Rwanda to the south, and Uganda to the north. Far beyond the ridge on their left was the Central Congo Basin.

'Any updates on the situation where we're heading?' Shane asked as their heads connected with the Toyota's padded roof lining.

'There's a local Congolese army commander meeting us at the camp this afternoon. He'll give us a brief on security and what's what. Bottom line is that you and your chaps will have plenty of business, Shane.'

Michelle looked over at Fletcher and grimaced.

'Ah, don't worry, my girl.' Fletcher put a hand on her bare knee and squeezed it. 'No bloody rebel or poacher will dare mess with us once word gets out.'

'I hope you're right.' She sounded far from convinced.

'Seriously, though, I want you to go out with a local guide and either Shane or one of his cronies for the first few trips.'

'Thanks. Now I'm not just nervous, I'm petrified.'

'When are you expecting your first clients?' Shane asked.

'Chuck's coming out again in a couple of weeks to see how things are progressing, and Brigadier Moyo will be up here next month to check on his investment.'

'Chuck's coming back so soon?' Michelle observed.

'Didn't I tell you? He's got a stake in this venture now, as well as Moyo.'

'No, you didn't,' Michelle said.

Fletcher explained that, as well as providing extra funding to enable Michelle and Shane to carry out their respective roles in the DRC, Chuck had invested some of his money in Fletcher's initial set-up costs. He had provided cash to buy the vehicles they were travelling in, and for incidentals such as tents and camping equipment for the new hunting camp. 'It's why we didn't have to ship everything from Zimbabwe.' Moyo's chief input had been to secure the concession from the government.

'I don't know,' Michelle said. 'I just can't imagine too many rich, pampered American businessmen coming out to this place to hunt.'

'It's different.' Fletcher waved a hand in a vaguely Gallic gesture; Shane wondered if he had picked that up from the locals. 'Nobody's hunted where we're headed for years – not legally, at least – and there's game here that people from the States and Europe will never have clapped eyes on. I always like to offer something different for my clients, and word gets around. Chuck's been great. A one-man marketing machine. They'll come, all right, mark my words.'

Shane offered no opinion. He scanned the steep ranges of the volcanoes to the east, the dramatic inclines thick with a tangle of trees and creepers and God alone knew what else. He had a job to do here, whether the clients came or not. It would be hard country to operate in, but he found himself looking forward to getting out in it. Others might think him mad for wanting to crawl through a snake-infested tangle of vines in search of armed men who might try to kill him. To him it was a job – a calling, maybe. He wondered if he would ever, truly, be able to give up this world and settle down on a peaceful game farm or run a bush lodge.

The hill country gave way to open savannas, perhaps once the preserve of herds of plains game, but now covered in a patchwork of subsistence farms and villages. They whizzed through the town of Rutshuru, the capital of the *groupement*, or district, of the same name. It was a smaller version of Goma and, in Shane's view, just as ramshackle. At Kiwanja, they took the north-eastern fork of the road and started climbing again. Towards the next place he would call home.

The site Fletcher had chosen for their camp was a clearing carved from the forest on top of a small hill. Below them they heard a gurgling stream or river, but the jungle between them and the valley was too thick to see through. Beyond that was a panoramic view of the mountains, which here marked the border with Uganda. They were dressed in a thick coat of green, and crowned with wisps of white mist.

At the centre of the cleared patch, which was the size of half a soccer pitch, was the gutted shell of a mud-brick building, once whitewashed, now scorched by fire. Charred beams sagged between the walls like flayed, blackened ribs. The grass around the clearing was waist-high, stiff and serrated – a field of green bayonets, Shane thought as he ran a finger lightly along one wicked blade.

'The others, they will be here soon,' Patrice said. He was shorter than either Wise or Caesar, slight of frame, but his thin arms and legs rippled with well-defined muscles. He wore a new khaki shirt with the

Isilwane logo – a male lion's roaring head – embroidered above the left breast pocket, and matching shorts. On his feet were a pair of rubber gumboots which reached almost to his knees.

'What others?' Shane asked.

Fletcher explained that Patrice, a native of this part of the country, had organised a work party of ten men to help set up the camp. They should have been waiting for them at the clearing, but Fletcher shrugged and said, 'Ah, well, Africa is Africa. Some things don't change from country to country.'

Shane could not abide standing around doing nothing when there was work to be done. As soon as Fletcher had given him a rough idea of the layout of the camp, Shane gave his orders to Wise and Caesar.

The two young men seemed as eager as Shane was to get on with the work, and they manhandled heavy-duty canvas safari tents and bags of poles down from the vehicles' roof carriers and started unloading the trailers. There was no shade in the clearing and the three men began sweating heavily as soon as they started moving. Shane stripped off his shirt.

Fletcher spread a map of the Virunga Park and its surrounding areas on a fold-out table under the shade of the first trees at the edge of the campsite, and pored over it, with Patrice at his side.

'What about him?' Wise asked, gesturing towards Patrice with a thumb.

Shane was as disappointed in the guide's reluctance to join in the hard work as his men were. However, he did not want to start the venture on a sour note. 'He has to give the boss the lie of the land.

257

He'll be earning his money soon enough. Let's just get on with it.'

'Can I help?' Michelle said. 'I feel like a bit of a waste of oxygen at the moment.'

'Yeah, sure. Thanks,' Shane said, wiping his brow with the back of his forearm. 'Can you divvy the chairs, tables and bedding stuff into separate piles for each tent so the guys can fetch them once we've put the tents up.'

She worked and sweated alongside the men, and Shane had to try hard not to stare at her when her shirt rode up as she stood on tiptoe to pull a camp chair down from the roof carrier. He glimpsed a small tattoo above the waistband of her pants. Shane turned away and saw Caesar grinning at him. 'Back to work,' he grumbled at the man.

In an hour they had three green canvas walk-in safari tents erected. Finally, the work party organised by Patrice ambled in.

Fletcher went with Patrice to greet them, then assigned them to Shane.

'These men have no English,' Patrice said.

'Fine. You can translate,' Shane said, hands on hips, as he appraised the men. Their ages, he reckoned, ranged from fifteen to fifty. Generally, he thought them in poor health. Most seemed either undernourished or ill. Still, he had no one else. 'There are pangas, shovels and picks in the trailer. Tell them I want the central area and pathways between each of the tents cleared of this grass. It's a snake farm in here at the moment. Also, there are pit latrines to be dug.' Shane showed Patrice where he wanted the ablutions and the other four tents erected, and told Wise and Caesar, who were adept at erecting the tents by now, to help out.

Patrice spoke to the men in Lingala and they shuffled slowly to the back of the trailer to fetch their tools and stores. Patrice returned to the shade, where Fletcher was now sitting at the table in front of a laptop computer and satellite phone. Shane guessed Reynolds was trying to establish an Internet connection. It was important that they get communications up and running, but he seemed to have no need of the guide at the moment.

'Patrice,' Shane said, walking over to him, 'perhaps you can help with the tents.'

'I am like you, a supervisor,' he said.

Shane nodded. 'Then perhaps you would like to get out into the clearing and supervise your men.'

Patrice pulled a packet of cigarettes from his pocket and slowly, deliberately, shook one out and lit it. He squatted on his haunches and sucked in a lungful of smoke.

Shane waited for Reynolds to say something, but he was engrossed in the computer's screen, softly cursing as he tried to get the connection working. 'We will have to work as a team out here,' Shane said.

Patrice exhaled. 'My job in this *team*, as you call it, is to guide, not to work like a slave.'

Shane didn't know whether Fletcher was deliberately avoiding entering the confrontation or was simply lost in what he was doing on his computer. 'Fine,' Shane said, then turned and walked away.

*

The sun was a red semicircle over a craggy peak when Michelle lowered herself theatrically into a canvas director's chair in the centre of the clearing. 'Oh, my aching back. I haven't done that much physical work since I lived on my parents' farm.'

Shane opened the portable camping fridge and pulled out a bottle of Primus beer. The distinctive yellow brand, the beer's name and a map of the DRC was painted on the bottle, not printed on paper. He deftly ran the blade of a machete along the neck of the bottle and the top sailed off with a pop that sounded as celebratory as the uncorking of a bottle of fine champagne. 'It's not very cold – the gas fridges will take a while to cool down.'

'As long as it's wet,' she smiled back at him.

Shane repeated the trick for Wise, Caesar and Fletcher. Patrice sat apart from them, outside the circle that had gathered around a flickering fire in the centre of the clearing, on a rolled tent still stuffed in its waterproof bag. Shane had not pushed the matter of Patrice's noninvolvement in the work party, but, when he had led Fletcher around the embryonic camp and pointed out where everyone would be sleeping, he indicated the rolled canvas as Patrice's new home. 'I wasn't sure whether he was going to be staying with us in the camp or at his village,' Shane said. 'There's a tent there for him if he wants it.' The work gang had already been dismissed. Fletcher had tried to suppress a wry grin, but failed. He had obviously picked up on the tension between the two men, but decided to let things run their course.

'A beer, Patrice?' Shane called across the newly cropped grass.

'I do not drink alcohol,' the African called back in his French-accented English.

'You've done a good job, Shane,' Fletcher said, raising his beer.

'Hey!' Michelle protested.

'All right, all right. *All* of you have worked well. To a successful new venture.'

They raised their beers and Patrice vaguely lifted the hand holding his cigarette. 'I am going to spend the night in my family's village, monsieur,' he said to Fletcher, as he stood.

'The guys will help you with your tent, I'm sure,' Fletcher said. No one else made a move.

Patrice looked around the circle, then said, 'It is four kilometres from here. I will be back at dawn.'

'Try not to make too much noise, as we'll all be sound asleep after today's effort.' Shane raised his hands above his head and let out a lion-like yawn. Wise and Caesar smiled but said nothing. Patrice melted into the gathering gloom.

261

15

Shane lathered his face from a tin cup full of hot water and looked into a small mirror propped on a jagged section of the derelict cottage's ruined wall. As he shaved, he noticed the reflection of a movement.

He turned and saw Michelle emerging from the canvas doorway. She caught him looking at her, grimaced, then headed towards him and the campfire.

'You are so busted,' he said.

She blushed. 'Stop it. I'm single and over eighteen. Well over eighteen, in fact.'

'How's the old man?'

'He's not that old. He's asleep. Did you hear voices in the night?' She used a cup to scoop boiling water from the large galvanised metal bucket resting on the slow-burning campfire and dropped in a tea bag.

'There was a little commotion.'

'Hey, what was that?' Michelle peered through the abandoned building's doorway. 'I heard something move in there.'

Shane wiped the remnants of shaving soap from his face with a green sweat rag and led her inside the ruin. Sitting on the floor against the wall were two African men, aged in their twenties. They looked tired and dishevelled in their hand-me-down clothes. One sported a badly swollen left eye. 'He put up a fight. The other one went down peacefully.'

'What! You captured them? Who are they?'

'Wise and Caesar and I didn't go straight to bed like we told Patrice. I figured that with all this expensive gear lying around, word might have got out amongst the local criminal element. We caught these two sneaking around just before midnight.'

Michelle frowned. 'Why didn't you tell me? Did Fletcher know about your little ambush plan?'

'Easy on there. We didn't want to worry you. Besides, you were safe.'

'Says who?'

Shane smiled. 'I was pretty sure you'd have someone big and strong and old and rich to protect you through the night.'

She balled a fist and punched him in the arm, eliciting a semi-fake cry of pain. 'I'm not a goddamned kid, Shane. So don't you treat me like one. And I'll be having words with Fletcher.'

Their banter was cut short by the sound of an approaching vehicle. It was a green pick-up truck. In the front were two men in camouflage uniforms. Patrice rode in the rear compartment.

Shane slung his SLR over his shoulder and strode out to meet the vehicle. The older and plumper of the uniformed men eased himself from the truck's cab.

He wore a maroon beret and carried the rank of a colonel on the epaulettes on his shoulders. Shane had studied the military insignia of the Congolese Army as part of his research into the country. The officer's tailored fatigues were starched and appeared new. His paratrooper's boots – they looked French to Shane – reached more than halfway up his calves and were polished to a mirror-like sheen. He wore gold-rimmed aviator sunglasses with mirrored lenses, and chunky rings glittered on several of his stubby fingers.

The other man, who had driven the pick-up, wore the same colour uniform, but that was where the commonality with the senior officer ended. His was faded and patched in several places and his footwear was a pair of scuffed gumboots. His chest webbing looked as though it had been run up on his wife's sewing machine from a patchwork of different coloured canvas. The wooden stock and butt of his AK 47 were pitted and scratched with age, and even from ten metres away Shane's trained eye spotted specks of orange rust around the muzzle. The soldier picked his nose with his free hand as he trailed the colonel. Shane had been schooled in the art of assessing an armed force's expertise, training, leadership, morale and equipment. The way these two men looked and acted told him a lot. Patrice brought up the rear.

'Francois, *mon ami, comment ça va?*' Fletcher called as he pushed open his tent flap and strode out to meet the officer. They shook hands and embraced like old friends.

Fletcher introduced Shane and Michelle to Colonel Francois Gizenga, the local military commander for the region encompassing the concession and the adjoining section of the Virunga National Park. The colonel apologised for not being there to meet them the previous day, as planned, giving as an excuse his command of an operation to mop up some pockets of anti-government resistance.

'Close to here?' Shane asked.

'Oh no,' Gizenga said, 'some sixty kilometres to the south-east. You won't be bothered by them. Believe me, no one will be bothered by them now.' His broad face lit up with a wide grin.

'A cognac?' Fletcher suggested.

Shane thought it a little early, and declined when Fletcher returned from his tent with a bottle and glasses, but the colonel accepted the offer. Michelle also said no and excused herself. 'We need to talk later,' she said to Fletcher as she left.

Shane, Fletcher, the colonel, and Patrice, who acknowledged Shane with little more than a cold glare, sat around a fold-out table under the shade of the awning that projected from the roof of Fletcher's tent. The officer's driver had returned to the pick-up and squatted in the shade on his haunches, his back resting against the vehicle. Wise and Caesar had relieved Shane on guard duty and were sitting outside the gutted building.

'So, Fletcher has asked me to brief you, Mr Castle . . .'

'Shane.'

'Very well, Shane, on the current situation here in my *groupement*.'

Shane didn't know whether the man had called it his district because he was born there or because he thought himself the local ruler. He suspected the latter.

'You are familiar with this area, Shane?' Gizenga asked.

'Never been here before. All I know is what little I've picked up from the Internet,' Shane admitted.

'Very well,' Gizenga said with a theatrical shrug of resignation, 'we start from the beginning. The *Parc National de Virunga*, PNV, as we call it, was created in 1925 during the colonial times and originally named Albert National Park, after the then king of Belgium. The reserve runs north-south along our border with Uganda and Rwanda.' The colonel traced the elongated green-shaded zone that denoted the protected area on the map in front of them. The park was partly split by a wedge of communal and privately owned lands along the Rutshuru River, and it was in this area, north-east of the town of Rutshuru, on the border with Uganda, that Fletcher's hunting concession was based.

'We are in what was once known as the *Domaine de Chasses de Rutshuru* – a hunting reserve, or a safari area, as you would call it.' With his finger, Gizenga drew a box around much of the white area on the map between the green of the PNV to the west, and another identically coloured area on the border. 'Over there,' he added, pointing past Fletcher to the east, 'a few kilometres away is the Bwindi Impenetrable National Park in Uganda, home to about half of the remaining mountain gorillas – about three hundred and twenty creatures in all.'

'Impenetrable?' Shane asked.

'*Oui*. It is named for a good reason. Here we are quite high, and this limits the size of the trees. Instead of rainforest with a high canopy and little undergrowth, we have smaller trees in thickly forested areas with a very thick tangle of vines, bamboo and bushes below.'

Shane nodded. He knew they were on the border of the Ugandan park, and had read a little about it, but wanted to know more about the side of the imaginary line where he and his men would be operating. 'You say this was once a hunting concession. When was it last used?'

Gizenga shrugged. 'Perhaps twenty years ago, maybe more, when Mobuto Sese Seko was in charge. Since his fall, and following the civil wars, this land has been taken over by refugees and others. The animals have mostly gone, replaced by small farms and people, with the exception of the more rugged areas, such as where we now sit.'

'It's called the Sarambwe Forest,' Fletcher intjected.

Shane leaned closer to study the map. 'No civilisation between us and the Ugandan border.'

Fletcher shook his head. 'Not unless you can call a couple of refugee villages civilisation.'

If Gizenga was offended by Fletcher's comment, he ignored it. He explained a little more of the park's history, including its name change under Mobuto Sese Seko's government, and the increasing interest in efforts to save the endangered mountain gorillas, which were mainly located in the Mikeno sector of the Virunga park, about forty-five kilometres south of their camp.

'Occasionally troops of gorillas have also crossed into our country in this area, from the Bwindi Impenetrable Park. If the forest on this side remains intact, and we keep poachers and militia out of here, perhaps one day tourists will come to the Sarambwe Forest to view wildlife.'

'To a hunting concession?' Shane asked. 'I don't follow you.'

'Our government believes that hunters will return before the backpackers,' Gizenga said. 'My men have been deployed to this area in force, with three aims. The first is to clear out the Rwandan Interahamwe – the Hutu militia who have lived in this part of our country for too long. The second aim is to make this concession safe for Fletcher and his clients to hunt, and the third is to stop local poachers and refugees coming here, killing wildlife for bush meat and cutting down trees for firewood.'

Fletcher leaned back in his chair. 'It's something you don't see every day in Africa, Shane. Forward thinking. The Congolese hope their own people – and the militiamen – will move out and stay away if there are soldiers and hunters operating legally in the bush. Even though we're hunting, we're doing more for conservation – by stopping the locals and foreigners from massacring the wildlife – than any other greenie in the country.'

It was an odd concept, introducing hunting to protect animals, but Shane knew that several of Africa's great national parks had begun life as hunting preserves, so perhaps it was just history repeating itself. The problem of Rwandan and other rebels hiding out in the DRC's eastern forests gelled with what he had read online, although Gizenga had left out any mention of illegal hunting by the Congolese Army.

Gizenga continued. 'Inside the Virunga Park there are anti-poaching patrols funded by international aid organisations, conservation groups and the UN. They, along with our soldiers, have done a good job increasing security and making the park safe for the return of tourists, but it is areas such as here, where you are operating, close to population areas, where there is still a problem. In past years small armies of rebel forces have swept through the park and beyond its borders, attacking and killing rangers and local villagers alike. The fighting has died down a little, although refugees have settled around existing villages and there is still a problem with robbery and subsistence poaching in and around the park.' Fletcher interrupted and told the colonel of the previous night's events.

Gizenga nodded. 'Crime is still a problem in these communities. The poaching, though, it is mostly for bush meat now. Sometimes they light fires to drive the game from the jungle into nets. As well as the antelope and hogs, they will catch monkeys and smoke the meat. Sometimes they will kill chimps and gorillas.'

'Are the bush-meat hunters usually armed?' Shane asked.

'They may carry spears, bow and arrow, or they may set snares. However, in this area there are also many, many AK 47s. We are restoring law and order, you understand, Shane, but you will encounter men with rifles.'

'What are our rules of engagement?'

The colonel looked at Fletcher, then back at Shane. 'We here in the DRC have been very impressed with the stance that our allies in Zimbabwe have taken against armed poaching. Our government has imposed a shoot-to-kill regulation in the national park and in designated safari areas, such as where we are right now. As far as I am concerned, if you see a man in this area,' Gizenga traced the borders of the concession with a manicured fingernail on the map, 'and he is armed, but not in the uniform of the Congolese Army, national parks or police, then you may kill him.'

'As far as you are concerned, Colonel?' Shane wanted more than one man's opinion. 'What does the law say?' Fletcher frowned at Shane.

'Monsieur, I *am* the law here.'

'What should we do with those two over there?' Fletcher asked Gizenga, pointing at the building. He explained the night's events to the colonel.

'I will take them into custody and hand them over to the police. They will be charged with robbery.'

Shane rubbed his chin. 'They didn't actually take anything, you know. We caught them before they could.'

'They will be charged with robbery, monsieur.'

Shane nodded. It wasn't his country. He almost felt sorry for the two men. He wondered what was in store for them.

After the colonel left, the work gang from the local village returned for duty – minus the two who had attempted to rob the camp. Shane had a reluctant

Patrice tell the men what had happened to their comrades, along with a warning that the same fate awaited anyone else who wanted to steal from the hunters.

'Tell them the wages they will receive will be good, and that we'll be looking for some men – and probably a few of their wives – to work here full-time. Those who apply themselves will be rewarded.'

Patrice scoffed, but translated anyway.

Shane supervised half of the men in a clean-up of the debris in the disused building. Wise and Caesar worked with another party finishing off the pit latrines and erecting a bush shower – a framework made from felled trees that would support canvas buckets with a nozzle attached. Patrice lay in the shade of the tree line, propped up against his still-rolled safari tent, smoking a cigarette.

Fletcher walked past the work gangs and let himself into Michelle's tent, where she had been since Gizenga's visit. Shane took a break from shovelling broken glass and charred timber, and lit a smoke while he watched. He heard Michelle's raised voice and, though her words were indistinct through the heavy canvas, he could guess what she was saying.

After a few minutes, Fletcher left the tent and walked over to the Landcruiser. He called to Shane: 'Colonel Gizenga invited me over to his camp for lunch to meet his officers. I'm going now. I'll be back before dark.'

'Everything okay?' Shane asked.

'I think we should let the whole team know next time you're running a night-time security operation. She's accused me of treating her like a "princess". Is that a bad thing?'

16

Fletcher had to drive to Goma to meet with some bureaucrats from the parks service to discuss the details of hunting quotas and permits, but before he left he wished the others well on their expedition to track the mountain gorillas in the Virunga National Park.

Michelle sat next to Shane in the front of the Land Rover Defender, and Wise and Caesar sat in the back. It was Sunday, so Patrice and the work gang had the day off. Shane was pleased to be away from the surly guide. He didn't know who would come to blows with him first – himself or one of his men.

Shane had encouraged Wise and Caesar to come gorilla tracking in order to help familiarise themselves with the terrain in which they would be operating, and to learn more about the wildlife they might encounter. While both could interpret the warning calls of a baboon, track a lion or tell the size, sex and condition of a rhino from its dung, neither man had ever seen a mountain gorilla in the flesh.

Shane handed them his dog-eared field guide to African mammals as he drove. Caesar flipped through the book and was astonished to learn that a male silverback could grow to be as tall as himself and twice his weight. 'Ah, that is one big monkey,' he observed.

'Ape,' Michelle corrected.

'Still looks like a monkey.'

'I saw chimpanzees when I was here with the army,' Wise said. 'They are like humans, those ones. They beat on the big roots of the trees like this,' he drummed a rapid tattoo on the Land Rover's aluminium door panel, 'to signal each other through the jungle.'

'It was good of Fletcher to organise the gorilla-tracking permits,' Shane said to Michelle.

'Hmmm,' she replied. 'He certainly is in tight with the local authorities.'

They drove as far as they could, until the track leading eastwards from the village of Rumangabo, the nearest settlement to the Bukima gorilla base, finally petered out. Amidst some fields of straggly maize and a muddy potato crop they met a Congolese guide, Henri, and a scout, Jean-Baptiste, who were waiting for them by prior arrangement. Fletcher's contacts had arranged for them to track the gorillas first and then end up at the Bukima base camp, instead of jumping off from the research base. Henri carried a well-worn FN rifle. Shane wondered if the weapon was for protection against wildlife or armed Rwandans, but he said nothing. The two guides wore brown parks uniforms with a yellow-orange patch on the left breast pocket that said *ICCN, Institut Congolais pour la Conservation de la Nature*, and a round patch on their right shoulder with the ICCN's Okapi logo on it.

Four skinny boys – Shane guessed they were in their mid-teens – offered to act as porters for the small party, but the men all declined. Shane looked at Michelle, who had brought a small day pack containing water, some bananas and her camera gear. 'I'll be fine,' she said. 'I don't need anyone to carry for me.'

'It is a difficult walk, mademoiselle,' Henri said.

'I said I'll be fine,' Michelle admonished the guide in fluent French.

Fletcher had viewed the mountain gorillas on a previous visit and, on his advice, everyone wore long-sleeved shirts and trousers, despite the oppressive heat of the morning. Michelle pulled on a pair of yellow chamois work gloves as they set off – Fletcher had warned her about stinging nettles.

Henri and Jean-Baptiste led them into the forest, and set a cracking pace, even though the lead man was using a panga to hack through vines and thick grass as soon as the path from the rendezvous point petered out. Shane kept himself in the peak of physical fitness and ensured that Wise and Caesar exercised between patrols, but soon all three men were sweating and huffing. From the tops of the hills they crested, Shane could still see the smallholding farms they had passed through earlier, a reminder that the loss of their natural habitat to agriculture was as big a threat to the gorillas as the activities of poachers.

Shane put his hands on his hips and paused for a second to suck a deep breath into his lungs. They had stopped in a rare natural clearing, on the knife edge of a ridge that afforded them a stunning view of dark dense valleys and peaks bathed a glittering emerald by the morning sun. He realised it was the combination of several natural factors that made this such arduous country to function in. He had climbed mountains in the army, he had operated at altitude, he had worked in stifling heat, and he had hacked his way through near-impenetrable jungle. However, he had never faced all of those conditions at the same time.

The little gap in the tangle of creepers and thick bush trees was an anomaly. As they resumed their trek he noticed that the entire surface of each mountain was covered in vegetation. As well as clumps of trees and bamboo thickets, there was a never-ending lat-ticework of vines to negotiate. The creepers crisscrossed at about waist height for a human, though underneath them there were crawl spaces where nothing grew because of the lack of light. The gorillas, Henri had explained before they set off, walked bent over, on all fours, on their hind feet and the knuckles of their hands, so they could move faster than humans, scurrying about for much of the time beneath the tangle of vines. The lead man, Jean-Baptiste, had no option but to keep hacking.

'*Ils sont là*,' Jean-Baptiste whispered.

'There they are,' Michelle translated for the others.

On the far side of the valley they were descending into, Shane saw a sapling, taller than most around it, swaying, although there was not a breath of wind on the hot, humid mountain slope.

Henri explained. '*Un* gorilla. He has grabbed the

tree to try and reach for leaves, to eat. He may try and break it.' On cue they heard a snapping noise and the sapling fell.

Shane looked at Michelle. Her breathing was shallow and rapid, almost as though she were hyperventilating. Unlike the men, she had spent most of her days in the Zimbabwean bush in her Landcruiser, not on foot. 'Breathe slow and deep, if you can. We're almost there.'

She nodded and tried to smile.

The guides said nothing to each other, but moved off with renewed vigour. Michelle grimaced. 'They're heading the wrong way, the gorillas are over there.' Jean-Baptiste and Henri were hacking a path on a ninety-degree tangent away from the apes.

Wise tilted his head back and sniffed. 'These guys are good. You can hardly feel the breeze, but they are taking us downwind of them, so the gorillas will not smell us.'

Shane nodded his agreement. Wise was good as well – Shane could feel no trace of any wind when he tried the same trick.

'They are moving as they feed,' Henri explained, picking up a freshly shredded length of creeper vine, the sap still sticking on his fingers. They stumbled after the tireless Congolese, stopping every now and then to whisper curses as they picked off vines covered with tiny thorns that continually snagged at their clothes and exposed skin. 'We will move ahead of them, in an arc, to . . . what is the word . . . ?' He made a T with his two hands, the fingertips of his right meeting the path of his left.

'Intercept them,' Shane finished.

'*Oui* – intercept. *Bon.*'

Shane brushed a vine from his face and felt the barbs rake his palm. Gloves would have been a good idea, he conceded. The skin on his arms and legs was by now covered in shallow scratches, the fabric of his lightweight shirt and hiking pants laddered in dozens of places. He made a mental note to make sure he, Wise and Caesar all learned from the lessons of this tourist jaunt before their first patrols.

There was still another half-hour of scrambling, sliding, climbing and slithering up and down hills before Henri held up a hand and shushed them to silence.

Michelle had felt, more than once, like she wanted to quit. She had been on the verge of asking the guide to leave her by the side of the trail, or send his assistant back to camp with her.

It would have been foolish and selfish, she realised, but, more than that, she did not want to appear weak in front of Shane. Plenty of other female researchers, including the pioneering Dian Fossey, had worked in these conditions. She had to show Shane, and herself, that she was as tough as any of them. What this walk was showing her, however, was that she was woefully out of shape for work on foot in this environment.

Michelle looked at Shane's broad, sweat-soaked back in front of her. The smell of him was acrid in her nostrils, but not at all repulsive. That odour, the presence of a man, had returned to her life only recently.

Fletcher had reminded her how good sex could be and, if she were honest with herself, how much she craved a male presence in her life.

She had accused Fletcher of treating her like a princess and he had not denied it. The look in his eyes had said, And what's so wrong with that? He had also treated her like a child, not warning her of the night patrol he and Shane had cooked up, and lavished gifts and indulgences upon her. It was nice to be spoiled once in a while, but not at the cost of being relegated to a mere chattel.

Shane was certainly not out to woo her, but she wanted him to be her friend. She had antagonised him initially, regarding his profession, and felt a little guilty about that now. On the few occasions they had been together in private she had enjoyed their chats and the way he started opening up to her. They talked about their families and their childhoods, but he was still prone to becoming moody and withdrawn. She wondered what demons from his time in Afghanistan and Iraq he might be hiding. It was nice being with him here, on the mountain, despite the punishing nature of the trek, just as it had been good to be with him in Livingstone and on the parachute jump. Coming so soon after her return to the wonderful world of sex, the feel of his muscled body strapped to hers in the little aeroplane had been almost overwhelming. She mentally chided herself. Fletcher was a good man, and one man in her life – in that way – was more than enough.

Michelle reached out to grab a vine and haul herself up yet another incline. At times it was like climbing a ladder, her feet not even touching the soil beneath the interlocking strands. Hand over hand, she dragged herself up the hill, her feet scrabbling for purchase.

Even though he was breathing heavily, Shane made the trekking look easy. Mercifully, at the top of the hill they reached another small clearing. She followed Shane's lead and dropped to one knee. Ahead of her she saw Henri's raised hand. She knew that meant silence. She slipped off her day pack, fished out a plastic water bottle and guzzled the now warm contents.

They waited, panting and sweating, on the edge of the clearing, which had been caused by the fall of a giant tree. Henri made a low two-part coughing noise, as though he were trying to clear his throat.

To her left, Michelle heard the rustle of leaves and, to her amazement, the voice of a mountain gorilla in reply. '*Hmm-ha*,' it coughed.

Shane looked back at her and she wondered if her grin were as wide and as silly as his. She saw the look of boyish surprise on his face and thought he looked too sweet right then to be a trained killer. She wondered how Fletcher had reacted to seeing the forest giants. Probably wanted to shoot one, she thought uncharitably.

Henri cleared his throat again and the gorillas replied. Michelle shifted position slightly to peer around Shane's protective bulk.

The silverback waddled into view, spreading his huge weight between his rear legs and his wide knuckles. He stopped in the clearing and turned to look at them.

'This group is named after a silverback called Rubago, or his western name, which was Marcel. The current leader of these gorillas is a descendant of the first Marcel, who was killed by poachers,' Henri whispered.

Michelle felt the hair stand up on the back of her neck and a lump rise to her throat as the gorilla locked eyes with her. Henri had told them, in the briefing before the trek, to try to avoid eye contact with them, but she couldn't. She was transfixed by the bottomless, jet-black pools, for how long, she would never be able to remember. He seemed to be questioning her, appraising her, trying to make up his mind about some issue of life-threatening importance. In essence, she realised later, he was probably doing just that. As the leader of a small family of imperilled individuals – a group lucky still to be alive, against incalculable odds – the silverback had to decide, right then and there, if he would trust this band of upright two-legged apes.

She glanced at Shane, who was rock-still in front and to one side of her. Michelle felt light-headed and realised she had been so mesmerised she must have stopped breathing. Shane might have been in the same state of suspended animation, for when the silverback ambled slowly off into the jungle, the ex-soldier let out an audible hiss of breath.

With the all-clear given, through a cough-word or two, the rest of the troop of gorillas filed past them. Michelle counted two more adult females, three juveniles and a very young one, before she had the presence of mind to fumble for the digital camera in her day pack. When she looked up and focused, she saw the youngster, perhaps the height of a human two year old, scamper up a sapling on the far side of the clearing. The spindly tree was too narrow to support even the baby and, as he neared its top, the trunk bent. The little gorilla, a bundle of spiky, fuzzy fluff, found himself dropping back to earth at an ever increasing rate and let out a little squeal. Michelle tried not to laugh out loud as her camera motor clattered off half-a-dozen frames.

Michelle lowered the camera as the toddler dropped the last metre to the ground and toppled over. He raised himself, shook off some leaves and waddled towards the humans, instead of following the rest of his family.

Henri had warned them that the younger members of the troop still found humans a novelty, and might try to approach them. The rule, if that happened, was that they should stay perfectly still. Visitors were discouraged from reaching out and trying to touch a gorilla, but if the animals tried the same gesture, they should just sit quietly and enjoy the experience. Michelle froze, her camera held near her chest. The little gorilla walked past Henri and Jean-Baptiste. He sidled around Shane – perhaps the man's bulk reminded him of his disciplinarian father – and knuckle-walked through the grass until he was close enough for Michelle to smell him. He sat for a moment, looking up at her, though she noticed his eyes weren't on hers. The gorilla stood on his little hind legs, reaching up towards her. Michelle's heart fought to escape her rib cage and she felt sweat break out anew all over her body. Tiny hands that looked as though they were encased in gloves of soft black leather reached up to her. The gorilla extended a finger and tapped the end of her three hundred millimetre telephoto lens. Michelle cast her eyes downwards and saw the reason for his curiosity. The youngster had caught sight of his own reflection in the glass of the lens. He moved his face closer, until she was sure his breath must be misting the surface.

Behind Michelle, Wise was slowly edging around Caesar to get a better look at the little primate. As skilled as Wise was in moving silently through the dry bushveld, he was still not yet attuned to the ever present threat of the vines that carpeted even the open ground like trip-wires. His foot caught a tendril and he pitched forward, landing heavily against Caesar, who let out an involuntary curse as he took his comrade's weight.

The baby gorilla shrieked. Before Michelle had time to admonish the two men, the jungle to their right erupted in a cloud of shredded leaves and trailing vines. The silverback bellowed as he charged into the clearing. Wise rolled to the ground and Caesar stood and turned in panic.

'No!' Michelle called over her shoulder.

The silverback headed towards them from a ninety-degree angle. Henri and Jean-Baptiste, at the head of the column, were too far forward to intercede. Caesar started to run, and Wise was clumsily clutching handfuls of long grass to pull himself upright.

Michelle reached out and planted a hand firmly in

the middle of Wise's back and pushed the man to the ground. He started to shrug her off, but she managed to hiss, 'Down!' Henri had warned them that to run from a charging silverback would only inflame the animal, and it might pursue them and attack. Against all instinct, they had been told to cower and not move in the face of a confrontation.

The little gorilla had panicked and run back to the centre of the clearing, but from there he had been uncertain in which direction to head. The silverback checked his stride for a split second to make up the baby's mind. He snatched the wayward child by his tiny arm and hurled him, forcefully, but with enough restraint not to snap the limb, into the jungle in the direction in which the others had disappeared. The youngster squealed again, then scarpered off.

Michelle stood and took two long strides after Caesar. It was Shane's turn to call a warning now, but she ignored him. She lunged for the fleeing black man and managed to grab the belt of his trousers and check his pace. The silverback stood upright, his height towering over the other cowed humans, and beat out a staccato rhythm on his huge chest. The sound was hollow but menacing. He shrieked and resumed his charge, heading straight for the standing humans.

Michelle held onto Caesar's belt, despite his twisting and reaching. She pitched herself forward, her other arm reaching around his narrow waist, and used her full weight to push him down. Unprepared for the tackle, Caesar fell face-first into the grass. Michelle smothered him.

The gorilla reached the prone forms with half-a-dozen strides. He stood over them, bellowed and rapped on his chest again.

'Quiet,' Michelle whispered to Caesar. She thought he might be whimpering under her. She heard the gorilla behind her, sensed his shadow blanketing her, but she dared not turn around to look up at him. She was terrified by the charge, but she knew her fate now rested in the mighty beast's hands.

The silverback grunted and coughed. He dropped to his knuckles, and looked around, his massive head swivelling as he glared a warning at the other humans in the clearing. Slowly he turned and, message delivered, walked back into the jungle.

'He's gone,' Shane said, crawling over to where Michelle still lay across a motionless Caesar. 'You can get up now.'

Michelle rolled over and started laughing.

There was a woman waiting for them at the Bukima gorilla-trekking and research base camp.

Shane spotted her from a hilltop, nearly a kilometre away, and later he would think it was her sheer presence that had made her so visible from afar. She stood in the middle of the encampment, a clearing dotted with a small circular wooden building, which he later learned was the grandiosely named visitors' centre, and two dome tents. She had her hands on her hips, her legs slightly apart, waiting for them.

As they moved down the forested hillside he glimpsed her again, every few minutes, when a gap in the foliage allowed. Her features became clearer. Jet-black hair, cut in a mannish crew cut. Tight white sleeveless T-shirt. Toned, tanned arms, narrow waist. Not as tall as Michelle, maybe five-eight, but a woman hardened and sculpted by months on the mountains. She stood in front of a mural of a silverback, which had been painted on the side of the visitors' centre. A Congolese soldier with an AK slung over his shoulder stood in the shade of a tin-roofed, open-sided cooking shelter, chatting to a pretty African girl who stirred a pot over a smoky fire. A group of eight westerners, mostly in their late teens or early twenties, paused with their two guides for a group photograph before heading away from the patrol post into the jungle.

'That must be Marie Delacroix,' Michelle said, pointing to the white woman.

Shane thought Michelle said the words with a mixture of awe and excitement. 'Never heard of her,' he replied.

'You mightn't remember the name, but you'll have heard of the court case.'

When Michelle mentioned a furrier in Paris, Shane's memory rewound to a series of reports on the satellite news channels he'd seen while working in Baghdad. The story had gone around the world. A group of animal rights activists had planted an incendiary bomb with a timing device in the warehouse of a fashion company that specialised in exotic furs. That in itself was not all that sensational; however, a female security guard had been burned to death in the blaze that consumed the building when the time bomb went off.

'She was one of them?' he asked.

'The police arrested and charged her – Doctor Delacroix was the public face of the animal rights group – but the case against her was dismissed by the court. There was no evidence to tie her to the actual attack and she had a rock-solid alibi.'

'Which was what?'

'She was here in Africa, back at her gorilla research base, when the fire took place – although the police still claimed she was the mastermind behind the bombing, and another two fires in Paris.'

'You called her "doctor"?' Shane asked. They were close to Doctor Delacroix now. He saw high, sculpted cheekbones; a wide, sensuous mouth; feline green eyes. With a different haircut, he reckoned Marie Delacroix could herself have been on the catwalk.

'She's a highly qualified, respected zoologist. *Time Magazine* called her the new Dian Fossey, though apparently she hates being compared with her. She thought Fossey was too weak on the poachers who hunted the gorillas in Rwanda.'

Shane gave a snort of surprise. From what he knew of the late scientist – which was largely courtesy of Hollywood – her hard line against the locals who threatened the mountain gorillas might have contributed to her death. He took another look at Marie Delacroix. There was a hardness about her.

Shane, Michelle, Wise and Caesar were covered in mud, their exposed skin checked with scratches, their clothes sporting runs and tears from the walk. Marie Delacroix looked as though she had just stepped out of a sidewalk cafe in her native city. 'You are Michelle, no?' she asked in accented English, not approaching them, hands still on her hips.

'Doctor Delacroix? It's an honour,' Michelle replied, wiping a grimy hand on filthier trousers. 'You know my name?'

The Frenchwoman smiled. 'Fletcher told me you would be here today.'

Michelle looked puzzled. 'He did?'

'*Oui*. We met when he came to trek with the gorillas. He told me he was bringing a researcher up with his hunting party. I understand you are to conduct a survey of his concession in the Sarambwe Forest, yes?'

Michelle nodded. Shane noticed that the other woman had not acknowledged his presence or that of his men. Michelle suddenly realised the faux pas and did the honours. Marie Delacroix nodded at the men but said nothing to them.

'I'd be happy to show you around, if you wish.'

'That would be wonderful, Doctor Delacroix.'

'Call me Marie, please. It will be nice to have another woman over the age of twenty to talk to!' They both laughed. 'I know the area of the new hunting concession well. There is a troop of gorillas that has occasionally strayed across the border from Bwindi into the Sarambwe Forest. When they cross, it is my job to monitor them on behalf of the Uganda Wildlife Authority until they return to Uganda. I will show you on the map the areas you may wish to focus on, when I visit.'

'You're already planning to visit us?'

'*Oui*. Fletcher has invited me to stay at his camp

287

tomorrow night. I will be there. He is a good man –
for a killer of animals.'

Shane weighed in. 'I wouldn't have thought you
would approve of hunting.'

She turned her head, still standing defiant and
aloof with her hands on her hips, and nailed Shane
with a well-aimed look. 'I do not, but sometimes one
has to dance with the devil, as the English would say.
I know of Fletcher's record against poachers in
Zimbabwe – and of yours, Shane. He told me all
about you. We need all the help we can get here to
stop poaching.

'Fletcher and I, we have talked at length, and we
have made the truce – the pact of temporary allies. I
am a realist. I know that I cannot protect the animals
that live outside the national park, and I know that
poachers, hungry refugees and Congolese farmers
pose more of a threat to my mountain gorillas than
American or European hunters. If a forest outside of
the Virunga is used for hunting antelope and forest
hogs, it cannot be slashed and burned to plant
bananas. If men with guns hunt legally in such a concession and prevent poachers from doing their
business, then so much the better. In a perverse way I
admire Fletcher for the work he has done in
Zimbabwe – this includes the efforts of you and your
soldiers.'

'We had the support of the police and the national
parks authorities in Zimbabwe. We worked well with
them,' Shane said. He was always uncomfortable taking credit for the efforts of others.

'You are too modest. This country is only just

rediscovering the economic value of wildlife, and the magnitude of the poaching problem. They are learning that one must fight fire with more fire. I will forgive Fletcher and the bloated capitalist killers he calls clients if you do one thing for me, Shane.'

'What's that?'

'Kill poachers.'

Michelle said, 'We've also had success in Zimbabwe with educational programs in the schools, to teach the kids about the value of wildlife and . . .'

Marie cut her off, still staring at Shane. 'This is a war. It is too late for mere words. I know that pig Colonel Gizenga has given Fletcher carte blanche to curb poaching in the concession. If you kill the poachers there, they will not make it into my national park. Perhaps one day Sarambwe will be proclaimed a park as well, and then you and your hunters will go home.'

My gorillas. *My* national park. Shane could see they were talking to one of the most dangerous personalities the human race could field. A zealot. Shane was a soldier, but it was people like Marie Delacroix who started wars.

'Fletcher is going to take me on a hunting trip. I want to see first-hand what it is that gives men such a hard-on over killing.'

Shane coughed into his hand to cover his laugh. He thought that if Marie carried a gun, the rich hunters had better watch their backs.

17

Shane held the prismatic compass up to his eye
and checked the direction in which Wise was
heading. The scout was all but invisible in the
gloom beneath the forest canopy, thanks to the camouflage uniform and his black skin. The route Shane
had chosen took them through a deep valley, where
the vegetation was more like a hot and humid jungle
rainforest than the vine-covered slopes where they
had tracked the gorillas.

The three of them wore matching tunics and trousers
printed with differing hues of green and brown, punctuated with squiggles of black. The pattern – US Army
jungle leaf, it was called – was familiar to Shane from
joint military exercises with the Americans in the tropical north of Australia, Thailand and the Philippines.
The uniforms had been a gift from a hunting client, one
of Chuck Hamley's Illinois National Guard buddies.
Shane had initially thought the clothing useless – particularly in Zimbabwe's dry, khaki-hued bush – but it
was perfect for their new environment.

Shane wiped beads of perspiration from his upper lip with a gloved finger. With their green fire-retardant Nomex uppers and soft grey leather palms, the lightweight military flyers' gloves were a favourite of special force soldiers. His face was painted with vertical stripes of black and green camouflage makeup, and an olive strip of rag tied around his forehead kept the sweat from running out of his hair into his eyes.

Wise looked back over his shoulder, and Shane held up a hand and pointed thirty degrees off to the left. Both his men were struggling with the intricacies of navigating with a map and compass, although Caesar grasped the theory quicker than his ex-military comrade. Wise had earned himself another classroom session in the tent later in the day.

Birds squawked and he heard monkeys scampering through the branches above them. Wise and Caesar could have been dropped blindfolded and naked a hundred miles from anywhere in their native bushland and still made it home for dinner the same day. In the jungle, however, they were as lost as cub scouts on their first outing.

Shane was not overly concerned. He was confident in his own ability to plot a course through the challenging terrain and enjoyed passing on his skills to others. Wise and Caesar, he was sure, would be fine after a few more training exercises. When they started patrolling in earnest they would have local guides to lead them through the jungle; however, it was vital that his men know how to navigate themselves in case they were ever split up and had to find their own way back to base.

Shane turned his head and motioned for Caesar, who was behind him, to move up. Shane appraised the other man's movements critically. He had taught them the art of walking silently through the jungle – a special skill at which the Australian Army excelled. He had shown them how to move painstakingly slowly, placing a heel with deliberate care and then gradually transferring the body's weight around the outside edge of the foot, while feeling and listening for the twig that might snap and give away a man's position. He had armed them all with secateurs, small snips usually used for pruning roses, which Caesar now patiently used to cut away a 'wait-a-bit' vine that had snagged on one of his canvas water-bottle covers. Shane nodded his praise as Caesar knelt, with the exaggerated slowness of a mime artist, beside him.

'Which way?' Shane mouthed the question silently.

Caesar fished the compass out of the flapped breast pocket on his tunic and held it up to his eye. He pointed to a stout tree. Shane made a slight correction and indicated for Caesar to replace Wise on point.

They moved on slowly, and Shane tried to ignore the mosquitoes that buzzed around the back of his neck and the thought of the unseen, unfelt leeches that were probably right now burrowing into the skin above his boots. Out of habit, he constantly shifted his gaze from left to right, and above. After every few steps he also turned to check on Wise, who was still creeping along behind him. In the treetops he caught the occasional glimpse of one of the many primate species that lived in the mountains. A flash of colour danced through the dark green as a red-tailed monkey leapt agilely from one branch to another.

As part of a training exercise for Wise and Caesar, he had mapped a simple three-leg triangular route out of the camp: to the east towards the Ugandan border and away from the village where the would-be criminals had originated; into the concession's forest to the north, and then off to the south-west until they rejoined the main track back to the camp. It was his intention that they march through the village on the way home, rifles slung, in full uniform. Shane wanted the local people to know he and his men were active in the area, in order to deter those who might be tempted to continue their subsistence poaching in the newly proclaimed hunting concession.

Shane's eyes fell on Caesar. He had stopped. Slowly the other man raised his left hand, palm open. Shane passed the signal back to Wise, who also halted. Shane crept, with even more caution than normal, to a position on Caesar's right. He looked at the Ndebele, who wrinkled his nose and softly sniffed the air. Shane mimicked him and caught the smell, faint yet distinct.

Smoke.

The three men crouched close to the dank floor of the forest, the smell of rotting mulch mixing with the sweat of their bodies to create a raw scent. Shane felt a tingle in his fingertips – the old sign of impending action.

They moved off, even slower than before, in the same order. It took them a full ten minutes to cover the next hundred metres, and with every painstaking step the smell of smoke became stronger.

Caesar dropped fluidly to one knee, stuck out his arm and gave a thumbs-down signal. Shane dropped to his hands and knees and crawled forward. Caesar was behind the massive wall-like root of a figtree, his left side huddled against the towering trunk, his AK 47 peeking around the girth of the forest giant.

Shane heard voices. He dropped all the way to his belly and leopard-crawled to a point on the ground to Caesar's right. He counted eight pairs of legs. They stood or walked around a slowly burning fire, fed by damp, freshly cut logs. He smelled the metallic tang of fresh blood, then noticed a skinned animal haunch propped against a tree. The words of the African men were muted; the low, conspiratorial tones of the guilty at work.

Three AK 47 assault rifles stood in a tripod formation, their interlocking barrels keeping them upright, close at hand, ready for action. Two wicked-looking pangas, their long and wide blades burnished from sharpening, lay haphazardly on the bloodied leg of bush meat, which he guessed the men were going to smoke, in order to cure it.

Shane looked over his shoulder. Wise had gone to ground and was facing away from him and Caesar, back towards the direction they had come from, his AK 47 pointing down their near-invisible trail. Caesar watched out to Shane's left flank. Good men, Shane thought. They had followed the drills they had rehearsed time and again.

He glimpsed hands and a face as a man bent down to place a heavy cast-iron pot into the glowing coals beneath some more meat, already laid on racks for smoking. If they were preparing a meal in the pot, these men were not going anywhere fast. He needed a better vantage point, so he gently shifted his body two metres to the right, moving with the patience and silence of a tortoise. His suspicions about the men being in no hurry were confirmed when he saw a man in a grubby white singlet and patched trousers stringing a rope hammock between two trees.

Shane motioned to Wise and Caesar to fall back, then crawled after them.

'There are at least three rifles in that group,' he whispered to them once they had stopped, out of sight and earshot of the poachers' encampment. 'The odds aren't worth us trying to take them out by ourselves.'

'Why don't we just open fire on them? We could kill them all before they even get to those weapons,' Wise interrupted.

Shane's glare hushed him. After a pause, Shane said, 'We do it by the book – our book. I know Colonel Gizenga thinks we can get away with shooting anyone we see, but five of those men are unarmed, and we don't know which five they are. It's up to the Congolese Army or police to arrest them. Whatever Colonel Gizenga's rules are, we're not assassins.'

He outlined his plan, and there were no questions when he finished. Wise and Caesar would retrace their steps and return to camp. Even if their map reading and navigation left something to be desired, they were more than capable of picking up their own spoor through the jungle. Shane would find a good vantage point and, hidden away, keep the poachers under observation until the other two could organise a local police or military force to apprehend the criminals.

Shane always had his two-way radio on his belt, so he would be in communication with the hunting camp as soon as his men returned. While he waited for Wise and Caesar to find their way home, he busied himself crawling in a circuit around the entire poaching camp in search of an observation post.

After an hour on his belly, slithering through mud and over decaying leaves and fronds, he found the perfect location. It was the massive stump of a tree that had been felled some time in the past – long enough ago that ants had been able to hollow out the inside of what remained. Nature – with the help of an illegal tree-feller – had created a mini turret that he could ease himself into and sit in in relative comfort. He looked around him for signs that some forest creature might have had the same thought, but aside from some tiny pellet-like droppings – perhaps from a shrew or mouse – it appeared he would have the hide to himself. He peered out at his quarry through an old knothole in the hollowed stump.

Three men had strung hammocks around the smoking fire and they dozed in the fetid, airless afternoon heat. A young man – more like a teenager – squatted on his haunches and tended the fire. Two others lay sprawled out on the ground, while the remaining two worked slowly at slicing flesh in thin strips from the remains of the carcass. Shane hadn't been able to see what the dead animal was before – aside from one leg – but it looked like it was probably a buffalo. Shane shook his head when he thought of the tourists who might have paid to see a mighty old bull wandering through the forest, or the money that might have gone back into the village coffers if an American hunter had been allowed to bag the beast as a trophy. He looked at the emaciated forms of some of the men – whether their condition was from mal-nutrition or AIDS he had no way of knowing – and had a softening of heart. Perhaps they had more right to harvest their own wildlife than some dentist from Chicago. No, he told himself, swinging the argument back in his mind, the three AK 47s and the smoking rack were a strong clue that these were not starving villagers setting snares to feed themselves – this was a professional gang hunting illegal bush meat for sale in the city.

'*Taipan, this is Niner. Radio check, over.*' Shane had connected the external earpiece to his MBITR radio so that the noise of incoming transmissions would be heard by him only.

'Roger, over,' he whispered. It was good to hear Fletcher's voice on the other end. Wise and Caesar had obviously made decent time on their return trip.

'*Taipan, this is Niner. Send sitrep, over.*'

Shane gave his summation of all that he had seen in a concise transmission. 'Estimate they are camping at least for the night, over,' he concluded.

'*Good work, Taipan. I've contacted the G-man and confirm that we will have a reaction force in your loca-tion by ten hundred hours tomorrow, over.*'

Ten o'clock the next morning! Shane swore silently. It had only just gone four in the afternoon. He had already been sitting in the stump most of the afternoon. He had, as always, enough food and water to last him at least twenty-four hours, but he had banked on a quicker response. They would be lucky if the poachers were still there by the time Fletcher had given him. He knew the 'G' man Fletcher referred to was Colonel Gizenga. 'Say again, over.'

'I confirm, ten hundred tomorrow, Taipan. Nothing we can do before then as G-man has an operation going on this afternoon.'

There was no point in Shane complaining. He was a soldier and it was his job to follow orders. He looked forward more than ever to the day when he had enough money to buy his own piece of Africa, as he whispered, 'Roger, over.'

Fletcher closed the conversation by telling Shane to send a sitrep every three hours. Wise and Caesar were manning the radio during the night. Shane kept a watch on the poachers as the dark swiftly infiltrated the jungle. He had assumed they would mount a piquet during the hours of darkness, but was amazed when the last one still awake hefted a log onto the fire, then curled up in front of it and soon started snoring.

Shane faced a long, lonely night. He ate a dinner of two high-energy fruit bars washed down with luke-warm water from his plastic canteen. It was times like this that he wished he had at least one other member on his team, so that two of them could have shared the vigil. It made him think of old Charles Ndlovu, lying buried in the plague-infested dirt of the Victoria Falls cemetery, in a traitor's grave. The more he thought about Charles the less he understood the man's reasoning. He remembered the tears of his wife, Miriam, and resolved that he would look in on her and her children as soon as he had the chance to return to Zimbabwe.

With care not to make a rustling noise, Shane opened his backpack – all three of them had carried full loads on the navigation exercise – and pulled out the black nylon case containing his state-of-the-art night-vision goggles. They had cost him a month's pay from his time as a security consultant in Iraq, but he hoped tonight they would prove to be worth every cent of the five-figure price. He slipped the harness over his head and switched them on. The hitherto impenetrable blackness now shone in an artificial lime-coloured daylight. The embers of the smoky fire glowed as iridescent pinpricks in the centre of his field of vision. The boy lay curled on the ground. He scanned the positions where he had seen the other men lying or swinging in their hammocks. All were still and more than one of them now snoring.

Shane looked again at the assault rifles, standing next to the meat-smoking rack, at least four metres from the nearest sleeping poacher. He couldn't believe a group of men who hunted and broke the law for a living could be so careless with the most important tools of their trade.

He considered moving in, grabbing the rifles and rousing the men from their sleep. He would have the advantage of surprise, but the men might scatter into the jungle. If they ran, he would be unable to nail all of them – he was quick on the trigger, but not that quick. Besides, shooting unarmed men in the back was not his style.

It was tempting just to take the unattended rifles, he thought to himself; however, when the men awoke and found their rifles gone, they would make a run for it – if they didn't try looking for him. Either way, they would be long gone before Fletcher and Colonel Gizenga and his men arrived on the scene.

If he simply did as Fletcher had ordered – sat tight and continued to provide sitreps on the men's position – he would end up as a witness, if not a participant, to a full-scale fire fight. No matter how many men Gizenga could muster, three AK 47s on full automatic would generate a lot of lead, and possibly casualties if the poachers were cornered into a fight.

The motto of the Special Air Service Regiment was 'Who Dares Wins'. The third option that slowly crept into Shane's mind was more than daring, it was crazy. A broad grin lit his face in the darkened confines of the hollow tree stump.

He forced himself to wait, though every nerve ending in his body tingled with anticipation, fear and excitement. He checked his watch. Three am. No one had risen to relieve the boy who slept closest to the rifles. Rasping snores competed with croaking frogs and chattering insects to fill the night air. Slowly, Shane slung his rifle upside down across his shoulders and backed out of the tiny hole in which he had hidden for hours.

It was bliss to move again, though as he crawled his legs ached as the blood resumed its normal flow.

He lowered himself to his belly and edged towards the jungle clearing, using only his elbows and the toes of his boots to propel himself. The K-bar was in his right hand. If one of the poachers woke now, and stumbled upon him, it would be the last mistake the man would ever make.

Shane heard the rustle of something moving through fallen leaves, behind him and to the right. He froze, and lowered his face into the mulch. As always when soldiering in a jungle there were things just as deadly as the enemy to contend with. He felt the brush of the fabric of his camouflage trousers touching his skin. He held his breath, forcing himself to stay still, though every primal instinct told him to kick and roll away.

He felt the weight of it now, pressing the material against him, transferring its own bulk slowly over the back of his calf. Slithering. He was a brave man, a professional soldier who had faced death many times, but nothing in creation scared him quite so much as snakes. He imagined its forked tongue darting in and out, smelling him, trying to work out what he was. The head reached his other leg now, its first touch as gentle as a lover's caress. He bit on his lower lip and tasted blood. What would he do, he wondered in sudden panic, if it started to wrap itself around his leg? By the weight of it, and the endless seconds it was taking to cross his legs, he thought it was probably a python. The snake experts said they weren't poisonous, though they could break every bone in a pig's body and swallow it whole if they chose to. The snake paused, lying across him like a door stop filled with lead shot. There was no warmth from its scaly body. It was probably drawing heat from him.

Shane listened hard for sounds from the poachers' camp. He cursed himself for not staying in his hollow tree stump. Who dares wins. What bullshit. Here he was now, almost pissing himself under the weight of a reptile. Still, he resisted the urge to jump up and flee. Slowly, almost cruelly, the snake prolonged its journey, its cold-blooded bulk warming itself on his pounding pulse. At last, he felt the flicking twitch of its tail, and the relief as the weight slid off him. He risked lifting his head an inch and turned to see the diamond-patterned serpent disappear behind a fallen log. He allowed himself a long exhalation of breath through narrowed lips.

Ahead of him the fire's embers glowed like beacons in the view through his night-vision goggles, which worked by amplifying any ambient light they picked up. He emulated the snake, transferring his weight with serpentine silence and care. Like the python, Shane needed to move quietly in order to catch his prey off guard. He sniffed the air, as the snake had, and watched the lazy smoke that licked the strips of curing meat. It was moving towards him, which was good. In Africa, staying downwind meant staying alive.

Shane made it to the stacked rifles. The drying racks shielded him from view, though not from the hearing of the nearest poachers. He would need to work in total silence. He rose to his knees, scanning left and right to confirm all the men were still motionless. He grabbed the ends of the barrels of two of the weapons with one hand and lowered the third to the ground, before lying all of them down. He dropped to the earth again, alongside the three guns. Even a cursory inspection told him what he had guessed, that the AKs were old and poorly maintained. Still, the Russian Mikhail Kalashnikov had purposely designed a weapon that could be dragged through tropical jungles and dust and bone-dry bushveld without cleaning and still deliver its deadly payload of copper-jacketed death every time. However, Shane knew there were some things even one of these mass-produced third-world killers couldn't withstand.

He took a handful of dirt from near the fire, where the coals had dried the soil. Slowly he let the grains slide from his fist into the barrel of the first of the rifles. A bit of soil alone might not stop the bullet's path, so he pulled a water bottle from his belt, undid the cap, and trickled a mouthful down the barrel. He laid the AK with its muzzle up, so the water would mix with the dirt. By morning it should have set hard. Unless the poacher who owned it had a sudden burst of self-discipline and decided to clean his weapon, he would never know his prized possession was hopelessly blocked.

He slid through the leaves and cradled the second assault rifle close to his chest. Slowly, quietly, he removed the banana-shaped magazine full of bullets. At the bottom of the magazine was a metal plate that could be slid off. He kept pressure on the plate as he jiggled it free and allowed the spring to ease itself slowly from the tin box of the magazine. Free of pressure, the rounds started to slide towards the bottom. He laid the magazine down so no bullets would escape. From his belt, Shane drew his Leatherman, and opened the tool so that its pliers were in his hand. He gripped the thin wire of the spring between the jaws of the snips at the fulcrum and squeezed. The spring snapped in two with a tiny ping of breaking metal that sounded as loud to Shane's ears as a blacksmith's hammer on an anvil. He held perfectly still and listed for movement. The poachers snored on as Shane reassembled the magazine. With its spring broken there would be no pressure to feed the bullets into the rifle's chamber. The first round the firer slid into the weapon would definitely be the last from that batch.

Shane picked up the third rifle and was about to remove its magazine to do something similarly devilish when he heard a cough. He laid the weapon down and rolled to his right so he could peer around the fire pit. He saw a pair of skinny black legs beyond the embers. He swore silently to himself. The man started to walk away from him, towards the edge of the clearing.

Assuming the man was off to answer the call of nature, Shane reasoned he had less than a minute to get away. He rose to his knees, pushed forward the rear sight of the undamaged weapon, and rearranged the rifles into their tepee formation, so that the muzzles rested against one another. He dropped again to his belly and leopard-crawled back towards the hollow tree stump.

The poacher was an old man with a spare covering of tight grey curls atop his bony skull. He wore a pair of ragged cargo shorts and was bare-chested. Back in the relative safety of his hideout, Shane watched as the man scratched his crotch and knelt and prodded the fire. He blew on the dying embers and coaxed some life back into them. Shane smelled the resultant smoke and counted his blessings again that he had moved off when he did. The poacher stood beside the stack of rifles, but did not spare them a glance. He farted loudly and ambled back to his hammock. Shane radioed a situation report to base.

As the first rays of sunlight struggled to pierce the jungle canopy, the old poacher who had almost disturbed him was the first awake. He pulled on a shiny British football shirt – its garish blue an odd choice for working clandestinely in the bush, Shane thought – and started packing an old canvas rucksack with his meagre belongings. Shane was annoyed that he had been unable to spike the third rifle, but consoled himself with the fact that if these men ended up in a fight it would be a pretty one-sided affair.

The old man – Shane presumed he was the leader of the band – roused the others from sleep. As they rubbed their eyes and donned their clothes he kicked dirt on the remains of the fire. Under softly spoken but authoritative orders from the leader, the youngest member of the group started retrieving the dried meat from the makeshift racks and stuffing it into a hessian sack. They were getting ready to move and, at this rate, would be out of the clearing before six o'clock.

Shane pressed the microphone of his radio close to his lips and whispered, 'Zero Alpha, Zero Alpha, Taipan, over.'

305

Wise acknowledged him almost immediately, in a soft voice, knowing Shane was still in hiding.

'Target is getting ready to move. No way, repeat no way, will they be anywhere near this location by the time you arrive, over.'

'*Standby for Niner, Taipan*,' Wise replied. Shane fumed silently while he waited for Wise to fetch Reynolds. If they had gone with his initial plan, for Wise, Caesar, Fletcher and any soldiers he could muster to return at first light, they might have been able to intercept the poachers while they were on the move.

Fletcher's voice hissed in Shane's ear. '*Colonel Gizenga's men are in position, Taipan. About one kilometre to the east of your position, line abreast from north to south. I will bring your men and reinforcements in from the west. We're leaving now, over.*'

'Roger, Niner, but I thought . . .'

'*Save it, Taipan. Aren't you the one who says no plan survives the first ten minutes? Gizenga's men finished their operation early and moved into position last night.*'

Shane was surprised. He was disappointed Fletcher hadn't seen fit to contact him earlier, but, as Reynolds had said, Shane knew a good plan was a flexible one. Quickly he told Fletcher that he had managed to sabotage two of the poachers' three weapons, though at least one could be brought into action again if its owner had a second magazine.

'*Good work, as usual, Taipan*,' Fletcher replied.

Shane brushed off the praise, asking instead, 'Confirm that you have the west flank and the military has the east, over.'

'*Correct. I'll send Wise around to the north and Caesar to the south. Your guys will be like a Zulu impi's horns, encircling the enemy. Either we'll drive the poachers into the soldiers, or vice versa, over.*'

'Roger, Niner. I'll follow the target, but tell the army that if they want to set an ambush to warn me first over the radio. I want to take cover if there's going to be crossfire.'

'*Affirmative, Taipan.*'

That was enough chatter over the radio. The poachers were shouldering their packs, so Shane simply ended the conversation with a single click of the transmit switch.

He checked his compass. The hunters and their heavily laden bearers were heading almost due east. Their route would take them into the centre of the line of Gizenga's soldiers. Shane had never worked with the Army of the Democratic Republic of Congo, but if the dress and bearing of Colonel Gizenga's driver was any indication it was likely the soldiers were poorly equipped and ill-disciplined. Still, after several years of war, some of them had to be seasoned fighters. Shane radioed Fletcher to pass on the new information.

After the gang had filed off, Shane followed them, though he was careful to stay out of sight. He was getting more used to tracking in the jungle, and found he could easily follow the trail of scuffed leaves, torn spiderwebs and bent branches.

Every hundred paces he stopped, dropped to one knee and listened. He rechecked the compass and saw the men had not changed direction. Shane calculated that he had travelled four hundred metres – quite a distance in the steaming maze of vines and swamp. He stifled a yawn and focused his senses on the trail ahead. He was tired after so little sleep, but he knew another shot of adrenaline would soon fire him up.

He started to stand, but froze when he heard voices. Not soft and secretive, like the tone the old poacher had used with his men, but shouted commands. Soldiers.

'Zero Alpha, this is Taipan, noises up ahead, I think it's your other blue callsign, over,' he whispered into his radio. Blue was friendly, red was enemy. He looked around and spied a thick tree trunk that would give him cover if the shooting started. He moved quickly, at a crouch, to its base and dropped to his belly.

'*Taipan, wait, out,*' Fletcher replied. Shane presumed his boss was trying to make contact now with the Congolese soldiers. For all the other man's faults, Shane trusted Fletcher's ability and experience. The hunter had been in fire fights with Zimbabwean freedom fighters when Shane had still been in primary school.

Shane heard rustling ahead of him, the sound of men running, taking no care to hide the sound of their footfall. The poachers had heard the approaching soldiers, which meant they might be coming back his way.

A gunshot went off somewhere in front of him. The report was muffled by the jungle's dense vegetation, and while he couldn't see who had fired, Shane knew it would spell trouble for him if he stayed put. 'Zero Alpha, Taipan. Contact, wait out,' he breathed, then hauled himself to his feet and ran.

Shane vaulted a fallen log and ignored the thorn-covered vines and creepers that snatched at his pistoning legs. He held the compass up as he ran, and saw he was now headed due west. With a bit of luck he would stumble upon Fletcher, Wise and Caesar.

'*Taipan, Zero Alpha. Head west. Repeat, west.*' Fletcher hissed in his earpiece. At least he was going the right way.

Shane cursed the soldiers for their poor noise discipline. They were acting more like beaters in a pheasant shoot than trained professionals. He'd heard them blundering about, even though he reckoned he was still a good hundred metres behind the poachers. The gang must have just about bumped into the army cordon.

His fatigue was gone, all his senses on high alert. Along with his increased awareness came an odd sensation of calm. This was his job.

He heard a bang and a man screamed, a primal keening wail of pain and shock. Shane couldn't see, but he reckoned the noise was a round exploding in the blocked barrel of the rifle he had filled with mud during the night. It was a dirty act of sabotage, but he'd long ago realised that there was precious little honour in warfare. He consoled himself with the thought that if the man were screaming – as he still was – then at least he might be captured alive.

Shane lost his footing as the land dropped away in a steep slope and found himself sliding on his bottom down a muddy creek bank. He held his rifle at the high port to keep it clear of soil and water as his boots hit the crystal-clear stream with a splash that soaked him to the waist. He stood and strode through the water. His left foot touched a rock and he was glad of the sure footing until his boot slipped on the slimy surface. He fell, just managing to hold his SLR free, and felt a sharp pain in his ankle. 'Fuck,' he said as he tried to stand again.

In his haste he'd made a mistake worthy of a nineteen-year-old recruit. He tested the ankle again by transferring his weight, and grimaced in pain. The joint buckled as soon as he tried to take another step.

Shane heard a further single shot from an AK 47, followed by loud cursing in an African tongue. The guy with the broken magazine, he reckoned. Shane's little tricks had provided good sport, but they would count for nothing if the gang of angry and wounded men came across him lying helpless in the mud. He heard an answering volley of fire, a four-round burst fired on full automatic, coming in his direction by the sound of it. The soldiers were running true to form. Pray and spray – shooting blindly on full auto in the hope of hitting something – was the mark of a truly undisciplined force.

'Zero Alpha, Taipan is down. Leg injury. I'm going to ground in the bed of a creek running north-south, over.'

Shane nestled into the bank of the stream and peered over the edge of the drop-off towards where the poachers and soldiers would soon appear.

'*Roger, Taipan. We're taking a bead on the gunfire and . . . Wait.*'

Shane pulled the wooden butt of the big rifle into his shoulder and looked down the barrel. If it came

310

to a shoot-out, this was as good a place as any to defend. He just hoped the Congolese Army didn't overrun the poachers and start shooting at him in their excitement. He heard them now, jeering and bellowing, punctuating each phrase with another burst of fire.

'*Taipan, this is Zero Alpha.*' Fletcher was panting as he spoke, on the run. Shane heard the same shots through the earpiece of his radio that were being fired in front of him. Reynolds and his team must be close. '*One of our number knows the stream where you are. We'll be there in a few seconds. Sit tight, out.*'

One of our number? Shane wondered who that would be. Perhaps it was Patrice. The thought of the surly guide coming up behind him with a loaded weapon wasn't reassuring.

The first of the poachers came into view. Shane captured him through the circular rear sight of the SLR, then placed the narrow blade of the foresight in the centre of the man's chest. The man was carrying an AK, but there was no banana-shaped magazine protruding from the bottom. Shane didn't have time to congratulate himself on his cunning, as the man was running straight towards him.

'*Arrêt!*' Shane bellowed, using the word Michelle had taught him for 'stop'.

The man slowed, then stopped as he looked down towards the stream and caught sight of the green-painted face at the end of the long rifle barrel. The poacher held up his rifle, as if to show that it was now useless. Shane motioned with the muzzle of his weapon for the man to drop his.

It looked as though the poacher might comply, until a second man elbowed him aside. Shane had been focusing his attention on the first man and had missed the approach of the second. This man carried a loaded Kalashnikov. He raised it to his shoulder and then pulled the trigger.

The man's aim looked true, but the bullets sailed high over Shane's head, showering him with shredded leaves and bark. Shane shifted his aim to the firer, squeezed the trigger twice and the poacher disappeared from sight. While he hadn't had time to damage the third of the gang's rifles he had quickly adjusted the rear sight of the weapon, setting it to fire at long range rather than the default setting for close combat. Raising the rear sight meant the marksman would fire high, to compensate for the natural fall of a projectile over a longer distance. The trick had probably saved Shane's life. He called again to the first man to stop, but he was running away, to his left, to the north, parallel to the stream.

'Shane! Coming up, on your left!' Fletcher called, not bothering with the radio.

Shane turned and saw blurs of movement through the jungle.

'One's heading your way!' Shane replied. 'He's got an AK but he's got no mag —'

Shane had lost sight of the fleeing poacher, but he heard him cry out, just as the first gunshot erupted. '*Non, non!*'

The deep boom of the heavy-calibre hunting rifle silenced the man's cry.

Shane pushed himself painfully to his feet and

limped northwards through the mud at the edge of the running water.

'Shane, behind you!' He looked over his shoulder and saw Caesar splashing through the stream. 'Are you hit?'

Shane tried to brush off Caesar's offer of help, but found that he could move faster leaning on the younger man's shoulder. The pair of them rounded a bend in the creek bed. Shane was speechless at the sight before them.

'Take the picture, Fletcher,' Marie Delacroix commanded.

She wore a tailored green shirt and matching fatigue trousers, nipped here and there to ensure they showed off her curves perfectly. Around her waist was a canvas webbing belt heavy with fat brass cartridges. She wore a leopard-print scarf around her neck and held a .375 Holland and Holland hunting rifle by the barrel, the stock balanced on her shoulder.

'No, Marie. I don't like the idea of pictures.' Fletcher stood opposite her, an identical rifle in his left hand and a pocket-sized digital camera dangling uselessly from his right by the carry strap.

'Take the picture,' Marie insisted again.

Shane and Caesar stopped. In front of them, Marie stood over the face-up body of the man who had been carrying the AK 47 without a magazine. Shane had been too late to tell them that their opponent may as well have been unarmed. She raised her hiking boot and planted it on the dead man's chest. 'Now, Fletcher.'

'What the hell is all this?' Shane finally managed.

Fletcher ignored the question and passed his rifle to Patrice, who stood, grinning malevolently, at his boss's side. Reynolds lifted the camera, which looked like a child's toy in his hands, and pressed the button. White flashlight lit the macabre scene and seemed to Shane to bounce off Marie Delacroix's wide eyes and perfect teeth.

'The huntress with her trophy, no!' she exclaimed.

Fletcher handed the camera back to her, and while Marie gleefully showed a hovering Patrice the image in the LED screen, Fletcher turned to Shane and Caesar, acknowledging them for the first time. He shrugged. 'She insisted on coming.'

'You brought a woman to a fire fight?' Shane couldn't hide his incredulity.

Fletcher held up his hands to stifle the protest, but Shane persisted. 'There were three armed men running about out there.'

'Yes, but you told me you'd managed to doctor their weapons. The soldiers picked up the wounded man. Spiking his AK 47 cost that chap half his face.'

Shane's ankle throbbed with pain and he was in no mood for mirth. 'First useful thing those dozy bastards have done all morning.' He jerked a thumb at the line of camouflage-clad Africans who were now wandering into view. Shane heard the sobs of the wounded poacher, who held a hand streaked with blood over the right side of his face.

'They did their job, all right,' Fletcher countered. 'They told me on the radio they'd captured the one guy and I heard you drill that other one just as we arrived. I knew it was down to one man.'

Shane couldn't hold his anger in check. 'Then you knew it was the man with no ammo in his rifle. I started to tell you, but —'

'You started to tell me something, and then Marie and I saw a man running towards us with a rifle. If she hadn't shot him first, I would have.'

'*She* shot him?'

Marie handed Patrice her rifle, took three paces and stood in front of Shane, hands on her hips. '*Oui*, s*he* shot the poacher. Are you such a Neanderthal that you think a woman cannot defend herself in the twenty-first century?'

'I . . . it's just that . . .'

'Don't be a male chauvinist pig,' she spat. 'You say a woman should not be in combat, a woman cannot kill these poacher *cochon*. You need to spend less time with soldier boys and more time with real people, *Monsieur* Castle.'

Shane ignored the insults. His objections had come out wrongly. However, he was certainly dumb-founded to have come across an ardent environmentalist standing alongside a professional hunter with a gun in her hands. 'I meant no offence. But this whole day has, pardon my French, been one gigantic cluster-fuck.'

'On the contrary, I would say. We have two dead poachers, six men in captivity and only one casualty on the side of good,' Marie said, giving a slow, contemptuous nod towards his twisted ankle.

Shane ignored her jibe and said to Fletcher, 'The soldiers have caught all the bearers?'

Fletcher nodded. 'The carriers surrendered as soon

as they realised they were caught. I have to agree with Marie, Shane, it's been a good morning.'

Shane fished his cigarettes from his breast pocket. The pack was damp from his sweat. He lit one, which made him aware his hands were still shaking a little. 'We should question the prisoners – find out who's behind this. We need to start looking for the men buying the bush meat.'

Fletcher shrugged. 'It's out of our hands now, Shane. The military will look after that. As long as we nail anyone who trespasses on our patch, I'm happy.'

'And I am happy that there are three fewer armed men on the mountain,' Marie said, smiling up at Fletcher.

'Don't be such a baby,' Michelle chided. Shane winced as she wrapped the crepe bandage around his ankle. He smelled soapy and clean, a vast improvement on the odorous, stubbled, camouflage-painted creature who had hobbled in from the jungle an hour earlier.

'You do know what you're doing, right?' he asked, drawing on a cigarette.

'Um, nurse, the bone saw, please.'

'Very funny.'

'It wasn't very funny this morning,' she said, her tone serious. Michelle had woken to a flurry of activity, with Fletcher striding back and forth from his tent to Shane's, where Wise and Caesar took turns manning the radio in between loading their packs with ammunition and cleaning their rifles.

Michelle had overheard only snippets of the conversations, but it seemed that Shane and his men had stumbled on some poachers, and the army, along with Fletcher and Shane's guys, were going out to round them up. She had felt alarmed, not at the thought that she would be left in camp alone, but that Fletcher and Shane would both be facing danger.

Her thoughts led her to Marie Delacroix, who had accompanied Fletcher on the anti-poaching mission. Fletcher had called Marie on her satellite telephone very early in the morning, though Michelle had been unable to hear the conversation. He had wandered a little way into the trees when he had noticed her watching him.

After the conversation, Fletcher had told Wise that he was going out to pick someone up, and had taken a portable radio with him. Michelle had guessed that Fletcher was going to fetch Colonel Gizenga or another army officer and she had been more than a little surprised when he had returned with the French environmentalist. There was no invitation from Fletcher for Michelle to accompany them. She guessed he had been worried for her safety and, while she had no desire to traipse off into the jungle in pursuit of armed criminals, she'd felt snubbed.

They seemed unlikely friends, Marie and Fletcher. Marie was at the far end of the spectrum when it came to animal rights, while Fletcher killed animals for a living. Yet they seemed to have hit it off. She felt a pang of jealousy.

'I was worried about you all this morning, especially

when I heard the gunfire, far off,' she said as she wound the last of the bandage around Shane's leg.

'Most of that was Gizenga's goons shooting up the forest.'

'Caesar told me you killed one of the poachers.' She looked up from his foot, into his eyes.

'Yep.'

She waited a few seconds, to no avail, for him to say something else. 'Just can't shut you up, can I? Do you want to talk about it?'

'Nope.'

'Might help.'

'Who says there's anything wrong?'

'How long has your hand been shaking like that?'

He looked at his hand and shrugged, then stared blankly at her.

'Don't you feel anything, Shane, about that man?'

He shrugged again.

'Is that it, is that what troubles you? The killing doesn't affect you?'

He looked down at his hand, dropped the cigarette, stubbed it out and then closed his fingers into a fist. The shaking stopped and she noticed the whites of his knuckles. 'You sound like an army shrink,' he said.

She gave him what she hoped was a sympathetic smile. 'If you don't want to talk to me, Shane, I'm sure Patrice would love to keep me company.'

Shane snorted. 'It was him or me, Michelle. Simple as that. The plan – the original plan, at least – was that we'd let the army round them up, arrest them.'

'Who changed the plan?'

318

'Just happened. Call it the fog of war.'

She shook her head at his unwillingness to say more. It worried her that he'd inadvertently described what they were doing as war. She thought it best to change the subject. 'Well, I can tell you, it was chaotic here, too, for a while.'

'How so?'

'You heard about the hunters, I suppose?'

'No. Tell me.'

She was surprised that Fletcher hadn't told him about the call on the satellite phone the previous afternoon. Fletcher had been contacted by two Texan oil men who had been visiting Kinshasa for talks with the Congolese government and, on the spur of the moment, had tried to arrange a hunting safari for the next morning. Fletcher had been over the moon and had started making preparations for Patrice to pick the men up from Goma. The arrangements had fallen through, however, when the men had phoned later to say their aircraft had been grounded for the day due to mechanical problems. Fletcher, Michelle told Shane, had been furious, but his temper had abated after Shane's message had come in about the poachers breaking camp. 'Then he was talking to Marie, and the next thing I knew he was bringing her back to camp.'

'It was confusing at my end too. The original plan was for me to hold in place until ten o'clock.'

'Just as well the hunters didn't arrive, or they would have been in the thick of your fire fight.'

'Yeah.' Shane reached for a fresh cigarette.

'What do you make of her?' Michelle asked.

'Sorry, who?' Shane looked as though his mind were elsewhere.

'Marie Delacroix.'

'Mad as a cut snake, as they'd say in Australia.'

Michelle chuckled. 'Seriously, don't you think it's weird that she would even give Fletcher the time of day, let alone go out on an anti-poaching sweep with him?'

Shane nodded. 'That's the connection. They've got one thing in common.'

'What?'

'They both hate poachers and want to see them dead.' Shane recounted the macabre scene of Marie posing for a photograph with her foot on the man she had killed.

'How did she act around . . . I mean, were she and Fletcher, you know . . . ? Oh, God, that all came out wrong.'

He smiled at her. 'Don't be silly, Michelle.'

'I'm not. It's just that —'

'You said it yourself. They're an odd pair, to say the least, completely mismatched. She's a ghoul – and she's not the first one I've seen. Some people get off on killing. She's bad news, and Fletcher's smart enough to see that. I'd say he's just keeping her on side. If he can show her he's just as into curbing poaching as he is hunting, then maybe she won't cause him any grief. You know, she could really put a spanner into the works on this concession if she wanted to.'

Michelle nodded. 'So you don't think they're . . . ?'

Shane smiled again, then fixed her with his dark

eyes. 'He's nuts about you, Michelle. You can see it in the way he looks at you.'

Michelle thought she caught a note of disappointment in the way he said that. 'You're all good now, soldier,' she said, fastening the bandage.

18

Michelle knelt at the base of the giant figtree and watched the chimpanzees through her binoculars. They were, quite simply, beautiful.

It was odd, she thought, to see chimps in the wild, three of them lolling about lazily in the branches of the neighbouring tree, two of them eating figs, the third dozing. Like most westerners, her only experience of man's closest living animal relative had been in a zoo and she'd remembered the captive apes chasing each other around, swinging from ropes, tapping on the glass of their enclosure, fighting with each other.

Here, however, these placid creatures had nothing to do but eat, sleep and live. There was no need for them to invent games to while away their boredom, or to fight with each other because of a lack of space to roam and forage. Of course, she knew they could be just as boisterous and violent in the wild, but today this lot seemed happy enough doing absolutely nothing.

She felt a hand on her shoulder and turned. Marie Delacroix smiled at her. 'Beautiful, yes?'

'Yes,' she said.

'There will be more chimps – unless the Congolese eventually butcher them all for bush meat – but we must keep moving if we are to find the gorillas.'

Michelle replaced the binoculars in the pouch on her belt and shouldered her day pack. Marie had set a stiff pace through the clinging swamps and pesky, snatching thorn thickets, and remained hard on Patrice's heels as the slopes steepened and they climbed closer into the heat of the sun. Michelle set off after Marie, wiping away the rivulets of sweat that stung her eyes. She glanced back to make sure Wise was still in sight. He grinned at her – more of a grimace, she thought. At least she wasn't the only one who needed more practice climbing jungle-covered mountains.

Shane was in Goma, at a mission hospital. While Michelle had done a pretty good job of cleaning him up after the brush with the poachers, a cut on his leg had become badly infected in the tropical conditions and he had started to develop a fever. Also, the doctor had wanted to X-ray his ankle. Fletcher had told her over the satellite phone of Shane's anger and frustration on learning he would have to stay overnight at the clinic. Marie had arrived at the hunting camp that morning, while Fletcher was still in town, with news from a contact in the Congolese Army that a troop of gorillas had been spotted in the Sarambwe Forest, on the Congo side of the border. With no gorillas still naturally occurring in the area, Marie had surmised the apes had strayed across from Uganda's Bwindi Impenetrable Forest National Park.

'We must catch up with them before they cross the border,' Marie said, not for the first time, as she glanced down at a map in a clear-plastic waterproof folder.

Michelle was keen for another gorilla sighting, though she found it amazing Marie could still be so excited, so driven to see the same creatures she had been studying for close to a decade. Dedication, Michelle thought, as she unhooked a barbed vine from her laddered khaki trousers. Perhaps it was more than that.

Patrice, who had reluctantly agreed to act as tracker and guide on the impromptu trek, slashed a creeper with his machete then stopped, the blade hanging by his side.

'What is it now?' Marie asked, the impatience plain in her voice.

Wise paused beside Michelle and wiped his brow with the back of his uniform sleeve.

'*Merde*,' Patrice said.

'Shit,' Michelle translated, for Wise.

'*Oui*, the gorilla is one of the few animals which shits in its own nest, as the English would say,' Marie explained. The four of them stood around the pile of leaves, twigs and grass, about a metre in diameter, which was liberally dosed with coils of excrement, not dissimilar to those that might be made by a human – a two hundred kilogram human.

'It stinks,' Wise said.

'What did you expect?' Marie replied, dropping to

a crouch. She picked up a lump and squeezed it in her hand. Michelle heard Wise snort beside her, but decided that looking at him might force her to break out in an involuntary laugh as well. One thing she had quickly learned was that gorillas were no joking matter for Marie Delacroix. 'Not far.'

'We should turn back, madam. It will take us three hours to get back,' Patrice said.

'No, we continue,' Marie said.

Michelle looked at Wise, who simply shrugged. Fletcher had insisted over the phone when Michelle told him of their plan that Wise accompany the trek, for security reasons. The unfenced border was crossed by poachers, rebels and refugees, as well as wayward primates. 'We can spare another hour, I'm sure, Patrice,' Michelle said.

The African glared at her, then turned back to the tangle of green tendrils. He raised his machete and hacked at the bush as though it were a living enemy.

They passed and, in Michelle's case, trod in another nest. More of the fouled beds indicated the troop was at least eight-strong. Michelle felt the adrenaline course through her veins when Patrice halted again, his head cocked as he held up a hand for silence. She heard it too, the two-part cough, like a smoker clearing his throat.

'There,' Marie whispered, pointing through a thinned-out bamboo thicket.

There was a grunt and the hollow *tom-tom* of the young male's fingers on his leathery chest as he caught sight of the humans, who crouched in unison. Michelle noticed Wise's fist tightening on the pistol

325

grip of his AK. 'It's okay,' she mouthed to him, remembering the panic of their first encounter with gorillas.

Michelle slowly parted the blades of long grass obscuring her vision and saw the black shapes take form in the shadows, not ten metres from where they knelt. The silverback turned and stared at her. Instinctively she lowered her eyes, not wanting to challenge him. When she glanced back up she saw the patriarch had reclined on his butt at the foot of a tree and was gnawing on a stick of green bamboo. She looked at Wise and then followed his eyes and he turned to the right. He pointed up into the branches of a young tree with the tip of his machete.

Michelle craned her head and saw the young gorilla, not much taller than a human five year old, staring back at her. She smiled and fished her camera from her pack.

'Gorillas are generally not climbers,' Marie whispered to her as they both watched the little one. 'They grow to be too bulky and heavy to be arboreal, but when they are young, like that little girl, they like to explore, as all children do. We must give her some space so that she does not feel cut off from the silverback and her mother, and vice versa.'

Slowly, Marie began to stand and take a few steps backwards. To their left the rest of the gorilla family was also rising, moving away from the humans who had interrupted their afternoon feeding and siesta time.

'Patrice,' Marie hissed. The guide ignored her and started walking towards the tree in which the young ape still clung, staring down now at the human who was approaching her. The gorilla started to climb down, but stopped as Patrice crept closer. She scampered back up to her original position.

'Idiot,' Marie said, shaking her head.

The silverback and his females and other children were all but out of sight now, the chief's huge bottom disappearing into the shadows, his indifference to the humans punctuated by a long, noisy fart. If they were worried about the youngster, neither the silverback nor his harem showed it. Michelle wondered if they had simply forgotten her. She'd heard of large families of humans inadvertently leaving a kid at a filling station on a family outing, so she had no reason to believe apes were any smarter than some human moms and dads.

Michelle heard the bite of a blade into wood echo across the hillside and turned back to where Patrice was. He hacked again at the trunk of the tree, whose diameter was no bigger than the circle her two hands would have formed with fingertips touching. A few more blows and the tree would fall.

'No!' Marie called, as loud as she dared. 'What are you doing, you imbecile?'

Patrice looked at the two women and grinned, pausing mid-stroke, droplets of sweat flying from his head and arm. 'You want to see these filthy apes, I will show you one. It will be good for your picture. Have your camera ready,' he said to Michelle.

She shoved the camera back in her pack in defiance. 'Enough, Patrice. Let it be.'

He laughed and struck the tree again, and again. The young gorilla's shriek only elicited another cackle from him. Wise scanned the trees where the other animals had just departed, his rifle held up at the ready now.

Marie stood and strode back up the path Patrice had covered. She had been using a walking stick during the trek, a cut-off sapling stripped of its bark. She raised it above her head and struck down, hard, across Patrice's back.

'Ow! *Merde!*' he cried as his final blow hit the gorilla's refuge tree. The slender trunk slit with a cracking noise and started to fall, slowly at first, then faster as the weight of the terrified, squealing gorilla played into gravity's hands.

Marie struck again, the second blow catching Patrice's arm as he raised it to shield himself. He took a step forward to escape the falling tree, putting himself in contact with Marie, who added her scream to the gorilla's as she fell backwards.

Leaves and vines flew through the air as the little primate leapt the last few metres into a shrub then, apparently unhurt, bolted off into the forest in hot pursuit of her family. Miraculously, the family had not returned to the scene of its missing member's calls. Patrice reached out and grabbed Marie's flailing walking stick, easily snatching it from her hand. Now he raised it over his head.

'No!' Michelle screamed. The distance between them was too far for her to travel before Patrice struck down. She looked around for Wise but he was nowhere in sight. Damn him! Had he run because he feared another silverback charge like their first encounter? 'Patrice!'

The African looked at her, the makeshift club still tightly gripped in his hand, and spat.

'*Cochon!*' Marie swore back at him. 'Drop that now!'

'A woman does not hit a man in this country.'

Patrice swung down, but before the walking stick could connect with Marie his hips were thrust forwards violently and his arms flicked back. He fell, face first, into the tangle of vines and grass beside Marie, who jumped to her feet.

Michelle saw Wise, standing over the prone Patrice, one foot pinioning the fallen man like a trapped bug. Wise's rifle was reversed in his hands and it was obvious to her now that he had snuck up behind the Congolese and slammed the butt of the weapon into the small of the man's back before he could hit Marie.

'Apologise to the doctor,' Wise said.

'Never.'

Wise bent and grabbed the dropped walking stick. He rammed its point down into the base of the back of Patrice's neck, where it met his spine. Patrice cried out in pain. 'I said, apologise.'

Marie spat on the ground, near Patrice's face. Wise leaned on the stick some more.

'*Désolé,*' he whispered.

'What?' Wise said coolly. 'Louder, man.'

'*Je suis désolé.*'

'On your feet. If you try anything on the way back, it will be a bullet instead of a stick.'

'That's enough, Wise. He's learned his lesson. Get up, Patrice,' said Michelle, taking charge. Marie and

329

the black man glowered at each other, while Wise kept his rifle at the ready. Marie's hand shot out and she slapped Patrice hard on the cheek. The African lurched towards her in retaliation but stopped at the metallic sound of Wise chambering a round in his AK 47. 'Enough!' Michelle repeated.

Marie glared at Patrice, unrepentant. 'If I ever catch you harming a gorilla I will kill you.' Her voice was calm now, an octave lower than usual. Full of menace.

'We must get moving,' Wise said.

Patrice, shamed by the two women, spat at Wise's feet.

Michelle moved to the centre of the three feuding people. 'Time out, everyone. Let's get back to camp. Patrice, lead the way, please.'

'So your *boy* can shoot me in the back?'

Michelle could see the muscles in Wise's face stand out as he clenched his jaw. He said nothing and, after a few more seconds of tense stand-off, Patrice retrieved his dropped machete and strode off back towards camp.

'Give him a few seconds' lead,' Michelle said to Wise. 'Let him cool off some.'

'*Oui*, and keep him away from me or I will kill him,' Marie said.

The return path was well marked so Michelle was happy to let Patrice storm ahead. Marie excused herself to go to the toilet on one side of the trek, so for a short time she and Wise were alone, out of earshot of the other two.

'Quite a day,' Michelle said.

Wise looked behind them, to make sure they were alone. 'Crazy.'

'Yes, he was, wasn't he?'

'I meant both of them. They are as bad as each other,' Wise said, slapping at a fly. 'That woman would have killed him. What he did was wrong, for the animal, but if she had a gun she would have shot Patrice. Just like she shot that poacher.'

'That was in self-defence,' Michelle said.

Wise looked at her as though he were about to say something, then he turned and walked away.

19

The boy had never seen people or stores the likes of which he encountered in the small town of Kasane in Botswana. It was paradise.

In Livingstone, Zambia, the nearest major settlement to the village where he had been born and might otherwise have died if his uncle had not agreed to take him hunting in Zimbabwe, there were many people and many stores, but they were not like this.

The supermarket, where he wandered the aisles, eyes wide, spoiled for choice by a million different types of food, was spotlessly clean and airconditioned. The air was almost too cold for him and he rubbed his arms as he selected chocolate bars, Coca-Cola and, best of all, a frozen ice cream. In Livingstone the shops were hot and dirty and the shoppers were thin and poor.

The people of Botswana were fat. Big, round-faced, healthy men, and beautiful women with swivelling hips and huge breasts that reminded him of American music video clips, which he had seen twice when he had stayed at his Uncle Leonard's place before the big adventure that had turned into a nightmare. His uncle had lived in a house of brick in Livingstone, which had once belonged to a *mzungu*. His uncle was so wealthy that he had satellite television which came from South Africa. But his uncle was a thin man, with a thin wife, and he was dead now.

He thought about home and his mother. Had she given up on him? Had she assumed that he was dead, like the others must surely be? His father had been terribly thin before he had died last year and it worried the boy that his last memory of his mother was of her coughing all the time. Her arms and legs were as skinny as sticks – just like his father's had been before he died. He missed his mother but he also dreaded going home. She would go on and on at him about going back to the school where the *mzungu* missionaries taught. He found reading hard – almost impossible, in fact – and he hated the way the other kids made fun of his slowness.

The boy left the chill of the Spar supermarket and let the heat of the day roll over him as he shovelled the chocolate bars and ice cream into his mouth and washed it all down with cold Coca-Cola. He would be a fat man one day, with a fat wife with huge breasts and a big round arse. Perhaps he would move to Botswana.

He ignored the stares of the Botswanans, who were not his people. He imagined that they might be jealous of the new running shoes on his feet, the Manchester United football shirt that smelled so fresh, and the LA Lakers baseball cap that he wore at a jaunty angle on his head. He had money in his pocket. But he still had the nightmares as well.

The boy had washed in the Chobe River after getting off the bus, and thrown away the rags he had lived in as soon as he had bought his new clothes from the Indian store in Kasane. As well as rotund Africans there were plenty of white tourists in Botswana. A man and a woman he walked past spoke like the man who had picked him up. He remembered the shock and humiliation of waking to find the German touching him, but he grinned with satisfaction as he recalled seeing him lying in the overturned car.

The boy knew he could not stay in Botswana. He had his temporary travel document in the pocket of his new baggy cargo pants. His money was almost gone, so he would have to go home to Zambia. He would look for the friends of his uncle and tell them what had happened, and they would give him an AK 47 and he would go back to Zimbabwe to hunt the elephant and the rhino again, and to kill the men who had killed his uncle.

He considered robbing one of the many tourists in Kasane, but decided it was not worth the risk. If he was caught by the police he would be sent to a Botswanan jail and he would never see his mother again or have the chance to avenge his uncle and the others. He walked past the shopping centre to the place where the minibus taxis were parked, and boarded one bound for Kazungula, a few kilometres up the road on the Zambezi River.

He left the bus with the other passengers and walked onto the ferry that plies the border crossing between Botswana and Zambia. His fellow travellers were all Zambian. He wasn't surprised as he couldn't guess what a big chubby Botswanan would want in Zambia. The others, eight men and two women, were poorly clothed. They eyed him enviously. No doubt some of them assumed he was a criminal, being so well dressed at such a young age. There was room on the ferry for one semitrailer and three cars. One of the smaller vehicles was a Toyota pick-up being driven by an old white man. The truck had the name of a Catholic charity on the side. The boy winced and pulled the peak of his cap down over his eyes as he sauntered past the man, whom he recognised.

'Daniel? Is that you under that fancy new hat? Glory be, but what have you been doing in Botswana?'

The boy pretended he hadn't heard, but the old man caught up with him and took his arm. The boy shrugged off the blotchy pink hand. He never wanted to be touched by a man again.

'Sorry, sorry, Daniel, but it's me, Father Timothy. At least say hello when I talk to you, boy.'

'Morning, Father, how are you,' Daniel mumbled as the rear ramp of the ferry was raised with the clanking of a chain. The ferry's diesel motor belched black smoke as its revs increased. They moved sluggishly out into the fast-flowing Zambezi.

'Daniel, you don't need to hide from me, you're not in trouble – even though we've missed you at school these past weeks.'

'Sorry, Father,' he said in a small voice. He wasn't really sorry at all, but he knew that priests always liked it when you apologised for your sins.

'Well, I won't ask again what you've been up to, or where you got the money to buy these nice new clothes, but I have to talk to you, my boy. Come, sit here with me.'

Daniel was reluctant to sit next to the priest. He thought again of the man in the car, but Father Timothy patted the metal bench that ran along the side of the ferry. Daniel felt trapped.

'I'm so sorry to have to tell you this, Daniel,' the priest began.

Daniel remembered the man visiting his mother, after they had buried his father, and her crying and praying the night after. His mother had told him that Father Timothy was a good man, and had pleaded with him to go back to school. He had ignored her. He didn't like the way the old man was looking into his eyes now. He looked down at the patterns on the metal deck of the ferry.

'It's your mother, Daniel. We tried to find you last week, but no one knew where you had gone. I'm so sorry, my boy, but she's gone to God.'

'She is dead?'

'I'm afraid so, son.'

His father. His uncle. The others in the bush. His mother. What had he done wrong to be left so alone in the world? The euphoria of walking through the supermarket, of strolling among the contented, well-fed people of Kasane, of planning his future life as a rich man, disappeared with those few words. He started to cry, and he didn't even flinch when Father Timothy wrapped an arm around his shoulders.

Timothy Ryan had ministered to drug addicts in his native Dublin, the victims of child sexual abuse in London, to murderers and rapists in a jail in Glasgow, and to victims of the AIDS plague in Zambia.

In his experience, for every lost soul who genuinely repented their sins, cleaned up their act, came back to the fold and embraced the word of the Lord, there were a dozen other failures or fakers who said what they thought he wanted to hear in order to get another free feed or a crack at the poor box after hours. He had become pretty good, if he were immodest enough to say so, at picking a liar.

He drove the Nissan in silence and glanced across again at Daniel. The boy had been vague about where he had found the money to buy his clothes, and that, to Timothy, was as good as a confession that he had thieved. It didn't surprise him that Daniel had turned to crime at a young age. His mother had been a good, hard-working woman who washed laundry for one of the *lani* lodges up the river, but his father had been a drunken bum more interested in blowing his wife's income on booze and prostitutes. The uncle, Leonard, whom Daniel revered in death, was well known amongst the local community as a poacher of note.

Yes, Daniel was cagey about his new duds, but there was no way he was lying about the rest of what had happened to him in Zimbabwe. If the man hadn't been already dead, Timothy would have king-hit

Daniel's uncle himself for taking the boy across the river on one of his poaching forays.

The easy thing, of course, would have been to do nothing, or to tell the police in Livingstone, which would be tantamount to the same thing. What would they care about the deaths of a few criminals in another country, save for the fact that their pay-offs might be a little light from now on? He could cross the border at Victoria Falls and tell the police in Zimbabwe, but he would likely get a similar response. Why would the cops over there waste their time investigating the shooting of men who had clearly, admittedly, been breaking the law in a country where the authorities had the right to shoot armed men on sight?

Timothy sighed as he turned off the new tar road linking Kazungula to Livingstone, onto the corrugated dirt track that led to the mission school and the orphanage. He hoped he had managed to talk Daniel out of arming himself or linking up with more criminals to cross back into Zimbabwe and avenge the deaths of the others. However, to save the boy from a continuing life of crime – and to see that justice was done – he couldn't take the easy option. Timothy Ryan would have to ignore the rule of law and dance with the very devil himself to get Daniel back on the straight and narrow.

Sister Margaret's beaming black face was at the window as soon as he pulled up, welcoming him and his truck-load of Botswanan fruit and vegetables. 'Hello, Father,' she said. 'And who's this with you? Young Daniel! Oh, praise be.'

After exchanging the minimal amount of pleasantries with the nun, Father Timothy said, 'Sister, did you by any chance keep the card of that lady journalist who visited us last month?'

20

Michelle chewed the inside of her lip as she
drove Fletcher's Landcruiser on the road
which had once been a flowing river of lava.
She ignored the spectacular views of the mountains to
her left and, for the time being, Wise, who was seated
beside her.

She was concerned that Fletcher was not taking
Patrice's insubordination seriously enough. She had
explained what had happened during the gorilla trek
on her return to camp the night before. 'Marie's a hot-
head and Patrice is too arrogant for his own good.
They must have just goaded each other on. It'll probably be the last time they ever go out together,' he had
said, brushing off her concerns.

In a sense, he was right, and that was what bothered her. Both Patrice and Marie had acted more than
a little crazy on the trek. She understood that Fletcher
needed Patrice's experience – no matter how difficult
a character he was – and that she, at least, would
probably come into contact with Marie on a regular

basis. Particularly if the wayward troop of Ugandan mountain gorillas stayed on the Congo side of the border. She had willingly agreed to Marie's plea that she keep close tabs on the primates, to help protect them from poachers and even Fletcher's organised hunting trips. No one, including Fletcher, wanted the endangered creatures caught in the crossfire. Fletcher had sent Patrice away from the camp on three days' leave as soon as they had returned.

Michelle swerved to avoid a timber scooter piled with fruit and honked her horn to scatter a scrawny hen and her chicks off the road. The kilometre peg on the verge told her they were close to Goma.

'Do you want to come to lunch with Shane and me after I pick him up from the hospital?' she asked Wise.

The Zimbabwean shook his head. 'No, I think I will go to a bar to . . . to perhaps meet some people.'

Michelle smiled. She knew exactly what Wise had in mind. He was a soldier who had been out in the bush for too long. She just hoped he played safe, but she didn't know him well enough to ask if he were carrying condoms. It wasn't the sort of thing men and women discussed in Africa, and that, she mused, was one of the root causes of the continent's biggest problem. She noticed how he looked out the window to hide his embarrassment. He was a good man, she thought, though he was not his normal chatty self – hadn't been, in fact, since the gunfight with the poachers in which Shane had been injured. 'Okay, here we are. Beautiful downtown Goma. I wonder if it looked any better before the earthquake.'

'You can drop me anywhere, Michelle.'

'There's a bar over there – how about that one?'

The hint of a smile broke through his brooding. 'As good as any.' They arranged to meet at the same spot at five pm – in four hours' time. 'Be careful around here,' Wise said as he closed the door.

It should have been her telling him that, she thought, as the young black man entered the shebeen. The Landcruiser practically rocked on its springs from the thumping beat of the music booming from the bar. She put the truck in gear and headed out of town towards Nngunga.

Part suburb, part squalid refugee camp, Nngunga was a temporary resettlement village which had been housing people displaced by the eruption of Mount Nyiragongo years earlier. It wasn't meant still to be functioning, but the rebuilding of the homes of Goma's poor would take money, will and materials. There seemed to be precious few of any of these.

Children clustered around a rusty water pump took turns at swinging on the handle to fill an assortment of odd-sized containers. They broke their work-play to wave at her and chase her truck down the black lava tracks between clusters of semipermanent dwellings. The original tents provided by the UN and other NGOs after the eruption were still standing in some places, their canvas mildewed and faded. Over the years, enterprising villagers had scrounged bits of wood, corrugated iron, plastic sheeting and cracked asbestos tiles which they had nailed and tied to frames erected on and around the emergency shelters.

Michelle had heard enough about Goma's original hospital – still in a state of disrepair since the eruption – to know she never wanted to see it. She'd heard of a single bloodstained wooden table used for birthing and operations in a room which looked more like a medieval torture chamber than a place of healing. At least in Nngunga the missionary doctors and nurses had a new tent and clean linen. She saw the Red Cross emblem next to a Catholic charity's logo on the sign and pulled over. She shooed away the horde of children following her as politely as she could.

Shane was sitting outside the clinic tent on an upturned packing crate, next to a young white woman wearing tan slacks and a white shirt, perched on a fold-out camp stool. Shane was smoking, emphasising some point with a stab of his cigarette in the air. The woman had an elfin look with big brown eyes and short brown hair. Her olive skin was blemish-free. She laughed at whatever Shane had just said. She was very pretty.

'Well, you look as though you'll live,' Michelle said as she navigated her way along a pathway flanked by discarded empty plastic water bottles.

Shane waved and the woman looked down at a nurse's watch pinned to the front of her shirt. '*Scusi*, Shane. I have to get back inside. I hope your leg is fine, but if it is not, you can always come back and see me. *Ciao*.' She smiled and excused herself from meeting Michelle with a wave, then walked back inside.

'Who's your friend?'

Shane stubbed his cigarette out on the ground

343

then transferred the butt to his pocket. 'Pretty, isn't she? Italian.'

'Did you get her phone number?'

Shane laughed and stood. 'She's taken. Do I detect a note of jealousy?'

Michelle laughed. Too loud, damn it. She felt her cheeks starting to colour. 'Where's her husband?'

Shane pointed skywards with a finger and Michelle was momentarily confused.

'She's a nun, Michelle.'

Now her laugh was genuine. 'Hungry?'

'You bet,' he said as they walked side by side to the Landcruiser. 'I figured the poor bastards I shared the tent with last night needed my slop more than I did.'

'Where do you want to go? Fletcher tells me the Hotel Karibu, out on the lake, is nice.'

'Haven't you had enough of Fletcher's Yank businessmen and Eurotrash?'

'Where do you propose, then?'

'Anna Maria – Sister Michael, once she takes her final vows – suggested a cafe in town. I've got the directions.'

Michelle started the Cruiser and turned back towards town. 'Final vows? You mean she's not a for-real nun yet? You still might have a chance.'

'Nah, she's too short for me.'

Michelle slammed on the brakes to avoid running into another Japanese four-wheel drive with the name of a well-known international charity emblazoned on the side. She leaned on the horn. Had Shane just been referring to her height? She was much taller than the nun.

344

'So, where is this place?'

'Next block, if the sister's as good with her directions as she is with a sponge bath.'

'Ewww. You're disgusting.' Michelle pulled over. 'We can walk from here.'

The backdrop of emerald hills and the resting volcano was very different from flat, dry Zimbabwe, but the sidewalk could have been in any African town. Michelle politely waved away the children pestering her for a ballpoint pen, smiled at the women in brightly printed traditional dress who sat patiently behind small pyramids of fresh fruit and vegetables, avoided a mangy dog and screwed her nose up at whiffy trees which obviously doubled as public conveniences after hours. Music blared from speakers and ghetto-blasters outside virtually every shop, bar and cafe. If it were this loud outside, it must be deafening indoors, she thought. There was rap and Hindi pop, African township music – Kwela, they called it in Zimbabwe – even some ancient Motown; but underneath it all was the beat, the thumping bass pulse of Africa. Her mind conjured a half-remembered line from an old safari movie – 'the drums, the drums, those damned drums'. The noise was life and in the millennia since man had first made music it had inspired him to dance, to love, to sing, to pray, to kill.

'There must be a government department somewhere in every African country with warehouses full of confiscated illegal treble knobs,' Shane said.

She smiled. 'So, where are we going?'

Shane pointed to a sign propped against a building

with cracked walls and a shattered front window. 'There. Tora Tina. That's the place.'

Outside the small cafe were metal tables and chairs and they were seated by an African waitress, whom Michelle addressed in French. 'What's on the menu?' Shane asked.

Michelle rattled off the short list and they settled for a plate each of beef and chicken brochettes. 'They're on skewers – like shish kebabs or satay,' she explained. 'What about a drink?'

'What do you recommend?' Shane asked the waitress.

'Me, I like Guinness,' she said in passable English.

'Long way from Ireland, but why not,' Shane said.

'With Coca-Cola?' the waitress asked, taking down the order on a notepad with a pencil barely an inch long.

'Coca-Cola on the side?' he asked.

'No, *monsieur*, we drink the Guinness mixed with the Coca-Cola.'

Michelle raised her eyebrows, but Shane just shrugged and said, 'Just when you think you've seen it all in Africa . . .'

The food was good and killed the conversation as they stared out over the colourful, noisy parade of Congo life from their vantage point above the street. The skewers of meat were served with French fries – *frites*, the waitress called them – and mayonnaise. 'A little piece of Belgian colonialism lives on,' Michelle said. After he had finished eating, Shane excused himself to find the bathroom.

'Your husband, he is very handsome,' the waitress

whispered to Michelle as she cleared the plates. 'Do you have many babies?'

Michelle laughed. 'No. I don't think he's the marrying kind.' Michelle wondered if she were. The girl looked confused until Michelle explained they were just friends.

'Where do you think you'll end up, Shane?' she asked when he returned.

'Six feet under like the rest of us, I suppose. Seriously? Here in Africa. Perhaps not in the DRC, but somewhere with red dirt, blue skies and as few people as possible. What about you? Presumably you'll go back to Canada one day.'

She had no idea. 'It gets in your blood, this continent, doesn't it.'

'I was born here, remember. Australia was a nice place to kill some time, but I think I always knew I'd come back one day. How long can you keep living out of a tent, following animals around and recording what they eat and shit?'

She laughed. 'Probably as long as you can live hunting human beings.'

'If that's the best you've got, then you'll be on your way back to Canada in a year, maybe eighteen months.'

'Is that as long as you're going to stay with Fletcher?'

'Truth is, I don't exactly know what I'm going to do when I've made enough money to buy my own place. What I mean is, I don't know what I *can* do. Soldiering's the only trade I know.' He finished the last of his black-coloured drink and grimaced.

'You could become a professional hunter – of animals.'

He shook his head. 'Not for me.'

'So, you're happy to hunt and kill people, but not, say, a wildebeest.'

'No wildebeest ever tried to kill me.'

'You could farm,' she suggested.

He gave a derisive snort. 'In case you haven't noticed, the Government of Zimbabwe has put in place certain disincentives for white farmers. Same thing's coming in South Africa and Namibia – by more peaceful means, perhaps, but buying a farm in Africa's like leaving your truck in the main street of Goma with the doors unlocked and the engine running. It might be there tomorrow, but you wouldn't want to bet on it.'

'You could run a safari lodge . . . and prey on all those rich women who come down with khaki fever.'

He looked as though he were considering it, nodding sagely. 'Too many jealous husbands. Bad for tips if you steal from your clients.'

'So what do you want to do? Just buy a piece of land and sit on your ass like a hermit?'

He leaned back in his chair and stretched his arms out. 'Well, since you put it that way . . . yeah.'

'Might be lonely?'

'Depends.'

'On what?'

'On how many endangered animals I've got roaming my plot of land.'

'I don't follow.'

'Well,' he said, leaning forward, resting his elbows

on the table so he was closer to her, 'the more threatened species I have, the more keen, unattached,
wide-eyed postgraduate students I can get to stay in
my purpose-built research camp.'

'Aha. A cunning plan. What makes you think these
impressionable – and presumably overwhelmingly
female – researchers would pick you?'

He sat back again and said, 'You tell me.'

She wadded a serviette from the table and threw it
at him. 'You do Coca-Cola and booze – no self-
respecting girl's going to come and camp with you.'

'That's what I'm counting on. I only want the bad
ones.'

She laughed again. He was the only person she did
that with these days. 'Come on, let's go to a bar.'

'Now you're talking.'

'Don't get any ideas. I told Wise we'd pick him up
about now. There might be time for you to have a
lemonade.'

After Wise had waved goodbye to Michelle, he
entered the bar, letting the familiar, welcome shebeen
fug overwhelm his senses. The beat from the boom
box reverberated through his chest, the deep bass
connecting with his own frayed nerve endings. The
smells weren't pleasant, but they were, in their odd
way, comforting reminders of the bars he hung out in
back in Bulawayo. Beer. Urine. Vomit. Sweat. Perfume.
He had a lot on his mind. He was looking forward to
talking to Shane about what troubled him, but, for
now, alcohol would help allay his concerns.

'Primus,' he said, pronouncing the last three letters as 'moose'. It was as close as he got to a French accent beyond the clumsy '*Bonjour, mademoiselle,*' he offered to the big-hipped maiden standing next to him, paying for a Guinness. She smiled at him and said something he didn't understand. It didn't sound angry, and she punctuated the foreign phrase with a wink.

Bloodshot eyes followed his movements as he gestured for the girl to join him behind a rickety tin-topped table set in front of a long wooden bench. Wise glared back at the three Congolese men sitting at a table in the corner, the darkest part of the bar. He drained most of the bottle of beer in his first two swigs. He wanted release. The beer might help him get it, but the woman would guarantee it. She wore a stretchy pink top with only one sleeve, which gave a tantalising view of her deep cleavage and smooth mahogany skin. He guessed she was part white – maybe the daughter or granddaughter of some long-gone colonialist. He preferred his women as dark as himself, but he wasn't a racist. He smiled at his own joke and the girl, taking it as a compliment, ran her tongue around her full lips.

Wise had wanted to talk to Shane sooner, but there hadn't been the right time. Shane had gone to the hospital and the mad French doctor's run-in with Patrice had robbed him of a chance for a quiet moment with Michelle on the gorilla trek. On the journey from the hunting camp down to Goma, he'd had doubts about the worth of saying anything at all. Michelle obviously liked the French scientist, despite her crazy outbursts, so it would have been hard for him to voice his concerns. He needed to talk to a man, as only a brother would understand talk of the madness of women and not take it the wrong way. He'd tried broaching his concerns with Mr Reynolds, but the boss had rebuffed him.

He drained his beer and burped, then pulled out his wallet and withdrew some notes. He passed the money to the woman across the tabletop, which was slick with condensation and spilt beer. He nodded to his empty and her half-finished drink, then to the bar. She frowned, but snatched up the money and swayed her way to the counter. Wise watched her arse as she walked and felt the pump of blood to his loins.

He thought about Shane while he waited for the girl to pay for the drinks. Shane was a warrior who had fought and killed in many places around the world, and Wise admired him for his skill with the rifle, and his discipline and craft in the bush. Wise had never known a better life. His time on anti-poaching patrols had been better paid, more exciting and more fun than his army service. He had hated the Congo as a soldier, but now, with money in his pocket and food and beer in his belly, he could savour the experience of living in a different country. He patted his jeans pocket to make sure the condoms were there.

The one problem with Shane, Wise mused as he nodded a curt thanks to the girl and pushed the change back across the table to her, was that he was growing tired of the killing. He had seen it in Shane's eyes. The deadness there. Wise had come into contact with killers in the army. There were three kinds, he reckoned. First were the wild-eyed crazy ones, who were fascinated, obsessed, with the blood and gore. These were the ones who bragged about body counts and mutilated their vanquished foes. Second were the humane men, the ones who did what they had to do, but were racked by guilt afterwards. These were the ones who cried at night in their tents or, in extreme cases, ended their own lives rather than live with the reality of what they had done. Third were the ones like Shane. They killed because it was a job, and experienced as much joy or horror as a woodcutter might experience felling a tree, or a farmer would feel driving his tractor.

Shane would either grow bored with killing and retire from it or, and Wise feared this might be more likely, one day the dam of human emotions he kept inside him might break, letting out a flood of grief and shame and horror that could drown a man from within. A woman would help him. It was plain to Wise and Caesar, for they had discussed it several times, that Shane wanted Michelle. Wise was of the view that a man should take what he wanted, when he wanted, but Caesar had pointed out that such a course of action might cost them all their jobs. Caesar was smart, but he spent too much time with his head in a book or writing to his girlfriend.

The girl arched a plucked eyebrow and did that thing with her tongue on her lips again. Another man entered the shebeen and mumbled some foreign words of greeting to the trio in the corner. He looked about and, for a second, locked eyes with the girl. She nodded back to him. Wise assumed the man was either another of the prostitute's customers or her pimp. Well, he would just have to wait his turn. The man turned and left the bar.

Wise grinned. If Shane didn't realise the benefit of hot, wet flesh, that was too bad for him. The afternoon dragged on at a leisurely pace. As the beer relaxed him, Wise took to the middle of the bare concrete floor to dance to a couple of numbers with the woman, his hands beginning the inevitable process of exploration as she gyrated against him. When he had finished his fifth beer, she stood in silence and held out a hand. Wise needed no further encouragement. He rose and let her lead him out a rear door and into a small courtyard which smelled even stronger than the shebeen.

'Antoinette,' the girl said, pointing to her ample bosom with her free hand.

'Wise,' he said, and she smiled and nodded.

'Come.'

She led him across the courtyard to one of a half-dozen identical doors set in a long rendered building with a rusty tin roof. He felt the sweat spring from his pores as they entered. The girl stood next to a timber bed with a thin foam mattress and pulled the one-sleeved blouse over her head. She was young – maybe not yet twenty – though she had the cold eyes of her trade, a look that would stay with her until she died. Oddly, and a little embarrassingly, the eyes reminded him of Shane's. He banished the thought as he watched her unzip and slip out of her skirt.

Wise heard footsteps in the courtyard and turned.

'*Ici*,' the girl said. He looked back and saw she had lifted one plump breast in her hand and, head bent, was teasing the erect nipple with the tip of her tongue.

Suddenly the door flew open and banged against the wall with enough force to shake loose a chunk of plaster. Wise saw the girl dive for the bed and knew instantly, through his beery fog, he had been set up. He had been right to be suspicious of the movements outside, and wrong to be tempted by more alcohol and the girl's body. As he pivoted on the ball of his left foot he raised his left arm to his face to protect him from whatever was coming and reached around to the small of his back with his right hand.

The man who had briefly entered and then left the shebeen earlier in the afternoon charged through the doorway, a panga held above his head. He slashed down and there was nothing Wise could do to stop the blade slicing into the flesh of his arm. The man whooped at the spurt of bright blood and drew back for another chop.

The nine millimetre Browning self-loading pistol tucked in the rear of the waistband of his jeans was cocked and loaded. After chambering a round before leaving the camp, Wise had carefully eased the hammer forward. The pistol had a single-action mechanism which meant he had to pull back the hammer again with his thumb in order to fire it. Under Shane's expert instruction he had practised the action until he could do it safely and quickly. Safe for the firer, not the target.

His first shot smashed through the man's sternum, slowing his forward momentum enough for Wise to sidestep the second sweep of the panga. A smaller man would have been knocked onto his back, but this bald-headed giant merely lurched back, like a drunkard, eyes wide as he stared down at the hole and spreading crimson stain on his white T-shirt. Wise fired again, the second bullet tearing through the man's throat, and this time he fell.

The prostitute screamed like a wounded animal, jumped off the bed and ran past him, to kneel beside the mortally wounded attacker, her hands caressing his face. Wise grabbed her arm and tried to drag her off him, to question her, but she turned on him, aiming long blood-red fingernails at his face. He warded off her first attack, smearing her hand with the blood from his arm. He winced in pain, his body only now registering the fact that he had been wounded. He grabbed a handful of the woman's hair and forced her to her knees, the pistol pointed at her head.

'Police!' he yelled at the top of his voice. '*Gendarme!*' he tried. He wondered how long it would take for the cops to respond to the sound of gunfire. Would they come at all? Goma had a justified reputation as a semi-lawless 'cowboy' town. Perhaps the smart policemen stayed inside their station when the shooting started.

'Wise!' a voice called from outside.

Wise kept a handful of the woman's braided hair and drew her to her feet again. With his back to the wall, he edged close to the open doorway. He peered around the doorframe into the courtyard.

'Thank God,' he said.

*

'Stay in the truck,' Shane ordered Michelle when they heard the gunshots. 'Reverse back up the road a hundred metres and wait for me there.' He opened the glove compartment. 'Shit, where's the nine-mill?'

'The pistol? Wise took it.'

'Fuck,' Shane said. He had given his own sidearm to Fletcher after being dropped off at the hospital. He'd reasoned he wouldn't need it overnight, and securing it might be a problem. Now he was unarmed. He left the truck anyway, ignoring Michelle's half-uttered warning. 'Reverse up the road, now!' he ordered her.

People had scattered from the sidewalk on either side of the shebeen and peered from behind parked cars and trucks and through neighbouring shop windows. He moved towards the bar's front door, sidling along the exterior wall. He risked a quick glance inside.

'Wise!' he yelled. 'Are you in there?'

He looked again and saw through the gloomy interior to a courtyard beyond. The open back and front doors created a draught and he smelled cordite above the usual malodorous signatures of an African watering hole. He took a deep breath and sprinted inside, pausing at a crouch bedside the bare brickwork below the wooden bar counter. He peeked around it and through the back door. No one in sight.

'Wise!'

He waited for an answer, and every second confirmed his fears. Outside he heard a siren. Now the police were nearly here, the smart thing would be to wait.

'Shane, Sha . . .'

He was on his feet, running. The voice was weak, racked with pain. He saw the row of doors, one wide open, and the black pockmarks of bullets through the single layer of rendered mud brick. There were at least twenty holes, maybe more. To punch through a wall it had to have been an AK 47. By the pattern it had been close to a full magazine, sprayed on automatic.

Inside, the brothel's room looked like an abattoir. Blood spattered the off-white, fly-specked walls. As his eyes grew accustomed to the gloom he saw three prone bodies – Wise, a near-naked woman and a bald-headed African with bullet wounds to his chest and throat. A panga lay next to the dead man's body. The woman stared at the ceiling, her eyes wide and lifeless. Wise lay on his side. He blinked when he saw Shane, then coughed. A spray of blood painted the bare concrete floor, adding to the swelling puddle.

'Jesus.' He kneeled and rolled Wise onto his back. There were four entry wounds that he could see, stitched in a line across his friend's chest, frothy blood bubbling out with every tortured wheeze. 'Wise, hang on, man.'

Wise blinked. 'Shane . . .'

'I'm here, mate. I'm here.' Shane whipped his T-shirt off and pressed it down hard on the wounds. 'You've got to hang on, Wise. Who did this to you?'

Wise moaned and blinked his eyes a few times. He focused on Shane as the other man fought to stem the bleeding and said, 'Marie . . . doctor . . .'

'What? *She* killed you?'

'N-no . . . Told him . . .'

'Told *who*, Wise?'

Wise blinked, then screwed his eyes closed tight with pain or frustration. Shane felt the first tremors beneath his hands as he pressed down on the wounds. Voices speaking French filled the courtyard as Wise opened his lips to speak again, the effort sending more spasms through his body. 'Hunts . . .'

'For fuck's sake, shut up!' Shane yelled out the doorway. He lowered his head to Wise's lips. 'Hunts what, mate?'

Wise's lips touched his ear in a macabre, tortured kiss as his head began to bob up and down and the shakes passed through his body. 'No!' Shane shouted. He had seen this too many times before. The room was filled with Africans in uniform and they stood, useless, with pistols drawn and assault rifles at the ready. He registered Michelle's pale face peering over the heads of the police and soldiers, her mouth agape in horror.

They could do nothing but watch as Wise died.

21

The city of Bulawayo, like the rest of Zimbabwe, was down on its luck, but driving down its wide, dusty, jacaranda-lined boulevards, Michelle almost felt as though she were coming home.

'I never thought Zimbabwe would seem like a haven.'

'You read my mind,' Michelle said over her shoulder to Shane, who was on the rear seat of Dougal's twin-cab *bakkie*. Michelle sat beside the pilot, who had collected them from Joshua Nkomo airport in his truck.

'Fletcher and Caesar couldn't make it?' Dougal asked.

'Fletcher's got a party of German hunters in camp. He couldn't leave them alone. Caesar's fighting off a bout of malaria, so I made him stay behind.'

'Shame,' said Dougal. Michelle shook her head. The one-word commiseration was a common term in southern Africa, which could be applied to everything from a broken fingernail to the death of a loved one.

Michelle looked back and saw Shane was staring silently out of the tinted window at the passing streetscape. She remained worried about him.

The sight of Shane standing and walking from that terrible room of death, bare-chested and spattered with Wise's blood, wiping his hands on his jeans, came back to her. More than the gore, it was the blankness of his eyes that lingered in her memory. He had walked past her and the jabbering policemen, who finally fanned out into a fruitless search for the killer.

She had found him out in the street, sitting in the gutter dragging on a cigarette, ignoring the cluster of onlookers.

'Shane. I'm so sorry. He was such a great guy,' she said, sitting beside him, tears rolling down her cheeks.

He stared straight ahead, exhaled, and flicked the half-smoked cigarette onto the roadway. 'He knew the risks.'

She was shocked, and rounded on him. 'How can you . . . how can you be so cold? He was your friend, Shane, and he just died in your fucking arms!'

He stood and said, 'There'll be things to arrange. Transport, death certificate, the funeral.' He walked towards the Landcruiser, not stopping to look back at her.

She stood in the steaming heat rising from the black volcanic roadway and screamed at him, 'Wise is dead, goddamn it! Can't you grieve for him?' Shane ignored her, climbed into the truck and started the engine. He sat in silence behind the wheel, staring out through the windscreen at the pyramidal green bulk of Mount Nyiragongo, which smoked ominously, like a crematorium chimney.

Her anger at Shane's apparent coldness had cooled by the time they returned to the hunting camp. She retired to her tent, leaving Shane, Fletcher and Caesar to toast their departed comrade in a macho-bullshit drinking session around the campfire. Fletcher, she noticed, had been similarly unemotional while talking to Shane about the loss of one of his employees. She knew soldiers had to get used to death, but this was unhealthy. At least Caesar, shivering through the onset of his returning malaria, had shed tears for his friend.

Fletcher had come to her tent later, reeking of beer, but she had feigned sleep and he had left her alone. True rest had eluded her for most of that night as her mind replayed the images and sounds of the day.

Dougal drove through Bulawayo to the cemetery on the Main Street extension. Like every other in sub-Saharan Africa, it was overcrowded and busy.

'They've opened up a new plot here in the old cemetery,' Dougal explained as he slowly navigated the narrow road between rows of headstones that looked to be at least a hundred years old. 'The new graveyard outside of town is about full, so the municipality's been trying to find more space between the old graves.'

They were going to lay Wise to rest amidst a jumble of fresh earthen mounds in what had once been a car park. Red mud clung to Michelle's shoes and cellophane from withered bouquets of flowers fluttered by in the strong, hot breeze. Dark clouds masked the sun's glare and promised seasonal rain that afternoon. Michelle saw wilted photos of young Africans cut down in their prime pinned to rough-hewn wooden crosses. She averted her eyes from a tiny mound on which someone had placed a pink teddy bear. A lump came to her throat. Wise deserved better than a pauper's grave amidst the victims of the AIDS plague. She hoped the boy's family would use some of the compensation money Shane had taken with him from Fletcher to erect a proper headstone one day. The easiest thing would have been to bury Wise in the DRC, but Fletcher had discounted that option from the outset, offering to pay to ship the casket back to the young man's home town. Shane had decided to accompany the body. It was how it was done in the army, Shane had said – when a man was killed he was escorted home by a comrade.

Michelle had deliberated about staying with Fletcher or returning to Zimbabwe for the funeral. Fletcher would be busy with his German clients, so she wouldn't have any more time than usual to spend with him. She hadn't been close to Wise – not as Shane had been – but she had liked the young African and had been near him when he died. On that basis alone she thought she should attend his funeral.

Then there was Shane. Although it should have been none of her business, the way he had acted since Wise's death worried her. The hard man facade didn't fool her. She reckoned he was hurting very badly and she wanted to help him, to comfort him. The realisation struck her there and then, in the cemetery. She cared about him.

The graveside service was brief. Michelle and Shane stood behind Wise's sobbing mother and stoic father. Shane had told her the old man was a bus driver, and Wise's mother a seamstress. Shane smiled and gently nudged Michelle in the ribs at the sight of the six attractive young girls on the opposite side of the open grave, who shot each other dagger-like glances every now and then. She guessed they were all Wise's girlfriends, though it seemed none knew of the existence of the others. She'd gathered that was Wise's style. Shane had told her on the flight from the Congo that he and Caesar had found a gross of condoms in Wise's kitbag. It was so unfair, Michelle thought. He'd been a strong, fit young man who excelled at his job which, despite some of her misgivings, was about protecting something precious. As the mourners moved forward to pay their last respects, Shane pulled a cloth badge from his pocket.

'What's that?' Michelle asked.

'It's a set of my old SAS parachute wings. Wise made a jump into combat and did a fine job.' He tossed them on top of the coffin, took a step back and stood briefly to attention.

'He was so proud of the work he did and he admired you greatly.'

Shane and Michelle both turned to face the voice and saw Wise's father standing beside them. 'I'm sorry for your loss, sir,' Shane said.

'Death is an all too common occurrence these days, Mister Castle,' the grey-haired man said, gesturing

363

around them. 'We thanked God when Wise returned safe from the fighting in the Congo. I tried to stop him working for you, you know.'

Shane nodded.

'But when we saw him, on leave,' the father continued, 'we noticed how he had matured, how he had become more responsible, how proud he was to serve with you. We knew he had made the right decision. Did he die quickly, Mister Castle?'

'He did. There was no pain.'

Michelle watched how easily Shane delivered the lie. Cold eyes. Unflinching nerve. A chill went down her back, even though she knew he was only trying to be kind.

'Will the police catch my son's killer?'

'That man should hope the police find him before I do,' Shane said.

Michelle could see it was no empty threat.

'I am a religious man, Mister Castle, and I believe one should turn the other cheek . . . but I am pleased you have told me this.'

Shane pulled an envelope from his shirt pocket and handed it to Wise's father. 'Nothing can compensate for the loss of a son, sir, but this is from Mister Reynolds.'

Wise's father put the envelope in the inside pocket of his threadbare black suit without opening it. 'He has a sister, studying at university in South Africa. She could not make it back in time for the funeral, but this money will go towards her studies.'

Michelle offered a few words of sympathy to Wise's mother and they hugged. The family slowly departed and the girlfriends sashayed past the grave, until only Shane and Michelle were left. As he stared at the cheap coffin at the bottom of the hole, she reached out and took his hand and he squeezed hers. She thought she felt a pulse through the grip, which was so firm it was close to hurting. 'It's a dangerous business you're in, Shane. Wise knew that.'

He nodded.

'Is it worth it?'

'I don't have a choice. This was where I was born, Michelle. No matter how violent, how bad it gets, I couldn't live anywhere else again.'

'I think I know what you mean. I'm not looking forward to going back to Canada. Where are you going now, straight back to Goma?'

'No. Being here at the funeral reminded me of some unfinished business I have to see to. I want to look in on Charles Ndlovu's widow, at Vic Falls.'

'Won't that just be opening an old wound?' she asked.

He looked away from her, back down at the coffin, then at the gravediggers, who hovered nearby, shovels in hand. 'I owe it to Charles. His family weren't responsible for what he did, and he was a good man.'

Fletcher had arranged for Dougal to fly Michelle to Isilwane Lodge and offered her the use of a Land Rover if she wanted to drive down to Main Camp in Hwange National Park to see how Matthew Towns' wild dog research was progressing.

Dougal drove her and Shane from the cemetery

back into the centre of Bulawayo and stopped outside a cafe, across from the old whitewashed colonial-era town hall. 'I've got to pick up a few things for the lodge on Fletcher's behalf at Haddon and Sly. Can I trust you two kids to say safe for half an hour while I'm queuing for meat and bread?'

They waved goodbye and Shane nodded a greeting to a green-uniformed security guard who stood outside the coffee shop, wooden baton in hand. 'Must be to keep out the party animals,' Michelle said.

Shane ignored her remark and followed the security guard's line of sight. Since his time in Iraq it was second nature to him, particularly being back in an urban area, to size up possible threats. He saw the gang of five scrawny teenagers in grubby clothes, across the road, loitering outside the iron-railing fence surrounding the municipal offices car park. Shane looked up and down their side of the street and saw no sign of trouble. The security guard obviously did a reasonable job of controlling his patch.

Inside the cafe was a world away from the struggling parade of humanity and crumbling public edifices beyond the wide plate-glass window. With its polished timber floors and liberal use of zinc-coated corrugated iron for decoration, the eatery wouldn't have been out of place in London, New York or Sydney.

The white maître d, with her platinum hair and French tips, blended into her surroundings as easily as a chameleon. Her style matched the decor and, as it turned out, the menu – chic, cool and expensive. A black African waiter showed them to their table. His bow tie looked as though it were strangling him, but he managed a broad smile and a friendly welcome that might have made him fifteen per cent in Manhattan. Shane wondered what tips were like in twenty-first century Zimbabwe. Not good, he reckoned.

Shane looked out at the streetscape and was transported back to Africa. A boy of eight or nine led a middle-aged blind man – perhaps his father – through the throng of lunchtime shoppers. Maybe one in twenty dropped a crumpled note in the boy's tin mug. People had long since given up using coins as currency in Zim. A two dollar coin, which in Shane's lifetime had been the equivalent of two greenbacks, was now worth less than a washer. Enterprising metal workers were picking up coins, drilling their centres out and using them for that exact purpose.

Unlike what he would have seen in the days of his childhood, there were very few white faces in the crowd outside. Zimbabwe's Europeans had always been in the minority, but their numbers had plummeted dramatically in the wake of the seizures of white farms in the first years of the new millennium. Those who were left were either diehards who had enough money to support themselves and cling to their principles, or those who simply couldn't afford to leave and start anew in another country. Many of the latter were elderly people living hand to mouth on government pensions which couldn't hope to keep pace with inflation. Stories of old white people killing themselves rather than seeking or accepting charity were, sadly, not urban myths. A grey-haired man in elastic-waisted shorts, carpet slippers and a patched off-white shirt shuffled past the window.

Life was just as tough for the average African, particularly those who supported the opposition party, but at least the blacks could usually count on the support of their extended family. If the old *murungu* aimlessly wandering the street had kids or grandkids, they were probably living in Perth or Shepherd's Bush or Ontario. If he was lucky they might be wiring him cash.

Shane turned his attention to the patrons of the cafe. As with the outdoors, there were more black faces than white, but the Africans were well fed. The men wore Armani and their women's hairdos were bigger than their backsides. Poorer women and their men, who had never seen a fashion magazine, favoured the reverse proportions. The whites were split between those who were still doing well – perhaps smart currency traders or import merchants making a fast buck on the country's inability to manufacture virtually anything these days – or the dispossessed former gentry squandering a few thousand Zimbabwe dollars on a weekly luxury of coffee and raisin toast.

'You don't like it here, do you?' Michelle asked.

He looked across at her and shrugged.

'Is it being in a city, or the people?'

'A bit of both, I suppose.' There was something else bothering him, too. Someone else. He couldn't look into those green eyes for too long without losing his concentration. He watched an Indian man chase a small boy in rags out of the fruit and veg store a couple of doors down. The boy weaved expertly through the honking traffic, two bananas clutched to his chest. The cafe security guard looked on with a pronounced lack of interest. Seemed the Indian wasn't one of his customers.

'Shane, who do you think killed Wise?'

'Could have been anyone. A friend of the guy who tried to roll him, the prostitute's pimp, maybe just a thief.'

'You don't sound convinced.'

'I'm not,' he said, sipping his coffee. 'But we'll probably never know.'

'You're holding something back.'

True, he thought. It was a physical sensation, not just an emotion. He had trouble breathing when she looked into his eyes, as though there were a hand around his lungs, restricting them. His stomach felt fluttery. It was a half-remembered sensation from his teens. First girlfriend, first kiss. Childish. Stupid. Incredible.

'You know he had a fight with Patrice.'

He nodded, pleased at the chance to say something half meaningful, rather than just stare at her. 'Yeah. Fletcher told me after Marie told him. Sounded like that prick Patrice was ready to have a go at her when you were on your gorilla trek.'

Michelle licked coffee froth from her lips. Shane looked out to the street again. 'Well,' she said, 'both Marie and Patrice were acting kind of crazy. Wise was just trying to keep a lid on things, and he did a good job. I don't think Patrice is mad enough to try to kill Marie but . . .'

'Wise might have been an easier target. You're a good mind-reader, Michelle.'

'I can't read your mind, Shane Castle.'

And of that, he was grateful, because when she smiled, exposing those perfect, even teeth, he experienced the shortness of breath again, damn it. There was no way around the fact that she belonged to another man, and that man was his boss. It was against his personal code and everything he'd learned and practised as a soldier to cut another guy out like that – although it did happen often enough, even in the regiment. SAS men attracted beautiful women but, like the proverbial moths, those women soon found there was a host of ways to get burned hanging out with fiercely competitive guys who spent most of the year away from home either trying or learning to kill other men. As well as not wanting to alienate his own source of income, he reckoned that if the impossible were to happen – if he tried to explain his feelings to Michelle and she reciprocated – then she would be out of a job as well. He'd joked about running a game reserve and accommodating researchers, but that was all it was – a joke. He might have enough for a plot of land somewhere, but he was a long way off being able to support a woman too. The teenager inside him wanted to grab her hand and tell her how he felt around her, but the army officer told him to stop acting like an idiot and get his mind back on his job.

He wasn't sure about Patrice. He'd raised his concerns with Fletcher, but been told the guide had a rock-solid alibi. Apparently he was home in his village while Wise was in Goma. Shane didn't share his boss's faith in Patrice's integrity – or that of his wife who had sworn her man was home. He hoped Caesar had the good sense to stay out of the guy's way while they were away.

'Time for another proper caffeine fix before we head back to the bush?' Michelle asked, breaking into his thoughts.

'Certainly.' Despite the pain and discomfort, he wanted this time alone with her to last forever.

When Dougal returned to collect them, they arranged that Shane, as well as Michelle, would travel in the Cessna to Isilwane. From there, Shane would borrow a vehicle and make the short drive to Victoria Falls to see Charles's widow, while Michelle drove down to Main Camp.

On board the cramped little aircraft, Shane reminisced about his first flight to Isilwane as they cleared the hills that marked the border of the national park at the start of the Matetsi Safari Area. Dougal buzzed a herd of sable antelope to clear them from the airstrip and put the Cessna down with hardly a bump.

Lloyd was there to meet them. 'How is the Congo?'

'Don't ask,' Shane replied.

'There was a woman here yesterday, looking for the boss,' Lloyd said.

'Really?' Michelle said.

'She is a journalist, from the television. I telephoned Mister Reynolds on the satellite phone and told him.'

'What did she want?' Shane loaded the last of their bags into the back of the old Series III Land Rover pick-up.

'She wanted to know how many clients we had in the last few months of the season, and where they were from. She also asked me about the anti-poaching patrols and how many men had been killed. But I told her nothing.'

'Good work,' Shane said, clapping Lloyd on the arm. One thing his time in the army had taught him was that journalists were bad news.

'Fletcher's never shied away from publicity in the past,' Michelle observed. 'Do you know where she went, Lloyd?'

'To Main Camp. She said she had heard that Mister Reynolds sponsored the wild dog research and she wanted to film the work there.'

'Uh-oh,' Michelle said, pulling a face. 'I'd better call Matthew and find out what's going on.'

'It's probably nothing. You know how these reporters are – if they're short of a story they just go back and rehash something that's been done before. What was the woman's name, Lloyd?'

Lloyd looked skywards as he searched his memory. 'Sally . . . no Sarah. Sarah Thatcher.'

The name rang a bell. Shane recalled the blonde television reporter from the story he had seen while still in Iraq. 'Same one who did the "war on poaching" story a few months back. Told you – same shit, different day.'

*

It was early afternoon and, as the drive to Victoria Falls was less than two hours from Isilwane, Shane told Michelle he would leave immediately and get the visit to Charles's widow out of the way.

The parched landscape he left behind had been transformed by a month of good rains. The mopane trees sported shiny, bright green butterfly-shaped leaves, and every herd of impala he passed was populated with tiny lambs, their ears looking too big for their dainty faces, spindly legs appearing barely strong enough to support their weight. The pans were full of water, and elephants wallowed gloriously in mud baths, revelling in their survival of another dry season.

Shane drove slower than usual, the rear of the empty Land Rover sliding away a couple of times as he rounded bends on the rain-slicked dirt road. When he made the main tar road, great clods of mud drummed on the aluminium panels inside the wheel arches as they flew free of the tyres' deep tread.

He could tell the Zambezi River was running high and fast by the tall plume of spray that was visible as he crested the hill that led into the town of Victoria Falls. He had the address for Charles's home from the old man's personnel file. He took a right turn into the industrial estate and followed the deteriorating road past the UTC garage, hardware stores and builders' yards until he came to a neighbourhood of modest brick houses dating from the 1960s. The whitewashed walls were spattered with mud the colour of dried blood where the rain had pelted into the grassless yard and flowerless beds. The roof was made of crumbling asbestos. With hunger, AIDS, inflation and unemployment to contend with, the people of Zimbabwe were a long way off caring about mesothelioma. Shane had been surprised to learn the country still mined the deadly fibre and exported it to Eastern Europe.

Outside the house was a new-looking Nissan Sunny taxi, its bright blue paint gleaming, tyres blackened. Someone had taken the time to clean the vehicle since the last rain, which had probably been that morning.

Miriam Ndlovu opened the door. She was a plump woman, dressed in a simple but neatly pressed blue cotton dress. 'Hello, Mister Castle. This is a surprise! How are you?'

'Fine, and you?' Her reaction was predictable – he hadn't telephoned to let her know he was coming because Charles had never had the phone connected. He thought he read something else in her face as the smile quickly vanished.

'What can I do to help you?' she said, as a young man, perhaps in his early twenties, appeared behind her. Shane recognised him from the funeral. 'This is my son – Charles's eldest – Fortune.'

Shane shook his hand and saw Charles's eyes in the son, who was tall and muscular, and well dressed in dark slacks, a crisp white business shirt and polished loafers. He wore a mobile phone in a leather pouch on his belt. 'How do you do, Mister Castle?'

'Please, both of you, call me Shane.'

'Fortune is a businessman. That is his taxi outside – he owns it,' Miriam said quickly, gesturing to the vehicle.

Despite the civility, Fortune, too, was unsmiling. He stood behind his mother poised like a boxer, easing his weight from one foot to the other, his hands held loose by his side.

'It must be hard to keep a car on the road these days, with the fuel shortages and the cost of spare parts,' Shane observed.

'People always need transport and, besides, my father made sure we were cared for,' Fortune began. A sharp glance from his mother stopped him from elaborating.

'Have you come from Mr Reynolds?' Miriam asked.

Shane was taken aback by the question. Fletcher had not even attended Charles's funeral. 'No, this was my idea. I just wanted to see how you and your family were getting along.'

There were a few pregnant seconds of silence before Miriam's innate sense of hospitality got the better of whatever it was that was concerning her. 'Please, come inside, Mister Shane. Tea?'

Fortune stood aside, but Shane felt the other man's eyes drilling his back as he moved past him and down the corridor to the lounge room.

Miriam motioned for Shane to take a seat on a velour-covered lounge. The home was neat and, despite its grubby exterior, it was freshly painted inside and the furnishings looked new. Shane couldn't help but wonder, uncharitably, if his old friend's deal with the enemy before his death had paid for the family's relatively comfortable lifestyle and the shiny car out front. In the hallway was a white top-loading washing machine, still covered in shrink-wrap plastic.

'We are not the only family in Zimbabwe with an automatic washing machine,' Fortune said, following Shane's glance.

'Hush, Fortune,' said his mother, returning from the kitchen with a tray bearing three cups of steaming tea.

'Don't think us ungrateful, Mister Castle,' Miriam continued as she lowered herself into a yielding arm-chair opposite Shane. Fortune remained standing. 'When I asked if you had come on behalf of Mister Reynolds, it was not to ask for money.'

Shane's confusion was mounting. 'I'm sorry, Miriam, but I don't think Fletcher Reynolds would have been offering money under any circumstances.'

'Oh,' she said.

'I simply came out of respect for an old friend, even if Charles did . . .' He saw the anger flash in Fortune's eyes and knew he had touched a nerve.

'My father did nothing wrong! Nothing!'

Shane sipped his tea, eyeing first the son, then the mother over the rim of the dainty, flower-patterned china. The cup, he noticed, was not the usual cheap dross found in the Chinese- and Indian-run discount stores.

'I meant no insult to your father, Fortune. I remember him as a good man – for all the excellent work he did in the national parks service and with my men and me. But the fact remains that he did do business with poachers, and Fletcher Reynolds could never forgive him for that.'

Fortune looked hard at his mother, who gave a small shake of her head.

'I do not understand this. You work with Reynolds,' Fortune said, his tone more accusatory than factual.

Shane nodded. He felt the hairs on the back of his neck start to rise. He'd lived in danger and on his wits long enough not to ignore his innate warning signs. 'Fletcher told me Charles went to him to ask for money, for you and your family, to be paid as a death benefit,' he said to Miriam.

The woman exchanged a few words in Ndebele with her son, perhaps clarifying the term 'death bene-fit', Shane thought. 'Yes,' she said. 'And the matter was settled.'

To Shane's knowledge the matter was settled by Fletcher telling Charles to get lost. Miriam, however, seemed to harbour no ill will over the decision, which had turned her husband into an informant for crimi-nals and an armed poacher. 'Miriam, did Charles say anything to you in the days before he died – anything that might have given you a clue why he did what he did?'

'A husband and wife discuss many things which are private, Mister Castle. Some things are best left unsaid, in memory of a good man. It's odd, though,' she said, putting down her cup and saucer on a pol-ished side table. 'Charles said you might come visiting one day.'

'He did?'

'Yes,' she said.

Shane waited for Charles's widow or son to say something else, but the room was silent. Again, he felt the physical manifestations of his unease. He drained his cup and placed it on the armrest of the lounge.

'What if we want money?' Fortune said.

Shane looked into the boy's hard eyes. 'You seem to be doing better than many people.' He disliked Fortune's tone and, at that moment, felt about as charitable as Fletcher had been. He had come to the house to check on his old friend's family and suddenly felt as though he were about to be shaken down. 'Find more passengers for your cab.'

'If you joke with me, *Mister* Castle, I could go to the police. It would not go well for you or your employer.'

Shane rarely played cards, but he'd been told on more than one occasion he had a good poker face. He stood and took a step towards Fortune. The boy was on the other side of the room, but still took an involuntary pace backwards. 'You don't want that any more than I do.'

Fortune swallowed, his bravado disappearing as quickly as it had surfaced. 'Please, please, Mister Castle,' Miriam said, hauling herself up out of the chair. 'No one bears any ill will over what happened. Fortune was speaking out of turn. No one in this room wants the police involved in this matter. It should be laid to rest, along with Charles.'

'But, Mother —'

'Hush, Fortune. Mister Castle has come to see us out of respect. Nothing more, it would seem. And for that,' she said, turning to face him and taking his hand in both of hers, 'we are grateful. Please forgive my son if he caused offence.'

'That's not necessary,' Shane said. 'I'd better get going, anyway.'

Fortune walked ahead of him to the door and opened it. 'Safe journey, Mister Castle. Please give our *regards* to Mister Reynolds.'

'I'll be sure and do that,' Shane said, brushing past him. He stepped out into the cloying heat, aware only at that moment that the house had actually been air-conditioned – an unheard-of luxury for the widow of a slain national parks ranger, and probably for the average commercial poacher. Yet Fortune had insisted his father had done nothing wrong. Shane looked at the shiny taxi cab and then, halfway down the garden path, turned and looked at the mother and son, still standing on the doorstep. 'It's good you have this cab, Fortune. I'd hate for you to end up like your father.'

Shane saw the fear flare in Fortune's eyes – as illuminating and sudden as a match struck in a darkened room – before the door closed.

22

L arry Monroe wondered how many of the Illinois National Guardsmen and women queued up outside the base medical centre at Camp Lincoln would die in Iraq.

The soldiers were members of a transportation company. They'd be running supply convoys in and out of Baghdad – probably one of the most danger-ous duties in the war. As they waited to be checked and jabbed prior to their deployment, they laughed and joked with the unnatural boisterousness of the willingly condemned. Proud to serve. Good to go. What a crock.

He pictured a body lying in the dirt, blood oozing from fresh wounds, the stench of bowels voided at the moment of death. He screwed his eyes tight to try to rid himself of the image, but failed. Unlike most of these boys and girls, he had seen death first-hand. It wasn't something to look forward to.

The sign outside the medical centre welcomed the citizen soldiers to *Company C, 205th Area Support*

Medical Battalion. Next to the letters was the emblem of the Illinois Guard, a yellow silhouette of Abraham Lincoln's head on a blue shield. He wondered what old Abe would have made of Iraq, of the African-American faces of nearly every other man and woman in the queue, of the black men Larry had seen killed.

'Major Monroe, sir? You okay?' asked the sergeant standing beside him.

'Sure, Bernice. Just a headache,' he replied to his chief clerk's enquiring look. 'How many more to process, anyway?'

She consulted her clipboard. 'Nearly halfway through, sir. Still forty-five to undergo medicals and four for return trips to the dentist.'

Larry nodded. He'd had to call Charles Hamley in to do the dental checks and patch-up surgery needed to get as many of these soldiers fit enough to die overseas. Chuck had made no complaint about the call-up, even though he'd been back in the country less than twenty-four hours, fresh off the airplane from yet another safari to Africa.

'Oh, my aching back. I spend too much time in the office these days, and not enough time in the practice. 'Bout the only time I look in people's mouths nowadays is when I'm in uniform.'

Larry instantly recognised the voice. He turned around and saw Chuck Hamley not more than a couple of yards behind him, stretching theatrically. Speak of the devil.

Larry had quit his own civilian job as a senior executive in a health insurance company in Springfield. He was moving with his wife and kids to

Utah in a couple of days, as soon as his week's military service was up. 'How you doing in there, Chuck?'

'Well, at least one of those boys' mommas is going to be pleased tonight. He's got a mouth full of cavities, impacted wisdom teeth that are keeping him on meds, and he needs root canal work ASAP. He's 4F for now. The only good news for him is that Uncle Sam's going to be footing his dental bill and he'll miss out on his sightseeing tour of the Red Zone.'

Larry nodded and made a note on his own clipboard. 'We had a guy knocked back because of asthma this morning. I thought he was going to cry. I don't know why these guys are so keen to go off and get themselves shot at.'

'By God, I wish I was young and fit enough to go. You should reconsider your decision to leave the guard. We need people with your experience now more than ever.'

'I've done my time.' In truth, Larry knew that Chuck was still in the acceptable age bracket for overseas duty and suspected his lumbago was not nearly bad enough to have had him classified unfit. He'd been as sprightly as a man half his age when stalking big game in Zimbabwe. Larry suspected the diminutive dentist hadn't received his call-up papers because of political interference. As for himself, Larry had been cured of the need he'd once felt to test his mettle in battle. The idea seemed ridiculous to him now.

Chuck said, 'Sergeant, give us a moment, if you will. Go sharpen your pencil or something.'

'Yes, sir,' the female noncommissioned officer said. She walked down the entry stairs of the medical centre and started randomly questioning soldiers in the line, checking to see if their paperwork was in order.

'Sounds like you might be going soft on us, Larry,' Chuck said.

'What do you mean? Because I'm leaving the guard?'

Chuck put his hands in the small of his back and leaned backwards, stretching his muscles again before straightening. 'Six months ago you would have sold your wife and car for a chance to go to Iraq or Afghanistan. Something you want to talk about, Larry?'

Monroe looked out at the line of men, hair clipped so closely the pale skin of their heads almost reflected the morning sunlight. 'No, Chuck, I'm fine.'

'Had me a great safari, this time around. You really should come back over again, Larry. I've got a beautiful sitatunga's head being shipped to me by Fletch next month.'

He shook his head. 'Thanks, but no thanks. Once was enough for me.'

'Look at me.'

Larry turned and looked at Chuck. The dentist was at least six inches shorter than he, but he had a commanding presence. They both wore the brown oak-leaf insignia of majors on their collars, so it wasn't an issue of rank. Larry didn't know whether it was the man's money or his nature, or a combination of both, but at times he could be downright intimidating. 'What do you want, Chuck?'

Chuck leaned closer to him, invading his personal space. Larry smelled cologne and wondered what the man's patients must think of its invasiveness. 'What I want, Larry, is your word, as an officer and a gentleman, that you won't betray me.'

'Whatever gave you the idea that I would?' Larry felt the sweat prickling under his arms.

The other man lowered his voice to barely a whisper. 'You're weak, Larry.'

'If you're talking about Africa . . .'

'What the fuck else would I be talking about?'

23

'The pictures are fantastic, Matthew, but remember you need to get a clear shot of each side of every dog,' Michelle said as she sat next to the young researcher in the Main Camp cottage which had once been her home.

'I know, I know,' Matthew Towns moaned theatrically and good-naturedly. 'But tell me more about the Congo.'

Michelle had been worried that she might come across as too meddlesome in the wild dog research program – which she had started – and had already proved herself right. Matthew was more than capable of carrying on her work, and she had to stop herself from stating the bloody obvious. 'It's so different from here,' Michelle said.

'Dangerous, too. It must have freaked you out with that guy getting shot.'

Worse for Wise, she thought. She would be interested to see when she returned what progress, if any, the police had made in finding the killer. 'It is dangerous, but the countryside is spectacular and the wildlife – the primates, in particular – like nothing you'll ever see down here. Coming face to face with a fully grown silverback was the most awesome experience I've ever had in Africa.'

'How are you getting on with the boss?' Matthew asked.

'Fletcher's great to work with and, for a hunter, he has a great affinity with wildlife.'

'That sounds like the textbook answer.'

Michelle felt herself start to blush.

'Helicopter?' Matthew cocked an ear, a puzzled look on his face. As he stood and moved to the window, the *thwop* of blades chopping at the heavy afternoon air getting noisier by the second, he said, 'Check it out. It's landing near the warden's office.'

Michelle shared Matthew's curiosity and walked out into the front yard of the cottage. In all her time living in Zimbabwe she had never seen a helicopter land in the park. She recognised the craft as a Bell Jet Ranger. On its side was a sign that read *Victoria Falls Helicopter Joy Flights*. 'He's a long way from home.'

They were joined by a small crowd, mostly women and children, who filed out of their modest staff bungalows to stare at the hovering machine. As one, the onlookers turned their backs or raised their hands to their eyes when the rotary downwash blew up a sudden fierce dust storm. The clouds abated, though, once the skids touched the ground.

Michelle wiped her eyes and blinked in surprise. 'Fletcher!'

He ran, bent double to keep his head below the

still-spinning blades, grinning broadly and clutching a bouquet of red roses. Petals dislodged by the wash followed in his wake as he crossed the distance to her. He was dressed in a cream linen suit, blue oxford shirt with a striped military-looking tie, and expensive brogues, now white with dust.

'Close your mouth or you'll start catching flies,' he said as he stopped in front of her.

'What . . . ? When . . . ?'

He took her in his arms and kissed her. She was dumbfounded; he was still supposed to be in the Congo. 'Do you have a bag?'

'What? Um . . . yes, my things are in the cottage. I only just got down here from Isilwane. I was planning on going out for an afternoon drive with Matthew and staying the night here in one of the lodges.'

Fletcher released Michelle from their hug and strode across to the young researcher. 'You must be Matthew Towns. Fletcher Reynolds.'

The two shook hands. 'It's nice to meet you at last, Mister Reynolds. It's great what you're doing, funding our research and all. Would you like to come out tracking the dogs with us this afternoon?'

'Sorry, Matthew, but three's a crowd and that chap in the chopper charges by the minute. Can't stay for tea. Michelle, grab your bag and let's go.'

'Go where, exactly?'

'Victoria Falls. I owe you a shopping trip, remember? Trying to make up for the last time I stood you up. I've got us a room booked at the best hotel in town.'

'Fletcher . . . I've got nothing to wear.'

'That's why we're going shopping. Now move it, girl!'

She shook her head and grinned at him when she realised he'd been staring at her. She wore a headset with a microphone attached, which allowed them to communicate over the noise of the helicopter's engine as they flashed over the green, freshly watered Zimbabwean bush.

'What about your German hunting clients?'

'They decided to leave two days early,' he replied, his voice crackly with static in her ears. 'It was a brilliant hunt. They got what they came for and opted for a couple of nights of comparative luxury in one of the big hotels on Lake Kivu. I was pleased to get rid of them, to tell you the truth. They were a pretty painful lot. Very Aryan, and very anal.'

'They didn't like the pit toilets?'

He laughed. 'With the tips they left, we'll have gold-plated flushing commodes on the mountain in time for their next trip!'

'That good, huh?'

He grasped her hand and squeezed it. 'Better than I could have imagined, Michelle. The Congo business is going to be a real winner for us.'

'Us?'

'You know what I mean.' The glee disappeared and he suddenly looked serious. 'I'm sorry I couldn't make it down here in time for Wise's funeral.'

'It was a sad service. Such a waste of a strong young man.'

Fletcher nodded. 'I didn't get a chance to ask you – where's Shane?'

'Oh, he went to the Falls as well – but by Land Rover. He decided to visit Charles Ndlovu's family to see how they were doing.'

Fletcher frowned and Michelle imagined it was because he still considered the old ex-ranger a traitor which, of course, he was. She thought it was good of Shane to take an interest in the welfare of the man's family, but right now she couldn't fault Fletcher for anything. The helicopter ride was extravagance incarnate, and she couldn't imagine how he would top it when they landed.

'See the spray up ahead,' came the pilot's voice over the intercom.

Michelle leaned forward in her seat and saw the plume of mist rising from the great cleft of the escarpment. 'A rainbow!'

Fletcher took her hand again and said, 'Hang onto your stomach.'

The township of Victoria Falls flashed beneath them in a heartbeat and the pilot pushed the nose of the chopper into a steep dive. Michelle gave an involuntary scream as she felt her tummy ride up and collide with her lungs. They were in the spray now, the sheer walls of the gorge on either side of them. Below them the churning white rapids elbowed their way through the narrows. Next she was pushed into the soft leather-upholstered seat as the helicopter clawed its way back into the perfect azure sky. The pilot made a few lazy circles up and down the Zambezi upstream from the Falls themselves and Michelle craned to see hippos polka-dotting the shallows and a family of elephants making briskly for the salvation of the river.

She looked across at Fletcher and saw her smile reflected in his face. It was a lovely, over-the-top gesture for him to collect her like this, and to remind her of his feelings for her. She hadn't had this much fun since her other flight over the same spot, with Shane, on the day of her first parachute jump.

Michelle looked back out of the Perspex window on her side, mentally chiding herself. Her moment of euphoria with Fletcher had been spoiled. Shane had popped into her head and she realised she was unconsciously comparing not only the two experiences, but the two men.

Fletcher was as immaculate as the bush allowed, in his new tailored suit and starched shirt, arriving like some modern-day knight on a steed powered by a jet turbine engine. Shane seemed always to be either in uniform or a T-shirt and shorts. His mount was a smoky Land Rover or a Cessna with no doors that smelled of sweat and old vomit. She forced herself to bring this train of thought to a halt. 'What a lovely view.'

'Not half as lovely as from where I'm sitting.'

She looked back at him and saw him leaning against the opposite wall of the fuselage, staring longingly at her. She slid closer to him, moulding her body into the crook of his, and kissed his lips.

A white BMW with an African chauffeur in a black suit was waiting to collect them when the helicopter settled onto the shimmering Tarmac at Victoria Falls Airport. Fletcher folded a handful of US dollars into the pilot's hand as he shook it.

Michelle felt self-conscious in her dusty green T-shirt and cargo pants as she slid across the car's cool, squeaky-clean leather seat. 'Where are we staying?'

'Just you wait. I don't want to spoil the surprise.'

They passed the hangar where she had completed her rudimentary parachute training, which brought a secretive smile to her face, then turned left and headed towards the town. She saw the sprawling, whitewashed Sprayview Hotel, where Shane had drowned his sorrows after Charles's funeral. It would be odd, she thought, if he were still in town and they bumped into him. Awkward.

'Left here, please, driver.'

Michelle groaned inwardly as they drove through the entry gates to Victoria Falls' largest casino, a garish new development dominated by a replica of the Great Zimbabwe stone tower, which looked as though it were made of papier-mâché.

'Classy, hey?' Fletcher said.

She tried to think of something polite to say, but he cut her off with a playful slap on her thigh. 'Don't worry, I'm only joking. We're not staying in this monstrosity, but they do have the most expensive shops for woman's clothes in Zimbabwe.'

She smiled at his use of the singular – woman instead of women – a peculiarity of the male Zimbabwean vocabulary. Inside the casino was a cool, moodily lit shopping mall, which boasted plenty of overpriced stock but very few customers.

Part of her felt as though she were betraying some ideal by even being seen in the midst of such opulence. Never mind that it was on the arm of someone suspiciously like a sugar daddy.

'Stop looking at the price tags,' he said. 'Just pick something you like. And you'd better find something other than those bloody hiking boots to wear.'

Michelle made a show of annoyance, but it was secretly kind of a nice to be indulged like this. She tried on four different dresses, finally settling for a floaty, strappy, maroon creation. She walked out of the changing room on tiptoes, holding her hair piled high.

'Well?'

Fletcher was sitting in an armchair. He dropped the fashion magazine he'd been flipping through onto the floor. 'My God.'

'It's a bit over the top.'

'Not for dinner at the Victoria Falls Hotel. Not for my girl. You look so good I'll have to go armed, to fend off the young bucks.'

She giggled and disappeared back into the change room, but then his words hit her. *His girl?*

She quelled her misgivings as she changed back into her cargoes and boots, but her heart fluttered almost to a stop as she re-emerged and he reached into the pocket of his suit jacket and produced a tiny box covered in black flock.

'Oh, madam!' squealed the African shopgirl, who had just finished wrapping the dress.

Michelle had the same reaction, though she was lost for words as Fletcher made a slow show of opening the little box.

He smiled broadly. 'Don't worry. It's not a ring.'
Inside were a pair of diamond earrings.

'Fletcher, they're beautiful. You're being crazy, though. All this will cost a fortune.'

'I've nothing else to spend my money on, Michelle. Come, you've got your evening dress. Now you'll need some things to wear around town.'

If the casino reeked of new money and excess, the Victoria Falls Hotel wafted bygone splendour and colonial decadence. In its own way, Michelle thought, the place was as over the top as the gambling den, but if she had to pick her luxury accommodation, this was the place.

The afternoon's shopping had been exhausting. The novelty had worn off for her pretty quickly and she had rushed through the purchase of her second and third outfits, some new lingerie and a pair of completely impractical, though gorgeous, strappy high heels to match her new dress. She had barely had time to shower and put on her new makeup before dinner, so there was no opportunity for anything else. Fletcher had sat in a lounge chair in the plush hotel suite, reading the *Financial Gazette* – one of Zimbabwe's few independent newspapers – while she showered. She'd welcomed the few minutes to herself. Even when they were together in the Congo, Fletcher was always coming and going on safari and she'd had time alone to read and work on her wildlife study.

She'd felt uncomfortable and constrained in the dress and heels when she'd emerged from the bathroom, pirouetting dutifully for his delighted inspection, though when they'd entered the dining room she had felt – for the first time in her life – not like a fish out of water among wealthy, sophisticated people. The wine had further relaxed her and she thought to herself how handsome Fletcher looked as they sat on the terrace of the restaurant sipping coffee and Amarula cream liqueur.

Fletcher asked the red-jacketed African waiter for the bill and reached across the white starched tablecloth to put his hand on hers.

'You know I love you, don't you, Michelle.'

She nodded. 'You were too good to me today, Fletcher.'

'That was just a beginning. I don't need you to say you love me, you realise.'

'It's been a long time since I've felt this strongly about anyone.' She sipped her liqueur.

'That'll do me, for now,' he said, squeezing her free hand. The waiter's return interrupted them, and Michelle used the pause as an excuse to depart for the ladies' room.

When she rejoined him they walked out hand in hand, across the internal courtyard to the old part of the hotel and upstairs to the suite. She was tired after the day's rush of events and wondered if he had considered that she might have wanted a room of her own. True, they had slept together several times, but even in the bush she had her own tent, her own space. As they walked down the corridor she saw a maid emerge from Fletcher's room and close the door. She curtsied to Fletcher and said, 'It is done, sir. As you asked.'

'Thank you,' he said, folding some Zimbabwean bills into her hand.

Michelle wondered what else he could possibly have thought of. 'I suppose I should have asked you if you wanted a room of your own,' he said, hand on the doorknob.

Suddenly she felt bad. How could he read her thoughts, her emotions? She was more like a churlish brat than a grown woman. This rich, handsome man loved her and had showered her with gifts, and she felt a strong attraction to him. Why the hell wouldn't he have assumed that she would want to sleep with him tonight? 'It's fine, Fletcher. Really.'

He opened the door and she was momentarily dazzled. Lighted candles, perhaps a hundred of them in the otherwise darkened room, sat on every spare inch of space, on side tables and the mantelpiece over the fireplace, on windowsills and the writing desk. They might have made the room unbearably hot, but the French doors to the balcony had been left ajar and the faint breeze coming up off the river made each tiny flame dance, and produced a comforting, shimmery aura of heat and light.

It would have been corny if it weren't all so incredibly beautiful. Michelle realised she had never in her life been truly romanced. It was a new sensation. She saw the vintage champagne in the dewy silver ice bucket by the bed, with two upturned crystal flutes. He'd forgotten nothing.

She stopped by the bed and scooped up a handful of rose petals from the cover and held them to her nose. As she drank in the intoxicating aroma she felt his finger running down her spine, from the base of her neck to the zip at the rear of her dress. She shivered at his touch.

'Nervous?' he whispered.

'Excited.'

She felt the coolness on her back as the zipper came undone, his lips on her shoulder. The expensive gown fell to the floor and she stepped out of it. She stood there in high heels and her new lingerie, unsure whether to make the next move or to wait for him. He had choreographed the entire day and evening, though he hadn't let her in on the script. Eventually, she looked back over her shoulder and saw him standing two paces away, arms folded, simply studying her in the candlelight. A slow smile played across his face and he nodded, as though to himself. He looked as though he were pleased with his creation.

His trophy.

24

Shane was nervous. Maybe even scared. It was a new sensation, and he didn't like it. He paced the drawing room at Isilwane Lodge, sucking on his cigarette like an asthmatic on oxygen.

The television reporter who had telephoned Isilwane looking for Fletcher had called again while Shane was visiting Charles's family and demanded Lloyd provide her with Fletcher's satellite phone number. Foolishly, the guide had eventually relented and Shane had returned to the lodge to find he had been set up.

'Why do *I* have to talk to her?' he'd protested to Fletcher down the crackly satellite call. He'd been surprised to hear that Fletcher had been in Victoria Falls on an unscheduled rendezvous with Michelle the previous day. They had almost crossed paths. 'Can't she go to the Falls and interview you?'

'I'm on a plane out of here tonight. I've got more clients on their way to the DRC and have to be back now-now.' The repetition of the last two words meant 'immediately'.

'Shit,' Shane had grumbled. 'I don't think we should be talking about the poaching problem up here. For one thing, it died down before we left for the Congo.'

'I know it did, Shane, and it was due to your good work. You've got a good story to tell, so do so. That's all these reporters want – a little colour. She'll make a hero out of you, and it'll be good PR for the lodge and the business. Trust me, I've been interviewed by the same woman before. She's on side. Her husband's actually ex-Australian Army, so she'll be soft on you.'

No amount of talk could persuade Shane that what he was about to do was wise, or would be easy; however, he'd taken the time to jot down some thoughts in his notebook about what he wanted to say in the television interview Fletcher had dropped him in. He wanted to help maintain working relationships between the lodge and the local authorities by talking about the good work done by national parks and police in controlling poaching in this part of Zimbabwe; to drum up more business for Fletcher by stressing that Zimbabwe, despite its political problems, was safe enough for hunters to visit; and, finally, to point out that controlled, legal hunting actually helped promote conservation of endangered species by raising money for the national parks service and promoting sustainable use of wildlife.

'The woman is here, boss,' Lloyd said. Shane had heard the vehicle pull up outside and it had sent his pulse racing.

'Great. I mean, show her in, Lloyd. Thanks, mate.' He put his notebook back in his pocket.

'Hello, Sarah Thatcher, Satellite News Network,' said the woman as she strode across the stone-flagged floor, hand outstretched.

He was surprised by the firmness of the woman's grip. She was pretty, dressed in trendy urban bush gear, but there was a hardness to her features that spoke of no-nonsense toughness. She handed him a business card and he pocketed it. The cameraman's name was Jim Rickards. Long hair, in a ponytail. 'G'day,' he said. An Aussie – not that it made the man an instant friend. Far from it.

'Thanks so much for agreeing to the interview, Captain Castle.'

He smiled at the woman's feigned fawning. 'I don't imagine you call your husband Major Williams, Ms Thatcher.'

'You've done your research, I see.'

'As I assume you have. I'm Shane.'

'Sarah. We'll have to watch this one, Jim,' she said in a theatrical aside to the cameraman, who had positioned two dining chairs in the centre of the drawing room.

Shane looked behind him and noticed that a stuffed buffalo's head would be in the shot. 'I'll move this way a bit, if you don't mind,' Shane said, sliding the chair two metres to the right, changing the backdrop to the innocuous view out of the French doors to the lawn.

'Light's better where it was, mate – if that's all right with you.'

'No, it's not – mate. I don't shoot animals and I don't want you setting me up to look like some big *bwana*.'

Rickards looked at Sarah for support, but she just

gave her TV smile and said, 'It's Shane's place, Jim. The garden will look nice in the shot, don't you agree?'

The cameraman shrugged, readjusted the digital camera on its tripod and then crossed to Shane, who had taken his seat, and affixed a lapel microphone to his shirt. At Rickards' request, Shane gave his name and his position, as head of security, as a sound check and tape identification for the video.

Sarah took her seat, attached her own microphone and pulled an A4 notebook out of her nylon day pack.

'Whenever you're ready, Sarah,' Rickards said.

'Shane, once again, thanks for taking the time to talk to us. As I explained to Mr Reynolds on the phone, we're doing a story about the war against poaching in Zimbabwe, including the great work you've done up here in your concession.'

Shane nodded, aware that everything he said from now on would be taken down and, probably, used against him. He put his palms face down on his trousers to try to soak up the sweat.

The reporter cleared her throat and said, 'Shane Castle, you're at the front line in Africa's battle against poaching. How *deadly* is this *war*?'

Shane had received some media interview training as a young officer cadet at the Royal Military College in Australia and Sarah's words reminded him instantly of something the PR officer instructor had told the class – journalists would always try to put words in an interviewee's mouth. He wasn't going to fall for that one.

'Well, Sarah, perhaps I could just start by saying a

few things about the current situation here in this part of Zimbabwe.' He followed his opening remark with the three messages he had prepared earlier, finishing with an assertion that legal hunting was helping with the sustainable management of wildlife in the country.

Sarah smiled politely, as though she had been expecting his considered words and corporate message. 'Yes, I'm sure that's the case, and no one would doubt you've done a terrific job controlling poaching.'

'Yes, we have been able to control poaching in this area by our close cooperation with national parks staff and local police.' Damn, he thought to himself, he had just fallen for her trick and used her words about 'controlling' poachers.

'Control, in the same way that one might eliminate pests? By killing them?'

He swallowed hard. 'They're your words, not mine.'

'You haven't killed any poachers?'

'Um . . . No, I didn't say that. With the help of the local authorities we have been very effective in . . . in ensuring that . . .'

'Effective in killing,' she said, smiling again. 'How many men have you personally killed, Mister Castle?'

Shane felt like a shipwreck survivor who had just climbed into a lifeboat only to find it full of holes. 'Look, what I was trying to say is . . .'

'Zimbabwe has a shoot-on-sight and shoot-to-kill policy when it comes to armed poachers in national parks and dedicated safari areas, doesn't it?'

'Yes, it does,' he said, almost relieved at being given a reprieve with a simple factual question.

'And, presumably, people like yourself involved in,' she made a show of checking her notebook, 'ah, yes . . . *security*, have the right to defend yourself?'

Shane fought to control his breathing. He was determined not to let her ruffle him, to make him lose his cool. 'That's correct, and as I was saying before . . .'

'So, you have fired your weapon, at poachers, in *self-defence?*'

'Yes.'

'And killed men.'

'What I have done is . . .'

'Have you or have you not killed people in your current job?'

He looked at the ceiling, unsure whether or not to answer the question. When in doubt, tell the truth. 'Yes.' At least, he thought, that might get her off his back and move on to a more relevant question.

'Unarmed men.'

'No.'

'Yes, Mister Castle. You were a party to the shooting of two unarmed men, in the same incident in which you and your anti-poaching patrol also killed several armed poachers.'

'No!'

'On or about the tenth of September this year you came across two unarmed men, bearers working with a gang of Zambian poachers you had just been in a firefight with, and ordered them to start running so you could have some sport with them before you executed them in cold blood.'

'Look, I don't know where you're getting your information from, but that is a complete and utter lie.

I have never, ever, in my life been a party to the shooting of an unarmed man and furthermore I reject —'

'You served in Iraq as a contract security officer, didn't you?'

Shane sat back in his chair and looked from the reporter to the cameraman. Rickards made a show of looking back down into the eyepiece of his camera. 'What do you mean by that?'

Sarah riffled through some papers at the back of her notebook, content to let silence reign for the few seconds it took. 'Ah, yes, here we are. I've got a printout here of a BBC story which names you as the suspect in the shooting of a wounded Iraqi man in Baghdad.'

He shook his head. 'You don't understand, he was —'

'He was an injured man, trapped in a burning vehicle, according to the story, who you chose to execute rather than try to capture or assist. Even terrorists are human beings, Mister Castle.'

Shane closed his eyes, seeing the burning man again, hearing his screams as the Americans urged him to let the guy burn slowly to death. He put his head in his hands, elbows resting on his knees.

'Mister Castle?'

Shane knew that whatever he said next would only tighten the hangman's noose. He had no idea what the woman was talking about regarding the so-called unarmed poachers, but his past seemed to be rushing up behind him like an out-of-control freight train.

'Keep the tape rolling, Jim,' Sarah whispered to the cameraman, before changing tack. 'According to

403

Zimbabwean police records, at least eight poachers have been shot and killed, supposedly in self-defence, on the Isilwane Safaris concession in recent months. How do you explain that number of deaths? That's more than have been killed in the entire country in the last twelve months.'

Shane looked up at the woman, then at the accusing lens of the camera. He saw his reflection, eyes red-rimmed, mouth slightly open. 'You killed a wounded man in Iraq, and at least two unarmed Zambian men here, in cold blood,' she spat at him. All pretence of politeness had vanished from her demeanour. 'Is this your definition of *security*? Eliminating all potential opponents, armed or otherwise?'

'I don't know who's feeding you this rubbish but —'

'Deny it. Tell me you didn't shoot that injured human being.'

He felt the rage rising in him and fought to contain it. He knew he should say something positive or clever to steer the interview back to what he wanted to talk about, but all he felt was contempt for the creature sitting opposite him.

'You wouldn't understand a thing about —'

'Try me,' she hissed. 'I've had guns pointed at me, bullets fired at me and, yes, I've had to shoot back. But I've never seen a man put another down like a dog, Mister Castle, like you did.'

Is that what he'd done? The screams filled his head. The laughter of the Americans. His fury at the insurgents who had tried to kill him and his human cargo and comrades all surfaced again. The dead bodies of his mates in the Range Rover stared back at him through the shattered glass. She was right – not in her interpretation, but in her facts. He had euthanased the Iraqi, as one might a suffering pet. He had justified it to himself over and over, yet there could be no explaining his actions, his motives, to this woman.

'Out,' he said.

'I beg your pardon,' Sarah replied.

Shane stood, removed the clip-on microphone from his shirt and tossed it towards the cameraman. 'This interview's over. I'm not going to get a fair hearing here and you've got your *facts* screwed up. Please leave the premises now.'

'But I'm not finished . . .'

'Oh yes you are. Get up,' he said to Rickards.

'Okay, okay, man, cool it,' the cameraman said. He unclipped his camera from its tripod and folded the legs under one arm. At the same time he dexterously transferred the camera to his shoulder and continued filming as he started to walk backwards. Sarah unplugged her lapel microphone to allow him to move unhindered.

'Please tell me you're getting all this,' Sarah said under her breath.

'Yep, and it's gold,' he replied.

Shane heard the whispers and followed them out, reaching out to cover the camera's lens with his hand. 'Get out now, please.'

'And thank you for the money shot,' Rickards said. He paused, defiantly, on the front porch of the lodge.

Shane's hand connected with the lens and Rickards toppled backwards, landing on his bottom on the gravel.

'Hey, that's assault!' Sarah said, loud enough for the camera's in-built microphone to pick up.

'Jesus – get up, you silly bastard,' Shane said, reaching down to give the man a hand up.

'Don't you touch me!' Rickards wailed, as though Shane were trying to grab him. He wriggled away on his posterior, the camera still on his shoulder and, no doubt, recording.

Shane shook his head. He knew he'd behaved badly – and blown the interview – but the whole thing was rapidly descending into the farcical. It would have been funny if it weren't all so tragic.

'I'll be in touch with Mister Reynolds,' Sarah called from the driver's seat of her rented four-wheel drive.

'Don't bother, you won't be welcome back here,' Shane said bitterly.

She started the engine as Rickards climbed into the back seat and swung the camera out through the window, its lens pointing at Shane. 'I don't need to come back here. I've got everything I came for.' She smiled again.

Shane lifted his right hand, with all bar the middle finger folded into his palm.

'Oh my God, Shane!' Michelle laughed. 'You gave her the bird? That's priceless.'

'You can laugh. I've probably lost my job over this.' He opened another two Zambezi Lagers and passed one green bottle to Michelle. He sat on the edge of the swimming pool at Isilwane Lodge.

Michelle swam to the side of the pool to accept her

beer from him. The cool water was bliss after the hot drive down from Victoria Falls. Lloyd had come to collect her after Shane's disastrous brush with the media. She didn't like seeing him down, and had hoped to talk through a few feelings of her own with him.

'You'll be fine. It's just a beat-up, I'm sure. They got sick of saying that shooting poachers was a good thing and now, to make it all newsworthy, they've got someone else to say it's a bad thing.'

'Yeah, you're probably right, but it still bugs me that she could get it all so wrong, or that someone could claim that I shot two people in cold blood.'

'That does sound very specific. Maybe Fletcher's got some enemies who want to get back at him. This is a small country and he's doing so well that perhaps someone's resentful.'

Shane nodded. 'I've thought about that. Now that he's built up the business there's always the chance that one of his senior army or political allies might want to take over the lodge as a going concern. It's possible someone could be spreading lies about Fletcher, but it irks me that someone would say it was *me* who did the killing. That's personal.'

She noticed the way he stared off into the distance as he drank from his beer bottle. There was more to the way he was feeling than a poor performance in front of the camera. He was tougher than that, she thought.

'You said she asked you about Iraq as well?'

'Yeah. That was below the belt.'

'What did she ask?'

He looked down at her and set his drink on the pavers beside him. 'I killed a man in Iraq, Michelle.'

She shrugged. 'I never wanted to ask, but I guessed you would have. You were a soldier.'

'No, this was when I was a contractor. It was just before I came back to Africa.'

'Still, it was your job.'

'It was an insurgent. A terrorist. The fire fight was over and he was in a burning car.' He looked away again.

'He was wounded and you shot him.'

'You know?'

'That reporter isn't the only one with access to the Internet, Shane. I've Googled you as well as Fletcher. I wanted to know what sort of people I was working with. I must admit, I was a bit disturbed when I read the first reports, about you being investigated by the Iraqi police and all, but I had to look a little harder to find the press release from your old firm that said the investigation had been dropped and you had been cleared of any wrongdoing.'

He smiled.

'What's so funny?'

'I didn't even know they'd put out a press release about me. Well, I'm sure Sarah Thatcher didn't get that far in her research, but thanks anyway.'

'What for?'

'For not judging me.'

'I did judge you, Shane. I weighed all the evidence I had about you, your past and your job here in Africa, and added in some evidence from the time we've known each other. The verdict was you're not a bad guy.' She leaned over and punched him on the thigh.

He smiled again, but once more his eyes roamed out towards the granite kopjes in the distance. There was more on his mind than the reporter's unfair and misguided questioning, though it didn't seem he was in a mood to open up. At least on that front he was back to normal.

'I didn't ask you how your date with Fletcher was,' he said, changing the subject.

She shrugged. 'Nice.'

'All champagne and caviar and five-star hot and cold running servants?'

'Stop teasing. It was romantic, though.' And no expense spared, she thought to herself. 'Tell me, what does a big war hero like you do to impress a girl?'

He looked at her, as if trying to judge the seriousness of her question. She stared back at him silently. He scratched his chin. 'Tell her I love her, I suppose.'

'No fancy dinner, no grand gesture, no diamond earrings?' She placed her index finger behind her right earlobe and batted her eyelashes.

He squinted down at her, as though unable to see the stud. 'Only if I thought the girl was a shameless materialistic gold digger and I was so old and butt-ugly it was the only way I'd get her to notice me.'

She flicked her hand and splashed water up into his face. 'Meanie!'

'You started it.' He stood and leapt high into the air. As he descended he raised his knees and clutched them to his chest, hitting the water in a bomb that sent a wave over the edge of the pool, with enough force to send their beer bottles rolling.

Michelle came up for air spluttering, hair plastering

her face. She lashed out at him blindly, splashing more water at him, but he was too fast for her. She shrieked with laughter and begged for him to stop. When he did, she started splashing all over again, and he reached out and grabbed her wrists to still her.

'Enough!' she yelled.

He laughed and, as she shook the hair from her eyes, she realised it was the first time she had ever seen him really do so. His face looked so different, softer, more open. He released her wrists, took a step back from her in the water, and said, 'Sorry, hope I didn't hurt you.'

'Not at all. God, I haven't laughed like that for ages.'

'Me either,' he said, then looked away. He put his hands on the edge of the pool and boosted himself up out of the water. 'Think I'm gonna go dry off. There are a couple of things I need to get done before we leave.' He walked away.

It seemed that whenever she got close to him he pushed himself away from her and retreated back into his shell. The journalist's questioning had obviously opened some old wounds, but it seemed there was more on his mind than she would ever get to know about.

She had also wanted to talk to Shane about Fletcher – particularly what Shane thought of him, not as an employee, but guy to guy. She'd woken that morning to breakfast in bed and Fletcher already dressed to travel. He'd said goodbye to her before she had even had time to finish her food. She was a little disappointed that he had to rush back to the Congo – she had envisaged a day spent together sightseeing or just lazing around – but consoled herself with the fact that he had come to Zimbabwe solely to see her. Their lovemaking the night before had been slow and tender. He knew how to make a woman respond, but seemed to have a set order about how he did things. When she'd grabbed for his manhood at one point, eager for him to enter her, he had removed her hand and told her to wait. She guessed he was being deliberately dominant, thinking that was what she wanted – but she'd simply been madly, infuriatingly ready for him at that precise moment. By the time he did get around to entering her she had been too distracted by his earlier brush-off to orgasm before he did, or even while he was inside her. She was sure, though, that in time they would get to know each other's moods more intimately.

Michelle sensed, from Fletcher's gifts and the elaborate measures he'd taken to create a romantic mood at the hotel, that he might be close to asking her to marry him. Some women would think she was mad to turn down a man like that. All that wealth aside, it would mean she could live her dream of a life spent in Africa doing wildlife research, without the added concern of not knowing where her next round of funding would come from. What worried her was that every time she considered her feelings for Fletcher, money always seemed to come up as a key point in his favour.

Shane dressed and checked the time. If he hurried, he might make Hwange Police Station before the CID office closed, which he guessed would be four pm. It'd mean a drive back to the lodge in the dark. Driving at night was never a good idea in the bush because many animals were on the move in the dark, but he had no other option. He and Michelle were due to start the long process of flying back to the Congo the next day, with a trip to Bulawayo in Dougal's Cessna.

'Hey, you look like you're going somewhere,' Michelle said, padding up the hallway towards her room with a towel wrapped around her body. She had left a trail of wet footprints on the stone floor and he did his best not to look at her legs.

'I'll be gone for the afternoon. Just need to visit an old contact.'

She cocked her head and frowned. 'Sounds mysterious. Have you got a girlfriend somewhere I don't know about?'

He fastened the Velcro of his watch strap and ran a hand through his wet hair. 'You see right through me. Tell Lloyd not to worry about dinner for me.'

'What are you up to, Shane?'

'Nothing.'

The old steam locomotive on a concrete plinth near the turn-off from the main Bulawayo-to-Victoria Falls road to the town of Hwange was a reminder that this was coal country. The Wankie Colliery – the business still kept the name the town had used under white Rhodesian rule – was one of the few things still working in Zimbabwe.

Shane drove past the monument, bypassing the town itself, to the sprawling police camp a little further down the road towards Bulawayo. The two-storey main building looked as though it dated from the seventies – the dying days of white rule. Inside, a constable in khaki trousers and a starched blue-grey shirt directed him to another building, which housed the Criminal Investigation Division. Shane followed the directions, walking past a parking lot crammed with police vehicles in varying stages of disrepair.

In the CID office a detective slouched in a chair invited him to enter. Shane vaguely recognised the man, and wondered if he were one of those who had come to Isilwane to investigate a shooting. 'What can I do for you, my friend?' the suited policeman asked without apparent interest in the answer. He sat behind a large wooden desk which normally seated three, judging by the number of chairs and a trio of battered manual typewriters which were probably older than Shane. Four deep wooden trays were overflowing with paper and carbon paper. The cramped office smelled of stale cigarette smoke and body odour, and its yellowed walls – once cream – were lined with rows of shelves full of tightly packed binders.

'My name is Castle. I work at Isilwane Ranch in the Matetsi Safari Area.'

The detective raised his eyebrows lazily. 'Ah, the premises of Mister Fletcher Reynolds. I have been to that place. What do you want with us, Mister Castle, with the name like the beer? It is late and I have to go home soon.'

Shane caught the slur in the man's voice and saw

413

the yellow in his eyes. The cop had been drinking. 'I know it is late, and I apologise for any inconvenience, but I am here on behalf of Mister Reynolds. He needs a copy of a statement he gave to police about an incident in which two poachers were killed.'

'Ah, but why does your master need such a document? He would have been given a copy at the time.'

'I'm sorry, but we had a small fire recently in the office at the lodge and most of our records were destroyed. A foreign hunter who was on safari when the two poachers were killed needs a copy of the statement from that incident as one of them injured himself jumping out of Mister Reynolds' vehicle when they came under fire from the criminals.'

The detective leaned back even further in his chair, rocking back on the two rear legs, and narrowed his eyes as he appraised Shane and the flimsy story he'd brought with him. 'I think there is more to this matter than you are telling me.'

Shane shrugged. 'I'm only doing as I was asked. I know this is an inconvenience so close to your finish time, but I wonder if you might also do me a favour.'

The policeman raised his eyebrows again. 'I hope you are not suggesting that you will offer me a bribe.' Shane knew full well the connotations of the word 'favour' in the Zimbabwean bureaucracy, and the policeman had caught the none-too-subtle reference.

'Of course not,' Shane protested. 'But I found this shopping bag lying by the side of the road and, as it's not mine, I thought I should hand it over to the police for safekeeping until the rightful owner can be found. However, some of the contents are perishable, so I

414

would leave it to the policeman in question as to how he would best store this stuff.' Shane hefted a red and white nylon shopping bag onto the desk.

The policeman looked through the window over his shoulder and quickly slid the bag to the floor beside him. He bent behind his desk and unzipped it. Shane smiled as he imagined the copper salivating over the plucked fresh chicken, five-kilogram bag of mealie-meal, bottle of Gilberts Gin and carton of Zimbabwean Newbury cigarettes. The detective looked up, the faintest hint of a smile curling his full lips. 'I will have to take this somewhere for safekeeping, my friend.'

The boot of his car, Shane thought.

'In the meantime, perhaps you might like to read through the folder of investigation statements. What was the date of the incident?'

The policeman left Shane alone in the room with a stack of ring-binders with dates marked on the spines. He worked quickly, unsure how long the man would be, or if any of his colleagues were likely to stumble upon him. The Zimbabwean police, hamstrung as they were by the government of the day, were not always the most efficient force, but they had inherited from their former colonial masters a passion for orderly paperwork.

Shane found a statement handwritten by Fletcher relating to the day when he and his group of American hunters had intercepted the two poachers in the *bakkie*, which Caesar had disabled by flattening a tyre. This was the pair who had produced an SKS semi-automatic rifle, which Caesar had unfortunately failed to notice when he'd given the vehicle a cursory search. Shane pulled out his notebook and jotted down a few details from the account. Stapled to Fletcher's statement was the report of the investigating officers, Detective Constables Dube and Mpofu. Shane ran his finger down the first page of the typewritten report, and then the next. Finally he found what he was looking for – a record of the types and serial numbers of weapons taken into police custody on that day. He ignored the details of the .303 rifle confiscated by Dube and Mpofu and focused instead on the impounding of the Simonov SKS semi-automatic rifle recovered next to the body of one of the poachers. The report said two rounds had been fired from the weapon's magazine, which tallied with Fletcher's account. Shane found the rifle's serial number and copied it into his notebook.

The policeman walked back in just as Shane was closing the folder. 'You have finished?'

Shane paused for a few seconds to think. 'When people surrender firearms voluntarily to the police, is there a record kept?'

The man pursed his lips. 'What business is this of yours?' The surrendering or confiscation of guns was a political issue. The government – more particularly, the President – was becoming increasingly paranoid about possible assassination attempts, so citizens who held military-style rifles had been ordered to hand them over for destruction. There were exemptions, but even a professional hunter such as Fletcher Reynolds had to justify the need for every pistol and rifle in his collection.

'Perhaps I should have alerted the desk officer about the goods I found on the side of the road . . . in case the rightful owner comes to the police camp looking for them?'

The detective looked out his window again and licked his lips. 'Yes, there is a register of weapons surrendered, what of it?'

'I need to see it.'

'Why?'

'To ensure that some weapons we handed over from Isilwane Lodge were properly catalogued and sent for destruction.'

'You are accusing the police here of corruption?'

Shane could have laughed at the irony of the detective's comment, but he kept a straight face. 'I am only following the orders of the lodge owner, Mister Reynolds, who is a good friend of the member in charge here at Hwange.'

'If he is a good friend, as you say, then he should know that no amount of money in the world would convince the member in charge or any other policeman here to risk getting caught trading in firearms.'

Shane saw the look of seriousness, bordering on outright fear, his question had evoked. It appeared life could be tough even for police in a police state. 'I understand, but you must appreciate Mister Reynolds has a right to know everything was handled correctly.'

The man shook his head in resignation and ran his finger along the spines of a row of folders set high on a shelf. 'Here. Be quick.'

'Thank you, *shamwari*,' Shane said.

'I am no longer your friend.'

Shane quickly scanned the folios in the folder as the man hovered near him, looking pointedly at his watch every now and then. There weren't many entries, as there were obviously few firearms left in the country to surrender. 'Thank you. Everything is in order,' Shane said, after coming to the end of the file.

25

Fletcher checked his gold Rolex, slyly admiring it yet again as well as noting he had less than an hour before his connecting flight would be called. Accents from both sides of the Atlantic and the broad vowels of Australia assaulted his ears as he roamed the duty-free shop at Johannesburg's Oliver Tambo International Airport.

South Africa was struggling to stay on track, politically and economically – the Mandela honeymoon was but a dim memory. Still, Jo-burg Airport's shopping concourse looked as though it could have been the international hub of any major city in the Western world. Two brand-conscious Afrikaner women dripping with gold and designer labels lugged baskets of tax-free booze to the checkout, while their husbands bought Springbok scarves and six-packs of Castle for nostalgic relatives lost to the white diaspora.

Fletcher stopped at the jewellery counter. He was working in the Congo – a country famed for its massive diamond pipes – and passing through the precious rock capital of the world, yet his tight schedule meant the most important purchase of the rest of his life would be made in an airport kiosk.

'I want a ring, please.'

'*Ach*, what kind of ring?' the white shopgirl asked. She had big hair and too much makeup.

'Diamond. Very big. Very expensive.'

The girl got up off her stool and her eyes widened. Fletcher guessed she must be on commission. 'An engagement ring, man?'

He nodded, and she gave him a look which mirrored his own concern. Why here? she seemed to ask, but she slipped easily into her patter instead. 'Perhaps sir would care to take a look at this selection – the top of our range.'

And vastly overpriced, no doubt, he thought. He knew nothing about jewellery or women's tastes. Jessica, his first wife, had gone for big, showy rings and chunky chains and pendants. He thought Michelle might like something more discreet.

'Yellow gold, white gold or platinum?' the girl asked.

'I don't know. Is platinum expensive?'

'Very, sir. The best.'

'Okay, then that narrows the choice.'

'She's a very lucky woman,' the sales assistant said as Fletcher held a glittering rock up to the fluorescent light. Its reflection sparkled in the envious girl's eyes, but all Fletcher could see was his tall, slender auburn-haired Canadian bride on his arm.

'I'll take it.'

With the ring safely in the inside breast pocket of

his suit, Fletcher took the escalators down to the British Airways Club Lounge. He figured he had time for at least one drink before he had to board the next of his connecting flights. He was going back to the DRC the long, slow way, first to Kinshasa and then on to Goma. He pulled out his cell phone and dialled Zimbabwe.

'Isilwane Lodge, good day.'

'Lloyd, it's Mister Reynolds. Is Miss Parker there?'

'*Yebo*, boss. One moment, please.'

Fletcher flipped through the pages of a coffee-table book about the Kruger National Park while he waited for Michelle. The book held little interest for him. He'd seen it all before. There was only one creature on his mind. 'Hello?' she said.

'Michelle, it's me. I'm in Jo-burg. I'm sorry I couldn't stay longer in the Falls, my girl.'

'I know. Still, it would have been nice to spend more time alone.'

'Yes, well, business calls, but I'm going to make it up to you.'

'You're doing a lot of that lately.'

'I've bought you a present today.'

'Fletcher, you don't have to keep buying me things. Don't tell me you've bought a wedding ring,' she laughed.

He took a breath. 'No. Chocolate-covered macadamias. Product of South Africa.'

'Hey, now you're talking. You really do know the way to a girl's heart, don't you?'

Fletcher wanted to tell her how serious he was about her, about the two of them being together forever, but he knew a phone call from an airport lounge was not the right way to propose. 'Can you get back to the Congo earlier?'

'Um, I'm not sure,' she said, sounding hesitant. 'I've still got to spend some time with Matthew and collect the vehicle from Main Camp. I was thinking of asking Shane to drive me down tomorrow, then maybe we could come back through the park in convoy. I love this time of the year – everything's so green and the bird life is fantastic.'

He didn't care about the bloody birds, and didn't want to think of his woman spending time with a younger man. 'Where is Shane? I'd like to have a word to him about coming back earlier as well.'

'He's out running some errand or other.'

'You're a hundred kilometres from the nearest civilisation. What "errands" can he have to run?'

'Search me. He doesn't tell me every little thing he does.'

'Sorry. I didn't mean to sound terse. I've got the Americans coming back in a couple of days and I'd like to get Shane and Caesar out on patrol to keep the poachers out of our way. You remember Anthony and the boys from New York?'

'How could I forget?'

He thought she sounded less than impressed, and changed the topic. 'Anyway, it's you I want to see. As soon as possible.'

'Yes, *sir*!' she said. 'Well, you might just have to wait, because I can't imagine what sort of a nightmare it would be trying to change flights from up here. But I'll see what I can do.'

He patted the ring in his pocket, which was next to his heart. 'I love you, Michelle. You know that, don't you?'

'Yes, Fletcher, and . . .'

The boarding call over the loudspeaker drowned the rest of her words over the poor connection. 'I'm sorry, I missed that. Are you still there, Michelle?'

He heard the dial tone and looked at the screen of the phone. His signal had dropped out. Johannesburg might give the appearance of a first-world locale, but he was most surely still in Africa.

Michelle had gone to bed early, and when she woke and looked at the glowing numerals of her alarm clock, she saw it was only just after midnight. Her mouth was dry and she instantly regretted the two gin and tonics and half-bottle of South African wine she had polished off over dinner.

Cicadas droned outside the open window as she parted the floor-to-ceiling mosquito net which surrounded her bed, and pulled on a T-shirt and shorts. She padded barefoot out into the hallway and immediately noticed the light was on in Fletcher's study, at the end of the corridor. Odd, she thought, as she had turned off all the lights before going to bed. She shivered, and suddenly felt vulnerable. She paused and heard the light *clack-clack* of a computer keyboard being worked. She had never seen Lloyd use the computer, and hoped it was Shane. She crept down the hallway, sidled along one wall and was about to crane her neck for a peep inside the study when she heard

Shane say, 'Come in, the door's open.'

'How did you hear me?' she said as she stepped into the open doorway.

'Sixth sense, I guess. Sorry if I woke you.'

'No, it's okay. What are you doing up so late, surfing for porn?'

He laughed. 'Not on this computer – the connection's too slow. Just catching up on some virtual paperwork.'

'I've never seen you use the computer.' She walked into the den, with its manly decor of old army and rugby team photos and other memorabilia of Fletcher's life as a scholar, soldier and hunter. There was even a cricket bat, signed by some group of notable past worthies, sitting on top of a low bookshelf. Shane hit two keys and, by the time she had made it around to the other side of the desk, the screen was blank. 'You're hiding something.'

'No,' he said. 'It's nothing. Just checking some of my own files.'

Michelle looked around and saw the sheet of paper in the out-tray of the ink-jet printer. She snatched it as he swivelled in Fletcher's chair and made a vain reach for it as well.

'These are Fletcher's accounts. Payments he received from his hunting clients in the form of cash and international transfers. Why are you going through his books?'

'It's nothing.'

'Don't tell me it's nothing when you're sneaking around in the middle of the night. Has Fletcher done something wrong?'

424

Shane was silent.

'Are you doing something wrong? Cooking the books, Shane?'

'Don't be silly.'

She looked from the rows of figures back to him. No, she thought, Shane wasn't the criminal type – whatever that was. Neither, for that matter, was Fletcher, although he was a businessman operating in a third-world country with first-world clients who paid large sums of money in hard currency. She'd once spoken to a white tour operator who told her that anyone who ran a business in Zimbabwe and said he had never broken a law was a liar. She looked at the payments made. From what she knew of the hunting trade the prices tallied. The print-out also listed clients' names and trophies taken. 'I don't know. This all looks pretty legit to me, from what I know of his recent safaris.'

Shane nodded. 'That's the thing. Those accounts are accurate.'

'You almost sound disappointed. What's on your mind, Shane?' She shifted an open ledger and sat on the edge of the antique leather-topped desk. The surface was cool against the backs of her thighs. She suddenly realised her nipples were semi-erect and showing through her T-shirt, so she casually folded her arms.

Shane leaned back in the swivelling office chair and put his hands behind his head. 'Something's not right here, but I can't put my finger on it.'

Michelle glanced down at the hard-covered book she had just moved. She picked it up and looked at

425

the cover. 'Firearms register? Where did this come from?'

'Out of the armoury.'

'Anything incriminating in *here*?'

He shrugged. 'A coincidence, but no, nothing damning.'

'But you still think Fletcher's up to something?'

'That reporter who interviewed me made some pretty damning allegations about unarmed people being shot. She tried to accuse me of blowing away a couple of guys in cold blood.'

She suddenly realised how little she knew about the man sitting opposite her, close to her. He might have been looking for evidence of wrongdoing by Fletcher, but it was he who was illicitly prying into private records. 'Did you?'

'No, of course not. I didn't get a chance to ask her for more information – I blew the interview long before then by losing my cool. But it got me thinking.'

'Thinking what?'

'That maybe one or more of Fletcher's hunting clients got a little trigger-happy and that Fletcher had to cover it up – by planting a weapon on an unarmed dead guy, or possibly paying bribes to the Zimbabwean police to turn a blind eye.'

'In which case he'd try to recoup the bribe through extra payments from his clients, or inflated trophy prices.'

'Exactly,' Shane nodded. 'But, as you can see from the accounts, there's nothing to indicate any irregular payments.'

She saw, however, that he still wasn't convinced of

Fletcher's complete innocence. 'Fletcher's been good to you. To me, as well.'

'You should be careful, Michelle.'

'What's that supposed to mean?'

'He's no saint.'

His attitude was starting to make her angry now. She wondered if he were trying to drive a wedge between her and Fletcher. 'Who the hell is?'

'All I'm saying is, don't go rushing into something with the guy before you know more about him.'

She exploded. 'No one, and I mean no one, tells me how to run my personal life!' Michelle stood and marched to the door. She turned, hand on hips to deliver her final salvo. 'You're sad, Shane. You know that? I think you're just jealous of what Fletcher and I have and you're so screwed up inside you can't bear to see two other people happy.'

He said nothing – just sat there and stared at her. She turned and stormed back down the hall to her bedroom.

Shane didn't allow himself time to dwell on Michelle's accusation – perhaps because it might be true, and he didn't want to think what that said about him.

He called up the accounts spreadsheet on the computer again and scrolled down, page after page. He paused to pinch his eyes and refocus. It had been a long day. In front of him on the glowing screen was a list of recent purchases made for the business. There was Fletcher's new Land Rover Discovery – which had cost a small fortune, a tractor for ground maintenance,

427

a generator, thatching and paint for the lodge, and a new Nissan sedan. Shane had never seen a small car at the lodge – it would have been quite impractical for the bush, in any case. He walked over to the battered metal filing cabinet. In the past he had needed to pull out the vehicle licence book – in reality, just a single sheet of paper – for his Land Rover when its insurance had come due, so he knew where Fletcher kept his vehicle records. He found the hanging file marked *Vehicles* and took it back to the desk and opened it.

He sifted through the licence books for the old Land Rovers and the Discovery, but there was no document for the small town car. Also in the file was a sheaf of insurance policies, held together with a paperclip. He flipped through these and saw they corresponded to the vehicle licences. All except the last one. It was an insurance cover note for a Nissan Sunny sedan, dated to take effect from the same day the vehicle was purchased, from a car dealer in Victoria Falls. Someone, presumably Fletcher, had drawn a line in pen across the piece of paper and scrawled beneath it, *Transferred to FN* followed by a date – a week later than the car's purchase date – and a mobile telephone number. Shane wrote the number in his notebook, closed the folder, took out his cigarettes and lit one. A chill took form in the depths of his heart and was pumped through his bloodstream.

Shane changed quickly into fifth gear and Michelle watched the speedometer needle on the Mercedes dashboard pass the one hundred and sixty kilometre per hour mark. They were forty above the speed limit and the Merc felt as though it were flying.

'Fletcher would have a fit if he knew you were driving his prize possession – let alone breaking the law in it,' she observed.

'I know.'

Michelle had regretted her terse words to Shane the night before even as she had uttered them, and although she wanted things to return to the way they were between them, the frosty silence had lingered over breakfast and in the car. As awkward as it was, she needed a lift down to Main Camp to pick up the other Land Rover she had left there when Fletcher had whisked her away in the helicopter. Also, she needed to spend at least some time with Matthew before returning to the Congo. Michelle had initially envisaged a slow, pleasant drive through the national park with Shane to collect the other truck, but speed was of the essence to him today apparently, and he had commandeered the fastest vehicle in Fletcher's fleet and taken them out to the Bulawayo–Victoria Falls road.

The big diesel ate up the kilometres and they passed little traffic on the drive south. Fletcher was able to import fuel from neighbouring countries, but most other Zimbabweans couldn't afford or access other sources. As a result, the roads were quieter – and safer – than ever before. Still, the high-speed ride was unnerving. Shane slowed to fifty when they re-entered Hwange National Park and they were soon outside Matthew's cottage.

'I'll see you back at Isilwane tomorrow afternoon,' she said, closing the door. He didn't get out of the car and simply nodded. 'You still haven't told me what's so important that you have to go racing back to Victoria Falls.'

'You don't need to know.'

'*Need to know*? You're not still in the army, Shane. Tell me if it has something to do with Fletcher. I *do* need to know if it concerns him.'

'See you tomorrow.' He put the car in gear and the tyres spun as they fought for grip on the dirt verge outside the cottage. All that was left of him was a cloud of dust.

'You do make dramatic entrances and exits,' said Matthew, as he emerged to greet Michelle.

'Sorry, Matthew, can you give me a minute? I have to make a phone call.'

'Sure.'

Michelle had the portable satellite phone with her and, while she knew it was an extravagance, she suddenly felt the need to hear Fletcher's voice. She dialled and waited what seemed an eternity for the long-distance connection to be made.

She wanted to tell him about Shane's allegations, and his unusual behaviour. She wanted him to explain his spending. Perhaps there was an offshore account, for tax purposes – that wouldn't be too bad, surely? She could forgive some creative accounting, but what Shane had suggested, that Fletcher might have been covering up unlawful killings, was something she couldn't quite believe.

He answered, his voice barely a whisper.

'Fletcher?'

'Michelle? Is everything all right? Are you okay?'

She soothed his initial surprise by saying, 'It's all right. I'm fine.'

'Michelle, I'm in the middle of a hunt. We've got a forest buffalo cornered, I really can't chat. Can I call you later?'

She frowned. Was she being silly?

'Michelle?'

'It's okay. It's nothing that important. We can talk later.'

'Sorry, my girl. I'll try to call tonight, all right?'

'Yes, that'd be nice. Bye.'

She ended the call. It wasn't all right, at all, but there was nothing more she could do for now.

Shane parked the Mercedes at the Sprayview Hotel on the way into Victoria Falls and took out his mobile phone. He opened his notebook and dialled the number he had written down from the cancelled insurance policy.

'Fortune Ndlovu,' said the voice on the other end.

Shane nodded to himself. He was right. He spoke with a phoney American accent when he asked to be picked up by cab from the hotel and taken to the airport. 'I'll be there in five minutes, sir,' Charles Ndlovu's son said.

Shane waited in reception, behind a large potted plant, and watched the shiny blue Nissan Sunny cab pull up. He noted the registration number was the same as that on the insurance policy originally taken

431

out by Fletcher. He strode across to the car and jumped into the back seat.

'Airport, sir?' Fortune said from the driver's seat, then turned to look at his passenger. 'Hey, you —'

'Drive, Fortune.'

'Get out of my cab. I don't wish to see you.'

Shane reached behind his back and pulled the Browning pistol from the waistband of his trousers. He kept the weapon low, out of sight of a group of tourists milling about outside reception, but Fortune saw the hand gun. 'Drive,' Shane repeated.

They turned right and headed back out of town. Shane saw Fortune eyeing him in the rear-view mirror and noted the boy's panic. 'I don't want to die, Mister Castle.'

'I didn't imagine you would. We're going to talk as you drive, Fortune. Why did Fletcher Reynolds give you this cab?'

'He didn't give it to me, he sold it to me.'

'On paper, maybe, but that was a sham. I checked his accounts and saw you paid less than the equivalent of a hundred US dollars for this car. It's almost brand new. Why did he give it to you? Was your father blackmailing him?'

Fortune looked confused. He opened his mouth to speak, but seemed to think better of it.

Shane carried on with his theory. 'Your father worked out that Fletcher Reynolds – or possibly one of his hunting clients – shot an unarmed man in the safari area. I was nearby, but I didn't see the shooting. There were two men, poachers with dogs, but only one of them was armed, with an old rifle. Fletcher and his clients came upon the men and reckoned they opened fire on them. I don't believe that. I believe that someone in the hunting party fired first and killed those men. There was no second rifle, so Fletcher planted one of his, an old Russian SKS semi-automatic, on the unarmed dead guy.'

'What does this have to do with me or my father?'

'You're not going to tell me?'

Fortune shook his head, so Shane continued. 'Your father told me he had seen an SKS in Fletcher's armoury and that he would instruct the other two members of my team how to use the rifle, as part of their training. That never happened, and I forgot all about it. But I think that when Charles went to the safe he found the SKS was missing and he confronted Fletcher about it. He found an entry in the firearms registry book that said the rifle had been handed into the police as part of the government's plan to get people to hand in unneeded weapons, but I checked the police records and they never received such a rifle from Fletcher – though they did impound it when they collected it from the crime scene. Charles put two and two together and worked out that Reynolds had planted the gun on the dead guy. I reckon Charles started blackmailing Fletcher, who was probably covering up for one of his clients who had done the killing and would have been charged by the police if anyone found out. This cab was part of the payment. It might have looked suspicious if you started throwing US dollars around town, but a car sold to you – even at a discount – wouldn't have raised any eyebrows.'

'So, if you have all the answers – if my father was extorting money out of his employer – why did he end up dead, shot as a supposed poacher?'

'Two possibilities. One, he may have got too greedy and Fletcher set him up – maybe killed him and made it look like he was a poacher. However, to do that he would have needed the cooperation of his hunting client, a rich American dentist who was with him on the day Charles died, and I can't see a Yank millionaire being involved in something so grubby. The second is that your father really did turn bad. If Fletcher murdered him, I'll see him brought to justice, Fortune, but I'll need your help. You got the cab, so you must know the truth.'

'The truth?' Fortune broke into laughter. It started as a chuckle and ended up in great bellows that filled the cramped confines of the little car. Shane raised the pistol, wondering if the boy were unstable. As the laughs subsided, Shame noticed a tear rolling down Fortune's ebony cheek.

'What is it?'

'The truth,' Fortune said, sniffing, 'is neither of those things you suggest. The truth, Mister Castle, is so terrible, so evil, you won't believe it.'

26

The national park was like an old friend to Michelle – her best friend, she sometimes thought. During the course of her research she had driven nearly every accessible road and track. She knew every major waterhole and seep, every river and vlei; the locations of dens, the semi-permanent homes for the young of wild dogs and hyena; the burrows of bat-eared foxes, and the favourite mud pits of rare rhinos.

She stopped for a sandwich at the hide overlooking Masuma Dam and paused to reflect on how her world had been shaken. It had been a rocky, unpredictable ride since she'd first received the email advising her funding had been cancelled. Fletcher's rescue – both of her work and her near-lost love life – seemed to have brought as many hurdles as rewards.

The dam was three-quarters full now that the rains had arrived in earnest, and there was little game to be seen, apart from a basking crocodile and a herd of a dozen waterbuck. Three of the younger antelope were moving closer and closer to the croc, as if silently daring each other to touch it. The lead buck lowered its head until its nose was barely a few inches from the reptile's snout.

The attendant at Masuma, a smiling African dressed only in baggy shorts and a torn T-shirt, strode fearlessly across the open ground beside the dam, uncaring of what predators might be lurking. He carried a twenty litre jerry can of diesel on his shoulder, to refuel the pump which kept the dam partially filled in the dry months and fed water to the picnic area and small campsite year-round. Michelle envied the man's confidence and his life as just another one of the bush's natural inhabitants. Did he get lonely out here, she wondered, spending months at a time away from his family, and with so few tourists passing through the park in these troubled times?

The thatch-roofed stone shelter where she sat was dark and cool in the midday heat. A fish eagle called from its perch in a dead tree and she heard the return cry of its mate somewhere out of sight. They would be together once one of them caught something. The birds, with their distinctive snowy heads, mated for life. Would she and Fletcher spend the rest of their lives out here in the African bush?

She thought again about Shane and the hurt she feared she had caused him, yet she could not deny that she resented the way he suddenly seemed to be hell-bent on unearthing some flaw in Fletcher. She wondered if Fletcher really had covered up an illegal shooting. The death of a poacher – her sworn enemy as well as his – was of comparatively little concern to her; but what was more troubling was the idea that Fletcher might have killed an unarmed man, or been involved in the cover-up of a crime. Shane hadn't even asked his employer about the journalist's allegations. She resolved she would ask for straight answers as soon as she was reunited with Fletcher.

Michelle was worried about Shane for reasons other than his covert investigations of her lover. He was like a ticking bomb, she thought. She wondered if he ever let his emotions out. Did he have nightmares? Did he cry in the dark when no one could see him?

It would be just her, Fletcher, Shane and Caesar when she returned to the Congo – she didn't count Patrice as a friend or confidant, and Marie would only ever be an occasional visitor – so it was vital she make her peace with Shane before they boarded the plane to return. There was still a long drive through the park to Isilwane, so she drained her Thermos cup of coffee and waved goodbye to the attendant trudging across the plain below her. She would cook Shane dinner tonight and they would share a bottle or two of wine. He was one of the few people she could talk to honestly and she realised that even after only a day she was already missing his company.

Shane thought about Michelle while he sat, smoked and waited in a chair on the lodge's lawn in the long afternoon shadows. He stubbed out the cigarette. He wanted a beer, but knew he would need a clear head when the woman arrived.

He would have to tell her. It would probably drive her away, forever, but she needed to be warned, so that she had time to get out of Africa. His dreams were over as well. He had not raised enough money to buy a place of his own, so he would have to find other work. The prospects of a job for a white male in Zimbabwe or South Africa were grim at the best of times. He would inevitably be tarred with the same brush as his employer, despite his innocence. There was always Iraq, he supposed. More death.

He held out his hand and stared at it. The tremor was so slight he might be imagining it, but he knew he could only soldier in the killing fields for so long. A return to the army might kill him in other ways. It was ironic. He had seem so much action, so much excitement, that a training or staff posting in Australia would bore him senseless, yet he didn't really think he could face too much more death either. He wasn't crazy yet, but he knew he was far from normal, emotionally. What might cure him? Love? A woman? Michelle Parker? Maybe, but she would soon be gone. The sooner he got it sorted, the better.

Shane had dismissed Lloyd – sent him off to the staff compound early for the night, with orders not to disturb him and the woman. He didn't need the guide and caretaker to announce her arrival, as he heard the growl of her Landcruiser. He wiped his hands on his trousers and stood. He took a good look at the cool, masculine interior of the hunting lodge as he walked through it. He might not see it again after tomorrow, when he planned on returning to the Congo – for the last safari.

Sarah Thatcher was getting out of the four-wheel drive when he walked down the steps. She pursed her lips in disapproval. 'This better be good, Mister Castle. I've delayed my flight back to South Africa for you.'

'You may as well go back to calling me Shane if we're going to be working together.' Her hands were full with her notebook and a videotape, which gave her an excuse not to shake. 'Come inside.'

Rickards followed them with his video camera and tripod. 'I've got a sense of déjà vu. You're not going to punch me again, are you?'

'No, no "money shot" this time.'

'But I want it all on tape. Everything you told me on the phone. That's the deal,' Sarah said.

'If you stick to your part of the deal. I need to see the video. I need to know what your eyewitness saw, just to make sure.'

'I hope this isn't a waste of time,' she said. 'I'll play the tape while Jim sets up. It's a VHS dub.'

Shane took a seat on the leather lounge in the drawing room and with the remote control switched on the wide plasma screen television. Sarah inserted the tape in the player and sat in an armchair.

On the television, torsos and legs passed the camera's lens as the interview was set up. In the background he heard a boy's voice, whining a little, asking if he really had to tell the story to the camera. A woman's voice, soothing yet authoritative, told him it would be fine, and for the best. 'Is that thing on?' the woman asked, and the black face of a woman with a nun's headdress filled the screen.

'No, not yet,' he heard Jim Rickards reassure the nun on the tape. The cameraman, who was now setting up a portable light nearby, looked at him sheepishly and shrugged off the lie.

The camera's focus pulled back, shifted, and settled on the wide-eyed face of an African boy. Next, he heard Sarah's voice, behind the camera, starting the interview by asking the boy to state clearly his name, age and place of residence.

'Um . . . I am Daniel. Daniel Ngoma. I am fourteen years old, and I live in St Francis' orphanage in Livingstone, Zambia.'

'Thank you, Daniel. Now, in your own words, I'd like you tell us what you saw when you accompanied your uncle and some other men on your trip to Zimbabwe.'

Daniel dissembled at first, neglecting to say why the men were in Zimbabwe, only that they had been ambushed by armed men while walking in the bush.

'Tell us why your uncle and the men were in Zimbabwe, Daniel,' Sarah asked softly but firmly.

'Um . . . for a holiday.'

'Tell us why they were there – really.'

'Um . . . they were hunting.'

'Legally hunting?'

Shane almost felt sorry for the young boy. It had obviously taken a huge amount of courage for him to tell the sisters or priests who cared for him that he had been part of an illegal cross-border raid, let alone whatever else he had to reveal. Also, Shane knew from his own bitter experience how intimidating Sarah Thatcher could be in an interview.

'No, madam. Poaching.' He looked down as he said it.

After that first admission of a crime committed, Daniel held nothing back, answering all of Sarah's questions in a clear, strong voice. As he spoke, Shane noticed the passion well in his eyes and strengthen his delivery. Though Shane had as yet provided no details to Sarah, it was clear to him that the poaching expedition the boy had been on was the same one in which he and Wise had parachuted in to block the criminals' escape into Botswana.

'And what happened, after the gunfight in which your uncle was killed by the rangers and the white man, Daniel?'

Shit, Shane thought. I probably killed this kid's uncle.

Daniel told how he and two other men, unarmed bearers who had been carrying the illegal ivory, had run off into the bush, towards Botswana, without their booty. 'We carried no weapons, no ivory, nothing. We ran as fast as we could, but one of the men was hurt.' These, Shane knew, were the ones Fletcher and the American hunters – Chuck's national guard buddies – had gone off to track.

'What was wrong with him?'

'He had been shot in the leg.' Daniel leaned down, the cameraman skilfully dipping the lens to follow his actions as he pointed to a spot on his skinny ebony calf. 'This man was bleeding, very badly. We could not leave him in the bush. The other man, his brother, carried him on his back.'

'What happened then, Daniel?' Sarah asked,

patiently drawing out the boy's story and, Shane thought, deliberately building to a climax for the television viewers.

'Other men were following us.'

'Were they Zimbabwean men? Black African national parks rangers, Daniel?'

'No, madam, they were *wazungu*.'

'White men, you mean.'

Daniel nodded. 'The men I was with said that we would be caught soon. They decided that they should give themselves up, as there was no way they could escape the white men. We could see them catching up to us. They told me to run ahead, to try and make it into Botswana, where I would be safe.'

'And did you, Daniel? Did you leave those men?'

He shook his head. 'I was scared, madam. I wanted the white men to find these other men, my colleagues, and to let them go. They had no ivory, no guns, so I thought that they would be set free.'

'And were they?'

He closed his eyes then, and when the single tear forced its way out from between his tightly shut lids, Shane had to swallow hard to keep his own emotions in check. Daniel brushed away the unmanly sign quickly with the back of his hand, embarrassed by his weakness. He took a deep breath. 'No, the white men did not set these men free.'

'What happened, Daniel?'

The boy looked straight back at the interviewer and said, 'They killed them.'

'Who did?'

'The white men. I hid behind a termite mound and

watched. The Zambian man who was not wounded stood and put his hands up when the *wazungu* arrived. He said, in English, "Please do not hurt us. We are unarmed, and we had no part in this business."'

Sarah said nothing and, after a few seconds, Daniel resumed. 'A man with white hair said, "No, you are poachers. You can die like dogs or you can die like men. I will let you start running, either with the wounded man or alone, and then we will hunt you."'

Shane heard a faint gasp from behind the camera, as Sarah betrayed the soul beneath her no-nonsense professional exterior.

'The men stayed, but then the *mzungu* with the white hair started firing into the dirt around them. Eventually, the man picked up his wounded brother and started walking away. The other men were laughing and calling things out – bad names for black people.'

'What happened next, Daniel?'

'The man carrying his brother made it about one hundred metres, and then the white men started firing at them. Their first bullets were in the trees and on the ground, and this made the man stumble and fall. He picked up his brother, and then the gun firing began again . . .'

'They killed them. Both of them.'

Michelle got her second puncture less than a kilometre from Isilwane. She swore and banged the steering wheel as the Land Rover coasted to a halt, but she realised no amount of anger would fix a flat tyre.

443

It was just bad luck. She had changed the first wheel near the hot springs at Manzi Chiesa, watched by a curious herd of zebra as she unbolted the spare wheel from its bracket in the rear tray of the Land Rover. It was a task she had performed countless times in Africa and the job was soon done. Getting two punctures on the one journey was not unheard of, but it was a pain in the ass. There was a full puncture repair kit in the vehicle's toolbox, and a set of tyre levers to take the rubber off the wheel, but she had done that once before and she knew it was a long, hard task. As it was getting dark she thought it better to walk the short distance to the lodge and get Shane or Lloyd to bring her back out with an inflated spare from one of the other vehicles. Lloyd could mend the hole tomorrow. There was some risk, walking alone in the bush unarmed, but she would stick to the road and be inside safe before any lions or other nocturnal hunters roused themselves. She hoped.

Arriving on foot meant the occupants of the lodge didn't hear her. She wondered who the strange Landcruiser belonged to. Fletcher's Mercedes, which Shane had taken to Victoria Falls the day before, was parked in the driveway. Michelle walked up the steps into the foyer and heard voices. She slowed her pace, her curiosity growing when she noticed the abnormally harsh light emanating from the drawing room.

As she reached the doorway she saw Shane, sitting in a chair opposite a man and a woman seated either side of a tripod-mounted television camera. A bright light was shining on Shane's face. He looked like an

animal caught in a spotlight. Why had he been foolish enough to invite the television crew back to the
lodge? By all accounts – assuming these were the
same people – they had savaged him the last time he
had spoken to them.

She was out of Shane's line of sight and the light no
doubt prevented him seeing much further than his
interviewer, so she paused, in silence, to listen to his
words, and the reporter's questions.

'So, Mister Castle, you say you were not involved in
the shooting of two unarmed Zambian men – bearers
for the gang you and your offsider *had* been engaged
with in combat?' the woman asked.

'That's correct. Once all of the armed members of
the gang had been accounted for, my priority was to
take care of my man, who had been injured. It was my
judgement that the unarmed bearers – including the
boy in your story, Daniel – should be allowed to get
away.'

'Why was that?' the reporter asked.

'They were no threat and we were not a police
force. Our mission had been to support the national
parks rangers in protecting wildlife and stopping the
armed poachers from escaping with their ivory. We
were also able to disrupt the poachers, who had been
in the process of setting up an ambush with the intention of killing the rangers who were pursuing them.'

Michelle had not seen his first interview with the
Englishwoman, but she was impressed by how he
was handling this one. He looked cool and in control
– as he normally did.

'So, what did your employer, Fletcher Reynolds,

and the American hunting clients he was escorting on the day, do after your fire fight with the poachers?'

'They arrived late – after the action was over. They seemed . . . disappointed.'

'Disappointed?'

Shane paused to clear his voice. 'Fletcher – Mister Reynolds – told me he would take the hunters on a scouting expedition to follow the tracks of the men who had escaped. It was my impression that this was all Mister Reynolds intended – to show the men a practical lesson in bushcraft.'

'You've heard what Daniel Ngoma said happened next. Do you believe the men he saw kill – murder – two unarmed Zambians that day were Fletcher Reynolds and his hunting clients?'

Shane stayed silent for a couple of seconds as though contemplating his next words. Michelle was horrified. She couldn't believe that Fletcher would have murdered anyone. If anyone had been shot, it must have been in self-defence. 'Yes I do. There were no other Europeans in the safari area on that day.'

'And why, Mister Castle, do you think Fletcher Reynolds and/or the men who were with him, would have murdered those men? For fun?'

'No. For money.'

Michelle felt dizzy. She couldn't believe what Shane was saying, but the reporter was making him spell it out.

'You mean, they wanted to rob these two unarmed Zambian men? Surely they wouldn't have been carrying much money, or any valuables. You said you had already recovered the ivory.'

446

'It is my belief that the men with Fletcher Reynolds, his hunting clients, had paid him a significant amount of money to go hunting and that Mister Reynolds delivered on his part of that deal by leading them through the bush to where those two men were . . .'

'What you're saying, Mister Castle, is —'

'What I'm saying is that Fletcher Reynolds was paid, and not for the first time, to organise a safari – a hunt – where the trophy was a human being. He was running a manhunt.'

'No!' Michelle screamed, then ran for the front door, out into the dark African night.

27

S hane found Michelle outside, on a garden seat. From the glare of a security floodlight he could see her eyes were red from crying.

'I don't believe it. Not a word of it,' she said as he sat down beside her. He handed her a bottle of Zambezi, but she shook her head.

'Here, drink it,' he insisted. Reluctantly she took the bottle from him.

'But how do you know for sure, Shane? That Zambian boy could be lying. Couldn't they have been fired on and shot back in self-defence?'

'I'm pretty sure that's how it all started,' he said, pausing to take a drink. 'I think it started with Chuck Hamley – he's certainly in this thing up to his neck. A few months back when Hamley shot a poacher he probably did so because he thought his life was in danger. Fletcher took the rap for it, and got away with it, but I think that's when the money started rolling in. It coincides with my employment – and the funding for your work.'

'Blood money?'

'That's one way of looking at it. Hamley was willing to pay again for the thrill of shooting a human being, and so too were the men he recommended Fletcher to. The hunters who killed those two unarmed Zambians were Hamley's national guard buddies from the States. I remember them.'

'But how do you *know* all of this, Shane?'

He told her of his visit to Victoria Falls earlier in the day, and how he had persuaded Fortune Ndlovu to talk to him.

'I got it wrong. I thought that Fletcher was being blackmailed by Charles Ndlovu because he'd planted a rifle on a dead man's corpse to make it look like he'd been an armed poacher. Charles was smarter than me. He told his son that he went to Fletcher to confront him over the missing gun and that he had worked out that Fletcher's actions were premeditated. Charles had the missing piece of the puzzle that I couldn't see. Fletcher knew Caesar and I had been watching those poachers and that only one of them was armed, with an old bolt-action rifle. He knew he'd get the drop on them, because Caesar and I had them under observation and we'd disabled their vehicle. They were sitting ducks. All Fletcher needed was another weapon so he could later convince the police that he and his hunters had been in mortal danger. He left the lodge with that old SKS semi-automatic rifle not as a back-up weapon but as something to plant at the scene of a crime to justify his actions. He went there to kill, Michelle. It was premeditated murder.'

She shook her head. She desperately wanted it all to be some terrible mistake. 'Why didn't Charles tell you, or go to the police when he worked it out? It just doesn't make sense.'

Shane took a long pull on his beer bottle. They were alone at the lodge. Lloyd was in the staff compound, and the television reporter and cameraman had left for a night drive back to Victoria Falls. They had more research and filming to do there in the morning. 'Tell me, Shane,' she prompted.

'Charles had AIDS. He was dying. He knew there would be no death benefit for his family if he simply died of his illness while doing his job. But he had another plan to make the most of Fletcher's safaris.'

'What do you mean?'

'He sold himself. To Fletcher.'

Shane was staring out into the night, and she saw the pain, plain on his face. 'His son told you all this?'

'The funny thing is that the boy thought I knew all about it. Charles must have kept my ignorance a secret from him. Maybe he figured one day I'd come looking for the truth about how he died – that I'd work it out. Charles needed money and he knew that Fletcher had clients – including Charles Hamley – who would pay big-time for the opportunity to kill a human being. Charles also knew he was going to die soon, so he made a show of leaving the lodge, pretending he'd defected to the poaching gangs. Fletcher backed him up with a cock-and-bull story about Charles leading our patrols away from where the poachers were really operating. When it was time – when Chuck Hamley was next in the country on

450

safari – Charles Ndlovu walked out into the bush, to his death.'

She remembered the day. The start of the rains. Shane had tried to keep her at the lodge, to stop her from tagging along, but she'd been worried about Fletcher's safety. It was the most emotional she had ever seen Shane, when he had brushed past her in the pouring rain. She looked across at him now.

There was a tear running down his cheek. He got up and walked away from her.

Shane breathed deeply. He wiped the errant sign of weakness from his face with the back of his hand. This was not the time to fall apart. Breaking the news to Michelle was something he had dreaded, not least of all because he was sure she would be gone the next day, back to Canada.

He'd promised Sarah Thatcher he would dig through Fletcher's records to see what else he could come up with. In a court – if this bizarre situation ever made it that far – Fortune Ndlovu's testimony would be hearsay. Besides, the young man had made it quite clear he would have no part in any legal action against Fletcher, Charles Hamley or anyone else, and if contacted by the police he would deny ever having spoken to Shane. Fortune wanted to protect himself, his mother, and their meagre wealth.

Shane and Sarah needed more information to bring Fletcher down, to stop his trade in human life. He went into the den and turned on Fletcher's computer again. He had trawled through the document folders and sent and received emails, but found nothing incriminating. In a few messages to and from Hamley there were references to 'unusual trophy requests' and mentions of hunting 'primates'. That struck Shane as odd as hunters only shot monkeys in Zimbabwe if they had become problem animals. The same went for baboons, although these were sometimes killed for sport and bizarre trophies. He wondered if 'primates' actually referred to humans. Even if it did, it would be tough convincing a policeman or court of the link. He found Fletcher's picture folder and double-clicked on it, revealing dozens of the thumbnail images of hunting parties and individual shots of Fletcher, a particular hunter and the trophy he had taken. Of course, Fletcher wasn't stupid enough to keep pictures of his clients posing with dead humans. When he right-clicked on a picture, and then selected 'properties', he found that Fletcher had entered a caption for each picture, giving the date, the client's name and the relevant measurements or weight of the trophy animal. That was interesting.

He heard footsteps in the corridor and Michelle's tall, slender frame was silhouetted in the doorway. 'Can I come in?'

'Sure,' he said.

'What are you looking for now?'

'A picture of a man – one of the Americans.' He scrolled through the pictures as he spoke, finally finding the group he was after. He clicked on the image of Charles Hamley's fellow national guardsmen. Only one of the men was not smiling. He opened the caption box. He found the name of the frowning man third from the left and wrote it down. He knew that in another file he would find contact details for all of Fletcher's clients. Bingo.

'Shane, are you okay?'

He knew she was referring to his emotional reaction outside. It angered him that she had seen his weakness. He didn't want her pity. Also, he realised that if she were too sympathetic he might just break down completely. There was too much to do to let that happen. 'I'm fine. You should get some sleep. It's late, and Dougal will be here early tomorrow.'

'Dougal? Why? We're not due to go back to the Congo for two more days.'

'*We* aren't going back, Michelle. I am.'

She put her hands on her hips and stood opposite the desk from him. 'Are you telling me what I can and can't do?'

'You've got most of your things with you. Dougal will fly you to Bulawayo and you can catch the South African Airways flight to Jo-burg. You'll probably be in Canada the next day. Are you all right for money?'

'Hold on there, buster. You can't just fucking send me home. I'm coming back to the Congo with you. I want to confront Fletcher about all this and see what he has to say for himself.'

'If you confront him, you might end up dead. Unless you want to stay with him – even after what he's done.'

'Shit, Shane. Of course I don't want to be with him now. How could you think that?'

'Love?'

'I don't love him, Shane. Even if I thought I would

453

have eventually fallen for him, it could never happen now. Even if he'd only planted a gun on a dead man I still couldn't have shared a home with him. But I'm not cutting and running.'

'It's too dangerous for you to go back to the DRC. I'm going to get the evidence we need to nail him – to expose him to the world. He probably knows enough senior people in the Zimbabwean police force to get him off any charges – even if they could be bothered laying any. After all, it's Zambian poachers who were killed – apart from Charles, and his death was more like assisted suicide.'

'You said the evidence "we need". Who's we?'

'Sarah. The reporter. If we can't find a court in Africa to try Fletcher or his clients I'm going to try to get something on video, secretly, so we can out him to the world's media. That might prompt the American authorities – the FBI, maybe – to check out his safari clients.'

'You need my help,' Michelle said, leaning forward, her palms planted on the desktop. He smelled her shampoo.

'No.'

'No one's closer to him than me. I can get him to open up. Maybe wear a wire.'

'No way.'

'*No way?* Why do you think you can keep me out of this when I'm already a part of it?'

He looked away from her blazing eyes, back to the computer screen. 'Because I couldn't live with myself if anything happened to you. I care about you too much.' Shit, he thought. He'd said too much. He

454

wanted her to get on the plane tomorrow and disappear.

She stared at him, mouth agape.

From the corridor outside the office they heard a clatter, like something falling.

Shane got to his feet. He looked around the office for a weapon, then picked up the cricket bat, a memento of Fletcher's boyhood. He put his finger to his lips and walked around the still-stunned Michelle. He moved to the doorway and reached around into the hall and switched on the lights.

He crept out of the office, dropped to one knee and retrieved something. 'This,' he said, holding an assegai, a short Zulu stabbing spear, as Michelle poked her head through the doorway, 'fell from the wall.'

'How did that happen?' Michelle asked.

Shane moved down the hallway, which led to the kitchen. He switched on the lights and noted that the rear door, which led out into the yard behind the lodge, was ajar. Michelle was close behind him. 'Someone forgot to lock up,' he said.

'Where are the staff?' she asked.

'The maid should be in bed in the staff compound – I'll ask her tomorrow before we leave if she locked the door. Lloyd's the only other person who has a key, but when I dismissed him before Sarah arrived he said he'd be off visiting a friend at another lodge tonight.'

'This is creepy,' Michelle said.

'I'm sure it's nothing to worry about.' Shane returned the bat to its rightful place in the office. 'It might have been one of the cats on the prowl.'

She looked dubious. The spear had been set

halfway up on the wall. It could only have fallen if someone had brushed against it.

'I'll check the lodge, lock up and set the alarm.'

'Okay,' she said. 'Um, Shane?'

'Yeah?'

'Well . . . there are two single beds in my room, and I know this sounds a little wimpish, but . . .'

'You want company?' He arched a dark eyebrow, and she smiled at the comic gesture.

'*Single* beds, I said. Would you mind?'

'Of course not,' he said.

Michelle had changed into a T-shirt and short grey running shorts. She climbed under the sheet. It was a hot night, and cicadas in the trees competed with frogs in the ornamental pond outside the bedroom window to see who could keep the most humans awake for the longest.

'You're not getting into bed?' she asked. He reclined, fully clothed, atop the bed next to hers, a squat black pistol from the armoury sitting on the blanket. 'You're making me nervous, Shane.'

'I'll get some sleep during the day tomorrow. Night, Michelle.'

'Night, Shane.'

He listened to the night sounds, psyching himself up for the long, sleepless hours ahead. Staying awake, no matter how tired he was, was a skill he'd developed in the army. Just as valuable was his ability to fall asleep any place, any time, when the opportunity presented itself.

He felt foolish. Michelle had said nothing about the feelings he had expressed for her. Perhaps she thought he cared for her in a brotherly way. She looked angelic, curled under her sheet, her hair strewn across the white starched pillowcase.

Twice he thought he heard footfalls – once outside in the garden and once inside. Each time, pistol in hand, he crept silently out of the room to investigate. On both occasions he found nothing, though the hairs standing up on his arms and the back of his neck told him his suspicions were not likely to be unfounded. The other thing military life had awoken in him was a primeval sense of impending danger.

He checked his watch. It was three in the morning, according to the luminous dial. Michelle shifted under the sheet, stretched, then sat up. 'I need to go to the bathroom.'

'I'll come with you.'

'You will not!'

'At least let me check.'

'Now you really are giving me the creeps.'

He slid off the bed and walked out into the hall, flicking on the lights. 'It's okay,' he said. 'Nothing to worry about. I'll be right outside the bathroom door.'

'Bullshit. I'm not going to have you listen to me pee, Shane.'

He shrugged and got back onto the bed, the pistol still in his hand. Michelle shook her head and walked out into the hallway in bare feet. He smelled her scent in the room, and tried not to think about what it would be like to have her curled up in bed next to him.

Shane heard the toilet flush and the bathroom door open and close. His ears picked up another tiny noise and it took him a second to identify the beeping. The alarm! He was on his feet, reaching into his pocket, when he heard her piercing scream.

'Do not move,' Lloyd said.

The African guide stood in the hallway, one arm wrapped around Michelle's neck, his other hand holding the wicked point of a skinning knife against the pale white skin of her throat.

'Shane!' she yelled.

'Quiet. I don't want to hurt you,' Lloyd said to Michelle. 'But I will kill you unless Shane does what I say.'

Shane held the pistol in his right hand, extended, pointing at Lloyd's head. The other man countered by pushing the knife until a tiny drop of blood welled and ran down the blade. 'Drop it, Shane.'

He reluctantly obeyed, letting the Browning clatter to the floor. 'What do you want, Lloyd? Have you come to rob us?'

Lloyd laughed. 'You think I am that stupid? I should kill you just for that. I overheard you, tonight, talking about Mister Reynolds. I will not let you ruin that man.'

'He's a killer, and so are you if you're helping him,' Michelle hissed.

Shane was impressed by the way she had regained her cool, despite the knife that had cut her already. She was tougher than he had imagined.

'Kick the pistol to me,' Lloyd said. Shane obeyed and Lloyd slid his knife into a pouch on his belt and dropped to one knee to retrieve the gun. Feeling his grip relax on her for a second, Michelle tried to wrench herself away. She broke free of his arm, but Lloyd reached out and grabbed her wrist, then yanked her back with enough force to make her cry in pain. Shane held up his hands, urging both of them to stay calm.

Lloyd rammed the barrel of the pistol into Michelle's temple. 'Don't be so stupid again or I will kill you.' He used his other hand to deftly draw the knife again from its sheath. As well as having his arm wrapped around her waist, he now held the blade against her belly.

'What do you want, Lloyd?'

'The satellite phone. What have you done with it?'

'So you've already checked the lodge out?' Shane asked.

Lloyd smiled, obviously pleased with himself. 'I know the alarm codes. After I overheard you, I left. When you set the alarm I came back in, via the front door, and searched the lodge, then let myself out. I saw you keeping watch, through the bedroom window, and I prayed I would get a chance to separate the two of you.'

'Sounds like God is on your side,' Shane said.

'Do not blaspheme,' Lloyd said. 'God punishes those who take His name in vain.'

'Where did you learn that, from Charles Hamley?'

'He has been a good man to us – to you, as well. Why are you trying to ruin everything for Mister Reynolds, Mister Hamley . . . all of us?'

'It's wrong, Lloyd. If you can't see that, then your God won't forgive you,' Michelle said.

'It's easy for you whites. If Isilwane closes, you can leave and find work elsewhere. My family and I will starve. Enough! Where is the phone?'

'Hidden,' Shane said. 'And the landline's out of order. Typically Zimbabwean, eh?'

'Get the phone now, or I will shoot her,' Lloyd said, gesturing to Michelle with another painful jab of the pistol's barrel.

'You're probably going to kill both of us anyway,' Shane said nonchalantly.

'I am sure Mister Reynolds will spare your lives – in exchange for your silence. Besides, I heard you admitting that you have no real proof of what has been happening.'

Shane nodded, as if Lloyd had scored a crucial goal in their match of wits. 'So we have no proof, and you are offering us a way out?'

'No,' Lloyd corrected him. 'It is up to Mister Reynolds to offer you a way out. Me, I would shoot you now.'

'Then I don't suppose we have much choice,' Shane said. Lloyd smiled and nodded.

'That's right. Where is the phone?'

'I locked it in Fletcher's desk drawer.'

'Then let us go and retrieve it,' Lloyd said.

'How about you put that knife away? I'd hate you to stab Michelle accidentally. You've got a pistol at her head.'

'How about you do as I say, for a change,' Lloyd said.

Shane shrugged and moved ahead of the other two, down the hallway to Fletcher's study. Once inside, he sat at the desk. Lloyd stood on the opposite side, Michelle still in his grasp, the knife and gun still touching her.

'Keep your hands where I can see them – one palm-down on the desktop while you unlock the drawer.'

Shane fished the key to the drawer from his pocket, unlocked it and withdrew the telephone, which was a little larger than a standard mobile phone. 'What now?'

'Dial the number for Mister Reynolds.'

Shane punched a series of digits and held it up so Lloyd could hear the dial tone. A groggy-sounding male voice on the end said, 'Hello?'

'Want me to hold it to your ear?' Shane asked.

Lloyd looked momentarily confused. Clearly, he did not want Shane standing close enough to him to pose a threat, yet he had both his hands full.

'Hello? Who's there?' the voice said from the phone.

Lloyd hesitated a moment longer, then slid his knife back into its pouch. 'Reach across the desk and hand it to me,' he said impatiently to Shane. Michelle watched on, not daring to speak.

Lloyd took the phone from Shane's hand, held it to his ear and said, 'Hello, sir. It's Lloyd.'

'Who the bloody hell is Lloyd?' Shane heard the angry, sleepy voice bark. It wasn't Fletcher's voice.

Shane reached across to the filing cabinet and snatched up the cricket bat.

Lloyd saw the movement, and understood that he had been tricked. He dropped the phone and turned the pistol towards Shane. 'Nooo!' Michelle screamed.

461

Shane swung from the far side of the desk as Lloyd pulled the trigger. The only sound in the room was the satisfying crack of old willow connecting with skin and bone. Lloyd toppled, wide-eyed, to the floor, dragging a shrieking Michelle down with him.

Shane vaulted across and stood over Lloyd. When the other man started to move, he delivered another blow across the back of his head, then reached down for Michelle.

'Oh, my God, Shane!' she cried.

He lifted her to her feet and she instinctively pressed herself against him. Shane looked down, to make sure Lloyd was unconscious, then wrapped an arm around her. 'I never sleep with a loaded pistol, Michelle. People only do that in the movies. I had an empty magazine in it, and a full one in my trouser pocket. If you go to bed with a loaded gun you might pull the trigger in your sleep or, worse,' he added, pointing down at Lloyd, 'some bastard might sneak in and get the drop on you.'

'So you knew it was not loaded.'

He nodded. 'I would have just clobbered him straightaway if he hadn't had that knife pointed at you.'

She smiled up at him. 'My hero.'

They both started laughing.

Shane dragged Lloyd outside into the lodge's work-shop and bound his hands with rope. He tipped a bucket of water over the African's head and slapped him a few times, eventually reviving him. Shane checked his pupils. 'You'll live, you fucker.' He gagged Lloyd with a strip of duct tape and left him propped against one wall. He knew the laughter he and Michelle had shared was just a release of nervous tension, but he was still wired after the scuffle – and from holding Michelle to comfort her.

'How is he?' Michelle asked as he walked back into the bedroom. She was standing by the dressing table, a hairbrush in her hand. Her long hair almost gleamed.

'He'll be seeing stars for a few days. We'll have to think of something to do with him while we're away.'

'So you've accepted that I'm coming with you, back to the Congo?'

He leaned against the doorframe. 'I get the feeling that it wouldn't matter what anyone said to you – you always do what you want.'

'Most of the time,' she said, smiling.

'Lloyd's tied up. There's no one else here, so I can leave you in private, if you like.'

'I thought I was going to die, when he grabbed me. When he made you drop the gun, I thought . . .' She put the hairbrush down and took a step into the middle of the room, arms folded protectively across her body.

'It's okay, you're safe now. I'll pull up a chair in the hallway, if you like.' His carotid artery was pounding in his neck.

'No, you don't understand. What I was worried about is that I might die without . . . without saying . . .'

He moved across the room at the same instant as she, with an urgency that made it more of a collision

463

than an embrace. Their tongues sought each other's mouths as their hands ripped at buttons. They ground their bodies into each other, lust overtaking logic as they fought to tear away clothes. She pulled the pistol from his waistband and tossed it on one of the beds as his hand reached inside her shirt and roughly fondled her breast. His kisses travelled down her neck and she moaned as his tongue encircled her nipple, followed by his teeth. As her nipples hardened he pulled down her shorts and let his fingers linger roughly over the springy dark curls. Grabbing his hair, Michelle pulled his mouth back to hers as she unbuttoned him and slipped her hand inside, pulling him free, stroking. The bed was beside them, but it seemed an unnecessary journey. He lifted her, hands under her buttocks, and she encircled him with her legs. He ground against her, intending to tease her with the head of his swollen cock, but she was already aroused and he slid effortlessly into her. They kissed passionately, their bodies temporarily frozen by the exquisite pleasure they felt but had tried so hard for so long to avoid. Eventually he carried her to the antique dressing table and rested her on the polished surface as he moved inside her with long, pressing strokes.

Michelle's body moved with his. She held tight to his buttocks and kissed him and bit his lower lip as he rode her, and he responded in kind. As he felt her orgasm grow – the tensing of her muscles, the changes in her breath – she clutched him tighter, arms around his neck. Her body pressed into his, until she was almost off the table again. He knew she wanted him to lift her. As he straightened, clutching her in a crushing embrace, the changing angle drove him as deep as physically possible into her and she cried out her release. Her shudders flowed into his, and once again they were still, until their breathing returned to normal.

Later, as they lay naked on the bed, lights on, the weak summer breeze barely cooling the sweat on their bodies, he began kissing her, from her forehead down.

As she felt herself stir, Michelle realised that the sex was as different as the two men. Whether organising a safari or a date or making love, Fletcher was considered, methodical and planned. Calculating, even. Shane, however, was instinctive. Passionate. Honest. He possessed her now in a way Fletcher never had.

She lay back against the bedhead on the piled pillows and ran her fingers through his thick, dark hair as his tongue teased her tender nipples to life again. For a moment the horror of what Fletcher had done, of what they must begin to do in the morning, didn't exist. Shane paused, though, as his tongue flicked past her belly button on its journey south.

'What is it?' she asked.

'Your tattoo. I didn't see it in the dark before.'

'Poor Tinker Bell. Fletcher never liked her. What about you?'

'I want her.'

There was a pinch as he drew the little picture in between his teeth. She felt his fingers part her, again, as he continued to kiss her skin. When he moved his lips down and to the side, opening her with his fingers at the same time, Michelle looked down at the tattoo. 'She's all red, like she's blushing.'

Shane's now moistened finger moved lower between her legs, exploring every part of her as his tongue found her clitoris. He paused and looked up at her smiling face. 'Just like you.'

When they awoke, the sun streaming through the window, their limbs were entwined. Hers were tanned from wearing shorts, while he sported a soldier's tan, brown hands and face with a V below his neck, from wearing a long-sleeve uniform and trousers in the bush. That would all change soon, she thought, when he became a lodge owner. She'd make sure that he spent an inordinate amount of his time keeping the swimming pool clean, while she watched on, cocktail in hand. She smiled to herself as she watched him sleep. She knew she was being foolish. They hadn't gotten around to discussing a future together, and she had no right to dream that Shane would stay with her once they had done what they had to do.

She'd denied her attraction – her love – for Shane for too long, mainly for the sake of a man who she now knew was a cold-blooded killer. Michelle felt foolish for falling for Fletcher. Looking back, she saw the expensive dinners, the gifts, the helicopter ride, as more manipulative than romantic.

Her world had been shaken, but she felt right about being in bed with the handsome, dark-haired warrior, who looked peaceful at the moment. There was none of the doubt or self-analysis she'd subjected herself to over Fletcher.

'Hmmm, morning,' he drawled, eyes still closed, somehow sensing her watching him. He lifted an arm free and checked his watch. 'We should get going. Dougal'll be here soon.'

She grizzled a little, and moved her hand between their bodies, grabbing him. He smiled. 'Bad girl.'

'I can be.'

She looked up at him and, with her other hand, traced a line from his forehead, down his cheek, to his lips. He kissed her finger as she felt him harden under her touch. 'I knew, as soon as I met you, that I'd made the wrong choice, being with Fletcher.'

'I knew you'd see sense eventually.'

She pinched his cheek, hard. 'Goose.'

She placed her finger back on his lip, stilling his reply, and inched along his body, propelling herself with her toes, until she was poised over him. She had awoken aroused. It were as if her body couldn't get enough of Shane. She slid down on top of him; felt the glorious sensation of fulfilment, of being part of him. She kept herself close to him, her breasts flattened against his chest, the two of them barely moving. She felt his pulse through his body as she buried her face in his neck, her muscles delaying him, holding him for a few more precious seconds.

'God, do we have to go?' she asked, when it was over and they lay still.

'No, we don't,' he said, still inside her, hugging her. 'We can go to South Africa, Botswana, Namibia – anywhere.'

'You don't really mean that, do you?'

'No,' he said.

Shane radioed Lovemore at Robins Camp in the national park, and the ranger and his sidekick, Noah, were at Isilwane Lodge two hours later.

'This is highly irregular,' Lovemore said. 'It is only because you saved our lives that day with the elephant poachers.'

Noah dragged Lloyd, still bound, though his gag had been removed, roughly to his feet and propelled him towards the green national parks Land Rover pick-up.

'Like I said, I can't hand him over to the police – I think they're on the take,' Shane reiterated. He had told Lovemore of their suspicions about Fletcher Reynolds, which had been largely confirmed by Lloyd's attack the previous night, and the bare bones of how they planned to entrap the hunter. Lovemore had frowned in disapproval, but eventually he had agreed to Shane's request.

'I just need you to keep him locked up somewhere, on ice, for four days. That should be long enough. Even if I gave him to some honest cops, he'd still be able to make a phone call and tip Fletcher off.'

'I understand,' Lovemore said. 'We'll keep him under lock and key at the camp, but after four days I'm letting him go.'

'You cannot do this to me. I have rights,' Lloyd whined from the back of the truck.

Shane leaned into the rear of the vehicle until his face was no more than a hand's span from Lloyd's.

'You gave up your rights the second you put that knife to Michelle's throat. You're lucky I didn't kill you last night.'

Lloyd glared at him for a couple of seconds, but couldn't hold Shane's menacing gaze.

As the Land Rover departed, Shane heard the drone of Dougal's approaching Cessna. Michelle stood beside him and, with the rangers out of sight, clutched his hand. 'Let's get this safari on the road,' she said.

28

L arry Monroe started the engine of the Jeep
Grand Cherokee, then got out again. As he
scraped ice off the windshield, his breath
formed white clouds of condensation. Fall was
finally here, despite the warm weather of the previous weeks.

Now able to see, he wound his SUV through the
subdivision, past neatly trimmed lawns gleaming
white with frost. He smiled at the sight of smashed
pumpkins from the weekend's Halloween festivities.

He stopped for his regular morning coffee at the
Ibis, then pulled onto Main Street and headed south,
out of the valley. This was his favourite part of the
morning. For the next twenty minutes he would wind
through Sardine Canyon before hitting Interstate 15
and the inevitable traffic leading into Salt Lake City.
As had many professionals, he had left the city and
opted for a quiet life in the country, willing to suffer
the commute for the peace of the mountains. The difference was that the city he had left – Chicago – was

in another state and he had other reasons than quality of life for relocating to Utah.

He thought of Africa, as he did often, despite his best efforts. As the sun rose higher the light shone pink across the Wellsville Mountains, which had finally shed the last colours of fall from the cottonwood trees. He noticed the deer in the pastures and in the new subdivisions, where open fields had once been, and wondered not for the first time how much deeper into the hills the housing would sprawl. 'Might need to move further out,' he muttered to himself.

Another look at the deer reminded him that the hunting season was well underway. Once he would have taken part in the killing and called it sport. Not any more.

Larry switched on the jeep's radio and tuned to National Public Radio for some news. It was the same old story – more violence in Iraq, rising oil and gas prices – until the reader switched to international news. The first item was about the deteriorating political climate in Zimbabwe. He felt the colour drain from his face. Was it God who sent these reminders? He switched it off in mid-sentence.

When he hit the freeway he was thankful for the smooth flow of the traffic. He smiled as he saw the Wasatch Front and the peaks of Antelope Island with a fresh dusting of snow – the first of the year. The endless queue ran slowly as he passed a car wreck, then picked up again on the south end of town. He focused his thoughts on the day's business ahead as he pulled into the underground parking lot beneath the multistorey office block that housed the Utah headquarters of one of the nation's largest health insurers. It had been easy for him to walk into the vacant state general manager's slot – a godsend, if he dared use the term, that allowed him to escape Chicago. And Chuck. He'd not transferred to the national guard in his new state. It was a clean break.

He'd only just sat down in his corner office on the top floor, with its expansive views of an increasingly chilly Salt Lake City, when the phone on his desk rang. It was his secretary, Marjorie.

'Mister Monroe, there's a woman on hold who says she's from SNN television – it's an international call and she sounds English!'

He was as surprised as his excited assistant, and he asked the obvious question that he hoped had already been put to the reporter, 'Okay. What does she want?'

'She says she's doing a story on health insurance companies in the US, comparing fees with those that operate in Great Britain.'

Larry was a cautious man. It was why he had done so well in business. Sure, some folks said you needed to take risks, push the envelope, to get ahead, but Larry had always found the opposite to be true. He still rued the one time he'd taken a chance and gone with his heart instead of his head, and his God would never let him forget that mistake. 'I'm sure she'd be better off talking to head office, but put her through anyway, Marjorie. I'll give her corporate affairs' number.'

He waited for the call, feeling slightly ill at ease. He'd talked to plenty of journalists over the years, but they were mostly from the insurance industry trade publications. He'd never been interviewed by a television reporter, let alone one all the way from England.

'Larry Monroe,' he said.

Her voice was a little husky, and her accent was nice – sexy, even, but there was an echo on the line, which made it awkward for him to cut in on what she was saying – something about needing his help for a story she was putting together. 'I'm not sure if I can help you, Ms Thatcher. Say, are you calling from England? The line is terrible.'

He waited for his words to carry to her, and for her reply. 'Actually, Mister Monroe, I'm in Africa. In Zimbabwe, and I'm not really interested in health insurance.'

The fear gripped him, like a hand squeezing his heart. His immediate urge was to hang up, to throw the telephone at the wall, and to get in his SUV and drive as far and as fast as he could.

'Mister Monroe? You are the same Larry Monroe who travelled to Zimbabwe in September of this year and took part in the slaying of two unarmed men in the Matetsi Safari Area? What can you tell me about that, Mister Monroe?'

He coughed, and saw tiny pinpricks of light at the periphery of his vision. The blotter on his desk seemed to grow and shrink and the room started to spin. 'I . . . you don't know . . . what . . . ?'

'Take your time, Mister Monroe. I don't want to fly to America to get the information I need from you, but I will if I have to. I'll bring a cameraman, and producer,

473

and we'll camp outside your home or push our way into your office, so that all of your colleagues, your family and friends will know what you are, Mister Monroe. A murderer.'

What could he say? Barely a day went by without him thinking about that trip, and the death of those men, and the worry that some day he would get a telephone call exactly like this one. He had, when he had thought rationally about it, prepared a defence, and he struggled to remember the words he had so carefully crafted in his mind.

'Cat got your tongue, Larry?' she prodded. 'Okay, I'll be in Salt Lake City in a couple of days.'

'No, wait . . .' he stammered. 'Look, Ms . . .'

'Thatcher.'

'Thatcher, right. Look, I *was* on safari and something truly terrible did happen to us – my friends and me. We were fired on by armed poachers, and the professional hunter escorting us, Mister Fletcher Reynolds, had to protect us by . . .'

'Oh, *protect*, was it? By allowing you to murder two unarmed men, one of whom was already wounded?'

'No, no. You've got it all wrong, Ms Thatcher.'

'Why weren't the killings of these two poachers – whom you say were armed – reported to the local police or national parks authorities?'

'You'd have to ask Mister Reynolds that. All I know is that our lives were in danger and —'

'How much did you pay Fletcher Reynolds for the privilege of hunting – of killing – another human being?'

He knew now he had already spoken to her for too

474

long, and that he, and his two friends, and that monster Chuck Hamley who set it all up, were damned. His best chance was that the woman was bluffing. They had made a pact, sworn an oath never to tell another soul of what had gone on. Larry had been against it, had wavered before Fletcher had led them in pursuit of the wounded man and his comrade. When he'd seen the spots of blood on the grass he had felt physically ill and had tried to pull out. The other two had forced him on, and he had at that moment, for the first time in his life, feared his buddies. He couldn't imagine who would have divulged their secret.

His wife had guessed there was something wrong after his return from Zimbabwe. God, he hated the sound of that name now. He had suffered nightmares, been withdrawn and moody, had hardly said more than hello and goodbye to the kids as they came and went to school. She had asked him to open up, but he had refused. He'd considered seeing a therapist but, even though he was sure they would be bound by doctor-patient confidentiality, knew he was too ashamed to tell anyone why he felt the way he did.

'I don't know where you got such a preposterous story, Ms Thatcher.'

'Don't worry, Larry. It wasn't one of your army *buddies*. Did they force you to take part in the killing?'

'Look, I really have had enough of this, Ms Thatcher. I don't know who's filled your head with this —'

'A witness,' she said down the line, and it shocked him to silence. 'A boy, *Mister* Monroe. A boy who was in the wrong place, at the wrong time, for the wrong reasons, but a boy with more courage than you, Larry. A boy who hid behind an anthill and watched as Fletcher Reynolds fired bullets into the ground and around that man and his wounded friend, until they started to run.'

Larry closed his eyes, but the spinning wouldn't stop. He was there again. He smelled the dust that stank of a herd of elephant that had passed through before them; he saw the hazy blue sky and the bright red blood on the brittle yellow grass; he heard the cries from the man who had been shot in the leg, the voice of the other, who prayed to God and to Fletcher Reynolds for mercy. He heard his friends – both successful professionals and businessmen – jeering like Klansmen. *'Run, nigger,'* Brad had yelled, firing his rifle close enough to the uninjured man to make him cry real tears of fear. Larry had tried to calm them, to reason with Fletcher, but the professional hunter had ignored him, turning to the two other American members of the hunting party to make the decision, to rein in Larry, the dissenter.

'I have this boy on videotape, in case you're wondering, Larry. I am going to tell the world what you did.'

'Not me!' he yelled into the phone. He heard the office door open and glanced up to find Marjorie looking at him, concern worrying her face. 'It's okay,' he mouthed, then impolitely shooed her out with his hand. 'Not me,' he repeated earnestly into the telephone. 'I pretended, but I aimed high. I did *not* shoot either of those men. What do you want from me?'

'I believe you, Larry,' she said. 'Someone else who saw you in Africa, after the hunt, guessed that you harboured some remorse for what you did – or, as you put it, what your friends did. This story is big enough to air across the English-speaking world, Larry, but if you help me, I might – and I stress, *might* – be able to keep your name out of it.'

'How?' He tried to control his breathing. He had said too much already, and wondered if he should just hang up and call his lawyer. 'You – or this boy witness you have – would have gone to the police already if you thought you had a strong enough case against me.'

'True,' she acknowledged.

Emboldened, he said, forcefully, 'In fact, you've got nothing. The word of a boy – what was he, one of the poaching gang? You've got hearsay. No one would be able to convict me or anyone else in a court in this country. In Zimbabwe, they'd probably give Fletcher a medal for killing poachers.'

'Well done, Larry, you've hit the nail on the head. No one expects convictions would be easy, or even possible. That's why the people who want to stop Fletcher Reynolds and his barbarous trade – pandering to people like *you* – have come to me. I don't care about courts of law. If a judge stops me from naming Americans on television in America, I'll broadcast the story in England, Canada, Australia, South Africa – everywhere else in the world. Of course, the good thing about cable and satellite TV is that I'm sure someone you know, somewhere in the world, will learn the truth about you, Larry, and hopefully tell your wife.'

He felt on the ropes again, close to passing out. 'Like I said, I didn't harm anyone.'

'I believe you, Larry. I really do. Now it's up to you as to whether it's your name or Fletcher Reynolds' that gets beamed around the world.'

'What do I have to do?'

'That's the spirit!'

29

Fletcher stood in the shade of the awning jutting from the front of his tent, fists resting on the fold-out camp table as he studied a topographical map. Colonel Gizenga reclined in a camp chair opposite him, legs crossed, an imported French cigarette in one hand.

'I'm concerned about what those Hutu rebels from Rwanda are up to,' Fletcher said.

Gizenga nodded his agreement. 'Our army, together with the United Nations peacekeepers, has launched a major sweep through the southern section of the park, heading north.' Gizenga swept a hand, as though that was all that had been required to move the dissident Rwandans. 'Some of them have returned to their own country, but others have continued towards us. We believe some will try to cross into Uganda, and hide out in the Bwindi Forest.'

Fletcher's expression was grim. It would not be the first time the Interahamwe rebels had used this route. In 1999 a group of militia had ambushed tourists waiting to track mountain gorillas in the Bwindi National Park, and several westerners had been killed. 'I don't care where you drive them, Francois, but I don't want my clients getting into fire fights with Rwandan butchers.'

Fletcher had warned Anthony, and Charles Hamley, who was due to arrive in two days' time, that a minor war was underway in the DRC's eastern border regions, not far from the concession, but neither of them had been deterred from continuing with his safari.

'This is an important business trip for us,' Anthony had explained down the line from the United States. 'We're bringing a new guy on our crew – this is what you might call a team bonding session, and it's very important. I'm sure you can keep us safe from a few raggedy-assed rebels.'

Chuck had been just as eager to return to Africa. 'I've some business dealings to discuss with your other clients,' he had said cryptically, 'which might be best done in your neck of the woods, away from prying ears, if you know what I mean.'

Fletcher had no wish to know what sort of business the millionaire dentist and a bunch of mafia thugs might want to discuss. As long as they paid their bills, they could count on his discretion.

'Shane Castle is due back any time now,' Fletcher said to Gizenga.

'I am concerned about that man. I do not like his attitude. Is it wise continuing to employ him?'

'He's good, Francois, which is why I've kept him on.'

Their conversation was interrupted by the tone of Fletcher's satellite phone, chirping from the table. 'Fletcher Reynolds,' he said.

The voice on the other end of the line was English, plummy. 'Hello, Mister Reynolds, my name is Will Delancy. I'm in the market for a safari and you've been recommended to me by a friend of a friend of yours from the United States.'

'Well, Mister Delancy, thanks for your call, but I'm a little busy right now. Perhaps I can get your number and call you back some time soon.'

'Afraid that won't be soon enough, old boy. I heard you were in the Congo and that's where I'll be tomorrow. I'm in South Africa now, on some diamond business, and have to come up your way to visit a mine. Flying the family flag and all that, you understand? Of course you do.'

'Again, I'd like to help you, but my camp's full for the next few days. Who did you say referred you to me?'

The man snorted a little laugh. 'Not silly enough to say something like that over the phone, old boy. But it's a friend of the Chicago dentist. Enough said? I'm only out in the Congo for a few days, Mister Reynolds, and I'm keen on hunting a particular type of primate . . .'

'Look, Mister Delancy, I'm sorry to disappoint you, but . . .'

'Double.'

'Pardon?'

'I said double. I'll pay twice your normal fee for the hunt, which, if my information is correct, makes that two hundred thousand dollars – American – for a day's work. I assume cash would be acceptable? I've got some other greenback transactions to make while I'm up your way, so it's no trouble at all.'

Fletcher saw Gizenga watching him, trying to eavesdrop on the conversation. He could take the booking and squeeze the Englishman in with the gangsters. If they didn't like it, he would take him out separately. Also, there was no reason for him to tell Gizenga, or even Chuck, that the man had offered to pay twice the going rate. With that kind of cash, Fletcher could buy another two four-wheel drives, or another couple of houses in Zimbabwe. 'All right, Mister Delancy. I think that perhaps I can accommodate you. I'll need your full name again, and passport details, so we can smooth your arrival.'

'Wonderful stuff. It's a bit of a mouthful, I'm afraid, but it's Captain, The Honourable William Standish Hobson Delancy.'

The Honourable! Fletcher smiled. This could open up a whole new line of contacts.

Fletcher took the rest of the Englishman's details and noted the time of his arrival at Goma. Gizenga gave him an enquiring look. 'A late starter. We'll need at least one more target.'

'We will be out of targets soon, if business keeps up like this,' Gizenga said. 'We have to find some more, unless some genuine poachers stumble into the concession again.'

They both turned at the rattling sound of a diesel engine. The Land Rover pulled into the clearing outside the newly refurbished cottage, and Shane stepped down from the front passenger's seat. 'That's what *he's* for,' Fletcher said.

Gizenga rolled up his map and, after a perfunctory hello to Shane and Michelle, left with his driver.

Michelle strode across the freshly scythed grass to Fletcher and rose on her toes to kiss him.

'It's so good to see you back, Michelle,' he said, giving her a quick hug, then releasing her as he became aware of other eyes on them.

Shane stood with his hands clenched loosely at his side, like a boxer waiting to go into the ring. They nodded their greetings to each other and Shane said, 'We didn't get a chance to talk properly, before I left for the funeral. When you've got a minute, there are some things I'd like to clear up with you. In private.'

'Well, don't let me get in the way,' Michelle said. Fletcher thought, from her tone, that she was glad of the excuse to get away from Castle. He was pleased to see Michelle throw Shane a disapproving, resentful look as she turned on her heel and walked to her tent.

'No time like the present,' Fletcher said. 'Take a seat.'

Shane sat where Gizenga had been, and looked over his shoulder, as though checking there were no one in earshot. 'I've been doing a lot of thinking.'

'Not a good pastime for a soldier,' Fletcher smiled.

Shane stared at him. 'If I thought too hard about what was going on up here – what you were doing in Zimbabwe – then I might have gone to the police, or tried to take matters into my own hands.'

'What are you talking about?'

'I've worked it out,' Shane continued, 'or, I should

add, I had some help working it out. Wise told me, briefly, before I left to go to hospital to get my ankle seen to, that he had watched Marie Delacroix gun down that man in cold blood. He told me he thought we should call the cops, but I told him to drop it and that we'd talk about it when I got back. I also told him not to say anything to you.'

Fletcher concentrated on keeping his face immobile, on betraying nothing. 'Go on.'

'Well, I imagine the silly prick went and did just that.'

'What has Wise's death got to do with me?' Fletcher asked.

Shane leaned forward on the table, palms down, narrowing the gap between them, and stared straight into Fletcher's eyes. 'I don't know, and to tell you the truth, I don't care. He could have caused you problems, and now he can't. I'd call that a satisfactory result.'

'That's a little hard, Shane,' Fletcher said, leaning back in his chair, uncomfortable with the intensity of the younger man's gaze, but nonetheless intrigued.

'This is a hard business, Fletcher. War is hard. But having the will to kill criminals, and the sense to make some honest money out of it at the same time – that's smart.'

Fletcher said nothing. He decided he would let Shane fill the void.

'I went to see Charles Ndlovu's widow. Now, before you jump to conclusions and put a hit out on her, don't worry, she didn't say a thing. Her line was that Charles had turned, and that he'd made some money by joining the poachers' team, but it didn't wash. There was too much money in that family all of a sudden. New furniture, new car outside, son in his own business. Charles didn't make that kind of loot by picking up an AK and heading off into the bush hunting kudu. I asked the widow if you had given her money and she couldn't meet my eye. Like I said, she didn't drop you in it, Fletcher, but I reckon you had a hand in Charles's death, and that you paid some money to his family in return.'

'That'd be a very entertaining story, Shane, if it weren't so sick.'

'It's okay, Fletcher. I don't have a hidden camera or microphone,' he unbuttoned his shirt, theatrically baring his chest, then continued. 'You can check for real, if you want. I don't expect you to confess, or to tell me the whole story.'

Fletcher pursed his lips and reclined further back in his chair, steepling his fingers in front of his mouth.

'I could go on, but you know what I'm going to say. There were too many holes in your stories, about how you always managed to stumble onto the scenes of the anti-poaching contacts, with hunters in tow. I always had my doubts that Caesar would have missed seeing that SKS in the pick-up. Don't say a word, but I reckon you probably planted that rifle on the dead poacher to make it look like he was armed. And another thing came back to me recently.'

'Do go on,' Fletcher said drolly.

'I remember you telling me, way back when I started, how you'd taken a poacher's leg off with one shot.'

485

'Indeed I did.'

'Except it wasn't you. You said to me, something like, "You'd be amazed what a .458 can do to a man". The problem was, you only ever hunt with your old .375. Chuck uses a Weatherby .458 and he was with you on that hunt. You're letting your clients do the shooting. They're paying you to hunt men, and kill them.'

'You said you didn't want a confession – and you won't be getting one, because I've got nothing to say to you about that, Shane. So what do you want?'

'In.'

Fletcher blinked in surprise. He searched Shane's face for any sign of deceit, but saw only those intense coal-black eyes glaring back at him. 'Explain?'

'I'm still short of the cash I need to set up my own game ranch. I need to make a whole lot more money a whole lot faster, and I think your business is a good way to do that.'

Fletcher laughed. 'Why should I give you any share of my *legitimate* hunting business?'

'I don't want a share of your buffalo, lion or elephant hunts. I want a cut of the real stuff. I've been helping you make serious money all along, acting as a beater, driving human prey into your clients' guns.'

Fletcher forced himself to stay immobile, silent, while he continually looked for signs of dissembling in the younger man.

'However, up until now, I didn't know what the game plan was – the big picture. Just think how much more effective I can be – we can be – if we're working together. I was finding poachers and killing

486

them – now I can find them, fix them, and lead you and your clients in to ambush them. We can do this smarter.'

He saw the earnestness in Shane's eyes, and something else. The greed. He had it himself, and he could see when other people were bitten by the bug. Shane wanted this plan of his to work, more than anything else. 'If this is some kind of threat, Shane, or a crude attempt at blackmail, it won't work.'

'It's neither. If you don't cut me in on a share of the profits, I'll walk. You'll be two men down – because I wouldn't leave Caesar here to your mercy. I doubt anyone would believe me or even have the jurisdictional reach to convict you if I went to the police, either here or Zimbabwe. I imagine you've got those bases covered.'

Fletcher couldn't hold back the first curls of a smile. Shane was thinking like him, exploring all the opportunities and risks. 'So, you'd just fade away into the bush.'

'You'd be taking a risk letting me walk away, and – I warn you – if you're thinking about killing me, I won't die easy. All I want is to be in on the deal. Quite frankly, I'm a little pissed off you didn't include me from the start.'

'You seemed a bit too high-minded to take part in the sort of hunting I do.' Fletcher realised, as he said the words, that he was tacitly admitting the truth, for the first time, to someone other than Chuck or one of his clients. He hoped he wouldn't regret it.

'I kill for money, Fletcher. The same as you. All I want is a fair share.'

'How much would you think was fair?'

'Twenty thousand per kill.'

'You're way off the mark.'

'Make me an offer, then.'

Fletcher licked his lips, a quick, snakelike gesture. Shane had talked him around very quickly, and he wondered if it were because he needed to share the guilt with another, and, thinking ahead, to have someone to share the blame – or take the fall. 'Ten thousand per target – that's how I refer to them – paid into the bank account of your choice.'

'Eighteen thousand, in cash. I'm not going to let you leave a paper trail that will lead the cops to me when you're on the ropes.'

Fletcher smiled. He liked the boy's style. 'Fifteen thousand, or you can pack your bags now and leave.'

Shane reached across the table. 'Deal. How about a drink to seal it?'

Fletcher stood and walked into his tent. The Johnnie Walker Blue Label was on a bedside table carved in the shape of an elephant. Beside it was his nine millimetre pistol. There was always a fallback plan if Shane got too greedy or tried to con him. He brought the bottle and two tumblers back out under the awning, and poured each of them a healthy measure. Fletcher raised his glass, but when Shane reached over to clink he held his hand back. 'Of course, you'll have to prove yourself.'

Shane kept his glass held in midair. 'You want me to kill an unarmed man? It wouldn't be the first time.'

'We'll see. What do you want to do about Caesar?' Fletcher asked.

'What about him? I haven't told him my suspicions. He's much slower than Wise, more naive in the ways of the world. I don't think we have to do anything about him yet. He's a pretty useful scout, so I want to keep him.'

Fletcher nodded his agreement, refusing to rise to the bait. 'Just keep an eye on him. It's still dangerous out there in the jungle. We can't remove every possible risk. Look what happened to Wise.'

Shane smiled, though it looked forced. Fletcher guessed that it had been hard for him to come to terms with the death of the black.

'So, can we drink on it? You won't be out of pocket, Fletcher. Now that I know what I'm doing, you'll clean up. These hills are what the Yanks would call a target-rich environment.'

Fletcher leaned forward and they toasted, though to what, he wasn't quite sure.

Michelle showered, noticing that the primitive canvas-bucket affair had been replaced by a portable gas-fired geyser, which delivered piping-hot water. She realised that this was just one more little luxury that Fletcher could now afford for his hunting camp because of his high-priced trade in human flesh. She scrubbed herself quickly, then dried off. So far she hadn't had to be alone with Fletcher. She was worried about how she would act; if she could convince him nothing had changed. What if he wanted to sleep with her tonight?

The cottage in the centre of the clearing, which

Shane, Wise and Caesar had worked so hard to clear out, had been rethatched and whitewashed by Congolese builders in the few days she and Shane had been away. Half of it was given over to a rustic lounge and bar area, and she heard loud male voices from inside. It was the despicable Anthony and his gangster cronies, including a new man, a dark-haired boy barely out of his teens who had leered at her on her way to the shower.

She had decided there was no way she was going to associate with those thugs. She hadn't forgotten Anthony's advances, and she was glad Shane was in the camp, in the tent next to hers. She only hoped that he didn't provoke an unnecessary fight with the criminals, lest he get Fletcher offside. They had passed, on her walk across the clearing, and he had given her the slightest of nods and winked, to confirm that the first phase of their plan was going smoothly. It was good knowing Shane was close by, but she was still very nervous.

Her next part in the sting would come tomorrow, when all the men were out hunting. She waved at the Congolese man Fletcher had hired as a chef, a necessity now that the client tents were full, and let him know she was ready for her dinner. She would eat in the privacy of her tent. As she passed the cottage she glimpsed Shane's erect, broad-shouldered silhouette in the doorway. She felt a pang of regret that they couldn't be together that night. Also, she was worried for his safety. If it all went wrong, there would be no shortage of men who would try to make sure he didn't leave the Congo alive.

She clutched her towel and toiletries bag tightly to her chest. She might be in danger too.

Shane walked through the doorway into the cottage and the conversation ceased. He looked around. It was like a scene from a Wild West movie, except the outlaws were in safari attire and armed with expensive hunting rifles rather than six-shooters.

'*Buona sera.*'

Anthony glowered across the room at him. 'Shane, I'm sure you remember Anthony, Sal and Eddy,' Fletcher said. Shane nodded, though no one proffered hands.

'Where's the newsstand guy? Joey, wasn't it?'

'He's taking a little vacation. Courtesy of Uncle Sam,' Sal, the construction guy, said.

Shane saw the young man standing next to him. He had a whitewall haircut – US Marine Corps issue, so named because there was bare skin all the way around the back of his head, from ear to ear, and what little hair there was on top was short. High and tight. His face was acne-scarred, the teenage wounds only recently healed. 'This must be your boy, right, Sal? The one who was in Iraq?'

Sal smiled, clearly disarmed by the fact Shane had remembered their brief conversation about his son. 'Yeah. This is Vincent. Just back last week.'

Shane strode across the floor and put his hand out. 'Shane Castle. I was in Western Iraq with the Australian Army in '03. Good to meet you, and good to see you home safe, brother.'

Shane thought Anthony and the others must have warned Vincent about him, as the boy's face registered pleased surprise. 'Yeah, likewise.' If he noticed Anthony's disapproving frown, he ignored it, and shook hands. 'They told me you was special forces. You musta seen some shit, huh?'

'Probably not as much as you,' he replied modestly. 'Hey, Patrice,' he called over at the surly-faced guide, who had obviously had barman added to his duties list since the arrival of the clients, 'drinks all round for my American friends – a double for Vincent.'

Urged on by Fletcher's furious nod, Patrice poured and served.

'Let's drink a toast to the United States of America, and the US Marine Corps – the only thing standing between god-fearing civilisation and radical Muslim fundamentalism,' Shane boomed.

'Fuckin'-A,' said Sal enthusiastically.

'Semper-fi,' Vincent roared, downing his drink in one gulp. He wiped his mouth with the back of his hand and said to Shane, 'Hey, you know, you're okay.'

'A word,' Anthony said, beckoning Shane with a tilt of his head.

Shane moved with him to the doorway of the bar as the others resumed their conversation. 'Fletcher tells me you're on our team now.'

Shane nodded.

'Tell you the truth, I was kinda surprised that you weren't part of the operation from the outset. In my world, it's one in, all in, you know?'

'Look,' Shane said. 'I probably overreacted when we last met, over what happened with the girl.'

'Yeah, well, maybe I had a little too much vino that night. I got to remember this ain't New York and not everyone knows me out here.'

Shane wanted to plant his fist in Anthony's pug nose. Instead, he smiled and said, 'Anyway, I'm apologising.'

'And I'm accepting,' Anthony said, clapping him on the back. He took a drink of his Scotch and Coke and said, 'Also, I felt bad when I found out that broad was Fletcher's goombah – that he was fucking her. That was disrespectful of me.'

'Yeah, it's usually the great white hunter who makes it with the client's girlfriend, not the other way around.' He needed some air, and he had work to do. He excused himself and went back to where Vincent was standing.

'How's your drink?'

'Hey, let me get this one,' Vincent said. 'Even though they're free for clients, right?' They laughed and Shane let Vincent order him a Primus beer from Patrice, who turned his nose up at Shane when he served the drinks. 'What's with that guy?'

'Patrice? Don't mind him, he's just a psychopath. Fits in real well around here.'

'Oh, okay,' said Vincent, not knowing whether Shane was joking or having a laugh at his expense.

'What I mean,' Shane explained, 'is that some men take to this business differently. You can joke about it, you can see it as kind of doing your duty, or you can become all fucked up and nasty about it, like Patrice does.'

'How about you?' Vincent asked.

'I'm a soldier. I'm doing what has to be done.'

Vincent sipped his drink and looked into it. Shane saw he was thinking hard, probably about the subject they were dancing around. 'I never saw combat,' he said quietly.

'What did you do over there?' Shane asked.

'I was a clerk.'

'But you're a marine, right?'

He looked up and nodded emphatically.

'You're trained to kill, right?'

Just another nod in reply.

'It's stuffy in here. We used to drink outside, around the campfire. You want to step outside and talk, Vincent?' Shane asked. He saw the uncertainty in the boy's dark eyes and waited as he looked around, to make sure his father and the other gangsters wouldn't miss him. Anthony was relating an account of two strippers and a can of whipped cream, which held everyone else more or less enthralled.

They moved out, and Vincent declined Shane's offer of a cigarette. 'Smart guy,' Shane acknowledged. 'You might outrun a bullet, but these'll get you in the end.'

'So, what's it like? Killing someone, I mean,' Vincent asked.

It was the question on the lips of everyone he had ever met, if they knew he had seen action in Iraq and Afghanistan. Most people never asked; some obliquely tried to draw it out of him; and every now and then someone came right out with it, like Vincent. He never really had come up with a good answer, and usually he tried to avoid it or stall, as he did now. 'Tell me first why you're here, Vincent.'

Shane casually slipped his hand into his chinos and felt for the record button on the digital voice recorder Sarah Thatcher had loaned him. There was a tiny lapel microphone pinned inside his shirt, connected to the recorder by a wire. Had he been talking to Anthony or Sal or perhaps even young Vincent in private in New York, they probably would have frisked him first, checking for a wire. He had gambled that out here they would be less vigilant about security.

'My dad, Sal, says that a man needs to prove himself.'

'You went to war for your country.'

'It wasn't enough,' Vincent said.

'It would be for most people, for most fathers.'

Vincent smiled. 'Yeah, well, I figured you'd know by now that our family is not exactly the Brady Bunch. *Capisce?*'

Shane exhaled a stream of cigarette smoke. 'Sure. But why this?' He needed to draw the boy out.

'It's something they've all done – all the older guys.'

'Hunting?'

'You could call it that.'

'Let's call a spade a spade, Vincent. Why are you here?'

Vincent looked out at the black curtain of jungle beyond the warm glow of the paraffin lanterns. Into the blackness that would soon enshroud his soul, Shane mused. 'I'm here because it's a rite of passage.'

Shane guessed they were someone else's words. He wondered what it was like having someone so evil for a father. He stayed silent, and knew, as Vincent would probably learn through police interrogations in the future, that the interviewee will usually fill the void, and incriminate themselves.

'I haven't killed a man in combat, so I need to kill a man here.'

Shane prayed to the gods of technology that the recorder was doing its job. 'I hope they're not making you pay as well.'

Vincent was relieved that Shane had stopped pressing him, and he chuckled. 'No, no. My dad's cousin Anthony's taken care of that.'

'It's a lot of money.' Shane made it sound like a casual observation.

'A hundred grand for a hit? Shit, that's cheap where I come from.'

Shane had enough, and he didn't want the boy to become suspicious. 'You'll do fine. Let's go back inside.'

'Hey, let me ask you something else first.'

'What?'

'How do you live with yourself, man? Killing like this, for money.'

'I'm a soldier, Vincent. Just like you. A warrior.' Shane thought he had never felt so disgusted with himself in his life.

'Cool,' Vincent said, and turned and walked back inside.

In the cottage, Fletcher and Anthony stood in a corner talking. They weren't smiling, and the others were giving them space, engaging in their own conversations but, Shane suspected, keeping an ear on the main event. Fletcher held a hand up to Anthony, as though asking him to hold his thought for a moment, then beckoned Shane over.

He led Shane to the bar, leaving Anthony brooding alone. Shane glanced across at Vincent and saw, thankfully, that the boy had joined his father's group and had not been buttonholed by Anthony. He'd feared that the mobster might press Vincent about what he and Shane had been talking about.

'I've got a problem,' Fletcher said.

'How can I help?'

'That's what I wanted to hear.' Fletcher explained to him that another hunter was arriving the next morning, an Englishman, and that he had planned on having the man tag along with Anthony and the rest of the Americans. However, Anthony had put his foot down and refused to let anyone else accompany them.

'I'm not surprised, given that Vincent has just told me that the purpose of this safari is to blood him into the family business. No wonder they don't want strangers around as potential witnesses – even ones who are just as guilty as they are.'

'I shouldn't have taken the extra booking,' Fletcher admitted.

'So, make the guy wait a couple of days. Send him gorilla tracking or something,' Shane suggested.

Fletcher shook his head and explained that the English nobleman was only in the Congo for a couple of days. 'Shane, you said you wanted in. This is your chance to prove yourself.'

'The guy will be expecting a professional hunter, not a gamekeeper,' Shane said warily. 'Where will we find a target? Have you got some guys in the bag somewhere?' Shane needed to find out where and how Fletcher found his victims.

'It'll take Gizenga at least a day to organise another one. He's got one of the poachers you helped capture lined up for the Americans tomorrow. I was thinking that maybe you could take the pommy out on a patrol. Who knows, you might get lucky.'

Shane rubbed his chin. As he'd suspected, the Congolese colonel was involved in the racket. 'I don't like going into anything without proper planning. What do you know about this guy?'

Fletcher explained the little he knew – that the man was an aristocrat of some sort, involved in the diamond trade, and had been recommended by one of Charles Hamley's associates.

'If I go into the jungle with some blundering upper-class twit he might end up getting us both killed by some wandering Rwandan militiamen. It's a big risk to take for fifteen grand.'

Fletcher glared at him. 'Are you getting cold feet or are you getting greedy?'

Shane smiled and shrugged. 'I'm guessing that Lord Haw Haw must have sweetened the pot to get you to take him on when you're fully booked.'

Fletcher nodded, accepting defeat. 'I like your style, man. Okay, double the normal fee. The usual arrangement with the clients is that if they don't get satisfaction, then they don't pay. If you get lucky and find a poacher, you'll make your money and prove yourself to me. It'll be a win-win.'

'Deal,' Shane said.

*

Michelle sat up in her camp cot as she heard the buzz of her tent zipper opening. She wiped her palms on the sheet.

'It's okay. It's me,' Fletcher said. She smelled the Scotch fumes and groaned inwardly. 'Can I come in?'

'Looks like you are already,' she whispered. The moment she had been dreading had arrived. She swallowed hard and tried to steady her breathing.

'I'm so pleased you're back.'

She felt the cot sag and squeak as he sat. 'Fletcher, I'm really pleased too, it's just that . . .'

'What. Not going cold on me again, are you?' He shifted himself closer to her, reaching out, his fingers touching her breast through the fabric of her T-shirt. She failed to suppress a shudder, and prayed he didn't mistake it for arousal.

'It's a bad time, Fletcher.'

'What?'

She sighed. 'My period.'

'Oh? Okay.'

'Fletcher, I'm sorry.'

'No, no. Think nothing of it. I want it to be just right – always perfect between us. In fact, I was hoping that we could go away, just the two of us, once the Americans are gone. I was thinking one of those nice old colonial hotels in Goma, on the edge of Lake Kivu.'

'That sounds nice,' she said, pulling the sheet up to cover her breast. She wanted so much to confront him about what he had been doing, to hear him say, to her face, that he had taken money to hunt human beings. However, she knew that such an outburst was too dangerous to contemplate.

On one level, she wanted to understand how a man who seemed to live by a code of morals could justify murder for profit, while, on the other hand, she was just plain mad – both at him and at herself for falling for him. She wondered if he had ever planned on telling her what he was really hunting – who he was killing. Did he think that in time he'd be able to justify himself to her? Either through fear or revulsion, she was starting to feel physically sick.

'There's something I want to ask you – some things I want to tell you – but not now. It has to be at the right time.'

Oh no, she thought.

'Don't look so worried. It's a good thing. You'll see.' He reached out and brushed a strand of hair from her forehead, then leaned close and kissed her lightly on the lips. 'Goodnight.'

'Night,' she said. A shiver passed through her body as he stood and let himself out of the tent.

30

Shane leaned against the bar in the cottage drinking Kenyan coffee from an enamelled tin mug as Fletcher outlined to the Italian-Americans the plan for the day, gesturing occasionally to a topographic map taped to the wall.

The hunters wore a mix of designer camouflage clothing which, properly accessorised, would have been as at home on the streets of New York or Los Angeles as the jungles of the Democratic Republic of Congo. Anthony had covered his bald head with a leaf-pattern bandanna, which Shane thought took first prize in the ridiculous stakes. Fletcher was dressed in his customary khaki, and Shane was in running shorts and a faded U2 T-shirt. He would, he had told Fletcher, get dressed and into character before Caesar returned from the airport run with his Lordship later in the day. The sun was already high in the sky and the humid air inside the room was thick with the smell of gun oil and sweat.

He'd only glimpsed Michelle once that morning,

and been confused by the way she had deliberately avoided his eyes as she'd hurried to the shower. He'd expected at least some furtive signal as reassurance from her. He hoped she was all right. They would have some time together alone, once Fletcher and his hunting party departed, and before the Englishman arrived.

'Ain't you coming with us, Shane?' Vincent asked.

Fletcher answered for him. 'As I mentioned to Anthony last night, I've got another client arriving today, an Englishman. Rather than delay our departure I'm assigning Shane to take him out this afternoon. They'll be operating well to the south of us,' Fletcher pointed to the map, 'so there's no risk of us getting in each other's way. Part of Shane's task today will be to recce this part of the concession to see if there has been any poaching activity lately. He may drum up some more trade for us for tomorrow.'

'Is this Brit guy hunting the same thing as us?' Vincent asked.

'He is,' Fletcher confirmed, 'but we may have better hunting than Shane and Mister Delancy today. We're in luck this morning.' Fletcher turned to face the map again. Shane marvelled at how easily and convincingly he lied. 'My contact in the Congolese Army radioed camp this morning to let us know that they had a contact with armed poachers not far from the Ugandan border, inside our concession, last night.'

Anthony, Sal, Eddy and Vincent crowded into a semicircle and studied the map like armchair generals. 'The army drilled four of the five poachers, but they say the fifth – probably the ringleader – got away. He's armed with an AK 47, and he knows how to use it. They're on his tail, and they think he's probably headed for home, in the village just to our west. The army has asked me, gentlemen, in my capacity as an honorary ranger in this area, to be on the lookout for this man and to kill or capture him.'

'All right!' Vincent enthused.

'Vincent, I'm not sure what your dad and the others have told you, but I'll run through our normal rules of engagement for your benefit.'

The coffee tasted bitter in Shane's mouth as Fletcher rabbited on about not shooting at women or children, or unarmed men unless he had positively identified them first as poachers. 'Any questions?'

'One man, in all that jungle?' Vincent sounded dubious as he leaned forward, studying the area on the map Fletcher had been pointing to. 'We're gonna have to be pretty damn lucky to find him.'

'This guy is always lucky, son,' Sal said, clapping Fletcher on the arm. 'He's got a nose for these scumbags.'

'As usual,' Fletcher concluded, tactfully avoiding Vincent's question – and whatever suspicions the other men might have that the whole hunt was rigged – 'your safety is my paramount concern. If there is unacceptable danger I'll pull us all back and either call for reinforcements or bring us back to camp.'

'What's acceptable danger?' Vincent asked.

Fletcher turned to him. 'All my clients know that this is not a one-sided affair. They come here having taken out the appropriate insurance, and having made their peace with their God and their family. This is not war, Vincent, as you knew it,' and Shane had to stop himself from smiling at the nice double entendre there, 'but it is the closest thing to it that money can buy. Never forget, gentlemen, that I am acting within the bounds of the laws of this land. It is *illegal* for an unauthorised civilian to be in the national park or a concession such as this in possession of a firearm and I am allowed – encouraged, even – by the government of this country to shoot poachers on sight.'

'Let's get some!' Anthony yelled, raising his Weatherby hunting rifle high over his head.

'Fuckin'-A,' Sal concluded.

Vincent lingered outside the cottage as the others began piling awkwardly into the Landcruiser with their rifles, hunting vests and ammunition. 'Shane?'

Shane cocked an eyebrow as he drained the last of his coffee.

'Any last-minute words of advice?'

'Keep your head down.'

From her tent, Michelle watched the heavily laden Landcruiser trundle out of camp. She assumed that Patrice and Fletcher would drive the gangsters most of the way to the killing ground, as the overweight hoodlums would probably have heart attacks if they had to walk.

She watched Shane toss the dregs of his coffee into the dying campfire and walk to his tent. She scanned the clearing to make sure none of the camp staff was loitering around, possibly spying on her, and darted next door.

Shane was bare-chested and pulling up his camou-flage fatigue trousers. She saw the sliver of white skin and dark curls beneath his hard, flat belly, and felt a momentary stirring of desire. 'Hey, don't you knock?' he smiled.

Michelle looked over her shoulder again, entered his tent proper and zipped the door closed. She sat down on his sturdy green plastic foot locker as he buckled his belt and pulled on a green T-shirt that hugged every ripple of his torso.

'Are you all right today?' he asked, prompted by her silence. He sat down on his cot and began lacing his leather and nylon combat boots, but looked up to await her answer.

She fiddled with the hem of her sleeveless khaki bush shirt.

He stood and sat down beside her, then wrapped an arm around her shoulders. 'I can get you out today, Michelle. I'll get Caesar to take you back to the air-port when he arrives with the Englishman.'

'No, no, I don't want out, Shane. It's just that it's hard for me to keep up the pretence, you know? Fletcher came to my tent last night, and . . .'

'Did he hurt you?' Anger flared in Shane's dark eyes.

'No. He never would.'

She felt worse than ever now, and wished she hadn't said a word. 'We didn't sleep together, Shane.'

He pressed her to him and kissed away the salty streaks. 'It's okay, Michelle. Whatever happened, it doesn't matter.'

'Nothing happened. I think he wants to marry me.'

'If all goes well we'll be out of here tomorrow. I'll treat us to the best room in the best hotel in Goma.'

'Funny, he said the same thing to me last night. I'm worried he might come after us, once we've got what we need.'

'I won't let that happen.'

She saw the steel in him now, in his cold stare, in the set of his jaw, in his clenched fists. 'We agreed, Shane. You can't kill him in cold blood. If you do, you're no better than him.'

'You suggested, I never agreed,' he firmly reminded her. 'But if everything goes well, he won't be bothering us.'

'Where will we go?'

He looked away, either pondering, or avoiding her. She wasn't sure which. She regretted the words as soon as she had said them. Had she assumed that they were inextricably intertwined now? A couple? He was a man, and no doubt prey to the same fear of commitment that most of his kind suffered.

'I don't care, as long as we're together,' he said.

31

The clear patch on the slope of the hill had probably once been a small subsistence farm. Now overgrown with a tangle of long grass and creeping vines, it was a step away from being overtaken once more by the encroaching jungle. For now, it would do just fine as a killing zone, Fletcher thought.

'*Contact. Target moving west, over.*' Gizenga's voice confirmed all was ready. Fletcher acknowledged the tally-ho call. Gizenga had told him that the target's weapon was empty. Fletcher had an AK 47 magazine half full of bullets hidden in one of the pouches of his vest, which he would plant on the body when he moved forward, as usual, ahead of the clients, to check the man was dead or incapacitated. This would add some verisimilitude to the production.

Fletcher looked across at the Americans, gasping and sweating despite the fact that they had only walked for a little over two hours. Even Vincent, the youngest and fittest of the group by far, was panting.

Too much time behind a desk, Fletcher guessed. He wondered briefly what the boy's future would be, in the dark world of organised crime. Despite what he now did for a living, Fletcher considered Anthony and his 'crew' little better than the poachers he had once genuinely hunted. He smiled at Vincent, who replied with a pained thumbs-up.

'Okay. Find a good firing position. Colonel Gizenga says his men are hot on the heels of the leader of the poaching gang,' Fletcher told the assembled gangsters.

He moved along the line of men, kneeling or lying on the edge of the forest, sweat cooling on the darkened backs of their shirts, eyes blinking as they scanned the sunny clearing. 'Move a little more behind the tree, Sal,' he whispered. 'Eddy, you might want to find a tree or a log, that anthill won't stop a 7.62 round.'

They adjusted themselves, fidgeting like raw recruits. Fletcher sighed inwardly. This lot couldn't even stay still without making noise. '*You should see him any second now, over,*' Gizenga confirmed. Fletcher scanned the opposing tree line, across the grass, and picked up the moving figure just as Patrice nodded to him.

'Here he comes,' Fletcher hissed to each of them, moving stealthily along behind them.

'Vincent gets first shot, okay?' Anthony reminded all of them, though he, too, peered intently into the scope of his rifle.

Fletcher knelt beside Vincent, who lay on his belly, his AR-15 assault rifle pulled tight into his shoulder.

It was the semi-automatic civilian version of the venerable M-16, the rifle Vincent had trained on and used in the Marine Corps in Iraq. Fletcher had every confidence that the boy would do well. Still, one never knew when it came to taking a life, as opposed to shooting on the rifle range. 'Steady, son,' he said reassuringly, patting the young man on the shoulder. Vincent glanced up at him, and Fletcher rethought his earlier optimism. He looked deathly pale now.

Fletcher could see the target's head and shoulders above the grass. The African paused to listen and smell the air. Obviously the man knew he was being followed, but he was unaware of what was in front of him. The target swivelled a second later, realising that he was cut off from moving downhill, around the clearing. He looked to his right and must have seen a shadow moving in the tree line at the top end of the grassland. There was no option for him other than to move through the long grass, which he did at a run. Fletcher recognised him as one of the unarmed bearers from the bush meat poaching party. An old man, with tight, frizzy grey curls. Fletcher saw his mouth was open, wide and pink, as he gasped for air under the sun's furious might.

'Ready?'

Vincent nodded.

'In your own time . . .'

The first shot rang out, but Fletcher knew immediately that things had gone wrong. Vincent yelled, 'Fuck!' as a bullet slammed into the trunk of the tree inches from his face. He slithered backwards on his belly, face buried in leaf mulch.

'Hey, what was —' Anthony's cry was cut short by a noise like fast-tearing paper and the ping and whiz of a bullet ricocheting off the rock he was about to lean on as he scrambled to his knees. A shard of stone flew off and nicked his arm. 'I'm fucking hit!'

Another gunshot echoed and Fletcher felt twigs and bark rain down on his head. He looked angrily across the clearing. The target had paused and dropped to the ground, out of sight in the long grass.

'Stay still!' Fletcher ordered. 'Nobody move. It's a sniper!'

'Bullshit,' Sal swore, and started to stand. 'Come on, Vincent, let's —' The bullets were ending conversations before they could begin. Sal screamed as his rifle was snatched out of his hand, as though grasped by an invisible bull whip and flung to one side. He shook his hand at the pain caused by the vibration of the gunshot. The expensive hunting firearm lay useless in the mud, its polished wooden stock shattered by a bullet.

'Two rifles – one silenced, and one AK,' Fletcher said, assessing the enemy's strength as he changed fire positions and dropped to one knee behind a once mighty fallen tree. 'Green one, we're taking fire, report! If it's your men firing, tell them to bloody well stop, over!' he barked into the radio.

'*Negative, negative,*' Gizenga replied. '*We are also being shot at. I thought it was your men, so I ordered my troops to go to ground!*'

Amidst the chaos and the shouting of the panicked Americans, Fletcher saw the target rise to his feet and start running, on a south-westerly course that would take him away from the hunters' rifles. 'No way,' he said to himself. He looked across at his clients and confirmed that all of them had their heads down. Anthony was almost crying from the pain of the little cut on his arm; Sal had his head in his hands; Eddy was lying behind a rock, and Vincent lay on his back, looking up at Fletcher, eyes wide with fear. Fletcher stood and brought the scarred stock of his old .375 up to his shoulder. He took aim at the running African, but the man dropped in the grass before he could fire. 'Bloody hell!'

'*Niner, this is Taipan, over.*' In contrast to the pandemonium all around him, Shane's voice in his radio earpiece was as calm as if the man had just asked him to pass the salt at the dinner table.

Fletcher had other things to worry about at the moment, and just hoped Shane wasn't going to add to his troubles. 'Taipan, Niner, go, over.'

'*Niner, we've got a contact down south. We're tailing one man armed with an old Lee Enfield. He looks like a bona fide poacher to me. I'm going to give his Lordship the green light, over.*'

Thank heavens, Fletcher thought. At least one thing had gone right today. 'Affirmative, Taipan. Take the shot. Things are going to shit up here, man.'

'*I can break contact if you need help, over.*'

'No. Just get it done. We're going to have to pull out of here, someone's shooting at us, over.'

'*Roger, Niner. We heard some automatic weapons fire earlier. Could be those Rwandan Hutus the army's chasing. I'd bug out quick if I were you.*'

'Affirmative,' Fletcher said. It was the only thing he

could do. Of their target, there was no sight, and another two rounds cracked over Eddy's head, giving him no choice. 'Patrice, give us some covering fire to the south. That looks like where it's coming from. The rest of you, let's move it!'

Ironically, the job of bandaging Anthony's arm fell to Michelle, who was ready and waiting with the first-aid kit when the Landcruiser disgorged its cargo of cursing, yabbering, angry white hunters.

'Ow,' he yelped as she applied a generous squirt of iodine to the wound. 'Look, Michelle, I want to say that I was out of line with what happened last time. I didn't know you and Fletcher was hooked up, okay?'

'Sure,' she said, pressing hard on the ends of the dressing to make sure it stayed in place and hurt him some more. 'Sounds like it could have gone better out there today. I heard you guys bumped into an armed poacher.'

'An army of them, more like,' Anthony said, rolling down his sleeve. 'We was lucky to get out of there alive.'

'Will you go back to the States now?' she taunted. 'Surely you just came here to hunt big game, not get involved in the war on poaching.'

He looked at her quizzically, as if trying to work out whether she knew what Fletcher really did. She imagined Anthony thought it was strange that Fletcher could have a girlfriend who was completely unaware of what really went on during the specialised safaris. 'Nah. Don't let the bastards get you down, I say.'

'Good for you,' she said, rinsing her hands in a bowl of water perched on a canvas camping stool.

Michelle could hear, but not see, Fletcher dressing down one of the Congolese camp attendants. Something about no toilet paper in the latrine and no soap in the guest tents. The Americans had complained. She could tell his anger stemmed from much more than that, though. She smiled to herself.

'What happened?' she asked when he walked into view, acknowledging her on his way to the cottage. He paused – almost reluctantly, she thought – to recount the afternoon's events.

'You seem more disappointed by the fact that the poacher got away than the fact that you were all nearly killed.'

His mouth pursed into a frown, then he turned and walked on. The big green Land Rover chugged around the bend of the dirt track and pulled up in the clearing. Shane and the Englishman got out, followed by Caesar.

'Hello there,' the new arrival said, as Fletcher ran a hand through his hair, forced a smile and strode across to meet him. 'Will Delancy.'

They shook hands. 'Sorry I couldn't be with you today. Come join us in the bar. How did it go, anyway?' Fletcher asked.

'Absolutely first-rate! Couldn't have been better. Your bird dog here is worth his weight in diamonds. We bagged one!'

Anthony and the others drifted across to the cottage from their tents to hear the Englishman's tale, and perfunctory introductions were made. Shane,

Michelle noticed, hung back from the crowd that had clustered around Delancy, smoking a cigarette in silence on the front step. She crept from her tent around the back of the cottage, where she could eavesdrop on the conversation inside without being seen. She peeked through a side window, behind the bar, her face hidden by a pot plant on the windowsill.

'You lucky son of a bitch,' Sal growled good-naturedly. 'Tell us about it.'

'Well, we were patrolling – I suppose that's what you'd call it? And all of sudden Shane and his gun bearer go to ground. I nearly ran into them. Bird watching at the time, of all things!'

With his bright orange hair, pasty white face and narrow beaked nose, he looked almost clown-like, Michelle thought, and his gestures and accent were those of an upper-crust wastrel. 'Then Shane points at this chap and low and behold, he sees us and freezes.'

'Who got him?' Vincent asked.

'Old Shane had his rifle up and ready but, ever the gentleman, he let me have first go. One's reflexes get pretty sharp from shooting pheasant. Before I knew it, bingo, one dead poacher!'

'Shit. No way,' Vincent said.

'Well done,' Fletcher said. 'What happened to the body?'

Shane had moved forward, unseen, and spoke up from behind Eddy. 'We checked him out, but then we heard voices and movement up ahead. It sounded like there were more of them, or maybe some of those militiamen. I didn't want to risk hanging around, and it would have slowed us down to carry him out.'

'Hmmm,' Fletcher said. In his hunts in the Congo so far, Michelle, guessed, there had always been Gizenga and his henchmen around to get rid of the evidence.

'I've got some pictures, if you'd like to see!' Delancy piped up.

'Fletcher normally don't let people take pictures,' Anthony said.

'That's right, Will. I'll have to ask you to delete them before you leave here, but I'm very interested in seeing them first,' Fletcher said.

'Of course. Mum's the word and all that,' the Englishman said. 'Here you go.' He pulled a small digital camera from one of the pockets of his tan safari jacket and brought up a series of images on the tiny screen at the back of the device. Michelle couldn't see them from her vantage point, but the Americans gave her a running commentary.

'Shit, look at that exit wound,' Vincent said.

'Looks like you musta got him near the heart,' Sal said. 'Blood everywhere.'

'Right through it, old boy,' Delancy confirmed. 'Look at this one. You can see the entry wound on the front of his chest.'

'His face is a mess, though,' Anthony said. 'Who did that?'

Delancy looked over his shoulder at Shane. 'Shane saw the body moving – must have been the death throes, I suppose – and made certain of things as he approached the bugger.'

Fletcher looked from the pictures across to Shane, who said nothing. Michelle saw the cold, hard look on the face of the man she had very nearly fallen in love with, and felt a shiver run down her spine.

'Show me where you were,' Fletcher said to Shane, taking him away from the others and leading him to the map on the wall of the bar, while the Americans urged Delancy to run his macabre mini slide show again.

Shane lit a second cigarette with the butt of the first, tossed the dead one outside, and bent to peer at the map. 'Right here,' he said. 'Where you sent us, about a klick in from the road. It was a good call.'

Fletcher said, 'You didn't hear the contact we had?'

Shane shook his head. 'Couldn't have. Too far away. But I heard automatic gunfire early on, to the east. There's definitely no shortage of people with guns out in the jungle at the moment. It must be the army taking on the Hutus. I heard a chopper as well.'

'Probably one of the UN helicopters. They're working with the Congolese Army to try to drive out the Rwandan rebels, back across the border.'

'Maybe you should call things off. It's not worth losing a client. Sounds like you ran into some of those militia guys. They're on the run and they're desperate.'

It was nearly dusk and Patrice was handing out frothing beers and tumblers full of Scotch and Coke. 'To tomorrow's hunt!' Anthony bellowed, raising his glass to clink against William Delancy's beer bottle.

'Tally-ho!' Delancy responded.

Michelle circled around the back of the cottage when she saw Shane and Fletcher slip outside. She wanted to hear their conversation.

'What do you make of Delancy?' Fletcher asked.

516

'He's an idiot. But he's a pretty good shot. Why?'

'I spoke to Chuck on the satellite phone this afternoon,' Fletcher said, looking back at the glow coming from the generator-operated lights in the cottage, 'he was uncomfortable that I'd taken a booking without his personal recommendation.'

'Fuck him,' Shane said.

Fletcher laughed. 'My sentiments exactly, though I expressed it differently. I told Chuck that Delancy was recommended by one of his friends.'

'What did Chuck say?'

'He said he'd check him out himself.'

'Wise move,' Shane said. 'When's Chuck arriving?'

'Ten tomorrow morning. We'll all be out on safari, so detail Caesar to pick him up from the airport. Michelle can babysit him here until we get back. Feed him some crap about her research.'

Michelle frowned at Fletcher's dismissive tone – had he been playing her all along, only interested in her research for what it would buy him? Also, she didn't relish spending any more time than she had to with Chuck, who gave her the creeps.

'Do you want me to take Delancy out again tomorrow?' Shane asked.

Fletcher nodded back towards the bar. 'No, they're all getting along famously in there today. I'm sure we can get Anthony and his crew to agree that we can all go out together. I want you to make sure that we don't miss our target. He's the last one Gizenga's got in captivity. If we cock this one up it'll be back to searching for real poachers.'

'You prefer killing the captive men – poor sods that

517

don't know one end of a rifle from the other, who've been released by the Congolese Army to run into your guns?'

Fletcher laughed. 'What a silly question. Of course I do. It's money for jam – let's go back to the party. Don't do too much soul-searching, Shane, or you'll have me crying in my beer as well. Think of it like I do – a means to an end.'

Michelle grimaced at Fletcher's self-incriminating wickedness. Shane's suggestion that they duct-tape a night-vision scope to the lens of the mini digital camera Sarah had leant them was a simple but effective way of allowing them to film at night. Michelle noted how bright Fletcher's teeth appeared in the lime-green picture on the camera's LCD screen.

Shane sat in the dark in front of his tent, reassembling his rifle and checking his magazines and ammunition.

He had seen Michelle creeping from behind the cottage and his heart had beat faster as he'd focused on keeping Fletcher's attention on him. Her bravery didn't make up for her lack of field craft. Still, he'd noticed that she was carrying the video camera, and hoped that she had recorded his last remarks to Fletcher.

She was a brave woman and it must have been hell for her, learning the man she was sleeping with was a killer. It would have been safer if she'd stayed in Zimbabwe or gone home to Canada, but Shane knew she was right – Fletcher would be far less suspicious if she were around. It was difficult for him, though, having her in the camp. He remembered the taste of her, the softness of her skin on the undersides of her slender wrists, the look in her eyes when she came. He'd said nothing, but he would have been gutted if she'd decided she had to sleep with Fletcher to maintain the charade. He felt his pulse rate start to rise, and knew this was not the time to let emotion cloud his thoughts. Better to focus on the mechanics of the job.

Fletcher had given him an old banana-shaped AK 47 magazine with five bullets in it. Fletcher carried one as well, with the idea being that when the Americans killed the 'poacher', whomever was closer would switch the empty magazine from the dead man's rifle with another containing bullets, before the Yanks arrived at the body. He pushed down on the top round, and heard the scratch and squeak of dirt in the magazine. He shook his head. The thing had probably never been cleaned. When he did it again, he felt the spring inside the magazine snap. It must have rusted away, he thought. He shook the copper-jacketed Russian-made bullets free and caught them in his left hand. He wouldn't need the magazine in any case and, not knowing what else to do with the rounds, he stuffed them in the side cargo pocket of his fatigue trousers. The magazine was history, so he tossed it aside. He had a hundred and twenty rounds for his own rifle, and reckoned that would be enough to see him through the next day.

32

His name was Mubare, although he didn't know it.

Mubare was not a man – he was a one hundred and eighty kilogram silverback mountain gorilla.

He stood one hundred and seventy centimetres tall, his massive head the size of a human's torso, his hands as big as dinner plates. All Mubare knew, or really cared about, was eating, having sex and protecting his family. He was very good at all three. That's why he was the silverback.

It was a fine day, which had begun with wisps of mist curling around the tops of the tall trees. The sun warmed his back pleasingly, drying the droplets of rain that remained from the previous night's shower. Soon it would be too hot to move and eat, which was why Mubare was leading his family on their normal early-morning foraging expedition.

He looked at the little black-haired human who sat watching him through the thicket of bamboo. He knew she was a female, by the smell of her, and that she was no harm to his family. Mubare saw humans often. He snapped off another green stalk and continued eating.

One of his females had given birth recently and he watched his tiny son, out of the corner of his eye, wander closer to the human. Mubare sat back on his bottom, scratched his privates and continued chewing his bamboo as he kept a wary eye on his offspring.

Marie Delacroix had been researching *Gorilla berengei*, the endangered mountain gorilla, on and off for seven years, yet she never tired of watching them, nor ceased to be surprised at the depth of her emotions towards these mammals. She held her breath as the little baby toddled towards her. It looked up at her and she knew, from past experience, that the source of its curiosity was his own reflection in the lens of her camera. She kept herself perfectly still, but couldn't stop a tear from rolling down her cheek as the baby reached up and first touched the glass of her camera and then, with his soft leathery finger, traced a line down the back of her hand.

The silverback grunted and the baby turned and scampered back to the safety of his family. It was time to move on. Mubare raised himself on his rear feet, kneeling forward on his knuckles, and kept an eye on the human as his females, sons and daughters lifted themselves and started moving on to the next juicy thicket.

Marie, who had long since dispensed with the need for a guide, waited until the silverback was moving, then stood and slung her rifle over her shoulder. She was worried, not because she had illegally crossed the border into Uganda to follow these gorillas, but because they had already crossed into the Congo once that day, and might yet move back into the Sarambwe Forest again. She had been alerted by a Congolese national parks ranger, who in turn had been told by one of Colonel Francois Gizenga's officers, that the troop had been seen moving across the border the day before. Marie had tried to contact Fletcher Reynolds, to warn him of the proximity of the gorilla troop to his hunting concession, but he had already left on safari with his clients. She had driven north from her base at Bukima, bluffing her way through army and UN roadblocks, until she had been close enough to walk to the hills where the apes had reportedly been seen.

Today was the first time she had ever carried a firearm on a gorilla trek. She had told her assistant, who had remarked on it, that it was because of the distant sounds of gunfire, of the army mounting yet another operation to try to oust whichever band of ragtag rebels was calling the Virunga park home this month. The gun was for her safety, she had said. However, secretly she replayed over and over in her mind the thrill of executing the poacher on her safari with Fletcher. From now on, if she came across an armed man who had no business in a park or other protected area, she would take the law into her own hands. It was risky, carrying a firearm into a neighbouring country, but Marie saw no alternative.

*

'Absolutely no way, Anthony. I totally and utterly forbid it,' Fletcher said.

'Half a million dollars, Fletcher. Just think about it. Five times the price of a human being.'

They had left the Landcruiser parked in the jungle, just off the dirt road, and had been slogging through a latticework of vines and thistles for the best part of two hours. Anthony had sprung the surprise request on Fletcher that morning and had been badgering him ever since. To no avail.

'Anthony, there is no way on God's green earth that I am going to be a party to the killing or capture of a mountain gorilla. It's simply not going to happen.'

Fletcher slapped at a mosquito on his neck, satisfied at the sight of blood on his fingers. He wished he could rid himself of Anthony and his mobsters as easily. Anthony, who had only just learned that there were mountain gorillas in the Bwindi Impenetrable National Park adjoining the concession, said he had been fascinated, as a child, by a taxidermist's shop in New York, which had a gorilla hand ashtray on its counter. 'Ever since then I wanted one of those things,' he'd said.

In addition, as if that request weren't dangerous or difficult enough, Anthony had explained that a Chinese-American 'businessman' with whom he had an 'association' kept a private zoo on a farm in upstate New York. The man had mentioned, in passing, when Anthony had told him of his travels to Africa, that he would pay half a million dollars for a baby gorilla. 'If his first offer was five hundred thousand,' Anthony had reasoned, 'he'll easy go seven-fifty or a mill. If I get a million I'll split it fifty-fifty with you, Fletcher.'

Fletcher shook his head.

'How about it, be a sport,' Anthony tried again, stopping to unhook a barbed vine from his tiger-striped camouflage smock. He was wearing the bandanna again today, which Fletcher thought was as absurd as his request.

'Once and for all, no!' Fletcher hissed. 'There are only a few hundred mountain gorillas left alive. I won't be a party to poaching or an illegal armed incursion into Uganda!'

Anthony snorted. 'Nah, but you'll kill people for money. How do you sleep at night?'

Sal and Eddy laughed. They stumbled along behind Anthony, along with Vincent. Shane had dropped back, presumably to check on Delancy, who was bringing up the rear.

Fletcher was constantly looking back, keeping an eye on all his charges and making sure Shane was alert – not that he needed to worry on that account. He'd had his doubts about Shane's sincerity, about wanting in on the business, and had half been expecting a set-up of some kind. His quick results with the English lord, however, had convinced him that Shane was serious. The gory picture of the dead poacher was proof.

He scanned the trees above them and the jungle ahead of Patrice, a near impenetrable tangle of vines and bamboo thickets. He had deliberately steered Gizenga towards higher ground, thick with vegetation and away from existing roads, in the hope that there would be less chance of them running into any Rwandan rebels – or other armed militiamen who had sought refuge in the concession and were now being harassed by the Congolese Army. The ambush yesterday had worried him. The whole operation would come tumbling down around his ears if he ever lost a hunter to a stray bullet.

Counting Delancy, he was looking at hunting fees of half a million dollars already from this trip. Minus the cuts for Chuck, Gizenga, and now Shane, he would still clear about a quarter of a million dollars for himself.

'Hey, Patrice, buddy! How about you? Could you use fifty grand?' Anthony called ahead to the guide. Patrice looked over his shoulder and raised his eyebrows at Fletcher.

'I'd kill you, if the UN anti-poaching patrols or the Congolese Army didn't get you first,' Fletcher told Patrice. The guide returned his attention to the creepers in front of him, hacking away with his panga. Overhead, monkeys chattered and leapt from tree to tree, their antics creating a light rain of falling leaves on the men far below.

'Boy, I'm outta shape,' Sal wheezed, wiping his brow with his bush hat. They were climbing steadily now, moving into the foothills of the mountains that constituted the gorillas' refuge in the Bwindi Forest across the border.

Fletcher checked his GPS. They were close to the stream where Gizenga would release the target. With soldiers positioned each side of its banks, the man would logically follow the watercourse as the quickest route down off the mountain. As if on cue, his earpiece hissed to life, as Gizenga called him, quoting their prearranged callsigns.

'*We are ready to release. Are you in position, over?*' Gizenga asked.

'Affirmative,' Fletcher hissed. He held up a hand to stop their movement, then beckoned Anthony over. 'Tell your men to stay alert. The army commander's just told me there's an armed poacher heading our way.'

'Okay.'

'*Niner, this is zero alpha, over.*' Fletcher reached for the radio handset again at the unexpected sound of Caesar's voice, calling from camp. He acknowledged the call.

'*Sah, I have Doctor Hamley here, over.*'

Fletcher sighed. He knew very well that Chuck should have arrived by now, and wondered why Caesar was stating the obvious, bothering him with such news while he was out on safari and about to go into action. 'So what, over?'

'*Sah, I am calling because Doctor Hamley wants to talk to you. He says it is urgent, over.*'

Marie Delacroix turned to face the sound of gunfire. It was getting closer.

Mubare, the silverback, heard the noise as well, and gave his characteristic warning cough. The rest of the troop of gorillas looked to him.

Another weapon answered, and this one was close enough for Marie to hear the *crack-thump* of the bullet leaving the barrel and echoing across the mountainside.

Mubare stood on his hind legs and faced Marie,

then beat a hollow-sounding tattoo on his chest, as if she, as a human, were somehow responsible for the bothersome noise. He grunted to his family and they veered off on a tangent, away from their south-bound feeding route, to the west. Marie held her breath as they filed past her. As he skirted her, Mubare gave her what she would have described from a human as an angry glare.

Marie took out her GPS and switched it on. While she waited for the gadget to compute her position, she pulled out her map. After a few minutes, the receiver gave her a position in degrees, minutes and seconds. Cross-referencing the figures on the map, she said, '*Mon Dieu!*' They were perilously near to the border of the Congo, much closer than she had imagined. If the gorillas kept on their present heading they would be out of their sanctuary and in the DRC again – in Fletcher's concession – in half an hour or less. She heard more gunfire to the east.

'Stop the target!' Fletcher hissed angrily into the radio.

'*Stop him? But what am I supposed to do, tell my men to kill him? I thought that was your job, over,*' Gizenga replied.

'Shit,' Fletcher swore to himself. He was cursed. He pulled Patrice aside and quickly issued his orders. He opened his day pack and pulled out his spare radio. He turned it on, checked the frequency and barked, 'Run!' at the guide, who turned and started jogging back the way they had come, brushing past Sal and

Vincent, and not stopping to answer Shane when he asked what was going on.

Fletcher had halted them within sight of the banks of the rock-studded stream down which the target would soon be clambering. It was shallow, and only about two metres across at its widest, its muddy banks lined with luxuriant ferns.

Shane moved past the sweating, mud-stained Americans, and came to Fletcher's side. 'What's up?'

'Get back to where you were and keep a lookout down the trail. Chuck Hamley will be coming up soon. He's driving to the nearest road junction and Patrice will guide him in.'

'Okay, but what for? Chuck's not due to go out on safari until tomorrow. Why the rush?'

'Just do as I say!'

Shane nodded and moved away, keeping Fletcher in sight.

Fletcher moved to Anthony and knelt beside him. 'Tell your guys to keep watch up that stream. That's where the poacher will come from. Shoot him as soon as you see him.'

'Wait a minute. How do you know which way he's gonna be coming? I hope this ain't a canned hunt.'

Fletcher sighed. 'Call it instinct, okay?' A canned hunt referred to the shooting of a drugged or captive-raised animal, a contest without challenge. Anthony was not as dumb as he looked but Fletcher had bigger problems than his clients working out his modus operandi.

'Where you going?' Anthony asked as Fletcher stood and walked towards the rear of the column.

'To take care of some business.'

William Delancy was sitting on a moss-covered rock drinking from a canteen of water, his back turned to Fletcher. Thank God, Fletcher thought. At least he'd been given one piece of luck. He raised his rifle high in the air and brought the butt down with a satisfying crack on the back of the Englishman's skull. Delancy fell to the muddy ground like a sack of potatoes.

Shane, who was watching for Patrice and Chuck's arrival, turned at the sound of the thud. His eyes were wide with surprise. 'What the —'

'Search him,' Fletcher ordered. 'His pack, his webbing – everything.'

'Hey, what gives?' Vincent asked, craning his head, looking back from his position behind a stout tree trunk.

'No problem. I'll explain later. Just keep your eyes peeled for that poacher.'

Sal and Eddy muttered something to each other, but Anthony, who had seen everything, hushed them and pointed back up the stream. For all his faults, Fletcher thought, Anthony was a man who knew when to butt out of other people's business.

Shane knelt over the Englishman. He checked his pulse. 'Well, at least you didn't kill him,' he muttered.

'There'll be time for that later. I want to hear him talk before I shoot him. Check that haversack over his shoulder. It doesn't look like a particularly practical piece of kit for a hunter.'

Shane lifted the canvas bag, which was slung crossways from a wide strap across the front of Delancy's torso, and undid the buckles. 'It's just a video camera in here.'

Fletcher knelt and looked in the bag. 'What do you mean "just a video"? Look, the bloody thing's gaffer-taped to the inside of the bag, and there's a hole in the canvas. This bastard's been filming us in secret.' He removed the camera and two other spare tapes.

'Why?' Shane asked as he opened each of the pouches on Delancy's belt, and the pockets of his hunting vest.

'Because he's a bloody journalist, that's why. Sent to expose what we're doing. Fuck!' Fletcher ejected the tape from the mini digital video camera, dropped it and crushed it under the heel of his boot. He repeated the action with the other two tapes.

'He killed a man yesterday. Even if he is a reporter, you can't just murder him,' Shane protested.

Fletcher put the camera back in Delancy's haversack. 'We're in the middle of the biggest operation the Congolese Army's run in this part of the country since the end of the civil war. William Delancy – or whatever his real name is – will die heroically, filming some of the action.'

Shane nodded. 'How did he find out about us?'

'I've got my suspicions.'

'Wise?' Shane asked.

Fletcher shook his head. 'He might have been part of it, but he wouldn't have had the contacts. When he came to me with his gripes he didn't say he'd been to the media. He just threatened to go to the cops.'

'Maybe he called the media after you fobbed him off – before you killed him.'

Fletcher shook his head. 'There was no way for him to make a call off the mountain, and Patrice made sure Wise didn't get anywhere near a telephone before he died.'

Marie Delacroix made the sign of the cross and looked skyward, uttering a short prayer of thanks for the stream in front of her.

She knew, from her time researching gorillas, that they disliked water intensely and would go to great lengths to avoid even getting their feet wet. As soon as Mubare came in sight of the running water, he stopped the troop. He stood there, looking up and down the watercourse, trying to work out what to do. Behind her, in the distance, Marie still heard the intermittent popping of gunfire.

'Turn back, turn back,' Marie willed the silverback.

His big head swivelled slowly, like a tank turret. Finally he made a decision, and the troop shuffled off, on their hind feet and knuckles, downstream. Marie cursed.

'What's that gunfire?' Vincent whispered.

'It's them Wandans, or something,' Eddy said.

'Rwandans, stupid,' Anthony corrected him. He looked over his shoulder, wishing Fletcher would hurry up doing whatever he was doing to the Brit, and get back on the line. 'Shush. I hear something.'

'It's like coughing. What the fuck is that?' Sal hissed.

'Quiet!' Anthony insisted. 'Holy Mother of God! Would you look at that.'

Vincent looked back at him, mouth agape. He took a couple of seconds to collect his thoughts then said, 'What do we do, Anthony, run for it?'

'No fucking way. Say hello to a million dollars, baby.' He raised the rifle to his shoulder and peered through the sights.

Mubare smelled human – and not the woman this time.

He uttered his warning call and the troop stopped. In the lead was the female who had sired his latest son, and she held the baby close to her. He tried to suckle from her pendulous breast, but she moved his mouth away for the moment, too intent on reading the silverback's signals.

Marie Delacroix heard men's voices, and started to stand, to get a better look down the course of the stream.

Shane heard the hmm-hah of the cough and it took him a second to recall it. 'Fletcher!' He looked up from riffling through the Englishman's pockets and nodded back towards the Americans. 'Gorillas!'

Fletcher rolled his eyes, turned and started to run, waving his rifle high over his head. 'Away, away! Anthony, no!'

The female gorilla looked across the stream at the running, yelling man, shrieked, and started to run.

The silverback bellowed in rage and splashed into the stream, against his better instincts, towards the source of the danger. Mubare hesitated, frustrated and enraged, as the unfamiliar sensation of water washed up to his knees.

Anthony squeezed the trigger, but Fletcher's yelling had spooked the primate too soon. He saw his bullet hit home in the female's right upper arm. 'Shit,' he cursed. By the time he chambered another round, the gorillas had disappeared into the jungle – all but one, that was. The baby, which had been clinging to his mother, had fallen. In her pain and panic, the wounded mother had run into the bush without him.

'Vincent, get up there and grab that baby!' Anthony ordered.

Vincent was the closest of them to the little ape, but he hesitated, looking back at his future boss. For three seconds he considered telling Anthony that he should get up off his fat ass and go fetch the baby gorilla himself. The ape crawled groggily on the ground, having landed on his head on a smooth river rock. Anthony glared back at Vincent and the boy came to his senses. He got up and splashed into the water.

The tiny bundle of black hair squealed in fear. He started to run, but Vincent, falling in the process as his foot slipped on a rock, managed to grab hold of the gorilla's left rear leg. He lifted the baby, grinning wildly, dangling him upside down as he stood triumphantly in midstream.

'Attaboy!' Anthony cheered.

The bamboo thicket at the edge of the stream

exploded in a shower of torn leaves and flying twigs as the silverback erupted from cover, bellowing as he ran. Vincent turned to see where the noise had come from but, before he could register his fate, the gorilla careened into him, knocking him flat on his back. The silverback, in a blur of black fur and bared white teeth, snatched up the twice-fallen baby and clutched him to his chest. With the back of his other hand he slammed Vincent's skull sideways, and the man's head ended its trajectory against the same rock he had slipped on. Tendrils of blood reached out into the flowing waters.

Gunshots erupted from the hunting party as men came to their senses. Fletcher stood, worked the bolt of his rifle and fired high over the heads of the fleeing gorillas, in order to see the troop off once and for all. The silverback, mercifully, was gone as quickly as he appeared. Their bullets did nothing but shred the bamboo.

'Vincent!' Sal screamed, staggering forward.

Marie Delacroix ran from the storm of gunfire, stooped low, tears blurring her vision, a mix of anger and fear pumping her heart full of adrenaline. She took care to give the startled gorillas a wide berth, heading north as the primates turned back to the east and the relative safety of the park.

She could hardly believe what she had seen.

That man.

That beast.

That devil, whom she had made a deal with.

Fletcher Reynolds, standing there, as plain as day, shooting at her gorillas.

Sal was still crying as he cradled Vincent's lifeless head in his lap. He spat vitriol at Anthony, uncaring that the man could have him killed for using such language.

'Suck it up, Sal. The boy's dead, but he died brave.'

'You motherfucker! You sent him to his death. I'm gonna kill you after I kill all them fucking apes!'

Fletcher moved between the two men and laid a hand on Sal's shoulder before he could stand. 'Enough! Our priority now is to get back to camp.'

'What's with him?' Anthony asked, gesturing to the Englishman, who now sat on the ground, his hands bound behind him with plastic cable ties. The wound on the back of Delancy's head was crusted with blood, the collar of his safari shirt stained deep purplish red.

Fletcher spoke loud enough for all of them, Sal, Anthony, Eddy and Shane, to hear. 'That piece of shit came here to spy on you and to expose you to the world's media.'

'What the fuck?' Anthony said.

'He came to get us?' Sal looked up from his dead son's face for the first time. 'You fucking asshole!'

Fletcher looked towards Sal and said, 'If I hadn't been occupied taking care of this spy, I would have been with you. If I'd let Anthony shoot the gorilla it would have been done my way. Properly. This man caused Vincent's death, and would have brought the downfall of all of us, Sal.'

Sal gently laid Vincent's head down on the carpet of

leaf mulch, stood and staggered over to Delancy, who looked up into his eyes, mouth grim, no emotion playing on his face.

Sal delivered a brutal kick into the Englishman's ribs, which sent him sprawling. Shane stood by, watching, his eyes flicking across each of the men.

'I say we do him, now,' Sal said, pulling a Colt .45 automatic pistol out of his shoulder holster.

'Nah,' Anthony interrupted. 'Fletcher wants to have some sport with him first, right?'

Fletcher nodded.

'Let's take him back to camp. It's going to get hot on this hill if the army drives those militiamen any closer our way,' Shane said. In the background, underscoring his words, was the ominous chatter of a light machine-gun.

Silence prevailed for a short while, except for the omnipresent twitters and croaks of the jungle's natural inhabitants. The men looked at each other, and their captive.

'Tell us your real name,' Fletcher said, looking down at him.

'Captain the Honourable William —'

Fletcher cut him off with a punch in the nose that made Shane wince with the sound of breaking cartilage, and left Delancy's face plastered with fresh blood. Fletcher turned his back on Delancy and Shane, and said, 'Anthony, perhaps you've got some particularly American ideas of how to make a recalcitrant prisoner talk.'

'Drop it,' Shane said.

He moved swiftly behind Fletcher and rammed the

muzzle of his SLR into the back of his head. 'Now!' he barked. Fletcher let his rifle fall to the ground. 'On your knees.'

Fletcher lowered himself to his knees, looking to the gangsters for help. Shane had timed his move as well as he could, when the minimum number of men were armed. Anthony had laid his rifle against a tree, and Eddy's was on the ground while he smoked a cigarette. Only Sal carried a weapon, his nickel-plated .45.

'Drop it, Sal, or I'll kill Fletcher.'

'What makes you think I give a fuck about him?' Sal brought his pistol up, straightening his arm.

Shane anticipated the mobster's reaction. He'd already thumbed the safety catch on his rifle and the barrel of his weapon had less distance to travel than Sal's. He swung the SLR up and to the left and fired two shots in quick succession. The first bullet took off the top of Sal's skull, while the second shattered his sternum, punching him back. He fell across the body of his son.

'Who's next?' Shane asked.

'Not me,' murmured Eddy, who dropped his cigarette and extinguished it.

'The quietest one's always the smartest,' Shane said. 'Pick up the other rifles and hand guns by their barrels and put them in a pile in front of me. Anthony, make like Fletcher and get on your knees.' To Delancy, still sitting tied and bloodied beside him, Shane said, 'All right, then, Geezer?'

'Oh, just fine, thanks. Took your bloody time, didn't you?' he gurgled through a throat thick with clotting blood.

'On your knees, Eddy, next to —'

'I could kill her now, Shane, but I thought you might like a sporting chance to get away – certainly a better deal than you gave poor Sal there. Hi, Anthony, Eddy. Long time no see.'

Shane looked over his shoulder. Chuck Hamley emerged from behind a tree and stood with an arm around Michelle's neck and a Glock pistol pressed against her temple. She, like Caesar, was bound and gagged. Patrice covered the Ndebele with an AK 47.

'Oops,' mumbled Geezer.

'Ah, Captain Delancy. I've been longing to meet you, sir,' Chuck said with false charm. 'Now, Shane, we can have a shoot-out, if you like – I'm sure you're a better shot than me, but I can guarantee you'll have this pretty lady's blood on your hands, just as I'll have her brains on my face.' He grinned at Shane.

Shane stared back at Hamley. Even if he took him out, Patrice would open up with the AK. It would be a slaughter. Shane lowered his rifle.

Fletcher, Eddy and Anthony needed no urging to hop to their feet and knock Shane to the ground. They stripped him of his pistol, his webbing, his canteens and his knife, till he was left with nothing but his camouflage fatigues and boots.

'Michelle?' Fletcher said, looking across at her. Chuck still held the pistol to her head.

She looked back at him. Chuck pulled the gag from her mouth, but she stayed silent.

'Why are you holding her, Chuck? Let her go now, damn it.'

'She's part of your problem, Fletcher. I'll explain,

but first tell me what's gone on here. What happened to Sal and Vincent?'

Fletcher recapped as Eddy bound Shane's hands with cable ties, then Chuck explained how he had taken the time to do some checking on William Delancy.

'From my quick phone call to Fletcher yesterday I found out that William here was referred by my old buddy Larry Monroe. You probably don't recall Larry, Fletcher, but he was one of your less than satisfied clients. One of the group who trailed the poachers to the Botswanan border?'

Fletcher looked shamefaced, Shane thought, as realisation dawned. 'That snivelling bugger who didn't want to shoot.'

'Precisely,' Chuck confirmed. 'I've been busy on the sat phone since yesterday, Fletch, as you should have been. I spoke to Larry, and he tried to con me for a little while; that is, until I persuaded him to tell me the truth.'

'How'd you do that? Did you pay him?' Shane asked.

'No, Mister Castle, as a matter of fact I told Larry I'd kill his wife and children if he didn't tell me all he knew about William Delancy. A far more persuasive approach than threatening to expose him through the media. Incidentally, I'm really looking forward to meeting this Sarah Thatcher. From the SNN website she looks very attractive. Where are you meeting her with the tapes?'

Fletcher stooped and picked up Geezer's hidden camera from its bag, holding it aloft for Anthony and Sal to see.

'The only other connection there was left to make, which I did via Fletcher's laptop and satellite phone today, was to find out who inside the camp had spilled the beans. According to Larry, Thatcher had part of the story, from an eyewitness, but had bamboozled Larry with a whole lot more information which must have come from somewhere else.

'I Googled Michelle – nothing there – and then Shane. I read all about Shane's little shoot-out in Baghdad and was surprised to read that our good friend William here was on Shane's team in Iraq. Small world, huh?'

'Michelle's got nothing to do with this,' Shane said.

'Very noble, and right on cue, Shane. Thank you,' Chuck said, obviously enjoying holding court. 'I had no reason to suspect Michelle at all until she made a rather pathetic attempt to overpower me with a shovel, just before we left camp. She must have overheard me radioing Fletcher about William, or seen the results of my Internet search.' He reached over his shoulder and rubbed his back, presumably where Michelle had hit him. 'I could only assume young Caesar here, Shane's loyal foot soldier, was in on the act as well. I searched her things and found some digital video tapes.'

Anthony clapped, slowly. 'Bravo, Chuck, but do you mind telling me what the fuck we're supposed to do now? We got four prisoners, two dead guys of our own and a mountain crawling with rebels, soldiers and poachers.'

Fletcher had stood there, open-mouthed, through Chuck's speech. He looked at Michelle, then Shane, then back at her.

'Why? You and I could have been happy together, Michelle. I would have given you the world, could have given you anything you asked for . . .'

She glared back at him. 'It's not about money . . . or about things, Fletcher. You're a murderer.'

'Let her go,' Shane said again.

Fletcher looked at him, his fists clenched in rage.

'You've got us.' Shane nodded at the Englishman and Caesar.

'No, Shane.' Both men turned to face her now. 'I'm not going anywhere without you.'

Fletcher walked over to Shane, who stood, defiant, with his wrists tied behind his back. 'You bastard.'

'No!' Michelle screamed.

33

'I still say we shoulda just capped the fuckers,' said Eddy.

'Nah, I like this,' Anthony said. 'A real hunt. Not one of them set-ups like Fletcher organises. Ain't that right, *bwana*?'

Fletcher frowned, though said nothing. Shane, his right eye swollen and his lip still bleeding from the punches Fletcher had landed on him, noticed that Chuck and Anthony were calling the shots now. Fletcher looked almost hollow, as though the soul he'd sold had finally been collected. Shane felt no pity for him. Since Fletcher's admission that Patrice had been following Wise on the day he died – and presumably had executed him on Fletcher's orders – Shane had promised himself he would kill the bastard.

'Make the call, please, Colonel,' Chuck said to Gizenga.

He nodded, raising the radio microphone to his lips. In French, he said, 'Attention all army and UN callsigns. This is Colonel Francois Gizenga. I am in

pursuit of four escaped poachers who were appre-
hended this morning after attempting to hunt
mountain gorillas. Descriptions as follows – one
white man and one white woman handcuffed
together, and one white man and one black man also
cuffed.' He repeated the broadcast in English for the
benefit of the Indian Army peacekeepers, who were
conducting operations with the Congolese Army
along the border to the south of the Sarambwe Forest,
under the auspices of the United Nations peace monitoring contingent in the Congo.

'Good,' Chuck said. To Shane, he added, 'In the
event that you somehow elude us, you'll probably be
killed by the first army or UN patrol you bump into.'

Shane didn't like their chances, particularly since
Gizenga's arrival at the stream half an hour before,
along with ten of his soldiers. The rest of his infantry
company, another eighty men at least, were fanned
out in the jungle on either side of the stream.

'I overheard one of Gizenga's men telling him that
the captured poacher they were going to herd down
the stream for Anthony's boys to kill, got away,'
Michelle whispered to Shane.

'Quiet there, honey, or I'll put your gag back on,'
Chuck drawled.

Rightly concerned that two ex special forces soldiers might be able to outrun and evade the hunters
and Gizenga's men, Chuck had ordered that Shane
and Geezer be 'handicapped' by having Michelle and
Caesar handcuffed to each of them, respectively, with
manacles provided by the Congolese colonel.

Geezer had winked at Shane as the young, fit

African's left hand was cuffed to his right, until Chuck had nodded a silent, prearranged command to Patrice. The tracker moved behind Caesar, swung back his arm, and then hacked down with his panga. Caesar had cried out in pain and dropped to the ground, dragging Geezer down with him, as the machete's blade sliced a deep, debilitating wound across the back of his right calf muscle.

Shane was faced with an impossible dilemma. He knew that he and Michelle could move fast, but could they live with themselves if they left Geezer and the horribly wounded Caesar to their own devices?

'All right,' Chuck announced. 'We'll give you fifteen minutes' head start, then we're coming after you. Colonel Gizenga, sir, please remind your men that they are here as the cordon – to stop our fugitives from running too far off to the flanks – and that either myself, Fletcher, Eddy or Anthony should be given first shot when one of the targets comes into view.'

'Of course,' Gizenga said. 'It is not the first time we have played this game.'

'Ready, everyone?' Chuck asked.

'Wait,' Anthony said. He moved close to where Shane and Michelle stood, under Patrice's watchful guard. 'Whoever gets Shane in his sights – kill him, but leave the broad alive. Me and her have some unfinished business.'

'Bastard,' Shane hissed. Michelle spat at him, but the spittle missed its mark, and Anthony just laughed.

'I'm going to fuck her while your body's still

chained to her,' he whispered to Shane. 'I hope you're still alive to watch.'

Chuck aimed his rifle at the sky. 'On your marks! Get set!' He pulled the trigger.

Both Michelle and Caesar were taken off guard by the sharp tug on their wrists as Shane and Geezer lurched forward, into the knee-deep waters of the stream, literally dragging them behind. Chuck and Anthony laughed out loud at the stumbling antics of the panicked white woman and the wounded black man.

'Fifteen minutes,' Geezer called, his pistoning boots sending geysers of water as high as his chest.

'Let's make the most of it,' Shane yelled back.

The stream rounded a bend. As soon as they were out of sight of the hunters, Shane and Geezer pulled their partners to a stop. Confused, Michelle asked, 'Shane, why have we stopped?'

'Caesar, jump on,' Shane said, without explanation, as he and Geezer linked left and right hands respectively, making an awkward yet functional seat for the injured man, whose left hand was now wedged under his buttocks.

'I can make it on my own,' Caesar said weakly.

'Shut up,' Geezer barked back at him. 'Keep an eye on your watch, man.'

'Let's move!' Shane ordered. Michelle splashed alongside him, on his right side, manacled as she was to that hand. Even though Shane and Geezer were burdened with Caesar, Michelle was hard-pressed keeping up with them.

'Breathe slow and deep,' Shane told her, seeing the

panic in her reddened cheeks. 'We can do this. We can beat these bastards.'

Behind them they heard shouting and gunshots. Shane guessed Gizenga's men were getting fired up for the hunt by loosing a few shots in the air.

'Time?' Geezer asked Caesar as they slogged through a stretch of water that was now up to their knees.

'Eleven minutes,' Caesar said. Blood dripped steadily from his wound, the tendrils of red overtaking them in the flowing water, underscoring how slowly they were moving.

'What's that?' Michelle asked.

Shane kept moving, but she pulled him to a halt, causing Geezer to nearly drop Caesar. 'For fuck's sake, keep moving,' the Englishman protested.

'Shut up!' she hissed. 'Listen, voices?'

Shane nodded and dragged them all towards an undercut bank of the stream. On the left-hand side of the gully they could hear men speaking French with African accents. He threw an arm protectively around Michelle, pulling her close to him and pushing her into the muddy bank at the same time. Caesar whimpered in pain and Geezer clasped a hand over his mouth. They heard footsteps tramping through the grass above them as the men moved along the edge of the stream.

They waited, hardly daring to breathe, pushing their faces into the dank mud, trying to melt from sight. If any of the men had looked down they would have seen the fugitives. If it were an army patrol, Shane thought, they might shoot them on sight if they had heard Fletcher's bulletin over the radio. When the noise of voices and footsteps receded, Shane peered over the edge of the bank. 'They're gone.'

'They must have been Rwandan,' Michelle said. 'They were trying to work out which way the army patrols would be moving.'

'It is fifteen minutes now since we left,' Caesar said.

They splashed back into the river as the first gun-shots sounded upstream.

'I don't care about your silly game,' Colonel Gizenga fumed.

'But you must stay with us,' Chuck Hamley insisted.

Gizenga ignored him and spoke rapidly in French into his radio. When he had finished issuing another order he said to the white men, 'Enough. I must go. My men are in contact with Rwandan Hutus. You are on your own. Me, I have a war to fight.'

'We should clear out,' Eddy said.

Chuck rounded on him. 'Those people are wit-nesses. They know what we've been up to. How would you like them going to the FBI and telling them you paid to kill foreign nationals for sport?'

'Hey, let it go, Chuck. You're the dumb fuck who let 'em wander off down the river. We coulda killed them and buried them by now!' Anthony said.

'Enough!' Fletcher commanded, regaining some-thing of his lost authority. 'The fact is that there are

four of them, unarmed, and four of us – plus Patrice –
all armed. Also, our fugitives *think* Gizenga's men are
still guarding the flanks. You call yourselves hunters?
Instead of making me sick with your pathetic squab-
bling, why don't you get on with the first *real* hunt of
your lives!'

'*Arrêt!*' the man ordered as he leapt from around the
trunk of a tree on the bank beside them.

He was African and elderly, by the look of it,
though the ghastly mask of bruises and suppurating,
pus-filled lacerations that covered the right side of his
face and stank from a dozen paces away made it
impossible to gauge his age. His one good eye was
wild with fear and fever. He carried an AK 47 and
pointed it at Geezer's chest. They stopped.

'The fool's got no magazine on that rifle,' Geezer
muttered.

The man barked an order in French. 'He says, shut
up,' Michelle translated. 'And hands up.'

'Bollocks,' Geezer whispered out of the side of his
mouth. 'Reckon he's got a bullet up the spout?'

'No way,' Shane whispered. 'On three. One, two . . .'

Shane and Geezer lunged forward, towards the
man with the gun, carrying Caesar, who screwed his
eyes tight waiting for the gunshot, and dragging
Michelle, who screamed. The foursome collided with
the injured man, who crumpled like a dead leaf under
their combined weight. When they were able to stand
again, Shane was holding the AK 47, shaking the
water from it.

'How . . . how did you know it wasn't loaded?' Michelle gasped.

Shane quickly explained that he recognised the wounded man as one of the bush meat poachers he had tracked, and that his injuries were caused by Shane blocking the man's rifle with mud so that it backfired. He had been held prisoner by Colonel Gizenga since then, and released as the day's 'target', armed only with an unloaded rifle and destined to be cut down by the American hunters.

The man whimpered, kneeling in the river, clutching his freshly aggravated wounds and distraught that his ruse had failed. 'Tell him to head that way,' Shane said to Michelle, pointing west, into the jungle. The man limped off without another word.

'Great, so now we've got a rifle with no ammunition – I feel much better,' Geezer said.

Shane smiled and reached into the side pocket of his sodden fatigue trousers. In his palm, their glittering copper casings more precious than solid gold, were five AK 47 bullets.

Patrice stalked ahead of the white hunters, his AK 47 at the ready, every sense alert. He moved quickly, but with deliberate care, scanning the mud on either side of the stream for footprints, the rocks for signs where a boot might have scuffed away the moss or river slime.

He was not afraid of the unarmed white people, nor particularly concerned that the others made sure he was up front, where danger was most likely. He had detested Castle since his arrival in the Congo. The man acted as though he knew everything about the bush, and he had refused to afford Patrice the respect he was due. It would be a pleasure to kill him. He would do so, at the first opportunity, and later tell Monsieur Reynolds that he believed the man had somehow armed himself, which was why he had fired first.

He saw tracks leading to the west. Bold footprints, but even though he was still twenty metres away, he could see it was only one man's spoor. Had the fugitives somehow managed to break their handcuffs and split up? Further down the stream, all looked quiet. A large tree had fallen across the river, forming a natural bridge. Again, even from this distance, he could see the uniform coating of furry green moss had not been disturbed.

With his undeniable skills as the premier tracker in these mountains, Patrice knew there was no human or animal that could elude his —

'What the fuck!' Anthony said as the bullet, which had entered Patrice's mouth and exploded out the back of his skull, whizzed past his ear. He dropped into the stream, crawling through the water, his knees fighting through the ooze on the bottom, desperate to find some sort of cover.

'Patrice is down!' Fletcher yelled, sprinting through the shallows and up the right-hand bank. He threw himself behind a tangle of exposed tree roots and peered forward.

Chuck had broken left, his body pressed into a recess in the side of the riverbank. 'Was that them?'

'How the hell should I know,' Fletcher called back.

'Eddy, get some cover, man!' Anthony yelled. His comrade was standing in the middle of the stream, looking left and right, as if unsure of which way to head.

It was an awkward operation. With no magazine, Shane had to yank back the cocking handle of the AK 47, which was on the right-hand side of the rifle, and feed a single bullet into the breech, then let the handle fly forward to chamber the round. Michelle's left hand was cuffed to his right, making the whole action even more cumbersome. In her right hand she held the precious stock of bullets – the same ones that had fallen from his broken magazine while he was cleaning it the night before.

Michelle ducked her head in anticipation of the next shot. The ejected hot cartridge of the bullet that had felled Patrice had shot out of the rifle's breech and hit her on the cheek, cutting and bruising her.

Geezer spotted for him, while Caesar lay limp against the cool wet bark of the fallen log. 'One man in the river, still standing, stupid prick. Take him, Shane.'

Shane saw Eddy, the quietest of the gangsters, looking as dazed as a hare trapped in a spotlight. He lined up the sights on his torso and squeezed. Eddy left a splash as he disappeared from Shane's view.

'Behind the fallen tree!' they heard Fletcher yell.

'Get some bloody fire down on them!'

Shane ducked as the first bullets, heavy slugs designed to take down a buffalo or an elephant, thudded into the natural barricade in front of them.

'Sorry, sorry!' Michelle wailed as a bullet slipped from her hand and disappeared beneath the water's surface with a plonk.

Shane took the time to lift his right hand and stroke her cheek. 'It's okay, Michelle. We'll be fine.' She winced as another bullet cracked a branch from the dead trunk, scattering woodchips over them. 'Take your time and find the bullet.'

Shane realised they had probably used up more than their share of luck already. It would take all his skill, concentration and training to tip the balance back in their favour now. It was dumb luck that he had the bullets at all.

'Reynolds will be the next to move,' Geezer predicted. 'He's the one with the balls.'

Shane nodded agreement and shifted his aim to the last spot where he had seen the hunter go to ground. Geezer, Shane would have been the first to admit, was a better shot than he. It had been he who had kept Fletcher and the gangsters so effectively pinned down the day before, with his silenced hunting rifle, as they had hidden on the edge of the grassy mountain clearing and given enough covering fire for the Congolese captive to get away. Shane had done the spotting, firing away with Caesar's AK 47 to add to the confusion.

'I found it!' Michelle exclaimed.

Shane looked over at her, proudly holding up the

missing round, glistening with water. 'Good girl. Dry it off for me, please.'

She leaned over and kissed him on the cheek.

'I love you,' Shane said as he watched the river-bank intently. They now had three bullets. And three targets.

'You do?'

'He's up!' Geezer exclaimed.

Shane saw the movement in the grass and fired. 'Shit. I think I missed him.'

'I saw it. My fault, mate,' Geezer admitted. 'I called it too soon. He probably just raised his bloody hat on a stick or something. Can't believe I fell for the oldest cowboy trick in the book.'

Michelle passed Shane another round. He yanked back the cocking handle and slid the bullet into the open chamber.

'He's moving!'

'On your feet!' Fletcher screamed. 'He's only firing single shots! Chuck, give covering fire. Anthony, with me!'

Shane swore as he saw Anthony lumber to his feet, obediently, instinctively following Fletcher, who was in his element as a warrior at war, issuing life and death commands through the smoke of battle.

'Chuck's not a bad shot,' Geezer observed casually as a ricocheting round forced him to lower his head.

'Down!' Fletcher barked. 'Behind those rocks. Anthony, prepare to give covering fire with me for Chuck.'

Shane had loaded the fresh bullet, but hadn't had time to draw a bead on either Anthony or Fletcher, who had now halved the distance between them, down to a mere thirty metres.

'We've got two bullets for three men,' Shane said.

Three more bullets smacked into the log, and Shane heard a hollow ringing after the second shot.

Michelle stared down at the water flowing around her. Her khaki shorts were running pink from someone's blood, either Patrice's or Eddy's. 'Some of us have to die,' she said.

'That log's falling apart, Shane!' Fletcher taunted them from upstream. He had noted, with satisfaction, that each successive round he pumped into the fallen tree dislodged a larger chunk of waterlogged, termite-infested wood. Their barricade looked sturdy, but it was more air than solid timber.

Chuck, who was lying alongside Fletcher now, on the opposite bank of the stream to Anthony, fired four shots in rapid succession. 'I see it too.'

'Give yourselves up and we'll finish it quickly!' Fletcher called.

'Why ain't they shooting back?' Anthony wondered out loud.

All three of the hunters ducked instinctively as a round went off.

'That didn't sound right,' Fletcher said.

'I didn't hear the crack-thump. Did that bullet come towards you, Anthony?' Chuck asked.

'Nope. Maybe one of them capped himself?'

Fletcher doubted it. He suspected a trap. He kept firing into the tree, another seven shots, until he started to become concerned about his ammunition. 'How many rounds do you have left?' he asked Chuck.

'Only five. I can't keep blasting away at that log.'

Fletcher looked across at Anthony, holding up a bullet, then putting a finger to his lips. The gangster looked confused for a couple of seconds, then grasped his meaning. He checked the bandolier around his waist and held up five fingers.

'Hey, I can see daylight through that log now,' Anthony called. 'You think maybe we got 'em all?'

Fletcher heard a low *thwap-thwap-thwap* noise, like the wings of some giant prehistoric jungle bird beating in slow time. The three of them looked up as the shadow of a white helicopter with black UN markings passed over them. As if in accompaniment, they heard a light machine-gun resume its chatter to their east, though closer than before.

'We can't sit here all day, just waiting them out. The peacekeepers are getting closer,' Chuck said.

'You want to go first?' Fletcher asked.

'There's only one way, isn't there?' Chuck said.

'You said to me on our first safari that you regretted being too young for Vietnam and too old for Iraq.'

Chuck nodded. 'We've come a long way since then, haven't we, buddy?'

'Yes,' Fletcher said. And all of it downhill. To this, the lowest ebb of his life, where he would have to move forward and make sure a woman he might have married, and a man he would have been proud to serve alongside in combat, were dead. He looked across at Anthony and signalled they would all move together. 'On three,' he mouthed silently, holding up three fingers.

'Fletcher, before we go . . .' Chuck began.

He was mildly irritated. 'Yes?'

'You have made my life complete.'

Fletcher wondered, for an instant, if he killed Chuck and Anthony, would Shane and his friend, and Michelle, let him walk away, or, if they were all dead, would their ghosts forgive him?

He shook his head and said, 'One, two, three . . .'

Michelle lay with her eyes closed, her face covered with her own blood, which had run profusely from the wound at her forehead.

Shane's body was underneath hers, holding her up out of the water, though he was face-down.

Caesar floated on his back, his khaki shirt stained dark with blood. The material of the Englishman's tailored safari jacket was just visible beside him, under the log.

Fletcher stood panting, on the other side of the log, his rifle pointing down at Michelle's face. He saw the blood, how it flowed from her hairline over her face. You can't fake blood, he told himself. He glanced across at the black man, and watched Shane for any sign of movement.

Anthony lumbered up to Fletcher and Chuck. Fletcher suspected the gangster had deliberately hung back as they had charged the barricade.

'Hey, where's the limey?' Anthony asked.

'I can't see the body,' Chuck said as he straddled the log, his rifle held in one hand.

The Honourable William Delancy, Geezer to his friends, lay three-quarters submerged in a hastily dug pit in the muddy bank of the stream.

He had only one shot left.

Anthony, the fat, lazy gangster, had already lowered his rifle. He would have been the slowest to react.

Chuck was sliding over the log on his butt, already bringing his rifle back up into his shoulder. Fletcher stared down at Michelle with a look that bordered on one indicating a complete and utter breakdown. Geezer fancied he could even see a slight tremor in the hands that held the stock of his ancient, scarred hunting rifle.

He thought, if he did say so himself, that he had done a particularly good job with the moulage – fake wounds – given his lack of props, although there had been no shortage of real blood to play with. It was the same way Shane had fooled Fletcher into believing they had killed a poacher the day before. They had made Caesar take off his shirt and lie down in the grass while Geezer had expertly applied the latex skin of the fake wounds to his face and chest, along with the theatrical blood. As well as being a peer of the realm and one-time special forces soldier, Geezer was a qualified combat medic. As part of the training he delivered for recruits to the security firm where he and Shane had worked, he had become adept at simulating the look of gunshot wounds. His work would put a Hollywood special effects artist to shame. It helped, he often said, having seen the real thing plenty of times.

Michelle's blood – and she was the star performer

557

who would make or break this little drama – was her own, brave girl. Using his Leatherman, Shane had unscrewed the fold-out bayonet – a nifty Russian invention from the old days – from under the barrel of the AK 47 and, at her insistence, cut his new girlfriend a nasty gash across her forehead. Head wounds always bled profusely, but also healed quickly. She would be fine, if Fletcher didn't deliver the coup de grâce to her in the next few seconds.

Geezer shifted his aim from Chuck, to Fletcher, then back to Chuck. Their second-last bullet, again at Michelle's suggestion – he envied Shane that girl – had been used to sever the handcuffs that had linked him and Caesar together. Caesar was lying there, face up, feigning death.

It was one of the easiest shots of his life, but if he picked the wrong target, and it all went pear-shaped, then his only regret would be that he wouldn't have a bullet left to turn on himself. Geezer squeezed the trigger.

Shane heard the shot and was rolling, pushing Michelle underneath him, into the water, before she could cry out, or before he knew which target Geezer had picked. The Englishman had taken his time – Shane had started to feel the first signs of dizziness from holding his breath for too long.

He burst from the water and screamed a primal war cry as he searched, bayonet in hand, for a target. From the corner of his eye he saw Chuck flung backwards over the log.

Geezer was yelling behind him, unseen, erupting from his muddy lair, with his useless rifle held high, no doubt.

Directly in front of him, across the slimy log, Shane saw the disbelieving face of Anthony the gangster. He was the closest target. Shane lunged, arm held stiff out in front of him, and thrust the bayonet into his throat. Anthony opened his mouth, but not even a scream emerged, just a gurgling sound, followed by his own blood. Shane had to lean back, using his whole body weight to pull the blade free from the sucking flesh.

Fletcher's instincts took over. He looked for the prime source of danger, and saw the man with the AK 47, standing on the bank of the stream, pointing the barrel at him. He was aware, too, of a fountain of blood to his left, and Shane screaming like a madman. He brought the rifle up into his shoulder and aimed at the mud-spattered Englishman.

'Drop your rifle, you bastard!' Geezer boomed, his voice stilling the madness around them. Michelle was crouching in the water, coughing and sputtering, Shane was beside her, their wrists still linked, though he was out of reach of Fletcher.

Geezer held his aim, but didn't fire. 'Drop it!'

Fletcher shook his head, smiled, and swung the rifle downwards, quickly, until the barrel was pointing at Michelle. She recoiled in the water, throwing herself to one side, falling at Shane's feet. Shane was no more than three metres from Fletcher, but it could have been three hundred for all the good he could do.

'You can't kill all of us,' Shane said. 'That's a bolt-action rifle. If you shoot her, so help me God, I'll cut your fucking limbs off one at a time while you're still alive.'

'I loved Michelle, Shane. I can't kill her, no matter what the bitch did to me.' He swung the rifle away from her and pointed it at Shane's chest.

'No, Fletcher. Don't do it. Just leave us be . . .' Michelle pleaded, as she stood.

'Stay where you are,' Fletcher called across to the Englishman, who checked his stride, his filthy face echoing the hate in Shane's.

Fletcher turned his malevolent stare back to Shane. 'I saved your worthless career, Castle. I got you back to Africa, paid you well, and you repaid me by fucking my woman. For that alone, I'm going to kill you.'

'No!' Michelle cried. Fletcher trained the barrel back on her.

Shane grabbed her wrist and moved her behind him, and Fletcher's aim followed his movements.

Beside them, still floating on his back in the water, was Caesar. Shane wondered if the young man had, in fact, been killed by a stray shot. He didn't dare glance down, but he felt a finger brush his ankle, beneath the muddy water's surface, deliberately pushing him away from Fletcher, towards the bank.

Fletcher, wild-eyed, raised the rifle to his shoulder. 'You're going to die a traitor's death, Castle.'

Caesar pushed himself up and out of the water, and Geezer took his cue to rush forward as well.

Shane's first concern was for Michelle, and he elbowed her to the side, away from him so that if Fletcher's bullet found its mark it would not hit her if it passed through his body.

'Geezer!' Shane called. As the Englishman splashed through the water, Shane tossed the AK 47 bayonet to him and he caught it.

Fletcher turned to face the new danger, the African in front of him, and pulled the trigger. The shot was so close that it punched Caesar backwards, straight into Geezer's path, knocking him backwards in the water.

Shane tried to rush back towards Fletcher, but was slowed by Michelle, even though she fought to keep up with him. Fletcher backed off two paces, working the bolt action of his rifle at the same time and chambering another round. He raised the rifle again to his shoulder and aimed at Shane. In the water, Geezer held a hand to the wound in Caesar's side, trying to staunch the blood.

'I love you,' Michelle whispered in Shane's ear. She wrapped her arms around him, blocking Fletcher's shot, and Shane tried to move her aside. 'No. I don't want to live without you, Shane.'

'I love you, Michelle.' Shane kissed her.

'The pair of you can have each other for fucking eternity.' Fletcher's finger curled around the trigger and he squeezed.

Marie Delacroix sobbed until she could cry no more. She had found the gorilla family, higher up the

561

mountain, and edged as close as she dared while they were in their highly panicked state.

The baby was safe, and the female, though still bleeding, was walking and managed to breastfeed the little one. The silverback prowled protectively around his troop, looking for someone to kill.

She retraced her tracks to the stream where the atrocity had happened. She had seen it with her own eyes, and she had wept, not only for the evil that had been done to her gorillas, but for her own stupidity.

Marie had danced with the devil – worse, gone hunting with him.

And she had killed. She felt ashamed now, of her joy in it, of the savage glee she had felt at taking the poacher's life. But, she realised with grim determination, at least she knew she could do it. She could pull the trigger, or plant the bomb, instead of just ordering someone else to. If the cause was just and if the target deserved killing.

She had seen him, tall and silver haired, standing among his fat, rich clients, firing his rifle even as the female gorilla was wounded and the baby nearly stolen. She could never forgive him for that.

Marie had no idea what poor wretch, or wretches, Fletcher and his goons were hunting today – they were on the far side of a big fallen log, and his body shielded the nearest from her view.

She centred the cross-hairs of the telescopic sights on the rear of his head, took a breath, as he had taught her, then exhaled half the air from her lungs. Then she squeezed the trigger.

Epilogue

'Okay, we're rolling,' Jim Rickards said. He focused the camera tight on Sarah's face and shoulders, so as to keep the microphone she was holding out of shot as she delivered her piece to camera.

'This part of Africa is no stranger to war, ethnic cleansing and human tragedy, but the last twenty-four hours have seen some of the bloodiest fighting in the Democratic Republic of Congo in years, and the loss of hundreds of lives, including those of several Europeans.

'The body of controversial French zoologist Marie Delacroix was discovered by Indian soldiers from the UN peacekeeping force in the Congo this morning. According to UN sources, Ms Delacroix, who will be remembered as much for her hardline stance as an animal rights activist as for her work with researching mountain gorillas, was caught in crossfire between Congolese Army forces and Rwandan militiamen.

'Information about the success or otherwise of the Congolese Army's push to remove the Rwandan Interahamwe rebels from their country is sketchy, as the military's senior area commander was also killed in a fire fight.

'Added to the European death toll are a white Zimbabwean man and five United States citizens, whose names are yet to be released. The US diplomatic mission here in the Congo is sending a team to investigate the deaths of the men, who were believed to have been on a hunting trip. In the meantime, a tide of humanity is surging out of this troubled border area between the DRC and Uganda.' Sarah paused as Rickards pulled back the focus to take in the dirt road down the hill and behind her, which was choked with a column of refugees.

Women carried their possessions in bundles on their heads, and their babies on their backs. A man wheeled a wooden scooter laden with unripe bananas, while another pushed a creaking wheelbarrow with a fly-blown haunch of meat in it. The column stretched back out of the shot, as far as the cameraman could see.

'That's great, Sarah. Got it all,' Rickards said.

'It's crap and you know it,' she replied, shaking her head. 'We can get a run with the French woman's death, and the Yanks, but we won't have the real story until Shane and Michelle and the others get down off the mountain. God knows how long that'll be, or even if they'll make it. We need something more than the audio grabs we took off the sat phone conversation with Shane. The sound quality was rubbish. I'm worried about them, Jim. We put them in this situation – all for a bloody news story.'

'They'll be fine. That Castle's a hard-arse and you've told the UN commander the reports about them being involved in gorilla hunting are ridiculous.'

'I know. The UN had their suspicions about this dead Colonel Gizenga fellow.'

Rickards kept the camera rolling and panned right to take in some long shots of the other end of the pathetic column of refugees. 'Hey!'

'What?' Sarah asked.

'Take a look,' Rickards grinned as he zoomed in.

Sarah put down her microphone and walked around behind the tripod-mounted digital video camera. She looked into the viewfinder and saw a monochrome image of the parade of displaced Africans. 'Whites!'

In the distance she could make out the growing features of three Europeans, trudging along in the phalanx of Congolese villagers. There was a tall, mud-spattered man carrying another – a black African with a bandaged torso – piggyback style.

The other two were a man and a woman, and Sarah recognised them immediately. Shane had an arm wrapped around Michelle's shoulders as they walked. He tilted his head to one side so it was touching hers, then turned his face and kissed her.

When they broke the kiss, Michelle reached over and wiped Shane's eyes, as though he were crying, which set Sarah off as well.

Acknowledgements

I was camped by a remote waterhole in Hwange National Park, Zimbabwe, in October 2006, some time after the first draft of this book was written, when the commander of a nearby anti-poaching patrol came up to me and told me a black rhino had just been killed.

Like the fictitious Lovemore and his men in *Safari*, the parks and wildlife service ranger in charge was keen to get to the carcass which, while only some thirty kilometres away, may as well have been on the dark side of the moon, as there was no vehicle – and no fuel, in any case – to move him and his men to the site in time.

My wife and I offered them a lift (though they would have had to have ridden on the roof as my little Land Rover only has two seats), but he was told to stay put as the police were on their way. They arrived some twenty-four hours later, and by then the poachers were long gone.

We had time to chat, and the patrol commander

told me of gun battles he and his men had been involved in – of rangers wounded and Zambian poachers killed in action. These men are in a war to save their country's wildlife. Underpaid, underfed and under-recognised, they are short of everything, except courage. I have the utmost respect for them.

For the record, I am neither anti-hunting, nor pro-hunting. Some of the most passionate conservationists I have met in Africa are also hunters.

All the camps mentioned in this book in Hwange National Park, Zimbabwe, do exist and while there is a Matetsi Safari Area on the north-west boundary of the park, near the Botswana border, there is no Isilwane Safari Lodge and certainly no Fletcher Reynolds.

Chewore, the black rhino mentioned in the book, is real (rhinos don't sue, so I'm sure she won't mind me using her name), and did have a bad habit of wandering into Botswana. At the time of writing, she hadn't been seen for a couple of years. I hope she is alive somewhere out there in the wilds of Zimbabwe, but I'm not holding my breath.

Mubare, the silverback gorilla, and his family do exist (at least I hope they still do), in Uganda's Bwindi Impenetrable National Park, across the border from the DRC. Tracking mountain gorillas is a challenging and expensive business, but if you are interested in wildlife, summon all your reserves of energy and cash and do it. It's worth it.

I am grateful to Matt Kay for his recollections of life in the Democratic Republic of Congo, and to Oskar and Linda Rothen and Kerryn Smith for their accounts of visits to the Virunga National Park and its surrounds. Annette Lanjouw worked on gorilla and chimpanzee conservation projects in the Virunga from 1987 to 2005. She answered pages of questions I had on the region, and I owe her a great debt of thanks. Likewise, my thanks go to Lulu Mitshabu, from the Catholic charity Caritas, who shared with me memories and pictures of a recent trip to Goma.

David Drakes read the manuscript from a Zimbabwean-born person's perspective, while Donna Bozowsky gave valuable feedback on Michelle Parker's Canadian background.

My friend in the US, Are Berentsen, helped with the descriptions of Larry Monroe's home in Logan, near Salt Lake City, Utah, and gave advice on African animal research projects, based on his own experiences in Africa.

In Zimbabwe, a number of people helped with suggestions and anecdotes, while our good friends Dennis, Liz, Don, Vicki, Sal and Scotty continue to keep us on the road and fuelled and fed – no mean feat these days – during our annual trips to Africa.

Thanks, also, to the relatives of young Matthew Towns and Dougal Geddes, who made donations to the Abbotsford Long Day Care Centre and Inner City Child Care respectively, in return for their names being used as characters in *Safari*.

As usual, my profound thanks go to my wife Nicola, mother Kathy, and mother-in-law Sheila, who continue to do a sensational, unpaid job as proofreaders. Without Nicola, there would be no five months of the year for me in Africa, and no books.

They say life begins at forty and for me it did, when my first book, *Far Horizon*, was published. For my new life, I have a number of friends at Pan Macmillan Australia to thank – Deputy Publishing Director Cate Paterson, Fiction Publicity Manager Jane Novak, Senior Editor Sarina Rowell, Publishing Director James Fraser, and copy editor Julia Stiles.

And thank you.